WHAT PRETTY GETS YOU

A NOVEL

CHANDRA HOFFMAN

Author of *Chosen*

FIFTH
GENERATION

First Edition

What Pretty Gets You
1st Edition © 2021 by Chandra Hoffman
Fifth Generation Publishing
Edited by Romy Sommer
Cover Design: Asya Blue
Author photo: Robin Trautmann

e-ISBN 978-1-7367258-0-1
ISBN 978-1-7367258-1-8

DEDICATION

With gratitude...
for Maia and Carolyn, who waited
twenty-three years for their story to be told

BOOK ONE

BOOK ONE

CHAPTER ONE

Maia

The first time I met Joel Carter, we didn't actually meet. It was one of those things where you start a conversation, and then it's too late to introduce yourself without being awkward. I was a kiosk vendor on the D Terminal of Philadelphia International Airport, Faces on Laces. I sold these plastic bar things you put on your shoelaces so they never come untied.

I'd stopped off to keep my one friend, Janelle, company at the sports bar on D. Salty slid me a beer, even though he knew the name on my ID—Sheila McHugh, age twenty-seven of Rochester, New York—didn't look much like me or match where I lived or what everyone called me. Janelle was on my one side, talking about not wanting to go home because her mom was giving her grief, and on the other side were two guys in suits.

My first glimpse of Joel—he was suck-in-your-breath-and-straighten-your-shoulders good looking, but there was something else. The way he talked—I'd never heard anyone so passionate about a place before. Maybe that's because I'm born and raised under the el train near Fishtown.

"You can feel a consciousness there," he was saying, "a lifestyle and a genuine commitment to being a decent human being, to lowering your environmental impact."

"What are you talking about—recycling?" the guy next to him asked and I was glad because I wasn't sure either.

"I'm talking about living in the middle of such natural beauty, you want to be a part of it, to preserve it for future generations. Everyone does. It's in everything you do—you bike to work, hike on the weekends, consume like a locavore. And the skiing is off the hook."

They kept talking, Vail and Beaver Creek, Breck and A-Basin, back bowls and corn snow.

It was hard to tell how old he was. Late twenties? Early thirties? But then I guess I was staring because both guys turned to me. Joel smiled and shifted his shoulders, an entrance to the conversation. I tucked my hair behind my ear. The guy behind him ran his eyes up and down me like a scanner, the way guys do.

"Sorry," I said, "but where are you talking about?"

"Colorado," he said like it was his name, something he owned.

"Joel Carter," he said, and he scooted his barstool back, telling us all about a place called Boulder, the green space and trails, the mountain biking, the incredible views.

"I'm originally from the East Coast, Jersey," he said dismissively. "Until I moved out there, I thought you had to go to Europe for this. I never knew America could be so beautiful."

He talked less to the guy next to him, more to me, what sounded like a fairy tale with dangerous mountain lions and rattlesnakes, snowy mountains and clean air. Without meaning to, I realized I was tilting towards him.

"When I was little," I blurted, "my dad used to read me this book about a girl named Heidi, who lived up in the mountains in Switzerland with her grandpa. He'd say, 'If you turn out as pretty as I'm afraid you're fixin' to, I'm shipping you off to the mountains with Grandpa and the goats.'"

Joel's snowy mountain stories reminded me how much I loved disappearing into the pictures of that book, sitting on my dad's lap, head on his shoulder, before he left.

"Your father sounds like a wise man," Joel grinned, crooked and cute. Behind him, Janelle was doing the heart thing with her hands.

"Hardly," I said, thinking how, of all the things my dad took with him when he left, including our parakeets and the blue suitcase, I always wondered why he didn't leave me that book, knowing how much I loved it.

Then Janelle got a call from her mom; her little boy needed a breathing treatment. We liked to ride the train together, keep each other company and watch for creepers. She tugged my arm and I stood up, and their eyes ran up and down again. I'm six feet tall; I'm used to it. Joel's was different though; he looked at me like an invitation, like I could just follow him into his fairy tale. Wrong; I had Mark, my boyfriend of six years, waiting for me.

Joel cleared his throat. "Hey, listen, you should definitely check out Colorado. Seven years ago, I was on track for Silicon Valley. I got headhunted by this startup, and they flew me out to Colorado. I never looked back. Sometimes, you have to take a chance to make a change."

"Yeah," I laughed and made like I was throwing a dart at a map. Thinking, *I'll just, you know, pick a place, pack up and go.*

I didn't tell him that girls like me, from the same-old Fishtown zip code with the same on-again, off-again boyfriend from middle school, those girls didn't stride through airports and take chances and hop on planes.

"You look like you're up for an adventure," he grinned, and I wondered what he saw in me that everyone else missed.

"Can I ask you something?" Joel said, searching my face like he was memorizing me. The breath caught in my chest.

I nodded, waiting, thinking, *Anything, ask me anything.*

But then his friend paid their tab, and Janelle was hanging on my arm, and Joel checked his phone. He said his flight to Denver was boarding, and it had been really nice to meet me, but we hadn't really.

I saw him again a week later, Thursday afternoon, early April, outbound. Turns out he was a regular commuter on the United flight between Philly and Denver. He'd fly in from Denver Tuesday morning and back out Thursday. He checked in at the gate next to my stand with a USA Today under one arm and a suit coat draped over his carry-on. Back then, before I knew Colorado, I wondered why he didn't have a heavier jacket. I thought it was all snow and skiing, year-round. I didn't know how variable the weather could be, how dry and clear the air was there, how a day could be sunny and make-you-throw-your-head-back-and-stare-at-the-sky beautiful, and a night could leave you shivering, huddled under a hand dryer in a public restroom.

If we hadn't talked at the bar, I wouldn't have been able to tell which place was home because Joel Carter walked with purpose going both directions. I used to think I'd walk like that one day, Birkin carry-on, clicking along like high heels don't kill my arches. Before all this happened, I imagined someday I'd have a job where if I wasn't there, someone would be calling to book me for a shoot, and I'd be click-walking-and-talking and people would move to the side because they could tell I was headed somewhere important. I watched Joel Carter pass, thinking how I envied his walk, loved his eyes, and incidentally, sort of hated my life.

⌒

He stopped at my cart one Tuesday in April—I thought he was going to say something about before, the bar, but he acted like he didn't even know me. He studied my trays and picked one out, right away. My impression: he was a guy who knew what he wanted. I couldn't have been more wrong. Or maybe I was dead on, and what he wanted was to have his cake and eat it too.

Janelle, who worked the watch cart, Time on Your Hands, coughed to get my attention and then reached out like she was going to grab a handful of his ass, making me choke on my Snapple.

"How much for these?" he looked up as I was wiping under my nose. He'd chosen the Barbie ones and I took it hard. I'd noticed that night at the bar that he didn't have a wedding ring and I hate when guys do that.

"Four bucks. For your little girl?" I was getting out a paper bag, just facilitating the sale then. Janelle and I always say don't mess with married men.

"For a little girl I know," he said, handing me a twenty.

I know this sounds stupid but I felt something zingy go through me when our hands brushed as I handed him the change.

I was just about to remind him that he was going to ask me something at the bar, when they announced his flight, pre-boarding for first-class passengers and those traveling with small children.

"I've got to go." He frowned slightly, a serious dash between his eyebrows.

"Alrighty, then," I said, blushing, sounding like an idiot. "Take care!"

He walked away, but before he turned the corner, he looked over his shoulder and flashed me this smile. It wasn't a gotcha-where-I-wantcha grin; it was more a hopeful tilt to the corners of his mouth, a crinkle around his blue eyes, that open door invitation.

"'Alrighty then, take care?'" Janelle drawled and snickered into her Dr. Pepper. "Where you from, girl, Georgia? Alabammer?"

She says I've got a serious fetish for men with dark hair and blue eyes. I guess she's right—I like the unexpectedness. Mark, my boyfriend, has blue eyes, and his hair is brown at the roots. This past New Years' Eve he'd announced he didn't want to go out. Instead, he came home with one of those peroxide kits from CVS and destroyed the bathroom and all three towels doing it. It looks okay, the blonde. It's a little brassy and he doesn't keep up with the roots. It would be one thing if he was growing it out, but then he messes with a new shade every couple of weeks. When I got on his case about the dark stripe at his part he'd said, "It's just hair for Chrissake!"

Tuesday night, I tracked clues to determine Mark's whereabouts. First, in the shoebox by the microwave was the stub of his paycheck and a receipt for a case of Bud Light and a WaWa hoagie slip. Funny; as idiotic as Mark can be about a lot of things, he's crazy about saving a paper trail.

The bathroom was still dripping, and it smelled like moldy shower and the Axe I'd gotten Mark for Christmas. Wet towel and martini glass boxers on the floor, a Bud can and razor ash by the sink. Another empty on the dresser in the bedroom and beside it, on deli paper, the dry stub of a cheesesteak, wormy onion ends dangling out. I balled it up and retraced back to the kitchen. I opened the fridge—no more beers—which means he took them to get his drink on with Nick.

I called Janelle but she said she had to stay home with Damien, that he was getting sick and her mom was giving her The Eye. I called my sister Scarlett but she was out with Rudy, her boyfriend since forever. I fell asleep waiting, on top of the covers, in my clothes.

When Mark got home, it was after midnight. He curled up behind me, smelling like beer and fry grease and smoke, familiar. He mumbled something into my hair about how he was off in the morning, and we should head down to jeweler's row.

"You've got a birthday coming up. Take a look at some rings."

I didn't answer. I rolled towards him and let him unbutton my jeans. I'll admit I thought about my crinkly-smile commuter man while we did it, and then Mark was passed out and I was freaking wide awake until the light outside the skinny window went from black to grey and the garbage truck started banging down the alley outside.

Wednesday night I went to Julie's Corner with Janelle. She was buying B-52 shots and Mark showed up after work, trying to get my attention by flirting with these patent leather girls from Temple.

Janelle snorted, "Girl, you got legs longer than I am tall and a face like Gigi-fucking-Hadid. If you'd do something with your nasty hair, you could have any guy in this place, in any place. Don't you see how guys look at you? Why Mark?"

I twisted my hair off my neck. "We've been together a long time, since seventh grade…" I hadn't told Janelle about our pending legal thing. Working side by side in the airport, people walking by all the time, we'd never talked about my dad leaving, why I don't live at home, or the modeling thing. Mark and I had been through plenty, but it was more like we were brother and sister in a messed-up family, soldiers from the same war zone. We took care of each other, and that counts for something, even if I had no intention of marrying him.

Mark bent over the back of some chick, helping her line up her pool shot, mashed up against her thigh, looking right at me, and I just waggled my fingers back at him. Whatever.

Mark and Nick disappeared, and when I walked all twelve blocks home, he wasn't there. At three in the morning, he showed up and we got in our usual fight about common courtesy.

"What am I supposed to think?" I sighed, opening up a trash bag. I'd already texted my sister.

"Just what I told you—me and Nick were brainstorming ways to get our legal situation sorted out."

I didn't answer, but he could see I was packing, throwing my clothes in garbage bags. Again.

"What? I'm taking care of things! You think you're going to financially save us? You still think some legit scout is going to spy you in the airport, fly you off to Paris? You think we're going to be rolling around some hotel bed in piles of your modeling money? You're almost twenty-fucking-years old, Maia!" and he whistled, a sound like a bomb dropping.

Mark was heating up mac and cheese, banging the pot on the stove, and our apartment was so cramped my shoulder slammed against his. Something about how sad and sharp and bony his was, like a little boy's, was almost enough to make me stay.

"I just meant—" Mark tried to stop me in the fishy stairwell, Scarlett waiting for me below, his face all sorry and soft. "I'll sort this mess out. And maybe, babe, maybe it's time you find a new dream?"

⌣⟶

I tilted my cheek against Rudy's cold car window while Scarlett drove us under the streetlights on Shackamaxon. It was Wednesday night, which meant Joel Carter, my commuter man was somewhere out there in the same city of brotherly love.

"Hey," Scarlett said. "No itching?"

I shook my head; whenever things are bad, I get these anxiety hives that start on the back of my neck and creep up my scalp.

"Okay," she smiled, "let's take that as a sign."

When I woke up Thursday morning, Scarlett was in the bathroom, and because my crazy sister likes to sleep with the windows open no matter what time of year, I heard geese honking, coming back to the city after a winter in Florida.

I rolled over and yelled, "Stupid birds! Don't come back! Just keep on flying!" What were they going to find here but some dirty water in Fairmount Park or get their babies run over by the cyclists down along the river?

"You want to borrow something cute for work?" Scarlett asked, toothbrush sticking out the corner of her mouth. I was feeling like Mark's warehouse winch couldn't hoist me out of bed to face the fact that I had moved back home and there was a pile of Glad bags with my life's belongings littering our crumby floor.

I'm seven inches taller than my sister, so I pulled on my own jeans but borrowed her sunflower T-shirt and black flats, significant only because these were the clothes I ended up wearing for the next five days. Then Scarlett made me sit on the toilet seat lid while she did my face and put my hair back.

"God, what I wouldn't give to have your cheekbones," she breathed as she brushed on powder. Her breath smelled like toothpaste. "Or your legs. Or your anything."

"Please," I told my sister, who is the hale-and-hearty kind of pretty, the kind where, when she's forty, she'll look exactly the same: rosy and curvy and creamy. Mom says she favors our dad, and she doesn't mean it as a compliment.

"It's true. And you know why I'm doing this? When you look good, you feel good, you know?" She held up the mirror for me.

I've got clear skin, winter-pale, with a few freckles and a straight nose. I think my eyes are a little too big and my lips too thin. With my hair back, my neck looks super long, like the game where you fold the paper and pass it around, and just make two marks where the neck connects to the head if both people draw in a neck. Scarlett says when I become a supermodel, it could be my signature, but I usually leave my hair down. It drives her and Janelle nuts.

"Beautiful." She snapped her compact closed with a puff of powder. Honestly, I went along because it felt nice to be fussed over, and because I knew my commuter would be coming through again that afternoon.

I put my wallet in my purse and made sure I had lip balm, enough money for lunch at the food court between the terminals and the ID of Sheila McHugh of Rochester, NY. Then, when Scarlett wasn't looking, I tucked my real license in my bra. Scarlett gave me a ride in Rudy's car and made me promise to come out dancing with them that night.

For no good reason, I hugged her when I got out of the car. I guess because that's what people do when they get dropped off at airports.

Thursday morning was slow. Janelle was off, so it was Anime Boy at her cart, and he'd asked me out when he first started, so now we ignored each other. I was wondering who'd watch my cart for lunch when I saw him coming through security—Joel Carter. He was doing his serious walk, like those rainy day Franklin Mills mall walkers in their jogging suits. His bangs ruffled as he walked.

Right past me.

No look, no smile, no snowy mountain fairy tales, no "can I ask you something?" Just that crease between his eyebrows.

Looking back, it's hard to say why I did it. It was one of those things that seemed like the only option at the time, but in reality was pretty stupid. I opened the cash drawer and tallied up the money. With the float, there was just over three-fifty. I put it in the mustard-colored envelope and marked down the amount. I straightened the merchandise, stacked the trays and pulled down the rolling screen, locking it.

"You closing down?" Anime asked. I made a noise that could've been yes or no, and he went back to Naruto and snacking on his cuticles.

I didn't know what to do with the profits for the day—too risky to leave them in the cash drawer. I put the float envelope in my purse and I swear I was planning to mail it back to Ritchie, all the way until I got to the counter and realized I'd need the money for my plane ticket to Denver.

CHAPTER TWO

Carolyn

"Do you see that right there?" The ultrasound tech swabbed the wand over my stomach.

"Is that a toe?" I asked, still giddy from having heard the heartbeat.

"He can never know you said that," she laughed, "that you thought it was his toe!"

He. A boy. A boy!

"I knew it," I said softly. Things had felt different from Sasha, bittersweet familiar this time. A little boy. Finally, a son for my husband, a brother for Sasha, a mama's boy, a second chance...

I took another deep breath, harder to do at almost twenty weeks.

A healthy boy and my cervix 'closed as it should be'—the good news was endless. Everything was going to be okay. Why shouldn't it be? I'd eat healthier, be better, carry him to term, he'd be an easy baby. I'd be more relaxed this time around; everyone says it's easier with the second. Then in the fall, Sasha would start preschool, I'd get my body back, my husband's work schedule would settle down. Everything would be fine!

The receptionist who had been keeping my daughter entertained with a princess coloring book out in the waiting area, just in case the ultrasound revealed bad news, knocked at the door.

"Somebody wants her mommy."

I hadn't wanted to bring Sasha but I'd texted Jackie, from Friday playgroup and asked for a ride to the clinic and/or watch Sash, and though I could see she'd read it, nothing. In the Uber on the way, Sasha watching Doc McStuffins on my phone, I got an Instagram alert—a photo of Jackie and Allison, also from Friday playgroup, getting together on a Thursday, pushing their kids on the swings #perfectBoulderday #playdatefun.

"As soon as the doctor's all finished, do you want to do something special, Sash?" I had no idea what it would be, buying time. She looked pouty and though she was almost four, we weren't far past our most recent public tantrum.

"That sounds fun!" the receptionist chirped. She was dressed in Strawberry Shortcake scrubs. I could smell her foundation from across the small room. "And as soon as Mommy's dressed, Dr. Michaels wants to have a word."

I worried about this while I tugged my clothes on, alone in the darkened ultrasound room with Sasha. I shimmied into the tight maternity jeans, shuffled into my hiking boots, thinking that the receptionist in her scrubs was no more likely to step into an operating room today than I was to go hiking in the mountains in my boots.

"Sash, honey, let me brush your hair." A quick draw, I had it out of my purse before she saw it coming; I'd spent the better part of the morning trying to tame her white-blonde tangles.

"No!" she shrieked, twisting out of my reach before I got in three swipes. As she spun away from me in the tiny exam room, she tripped over the cord of the ultrasound machine.

"Sasha!" I caught her arm, mid-fall, heart pounding. If she'd fallen, she could have smashed her head on the linoleum, a grade two concussion at least. "Be careful!"

In Dr. Michaels' office, I held her on what was left on my lap, in part to keep her safe, and in part as a buffer against whatever he wanted to talk about.

"So, they tell me you called in pretty upset again this morning," he settled behind his desk, put his glasses on to look over the ultrasound printouts, nodding.

"Yes, I couldn't feel the baby moving. I woke up and I couldn't remember the last time I—"

"Carolyn," he cut me off gently. "We had your regular ultrasound scheduled next Monday. We did a heart rate and cervical last week. You're nineteen and a half weeks, and let's not forget," he winked at Sasha, "you've carried this beautiful little princess to term..."

I nodded, my face hot. I buried it in the cool of Sasha's hair. No matter that I bathed her nightly, it still smelled like the pine bedding from the guinea pig cage at the preschool we had interviewed last Monday.

"Yes, but I ended up on bed rest for the last thirteen weeks!" I didn't add that because he'd cautioned me off running after our first loss, I'd also gained sixty-one pounds.

"Carolyn, what I'm saying is, you have got to relax." He stood up and crossed to me, opening the door. "It's better for you, and the baby."

This is something my husband said often too, but in Dr. Michaels' gentle voice, his hand squeezing my shoulder, his white jacket gleaming with authority, I could hear it. It wasn't a criticism, it was just instructions from the doctor, for everybody's well-being.

But what does that mean, relax? I understand the word, but it's like the term 'process your grief.' How does that look, in practical application? Does it mean not seeing the potential for disaster in everything from a left turn to a hair brushing mishap? Should I try, as they say in prenatal yoga, to return to the most simple of all, breathing? I gulped a breath.

"You've got a healthy little boy in there. Now, go on, and tell your husband the good news."

"Okay!" I tried to smile up at him. It's not easy for me to trust happy moments, but I let myself try. A healthy baby boy—a future unrolling in front of us like a velvet carpet. Right then, I knew exactly what fun thing we were going to do.

CHAPTER THREE

Maia

"Hi," I gasped to the flight attendant, out of breath from running down the jetway at final boarding. Everyone thinks if you're skinny, you're fit, but I can tell you, before Boulder, I never so much as jogged to catch a bus. The attendant was pissed, one hand on her hip, like my mom that morning when me and Scarlett snuck past her.

"You were lucky to make this flight." She glanced at my ticket, then handed it back.

Was I? I paused between the front seats, one hand gripping the leather. In a second, there would be no turning back.

My anxiety hives in full swing, traveling up my neck under my hair like goose bumps, I almost backed out, but there was Joel Carter in the second row, with an empty seat next to him. What was I doing? I scanned the plane like I was looking for 27E, a burning heat in my cheeks.

"Miss McHugh, we are trying to make an immediate and on-time departure," Grouchy Attendant snipped. "Please take your seat."

I'd never flown on an airplane. I took a deep breath and dropped into the seat beside Joel Carter, lacing my fingers over my jumpy stomach. He looked up from his iPhone.

"You?" His face split into that beautiful smile.

I bent my head to focus on my seatbelt, letting my hair fall between us like a curtain to hide my flaming skin. Then I tucked it behind my ear and turned to him, thinking, *now, quick, ask me anything.*

"Miss McHugh, this is not your assigned seat." Grouchy stood at our row, but Joel waved her off.

"It's all good. We…we know each other." He waited until she huffed off before tilting his head to me. "By the way, Joel Carter." His hand felt dry and cool in mine, like that expensive paper people use for résumés.

"Maia Kramer."

Joel tilted his head. "Who's Miss McHugh?"

"What?" The ticket, the attendant, my fake ID.

We looked at each other for a long minute. Then, Grouchy was back, asking coolly if we'd like a beverage before take-off and Joel ordered us both sparkling white wine.

"It's the closest thing they have to champagne." He clinked his glass against mine. "So, Miss-Maia-Kramer-McHugh, Philly girl who's never been to Colorado…." Joel's smile made the corner of his blue-blue eyes disappear.

"*Former* Philly girl," I corrected, twisting my hair up off my neck to cool it down. "You know, since I'm moving." I hadn't realized it fully, until I said it. "To Boulder," I added, since that was the place he'd said. I could barely picture Colorado on my fifth-grade U.S. States test, squarish, somewhere left of the middle?

"Is this the world's most incredible coincidence?" He stared at me like I was a souvenir from a country he hadn't thought he'd get to visit.

"I guess it must be."

I glanced up to see Grouchy buckle in backwards and roll her eyes. Jealous, I thought, but I was used to it. Other than Janelle and my sister, not too many girls ever wanted to be my friend.

"Amazing." Joel shook his head. "You're going to love it out there. First thing, Red Rocks, or we should hike Mount Sanitas, or maybe——" He stopped himself, but I'd heard it: We. I couldn't hide my smile. A future was unfolding, us, at the tip-top of rocky mountains, my hand tucked inside his.

The seatbelt sign pinged on overhead. The plane's white noise roared in my ears, and I reached for my glass—empty.

"So where are you staying in Boulder?" Joel asked.

"Um, I'll be looking for a place, more permanent, but, until then, what's that big hotel downtown? I have the address in my phone …"

"Boulderado?" Joel asked.

"That sounds right." I leaned back against the headrest, dizzy with the rumble of acceleration and lies.

"Are they picking you up?"

Picking me up? "Um, no. I thought I'd take a…" I paused, not sure what the public transportation was like out there, picturing gondolas swinging over snowy mountains, "an Uber or a cab?"

"Do you know how expensive a cab from Denver to Boulder is?"

I didn't.

Joel added, "Though I guess if you're sitting in first class and staying at the Boulderado, money probably isn't your first concern."

Buddy, you have no idea.

At the ticket counter, the agent had been a chipmunk-cheeked guy. He'd told me the ticket was $755, and I should buy three to six weeks in advance for optimal fares.

"What've you got in that big ol' pile of ones?" He'd smirked like I was a dancer as I counted out Ritchie's float. He told me he had a student fare of $362 without asking where I went to school, which was good, since I didn't.

That's when the anxiety hives started, a tingle on the back of my neck.

Then he asked for ID, and I almost walked away until I remembered Sheila McHugh. The real one pressed against my thumping heart. Only Mark and my lawyer knew I had it.

The plane ticket cost nearly everything in my purse and Ritchie's money, leaving me with exactly three dollars and twenty-three cents. The agent wrote his number on the back of a Subway napkin, wishing me a nice flight. "Look me up when you come back to Philly!"

And I'd sprinted for the gate, thinking, maybe never!

Grouchy offered us little ceramic cups of hot nuts. Trying to hurry past my mom that morning, I hadn't eaten breakfast. I was starving and more than a little queasy about what I'd just done.

"Listen, Maia. I have my car in long term parking. Why don't I give you a ride up?" Joel grinned. "I'm harmless, I promise."

"Thanks." I tried to smile back but the plane dipped and I closed my eyes against a wave of panic. Joel's hand was on our broad armrest, and he touched mine lightly.

"It's just a little turbulence. Are you a nervous flier?"

The fact that we were flying through the sky hadn't really registered. I'd been noticing how he smelled clean and woodsy, like my dad. I glanced over. Joel's shoulder looked substantial, muscled and round, so different from Mark's sharp angles, the kind of place a girl could rest her head.

Joel talked, mostly about Colorado, snowshoeing, mountain biking. When lunch came, a fruit and cheese plate, we bonded over silly food things: how we both hate overripe bananas and put ice cubes in our cereal to keep the milk cold.

"Pat's or Geno's?" he asked me—the Philly cheesesteak debate.

"Neither!" I laughed, sipping on my second wine. "Campo's Fire'n'Ice with cream cheese and jalapeños. Big dogs or little yappers?"

We agreed one hundred percent big dogs. He told me he had a yellow lab named Ben he took to the trails on weekends. I adjusted the image—now we were at the top of the mountain with a dog!

"When I was little," I told him, "I wanted a dog so badly I'd stand in the street and stare at the sun. My mom said if I did that, I'd go blind. I knew that was my only chance of getting a dog."

"I bet you were adorable." He ordered more wine for us both. Because of my mom, I'm not usually much of a drinker, and the wine hit hard, numb lips and a buzzing in my ears almost loud enough to drown out the panic over what I'd done—Ritchie's money, my cart, so much leaving—Mark, the night before, not to mention the jurisdiction.

"Last month," Joel said, "we were hiking Aiken Canyon and Ben started going nuts, and right up at the turn was this big ol' mountain lion. You know what to do if you see one?"

"Um, run?" I giggled. Definitely the wine.

"No! No." He took my wrist to show how serious he was, the fourth time we'd touched. Not that I was counting. "Never. You stand up big and you wave your arms and you open your coat and you roar as loud as you can. Maia, I'm being serious."

"I know." The laughter was bordering on hysterical now—it started with the image of Joel roaring down a mountain lion in his business suit, growing into giggles-at-a-funeral. What had I just done? I swallowed my panic with a hiccup.

"You're tall, you might be ok. But you have to pick up any kids or little dogs; they look for the smallest and weakest in the group."

Kids?

Joel smiled; he was still holding my wrist.

"I'm going to have to keep an eye on you out there, City Girl." He leaned toward me. "Tonight, if you're free, I'm taking you to Flagstaff House for dinner, up in the mountains. We'll get a window seat—amazing views, and their prosciutto-wrapped monkfish will blow your mind."

Now, in the picture, the town lights sparkled like a chest of jewels below, the dark mountains nestled around us, steaming plates of food and more bubbly wine between us on a crisp, white tablecloth.

I pictured calling Janelle, and Scarlett, repeating what Joel had said in the bar, "You have to take a chance to make a change."

But then our plane jerked like the R3 going off the rails. My forehead collided with Joel's temple and we jerked apart.

"Ladies and gentlemen, this is your captain speaking. Looks like we're heading for some unexpectedly rough weather. Please double-check your seatbelts and make sure all lap children are secure."

"What's happening?" I gripped the armrest.

The plane dropped like a stone. Across the aisle, a woman gasped, her mouth showing silver fillings as it hung open with the force of our fall.

This is what you get, Maia Jane Kramer!

Why did the voice in my head always sound like my mom?

"Flight attendants, take your seats immediately."

Grouchy's eyes were wide as she buckled in, facing us, her mouth a skeleton's grimace. Her teeth were all cigarette stained, and I was sorry for thinking mean things about her—she probably went home to cats.

I wondered, as my head snapped back and forth on my neck, if any of us was ever going home again.

"Whoa," Joel said under his breath. "Severe turbulence."

"Ladies and gentlemen, please double check your seat belts and again, make sure all lap children are secure. We ask if you have hot beverages on your tray tables, please place your cups on the floor. We're going to try and descend to a new cruising altitude. Looks like these thunderheads are bigger and a little bumpier than we—"

The voice cut out, and it was the Six Flags Free Fall, my thighs pressing against my safety belt. Our empty wine glasses went flying; my hair lifted past my cheeks.

People screamed—pretty sure I was one of them.

"Hang on," Joel said, through gritted teeth.

"I'm sorry," I whimpered to nobody.

"Shhh." Joel laced his fingers through mine.

19

The drop ended so hard I thought we had crash-landed on top of one of his fairytale mountains, but then the plane pitched right—no, we were still going. I heard the drink cart smash into the wall, then back. Across the aisle, the overhead bins burst open and the oxygen masks dropped from the ceiling.

Ours were nowhere in sight.

"Joel!"

He threw his arms over me, a human umbrella— "Look out!"—as we rolled left and suitcases came flying out of the open bins. One slammed off my shoulder. It sounded like the whole plane was breaking apart.

"Shh," Joel whispered, his lips against my hair. "We can talk, it means we don't need the masks. Shhh." He kept his arms wrapped around me. The wine jostled in my stomach, sliding up my throat.

"Don't leave," I sobbed into his shoulder, the same words I'd said to my dad that last time, raking bloody lines in my shins with my fingernails, begging him, *stay.*

He'd gone anyway.

"I'm. Right. Here. I've. Got. You." The plane shook so hard Joel's words came out like he was being punched with each one.

"She's bleeding!" Someone in the back screamed. "We need a doctor!"

I squeezed my eyes closed and kept my face in Joel's shoulder, thinking I'd been right; it was somewhere safe.

The plane swerved. We were going to die.

"You were going to ask me something," I whimpered.

"What?" he tilted his head down to the private space between us. His jaw pulsed against clenched teeth, and I reached up with my free hand to hold it.

We were the only people in the whole world; never mind it was ending.

I met his eyes. *Ask me the question now, before it's too late.*

The plane dropped again, and Joel tipped his face to mine, with purpose.

Our mouths collided, and then we were kissing, fireworks and sweet wine, hunger, his hand cupping the back of my head, steadying our mouths against the rattling, cementing us in this kiss. Our front teeth bumped, my arm wrapped around the broadness of him, holding on, thinking, *okay, there are worse places to die.*

And then, it was over.

I opened my eyes, pulled away. My fingertips slipped between us to touch my raw, wet lips.

The plane shuddered, a wet dog shaking off, tilted right. The drink cart rolled politely back into its closet by the cockpit.

"Alright, folks, sorry about that. Looks like we've found some better air down here. We've leveled off about fifteen thousand feet and are cleared for our thirty mile approach to Denver International—"

Joel pulled back. Had that just happened? Had we kissed? A tingling in my lips, the look on Joel's face, said yes.

DING DING DING! Call bells, the baby in the back still screaming. A different attendant was putting suitcases back in bins, walking with one hand on the chair backs, like a sailor just back on land.

"This woman is bleeding!"

"Is there a doctor on the plane?"

Joel awkwardly took his arm from around my shoulder and I waited, wondering if he was about to admit he was actually a doctor, and all the earlier dot com stuff about his job had just been casual lies to a stranger.

"Excuse me—" Grouchy was stopping at rows. She asked Joel, "Sir, are you a medical doctor?"

He shook his head and she hurried past with a first-aid kit in her hand. I noticed she didn't ask me.

"Okay?" Joel ran a hand up his face, making his damp bangs stand at attention. He glanced away from me. I let go of his hand, wiping mine on my jeans, noticing the way it shook.

I nodded, not trusting my voice.

⟨⟩

When the wheels touched down, there was a sprinkle of somber applause. We waited while paramedics wheeled off an old woman who'd been hit by a suitcase, a blood-soaked cloth against her wispy white hair. She reminded me of Babçi, Mark's grandma, who I used to love. I hoped she'd be okay.

"So." Joel gave a weak laugh. "Welcome, to your new life."

I couldn't make my legs move. People were waiting for us. Turns out, there is a specific way you're supposed to get off a plane. It was just like Babçi's funeral, how me and Mark were in the front row, and everyone expected us to get up first. They wouldn't leave before we did, but we didn't know it, and the poor organist kept going, three times through "Amazing Grace" before we figured it out.

"Here," Joel said gently, nudging past me out into the aisle. He took my hand like I was a little girl and led me off the plane, and I was glad he kept holding it as we walked. I blinked in the bright sunshine of the glassy terminal. My free fingers drifted to my lips again, remembering the hopefulness of our kiss.

"Look." He squeezed his arm around my shoulder and turned me, pointing to the mountains, way off in the sun-squinty distance. My eyes teared. "Look at those! Aren't they incredible? Think of all our adventures ahead! I can't wait to show you everything. You're going to fall in love, I promise."

I squeezed his hand back, and excitement rushed into my chest.

"How many bags do you have?"

"Um, none." I wondered if he could feel I was still shaking. If he did, hopefully he blamed it on the turbulence, not the fact that I'd just upended my whole life like my purse at security.

"Ah, I read about this. What's it called, The Hundred Thing challenge?"

I nodded, but I had no idea what he was talking about.

"You're going to fit right in in Boulder." Joel laughed, and I liked the way he held my fingers, how natural this was starting to feel, and I let myself smile back at him. "I can't wait to—"

"Daddy!" A little girl was running toward us.

CHAPTER FOUR

Carolyn

Since becoming pregnant this time, I have been blessed and cursed with the most acute sense of smell. While waiting for Joel at the airport, I could barely breathe from the sneakers of the teenage boy slouching beside me, suede mixed with the trapped stench of sockless sweat. The girl snapping her spearmint gum beside him had eaten something with green peppers for lunch, and the elderly woman rifling through her purse on the other side was a black tea drinker, carried the dander of cat with her and I was picking up something else, pine-something—a cleaning product, air-freshener, the scenting of her kitty litter—I couldn't quite get it.

I'd told Joel about it when it first started.

"The woman who gave her urine sample in the bathroom before me at Dr. Michaels' had asparagus last night."

He said that wasn't unique—asparagus makes everyone's pee smell off but only forty percent of the population can detect it. Originally, I tried to involve him, having me guess the type of cheese he was using in an omelet while I stood outside the kitchen, but he looked at me and said plaintively, "It's just Swiss, okay?"

He wrote it off as a quirky female thing, like how I know Sasha is about to wake up from a nightmare seconds before she does.

I tried to tell my mother about it, on our Sunday night phone calls between Boulder and Florida, but she thought I was talking about pregnancy aversions.

"You know, when I was pregnant with you, your father insisted on me making him scrambled eggs every morning, even though I'd have to gag into the sink. I nearly left him!"

So I was left to entertain myself with these peeks into others' lives through this (hopefully temporary) gift. The lady wriggling in her chair beside me at Dr. Michaels' waiting room that morning—brewing a yeast infection. The girl with the hunched shoulders and three bags of cheese curls in the airport shuttle reeked of vomit and defeat—bulimia? There'd been easy ones—a baby who needed changing, a woman I stood in line behind was a smoker, a vacant-eyed boy whizzing by on a skateboard had just gotten high. Others were trickier—a thickset man in mud-caked boots reeked of the sweet corn in animal feed and grassy manure, but also, hints of sesame oil. A farmer having an affair with the waitress at a Chinese restaurant?

These were the games I played, mental puzzles with olfactory clues. Joel traveled often. I was home alone with Sasha. I didn't really have friends, other adults to talk to.

Then there was Joel, stepping off the plane hand in hand—*were they? Had I imagined that?* —with a girl ten years our junior who stank of sweet wine, jet fuel and recirculated plane air. While I couldn't smell it, there was something else hanging between them—an otherness.

I kept sniffing, desperately, as Joel scooped up Sasha and the tall, blonde girl rubbed her neck, but I couldn't get it.

"We came to surprise you, Daddy!" Sasha patted Joel's cheek, eyeing the girl like a surprise babysitter she didn't want to be left with.

"You did! Maia, this is Carolyn, Car, Maia. We met on the plane. It was a crazy flight, terrible turbulence. Maia's just moving to Boulder." Then he touched the girl's shoulder—*see, I'm just a physical person with strangers*, the gesture said.

But I'd known Joel a long time.

"Well, welcome to Boulder, or Denver, I suppose," I said.

"I told Maia I'd give her a ride up to Boulder. She was going to take a cab."

"I thought we could…" I started, then stopped. Before, I'd imagined something different and urban, late afternoon at the Children's Museum, and then at a restaurant dinner I'd tell him about the baby—a healthy boy.

"What?" he asked. I had toted Sasha's car seat. It sat beside me like our faithful dog.

"Never mind," I picked it up by its straps. "We'll just go home now."

When we got into Joel's car at the long term parking garage (scents: sooty-stale exhaust, the rusty bouquet of aging metals, gritty cement) the two of us up front and Maia in the back with Sasha, I surreptitiously swiveled my head like a radar cone. On Joel, in his sweat, I caught hints of red meat and garlic, which confirmed the fact that he'd called me the previous night after a client dinner at Ruth's Chris Steakhouse. In his hair, the usual fake-fruit and flowers of my shampoo, that I bought in trial sizes and packed in his carry-on because he'd said, when he began commuting, that it reminded him of home. And in his clothes, more food smells, coffee and bacon—perhaps the complimentary breakfast buffet at his hotel?

On Maia, when I turned around to be doubly sure Sasha was buckled, I caught a whiff of a powdery floral deodorant, cherry Chapstick and, without a doubt, the metallic tang of adrenaline, fear's aftermath.

What had happened on that plane?

CHAPTER FIVE

Maia

Of course, she sat up front on the drive from Denver, her belly tenting the seat belt, doing the domestic thing; the plumber, the dog barf, preschool interview at noon on Friday, while I got the back seat beside his little girl.

I scratched my flaming neck. Sometimes, when the hives got really bad, they moved from the back of my neck to my face and I couldn't go out in public. Once, in the holding cell, the hives had gone to my mouth, and I'd begged the guard for Benadryl. I've heard they can swell your throat closed.

In the rearview mirror, Joel met my eyes once, and looked away.

"We went to the doctor, Daddy!" the little girl piped up.

When he didn't answer, she kicked the back of his seat with her sparkly silver shoes.

"Wait, you did? I thought that was next week? The ultrasound?"

"It was rescheduled. Anyway, it was fine. Uncooperative, healthy baby." The wife turned to her window, and I noticed her profile was blush-beautiful. Her hair was in a long, thick braid and she fit right in with the mountains outside, like the Swiss Miss on the cocoa box.

"What do you mean, uncooperative?" Joel asked.

"They couldn't find out the gender, but everything is ok. Dr. Michaels wants me back in two weeks, cervical check."

I flinched; I had no business here.

The landscape passing by the window was as foreign as the moon, cramped beige houses, no grass, just rocks and dirt and in the distance, those snowy mountains everyone was so crazy about.

"Why are you here?" His little girl turned to me, her amber eyes narrowed.

"Um." I tried to remember what I'd told Joel on the plane. Before. I swallowed. "I'm moving here."

"Yes," she said very carefully, "but how come, exactly, are you here, in *our car*?"

Nobody had an answer for that one.

Married, with kid(s)! I should have known. Back at the ticket counter, I'd made my return date for May 27—my birthday. I had three dollars in my purse and maybe forty dollars back in my TD Bank; I'd just given Mark rent and phone money. How could I change my ticket, get back to Denver, and then Philly, get the money back together for Ritchie? If I hadn't slammed out of our place with everything over my shoulder like Santa's sack, Mark might have some cash squirreled away. Fine. I'd find a way back home. I wouldn't tell anyone, not Scarlett or Janelle, definitely not my mom, what had happened.

The hour drive passed in thick silence, and subdivision moonscape gave way to hints of a town, with schools and shops and bike lanes, taller buildings, but all too reddish-brown and new to be anything familiar.

They dropped me at the Boulderado, this brick building, probably historical. Under the green awning and the eyes of the doorman, I got out.

Joel did too, though there was no suitcase in the trunk. He shook my hand, and I watched his mouth form the words, "It was a pleasure to travel with you—best of luck with everything."

I waited until they had turned the corner, Sasha's unblinking stare through the rear window of the Audi disappearing, before I opened my hand to examine the stiff paper he had pressed into my palm: his business card.

CHAPTER SIX

Carolyn

After leaving the girl from the airport at the Boulderado, Joel silently drove the fifteen minutes from town to our subdivision. Seven years ago, when we'd gotten married, and I'd dropped out of law school and followed Joel's job offer from New York, he was upset to discover we were priced out of what he considered the "true Boulder experience," although I suspected the sky-high real estate was an integral part of it.

Instead, his company's relocation service put us in a development off Jay Road, north of downtown; narrow, identical, beige townhouses bordered by farmland. Whenever the wind blew from the east, I smelled manure.

At home, we retreated—Joel presumably upstairs to unpack, me tempting Sasha outside with a bucket of driveway chalk to stop myself from stress-hoovering the chocolate and nut bars stashed in the appliance garage behind the Kitchenaid mixer my aunt gave us for our wedding.

Sitting in the driveway, as the sun dipped politely toward the foothills, loneliness drifted to me with the tumbleweeds. I drew an obstacle course with chalk—a river for Sasha to jump across, big fuchsia daisies for her to dodge, a ladder she had to pretend to climb—watching the oil derricks bobbing like East Coast shorebirds. Sometimes, even though I never even used the bathroom without Sasha trailing, and the baby tumbled constantly inside me, I felt physical pain at my loneliness, an ache near my sternum that no amount of chocolate could cure.

I replayed the airport scene in my head, questioning what I might have witnessed: before Joel saw us, had he been holding hands with that girl? I couldn't trust anything, not my sense of smell, not my own memory. Living in a world so insular, the space inside my head had become a vacant touring home, vaulted ceilings, hardwood floors, empty rooms—even Sasha's chatter felt like an intrusion.

Focus, I told myself, for Sasha's sake. *Relax.*

Jackie from the Friday playgroup came slowly up the street with Ella and Gracey on their trikes. Ella abandoned hers to join in my chalk obstacle course and I watched her carefully.

Our son would have been her age.

"This," Jackie sighed, waving her arm at the distant geologic beauty, the angle of sunshine warming our faces. "Last week it was snowing and now it's sixty-five. This is why we live in the best place on earth." It was nothing-speak, Colorado-propaganda filler.

"It's lovely," I agreed, wondering why she had ignored my text earlier. I was so out of practice here, with friends.

"So, did you hear?" Jackie said in a low voice. "Russ and I are giving it another go?" Their marital drama had been front-and-center for the past few playgroups, hashed over while we ate nutritional-yeast dusted popcorn and drank ginseng tea with waxy local honey. Last week, Jackie had given a detailed recap of make-up sex, inspired by her leader at Goddess Yoga.

"I hope it works out," I told her. Because I didn't drive, if Jackie moved off this street, I'd likely go days without talking to anyone but Sasha.

"Yes, it's for the—" Jackie stopped suddenly and I waited for her to say, "best" or "girls," but she surprised me, veering off topic. "Hey, do y'all want to come to dinner?"

In the four years since the playgroup was artificially formed from a sign-up sheet at Dr. Michaels' office, this was my first social invite outside of Friday mornings. This, I often thought, was what Joel and I needed in Boulder: Couple friends, BBQ friends.

"That would be really nice," I said carefully. "Let's talk about it when I'm in front of my calendar." Of course it was wide open, but I repeated the words I'd heard other women, those who had lives, jobs, older children with tai chi and rock-climbing club, say.

"No, I mean now, tonight. It would be good for us, to have some company, other people around. Buffer. You know."

I did.

Surprisingly, when I asked Joel, he agreed. I wondered, changing frantically into a billowing black maxi dress with the closet door closed to hide my body, did he know this was what we needed too?

We walked up the street with a six-pack clinking in our wagon, not holding hands, but connected by Sasha's. It was something, at least.

"So…" I stopped, not sure exactly what I wanted to say? "What was that girl's name?"

"Who?" he asked, the world's worst liar.

"That girl, from the plane. She should be careful. Accepting rides from strangers."

"What's that supposed to mean? She just moved out here. So she's independent."

"But, just, looking like…" I trailed off.

"So she's independent *and* beautiful! What's wrong with that?" Joel stared down the street toward Russ and Jackie's. "You worry too much."

He said that so often I could have cross-stitched it into his forehead.

"Taking rides from strangers is not independent. That's just stupidity. That's pushing your luck."

"Why are we even talking about this?" Joel frowned, a line between his eyes; his only physical vestige from our difficulties of the last years, whereas mine draped and pillowed over my body in layers of padded armor.

By some unspoken agreement, we both stopped, the exact distance from Russ and Jackie's for our conversation to remain private.

"The truth is," Joel said softly, in such a tone of heart-stopping confession that I looked down at our daughter's head, at the sloppy part of her white-blond hair, her vulnerable peachy scalp, and wondered desperately, *is this about to be a moment from which we cannot recover?*

To Joel, I said quietly, "Don't."

"Don't? Don't what? The truth is, Maia and I aren't exactly strangers."

Inside me, my son did a somersault, a reaction to the jetstream of adrenaline in his blood supply. I gripped the wagon handle, feeling like I wanted to run, but where?

Did I mention, years ago, I used to be a runner?

"Or at least, after today, it doesn't feel like it. We had an experience. It was a horrible flight. The worst turbulence I've ever been through. It made me think," Joel continued, "about a lot of things. There were a few minutes when I thought we," he corrected himself, "*I,* might die."

"What did you just say?" Sasha whipped her face up to Joel's, her chin jutting.

"Nothing, baby."

"Sash, look! Is that an eagle?" I pointed to a large bird of prey circling the neighborhood.

"Anyway, none of this is relevant." Joel started to walk again, cueing the conversation's end.

I exhaled, because he was speaking at normal volume again, defensive, irritable. But I wasn't finished.

"She should be careful." I lowered my voice, because we were right outside Russ and Jackie's, and I was about to commit the cardinal sin of Colorado. "Not everything, *everyone*, out here is wonderful. Bad things can happen to girls like that, even in Boulder."

And then I put a smile on my face and pushed open the gate.

CHAPTER SEVEN

Maia

I followed the flow of late afternoon walkers on Pearl Street. It was a no-car thing, a walking mall with shops, street performers and cart vendors. There was a guy setting up trays of silver jewelry so I stopped. He made a comment about my earring. It's one Scarlett gave me, looks like a little silver man shinnying up the rim of my ear.

"Nice stuff." I picked up a ring with a turquoise pattern. "Do you make it?"

"Some," he lied, I found out later. "I'm called Homer."

I thought he meant Homer like the fat dad on *The Simpsons*. But then he added, "As in, the guy who wrote *The Iliad*. Read it?"

"It's on my list." I told him how I used to work a cart too and was always dragging books along so I didn't fall asleep. "I mean, it's not on my actual reading list, but it's one of the books I know I should read, you know?"

"*The Iliad* will change your life," he said.

"Really?"

"You?" He looked me over, head to toe, pretending to reconsider. "Probably not." He laughed. It was nice, him joking with me, and I missed Janelle.

"How can you say that? You don't know me."

"Gorgeous girl, ten feet tall. You don't need Homer."

I asked him if he knew how a girl could get to Denver airport, cheap.

"Plenty of ideas, but not sure you want to stoop to that level. New in town?"

I nodded.

"Girls like you usually come with accents and rucksacks and Nutella. If you need to crash, my place's communal. Here…" He took out a Sharpie, wrote his address inside my wrist.

"Wow, thanks." I was suspicious and touched. Was everyone this nice out here?

When he lifted his linty fedora and resettled it on his head, I saw a patch of baldness.

A crowd surrounded me, a dozen girls running, wearing tiaras and boas and fluorescent sneakers, with their faces painted like Día de las Muertos. One girl grabbed at my hand.

"Come on, we have to find a man with a gold tooth and someone reading a Faulkner novel!" she cried, waving her phone in my face, and I pulled away, narrowly dodging a 12-passenger bike that turned out to be a bar, with an entire sports team pedaling, drinking from stainless steel flasks, and a man dressed like the Heidi book grandpa standing up on his pedals, singing,

"If I were the marrying kind
Which thank the lord I'm not, sir
the kind of rugger I would wed
would be a rugby…"

Some guy with purple hair bellowed, "Hop aboard, hottie!"

I stepped back to let them all pass, turning in a circle, a curious smile splitting my cheeks in this weird and wonderful new place.

"Welcome to Boulder," Homer laughed.

CHAPTER EIGHT

Carolyn

"So, Joel." Russ sounded like a talk-show host, affectedly sincere and loud. "Tell me how things are in dotcom Dom?"

The sun was setting, and the men were at the grill with the first of Joel's IPAs in their hands, remarking on the amazing spring weather. Jackie and I perched on her new Smith & Hawken patio set drinking strawberry daiquiris, mine virgin, as we watched the girls swing. Monkey bars spanned the top, I noted, making sure to watch that Sasha didn't try them—the number two cause of childhood arm and wrist fractures.

"I look at him in the mornings," Jackie nodded towards her husband, "when Ella and Gracey get into bed with us and I think, I almost lost all this. For what? Because he couldn't wipe down the counter after making spelt toast?" Jackie gulped from her drink, eyes narrow. "How are things with you two, with the travel and everything?"

"Fine," I said, wondering how much I could trust her. She cocked her head like a parrot, assessing whether this was interesting enough. I was about to mention the girl from the plane, see if she thought I should be worried, when Jackie jumped up to refill her drink. "Did I tell you we're starting a business?"

"What? No."

"Russ and I are doing stamp-making supplies, organic vegan inks. I got a zoning variance to put a cottage-style shed there, a home office, see those markers?" Jackie waved to a corner of the yard where the girls were weaving in and out of the ground markers in a shrieking game of tag. All I could see was a misstep, an ankle rolling, an eye socket going down on the splintered tops of the wooden stakes. How had I not noticed those when we first arrived, sticking eighteen inches out of the ground, the perfect height to impale a child? Accidents happen in the blink of an eye! I looked for Joel, but he was deep in conversation.

"Do you think they should play there?" I asked. Jackie was visibly annoyed that my question did not have to do with her business plan. "I mean, sorry to interrupt, but does that look dangerous to you?"

"Not really."

"When I was growing up, my piano teacher's son was running with a kazoo, and it went right through his soft palate. He had to have several operations, and still you could never really understand what he was saying."

"Well, we won't let them put the stakes in their mouths," Jackie said, but I could tell she was humoring me. "Girls, show Sasha your slackline!"

"Thank you," I said quietly.

After dinner, where Joel and Russ bonded over their mutual adherence to Paleo and I complimented Jackie's salad of grilled beets and roasted Brussels sprouts and wondered what I would eat later in my dark kitchen, Russ lit their fire pit. I scraped my chair along the patio next to Joel's. I wished he would sling his arm over the back and rest the V of his thumb and forefinger on my neck under my braid. It was something he used to do during my first (only) year of law school in New York, cupping the stress tendons to relieve my headaches. I put a hand on his knee, and he looked surprised, but not unhappy, so I left it there.

"So, Joel," Russ said, "Any sneak previews of when I can buy into a little bit of your company's magic? Always looking to invest. Don't want to keep all our eggs in one backyard business basket."

"I can't be specific," Joel said, "but I'm making a presentation to the Philly group at a conference in Puerto Rico next month. Looks promising."

"Ooh, business trip—are you going?" Jackie asked.

"Are you kidding?" I gestured at my stomach mound, tented under the black dress. Nobody from the Friday group knew what had happened with our first pregnancy, the boy who would have been Ella's age.

"What? You can fly whenever you want. You just need a doctor's note. I'd keep Sasha," Jackie offered. "The girls would be thrilled."

"Or take her with you," Russ said, sending a hard look to his wife. "Jackie brought Ella to Hawaii when we had a thing there. Swam in the pool, got their toes did at the spa. How much did those cost, hon, remember? Fifty bucks? To put toenail polish on a kid?"

I glanced at Joel, sipping his beer—he didn't say anything encouraging. He seemed lost in thought, and I wondered at what he had said, about worrying he would die earlier that day. About the girl.

"Leave her," Jackie said decisively. "We're good enough friends that even you should trust me by now. And there's no such thing as a 'vacation' with children. It's just parenting in a more challenging, unfamiliar setting."

"We'll talk about it?" I looked to Joel. Was it finally happening? Acceptance into her circle?

"The girls should check out the trampoline," Russ said. "Just got it for Gracey's birthday. Costco, two hundred and forty-nine dollars, for a twelve-footer and net. Great deal."

"Joel." I glanced at him, desperate.

"What?" He was three beers into the night, oblivious.

"We're not really comfortable with trampolines. Spinal injuries, multiple bouncers, and—"

Russ made a long-suffering face at Jackie, and she gave him an apologetic half-smile—for me, I realized—and stuck her fingers between her teeth, whistling like a football coach.

"I'm sorry," I murmured. Even living in a land of bear bells and coyote spotting, where children did not play in yards unsupervised because of mountain lions, I often felt like I was the only one with a true appreciation of how dangerous life could be. My vigilance was exhausting. I used it sometimes to justify the chocolate.

"Oh, this is the one who doesn't drive?" Russ said to Jackie, about me. "Guess I shouldn't get out the sparklers?"

"I-I brought glow sticks. They're in the wagon."

"Whee," Russ said flatly.

"Russell Grant," Jackie said, like he was the naughty boy at school the teacher secretly favored.

Joel shot me a look and I knew he was about to say something about how I needed to relax. Of course, he was right; they were all right.

"Sparklers will be fine," I lied.

Sasha crawled up on my lap, her feet in Joel's, bridging the space between us. He plucked blades of recently cut grass from between her bare toes and tickled them. I willed our eyes to meet, cementing this moment. Finally, he looked over, and smiled tentatively. I thought about Maia, from the plane. I pictured her out at a bar on Pearl Street with a host of boys in faded CU baseball caps and distressed jeans fawning over her. She was nothing to us. What I had smelled? It must have been the turbulence, fear, that was all. I exhaled and smiled back at him. *Relax.*

"The sky is my favorite color," Sasha said, tipping her head against my heart, and she was right; it was a breathtaking purple. The other three adults tilted their heads back, exposing their white throats, and made reverent sounds. It was the best part of the night.

Afterward, Joel and I walked home in comfortable silence, Sasha trundled into the wagon and wrapped in a blanket against the chill, near sleep as the wheels clunked over the seams in the sidewalk.

"That was nice," Joel said. "I actually had a good time."

"Me too."

"Why did you come to the airport today?"

"What?" We stopped walking. "Sasha told you, we wanted to surprise you."

Later, I would wonder how things would have been different if we had been honest with each other that night.

Joel looked at me like he had only once before in our whole ten years together—after the creditor called—like he didn't know me at all.

But then his phone rang, 9:00 on a Thursday night, in the wagon beside Sasha, vibrating and skittering like a trapped cockroach.

"Shouldn't you answer that?"

He stared at it.

"It must be about work," I said deliberately. "An emergency."

Hundreds, thousands, likely millions of wives did this every day, supplied their husbands with alibis, like a stage manager feeding a forgotten line from behind the velvet curtains. I didn't drive. I lived a thousand miles away from my parents who had followed their friends and nights of Quizzo to a senior-only community in Florida, who emphasized how much they liked us to "come for little visits." Feeling the weight of the baby inside me tugging me forward, I took the handle of the wagon from Joel and pulled on my own.

CHAPTER NINE

Maia

Joel D. Carter, CTO, didn't answer his phone.

I spent the night on the floor of the public bathroom at the end of Pearl Street, hitting the hand dryer button to keep warm and watching the battery life on my phone go down, the charger plugged in next to Scarlett's bed in Fishtown.

At sunrise, I called my sister. I could hear Mom in the background, how Ritchie had kept her up all night calling, trying to track me, or rather, his money, down, and she'd half a mind to call the police. *To report me!*

"This is the last thing you need, young lady!"

As if I didn't know.

Scarlett took the phone into the closet where Mom kept her cleaning business supplies. I could hear a broom banging the door, Mom yelling things for her to say, still slurry, and right then, I wasn't even a little bit homesick.

I didn't tell Scarlett where I was, so she'd honestly be able to say she didn't know. My sister hates lying, even for me.

"But you're okay? You have enough money?" You would have thought she was the older sister. I admitted I didn't.

"Listen, I have a hundred and eighty I can put in your account, but you have to give it at least twenty-four hours to clear." Then she warned me that Ritchie was really pissed, and if she had more money, she'd pay him back too.

"I love you," I said, "and not just because of the money."

"Be safe," she said.

After that, I called Joel again, to tell him he shouldn't go around picking up women in airports with a pregnant wife and kid at home.

"It's Maia. From the plane."

"I'm so glad you called! I feel terrible about yesterday, everything."

"You should! I mean, you're married? Why don't you wear a wedding ring?"

"I play racquetball, and if I jammed my finger, they might have to cut it off."

"Oh." I didn't know if he meant the ring or the finger, so I said something about not noticing a court on the airplane and he laughed and laughed.

"Look, I want a chance to explain. It's not what you think."

The phone hummed with silence, battery life ticking by.

"Sorry, that sounded ridiculous," he continued. "But everything is different for me, since the flight. Are you free for dinner, tonight, Flagstaff House?"

I paused, not as long as I should have. He'd said dinner and all I could think was how hungry I was.

"I don't go to dinner with married men."

"Please, I want to talk. This isn't what you think. I'm not…"

I waited.

"I'm not a bad person. What about lunch? I walk dogs at the Humane Society."

"I might be there; I might not."

"Okay," he said quietly. "Fair enough."

I found Homer at his cart reading *A Clockwork Orange* in the morning sun. It was cold, the city freshly washed in sparkles of dew.

"You again!" He seemed genuinely glad to see me.

"Me again."

"You want to talk about it?"

"About what?"

"Him, or her, or them, I guess. We are in Boulder. Hungry?" He offered me half his sesame bagel.

"Him," I said, sitting cross-legged on the bench nearby, trying to eat it slowly.

"And not really. It doesn't look like it has a happy ending."

"One's definition of happy ending depends on if you're a cynic, a romantic, or just horny."

"I hate that word," I told him. "It makes me think of gross old man toenails."

"So you are literary!" he crowed. "Do you have plans to see him again?"

"Sort of. I'm supposed to meet him at the Humane Society at noon."

"Is that good?"

"Well, I really like dogs," I said, and for some reason, Homer found this hilarious. "Could I walk from here to the Humane Society?"

Homer sighed like I was an annoying little sister, and told me to find him later, when I needed a ride.

All morning, I walked around Boulder in Scarlett's flats. Headache-thirsty, I spent my last three dollars on a smoothie at a place called Vitality.

"Can I have a cup of water too?" I asked, because I couldn't afford a bottle.

"There's an eco-filling station by the bathrooms."

Which it turned out was sort of like a drinking fountain, but not. Posted to the wall, there was a NOW HIRING board and an application. While I waited for my smoothie, I filled one out, using Homer's address and my cell, which was almost dead, and left it with the manager. Just in case.

Next to the library on Canyon I found a trail that followed a creek out of town. I can't do it justice, the way the cliffs, these huge red rocks hung over the water, this pencil thin trail and a scrap of road. It was like being a little kid, walking between your parents and feeling completely, utterly safe. Not that I have a lot of memories of that, but I have one. These rocks, they seemed to want to take care of me. Looking up at their shadowy caves, the happy tinkling of the creek beside me, I breathed deeply in the thin air. Just like Joel promised, I was falling in love with it all.

CHAPTER TEN

Carolyn

In our early days, before moving to Colorado where everyone reminds you of your good fortune, being picked by Joel was what made me feel lucky. I remember when we were dating the feeling of goldenness that surrounded him. *Everyone* loved Joel. His professors, his soccer teammates, my parents, even the surly landlord when we moved to Queens, would perk up to go a few rounds of "how bout those Mets" with Joel.

The year before we got engaged, my grandmother bellowed at the Easter dinner table, "Carolyn, if you let this one get away, you're not getting my amethyst earrings!" Joel was sitting right next to her; he thought it was adorable and dropped kisses on us both.

When Joel proposed, it was because of the Boulder job. He'd flown out to interview in early January and come home high on Colorado. He was in his final year of business school, and I was struggling through my first year of law at NYU. He'd called, asked me to meet him at Penn station, which was odd since we were long past the point where we met each other's trains.

"I want to take you to Lugo," he said, an Italian café on 33rd. I'd been buried in briefs, deep in torts the whole time he was gone. I hadn't gotten to do my run, my Central Park laps. I'd been living headachy days in the stuffy apartment on nothing but the Harry & David pear sampler my father had delivered every week.

It was noisy in Lugo. The ceilings are high, poor acoustics, and snow was falling outside the plate glass windows. Joel ordered a hundred dollar bottle of champagne, talking-talking-talking about Colorado, and the skiing he'd done with some of the team from Yakimori, the company where he'd interviewed, and the incredible bento boxes they had delivered for lunch, and how a massage therapist came to the office once a week, and Boulder was so progressive, so environmentally aware and fresh and clean compared to New York, how everyone had an attitude of respect for nature, for the outdoors. Mountain biking. Skiing. Crackling fires. I looked at the menu, lightheaded, wondering when was the last time I had eaten anything other than fruit.

"Last week, when the ball dropped, you asked if I had any New Year's resolutions. I do now: I want to get this job, ski every weekend, net eighty grand, and marry you."

Joel tells everyone I paused for at least a minute, that I made him sweat. I don't know that it was that long. I shouldn't have been surprised; we'd been together three years then. It was mostly the way it came out, at the end of his Colorado litany. Almost like an afterthought. And I was hungry, distracted by the smells of garlic and basil and cured meat coming from the kitchen.

I said yes. Joel kept talking and I remember thinking two things: that Boulder sounded almost too good to be true, and then, why not me? If I was careful, who is to say that we couldn't have a wonderful life? It was the first time since the accident that I let myself think of a happy future. He had asked me to marry him, to leave the city I had only just moved to, whose sounds and pace and public transportation left me on guard, unbalanced all the time.

"We could buy a house, maybe even a log cabin, and we'd ski every weekend. From the sounds of these guys, I'll be making more than enough to support us."

"Would I still go to law school?" I wondered out loud.

"I don't see why not. You might have missed the deadline for fall, but you could audit, or apply for an internship, or you could stay home and eat bon-bons all day! If the offer is anything like they were talking, I'll be taking care of everything financially."

Lightheaded, with the pangs in my stomach, that sounded perfect.

"Plus it would be a great place to raise a family," Joel added, and I felt so dizzy I reached across the table for his hand.

There was so much Joel didn't know.

CHAPTER ELEVEN

Maia

When Homer dropped me off at the Humane Society, he said, "Listen, tonight's kind of a potluck thing at the house. Don't worry about bringing anything. Seven o'clock."

"Okay, thanks." And even though he wasn't handsome, with his silly hat and thick jowls, and even though it totally wasn't my style, I was trying out a new version of Maia, so I leaned over and pecked his cheek. It surprised us both.

I squinted around the parking lot in the glaring sunlight, wishing for the millionth time I had put sunglasses in my purse the day before, but there was no sign of Joel's car.

I pushed the door open. Nobody at the desk. Down the hall, I saw a steel-haired woman in a jumpsuit dragging a skin-and-bones Great Dane. The dog's toenails skidded on the tile floor and he rolled his desperate brown eyes at me.

"Hello?" I called down the hall after her. "Excuse me?"

I looked around, saw nobody, so I followed them, pushing through the swinging door that said No Admittance. The woman in the jumpsuit had her back to me. She was filling a syringe, but she turned around and frowned. "This area is restricted."

"Sorry," I said. "I'm looking for a volunteer, Joel Carter?"

She checked her watch.

"Yeah, Joel's not usually late. He's not here. I could really use him, too. We're short-staffed today."

Both our eyes traveled to the Great Dane cowering on the metal table. He was enormous, but too skinny. You could tell he was old too; his watery brown eyes had a long story to tell. The hair under his chin and in the deep scars along his long legs was gray.

"Is he sick?" I asked.

"No," she sighed. "I've kept him as long as I could, but nobody seems to want a dog this big or this old."

"You're putting him down?"

She nodded. "Some hikers found him last month." Tears filled her eyes. "Chained to a tree up in the Flatirons. I can't even think about what this guy's past was like." She rubbed his head, and the dog licked her wrist, turning his big eyes to me. "He's a little skittish, especially around men, aren't you, Vader? But there's not a dangerous bone in his body." She put on her rubber gloves and my stomach soured. "I hate this part of the job. I'd take him myself, but my wife said enough—we've got six already." She laughed, more sad than happy.

Vader heaved a sigh and flopped on his side, offering his ribs to be rubbed. I worked my knuckles over them like a xylophone and he rumbled, a deep growl of pleasure.

"He likes that," she said, scratching around his ears, but then finally, "Well, this isn't going to get any easier. You can step out, or you can keep loving him up, while he goes. It's painless, for him anyway."

I should have recognized the feeling, standing on the edge of No Turning Back, but I just scratched my neck and jumped.

"I'll take him!" It was like getting on the plane, like there was no other option. Vader pushed his face into my palm. "I mean, how do I adopt him?"

"Does your landlord allow pets?"

"Yes." The lies flowed greasy and easy, like melted butter.

"We usually do a home visit the week before to make sure you're equipped for a dog, especially one this size. But this is a special circumstance, I guess."

I nodded.

When are you going to stop doing things like this?

"Well, how about that, buddy? An eleventh-hour pardon." She untied his leash and he leapt off the table. "He's good with getting down, but he has some arthritis, so going up stairs you'll need to give his hind end some support. It wouldn't hurt to get him on a supplement, glucosamine and chondroitin. They're not cheap, but it'll help his mobility."

Twenty-three cents to my name but still, I was better than death, wasn't I? The hives were traveling up behind my ears. I scratched as I followed her out to the front desk.

The woman handed me a clipboard of forms as the phone rang.

"Boulder Humane Society—hey, Joel."

My heart pounded.

"Oh thanks," she continued. "I appreciate the call. I could have used you today. But thanks for sending the new volunteer; I like doing paperwork more than euthanasia." She paused and looked over at the form I was filling out, using Homer's address, my dead cell phone.

"Maia Kramer," she said into the phone. "She's adopting Vader."

I started to giggle when she told Joel. No backing out now. It was better than letting him die, right?

Before I left, she handed me a gallon Ziploc bag of dry dog food, 'so you can transition if you're going to switch brands', a plastic bowl with his name on it, and finally, the leash attached to Vader's collar.

"We'll check in at the end of the week to see how things are going. Oh, and Joel says to tell you dinner, tomorrow night, meet him at six in front of your place and," she smiled at me, "he says wear something nice."

Vader and I walked from the Humane Society to Homer's. It took all of the afternoon and into the evening, both of us out of shape. Three times I had to stop guys and get directions for the address on my wrist. It didn't help that my poor dog kept looking up at me like, "are you sure this whole thing is a good idea?" no matter how many times I patted his head.

My heel blisters were bleeding by the time we got there, just before dark. The house was on the west side of Broadway, on a shaded section of Pine Street, painted lavender and leaning a little to the side. I left the dog supplies by the porch railing. I knocked, got no answer, so I pushed the door open. Inside, twentysomethings lounged on yard sale furniture. A long picnic table at the far end of the room was covered in a faded rainbow sheet and mounds of food. Vader cowered behind my thighs like a shy kid at Kindergarten.

"Maia!" Homer leapt up from a plaid chair with exposed springs. Everyone was intent on the TV, *Jeopardy*. Five guys and one girl looked me up and down. The girl turned back to the TV. There was absolute silence, and then a burst of answers, in question form. Someone had a notebook out; it looked like they might be keeping score.

I stood in the doorway, rubbing the prickly hair between Vader's eyes.

"I said you didn't have to bring anything," Homer said. "I haven't had dog since we went to King Wok."

"Ha," I said.

"Announcement! Everyone, this is Maia, who I told you might be coming to stay with me."

Raised heads, and the pierced eyebrow girl perched on a guy's lap droned, "That fucking dog doesn't stay here."

"Fuck yeah it does, if the goddess stays with it."

"What is the Great Wall, Alex?" they all yelled.

"I'll introduce you at a commercial." Homer took me by the elbow and Vader in tow, steered me over to the food table.

"Okay." His laugh was nervous. "It's clear-out-the-fridge night. The stuff at this end of the table is from less than a month ago, and it gets older and more question-able as you go."

Vader, whose head was level with the table, poked his nose around. I held him back by his collar, thinking it might be for his own safety.

I looked into a pot of tan liquid. Whole sections of a chicken drifted to the sur-face among strings of celery. The breastbone pierced the grease slick like the rudder of a sailboat. I took some slices of pale pink watermelon and a piece of brown bread.

Beside me, Vader whined, so I gave him the bread.

In the corner, there was a pile of rotting garbage in a bucket. Flies feasted on it, buzzing over to check out our plates.

"What is that?" I tried to keep the disgust out of my voice, mouth breathing, one hand on Vader's collar.

"Haven't you ever heard of composting? We compost our garbage, for the environment."

"Quiet!" a guy from the floor yelled and then, "What is Toronto, Alex!"

When Double Jeopardy began, a hush fell over the room. Homer got up for seconds and I noticed that his T-shirt was stained and the hair combed across a bald spot on the crown of his head was greasy. Here, he seemed less artist/hip Pearl Street vendor, more loser.

"So, uh, Homer, where's your workshop?" I asked. He was hunched over a plate of curry, yellow sauce running down his chin.

"Huh?"

"Your workshop, where you make the jewelry?"

"What?" the girl looked up. "Where Homer makes his jewelry? Ha!"

"Home-dog, you sly fox," Goatee Boy said, and then he bit down on the girl's neck, hard.

Homer turned maroon and suggested we go up to the roof to see the stars.

It was true, what the lady at the Humane Society had said; Vader needed me to stand with the fronts of my thighs against his hips to push him up the stairs at Homer's. He threw these heartbreaking looks over his shoulder like, 'sorry about the caboose'. I loved him already.

Through Homer's room, a bare mattress, snakes of computer cords and a ratty poster that read *Tetris—If You Dare*, we accessed a flat, tarry square of roof.

"Don't mind those guys," Homer dismissed his housemates. "They've been strung out lately. Programming."

I sat cross-legged on a tar-free spot and Vader settled next to me, grizzled chin on my knee, and my heart surged at his loyalty, my good luck.

Homer looked at us and shook his head.

"Listen, everyone said you could crash here for a while. They're cool with us, but they didn't know about the dog. That might be a problem."

Us?

"But tonight's fine. I'm not going to put you out on the street or anything."

With the sun behind the mountains, it was freezing. Homer went into his room, came back out with a scratchy blanket and threw it over both our shoulders.

"What's this?" He reached behind me, slid something out of my hip pocket, examining it. "May 27?"

"My return ticket." I took it from him, tucked it between my thigh and the rooftop. "But I can go back any time. I'm just waiting until some money clears."

Homer was huddling as close to me as Vader would tolerate; his breath reeked of curry and garlic. "But what are you going to do about this?" He nodded at my dog.

"I don't know, okay?" I snapped, realizing I hadn't really slept or eaten. He got out from under the blanket and huffed off, back inside the house where I could hear video game, the canned laughter of TV.

⌒

I must have fallen asleep, my head resting on Vader's back on Homer's roof, because when I opened my eyes, Homer was crouched over me and the sky behind him was dead black with a sprinkling of stars. Vader's growl was the roar of an approaching train. My eyes adjusted and I saw that Homer had his dick out of his pants and was yanking on it right over my head, mouth open, eyes half-closed. I could see the white, furry underside of his belly, the coppery hairs around his swinging balls.

I bolted to my feet and Vader scrambled to follow, his toenails clicking against the rooftop. He threw me a worried look, head hunched low.

"Jesus, Maia, I-I," Homer was trying to pull his T-shirt down over it, stuffing it back into his pants.

"Sicko!" I threw the blanket off my shoulders, an icy blast of night air on my skin. "You creepy Chester!" I grabbed Vader by the collar and hauled him down the stairs, made it outside before I threw up, pinkish watermelon on the buckling sidewalk.

I looked back once, my fingers looped in Vader's collar. Homer wasn't following us, but I'd left Vader's food and bowl back on his porch.

Together, we walked Pine Street toward Broadway, toward Pearl Street and the hand dryers. The clock on the bank said midnight. It felt too quiet compared to Philly, and it was brittle-cold, but there was nothing I could do about it.

"Hey, Buddy." Vader sat when I stopped on Pearl Street, looking up at me anxiously. "I really could have used some back up. We've got to be in this together, okay?"

I sank on to a bench, and he flopped his chin on my thigh again. By the street-light, I inventoried my purse. I had Sheila McHugh, mascara and cherry Chapstick, my dead cell phone, my empty wallet with my bank card and SEPTA pass, and twenty-three cents. I patted my chest, my license was still in my bra, and when I checked my hip pocket, I felt the stiffness of Joel's business card. In the other; nothing. I felt again, checked my purse. My return plane ticket was gone, lost, somewhere back on Homer's rooftop.

CHAPTER TWELVE

Carolyn

After Joel and I were married in my backyard in Cherry Hill, we honeymooned, (Jamaica; beautiful, romantic) and then loaded my parents' garage-full of silver-wrapped wedding presents into a U-Haul that was towing Joel's Accord. I remember walking through my childhood house before I left, the carpets steamed, the rooms empty, the FOR SALE sign listing out on the lawn.

My parents had announced it the same day I told them I was engaged. They were leaving New Jersey, following friends and better weather to Florida. Something about 'no home to come home to' made getting married and moving to Boulder loom even bigger than it was.

I sat on the floor in the old living room on the rectangle of dark peach carpet where the couch had been, where I had recuperated, my knee in a straight brace, the summer after the accident—*"I want her out here where we can keep an eye on her,"* I'd heard *my father tell my mother*—and how other than the police the first day, nobody came to see me. Not my boyfriend, not my supposedly-best-friend, Holly, certainly not the parents. It had just been me and the kousa dogwood tree outside the bay window, daytime television and the bowl of fruit my mother left on the coffee table before she went to work, so I would have something to eat, 'but only fruit, so you don't get fat while your leg heals.'

Five years later, the kousa was fuller, taller now, its branches heavy with creamy, star-shaped flowers. I would never see it again.

The drive across the country with Joel was the pendulum swing from the honeymoon. I was anxious without my daily run. I went three days on nothing but diet Coke and two pears, which I parceled out every twenty miles by carving off a sliver so thin you could see semis passing in the light that shone through it.

Neither of us is particularly relaxed during transition periods, but Joel was increasingly irritable on the drive to Boulder. We fought over music and audio books. Joel wouldn't let me put the windows down because he said the Midwest was too dusty. We were married now, and the lines were clear: he was the Pilot, I was the Navigator.

"You shouldn't drive tired," I worried at him.

"I've got it," he insisted, staring straight ahead.

Years into our marriage, I learned that the night before we left for Boulder, Yakimori had called him and renegotiated the salary; if he still wanted the job, thirty percent less than promised and only single year, renewable contracts.

"Joel, please." I reached for the volume knob and turned down his *Seven Habits of Highly Effective People*. We had just gotten through Chicago's traffic. "Please let's stop!"

"And waste what money on a hotel?"

We pushed on.

The tumbleweeds and jagged mountains outside Boulder were a welcome sight. The first day, I dug my sneakers out and ran mind-numbing laps around our neighborhood, terrified of getting lost, of mountain lions and bears. I marveled at this strange, red-rocked desert, the dryness, the smell of summer sage brush, the lack of East Coast green. Later, while I pushed unopened boxes along the beige carpeting to their respective rooms, Joel disappeared. He came home with a Labrador puppy. We didn't think about the carpeting or security deposits then. We were now married, with a dog!

Who said I didn't deserve to be happy?

In the early days, I felt hopeful about the turn our life had taken, invigorated by all the possibility of a new life here in Boulder's clean air. Everyone I talked to, from the checker at the Sprouts grocery store to the white boy with dreadlocks at Colorado Mountain Sports who fitted us for snowshoes, raved about how fortunate we were to have made the decision to move to Boulder, this exclusive land of chosen, golden people. This insistence that everyone out here is lucky, that this is the best place on earth, has never faltered.

CHAPTER THIRTEEN

Maia

I got the job at Vitality. Jenn, the manager with the short brown hair who had taken my application the day before, found me feeding Vader out of the dumpster when she came to open up Saturday morning. She didn't ask for references, just said that if I was Maia Kramer, I was early for my interview.

"Your dog's dehydrated and malnourished," her voice was as sharp as her jingling keys. She gave me some packing twine to tie up Vader and a large bowl of water.

"Because of the desert climate," she called to me. "The night and day temperatures are really varied. It's meant to get hot today, so be sure he has plenty of water. You're new to Boulder." It wasn't a question.

I followed Jenn around the rest of the morning, and she talked me through everything. I washed a lot of blenders. I learned not to put my hand too deep inside when trying to scrape the strawberry seeds off the glass. Jenn told me they had the blender blades sharpened every two weeks and replaced the motors every two months. Vitality was a crazy busy place.

Jenn kept throwing day-old bagels out to Vader. When I told her what I knew of his past, she went off about the college kids who came here and just ditched their adopted dogs when they left.

"It says a lot about you that you rescued him," she sniffed, sucking on a clove cigarette at the end of the day, both of us ruffling Vader's ears. I finished the last of my smoothie pour off. "If you want the job, I'll see you two tomorrow morning."

The Hotel Boulderado had an outdoor bar called The Corner, and I slid on to one of the leather stools under the patio heaters with their fake flames. I beamed at the bartender and ordered a glass of water with lime. Vader, curled at my feet, licked the soles of my new shoes gratefully, making the saddest, soft keening sound, like he knew we shouldn't be there.

Around me, everyone was in local uniform—intentionally shabby, faded and broken-in. Janelle would call it posh-poor. I would have fit right in, except, an hour earlier, I'd drained my bank account—forty dollars—at an ATM and blown the last of my money on a secondhand skintight black dress and platform Chinese dragon heels from a sidewalk sale outside Buffalo Exchange. Even the consignment stuff was expensive, but the salesgirls had fussed over Vader and fed him two slices of their veggie pizza that smelled amazing. I was calculating, as I walked to the bar, that after the dress, the shoes, new underwear, plus a pack of mint gum, I had $2.72 to my name until the money from Scarlett cleared, and no plan of where to sleep.

"Can I have another lime?"

The bartender slid two to me on a saucer, and I nibbled them, rind and all.

"You sure you don't want a drink while you're waiting?" he asked me again and I shook my head. "Something to eat?"

The sun was setting behind the mountains and it was so cold the goosebumps on my bare arms throbbed.

"Hey." The voice was warm in my ear—I hadn't seen him coming. I wanted to jump into his arms, but I managed to swivel elegantly on my stool and stand up.

"Joel," I said simply.

"I wasn't sure you'd be here." Joel made a move toward me, and Vader growled.

"Whoa, partner, stand back," I laughed, forgetting I was mad at him. After Homer, after feeling invisible in seas of strangers at Vitality all day, it felt so good to see his familiar face. "Vader's a ladies' man."

"So you've been in town how long and you've acquired a dog?"

"I saved his life!"

"How much do they charge to let that thing stay in your room?" Joel looked up at the hotel behind me.

"What?" and then I realized what he meant. For a second, I saw Joel's version of me, a Kardashian, breezing through fancy resort towns, flying first class, dozens of black dresses and heels, collecting stray animals. I felt a surge of longing to be her. Vader leaned against my thigh like a lamppost, thumping his whip-tail. "Oh, it's nothing."

"Not to change the subject, but… you look amazing."

Joel ordered a beer for himself and we sat. "What're you drinking, vodka tonic?" I nodded and he ordered me one.

"So," he said, and we each waited for the other to say something. I thought of our kiss, the magnet pull, how he'd felt like something safe, grown-up.

"The plane? Your phone call? What you said you wanted to tell me?"

"Okay. That." Joel took a deep breath, leaned closer. "For starters, yes, I'm attracted to you, and yes, obviously, I'm married."

I frowned. My drink arrived and I sipped. It was so strong it made the hairs inside my nose burn.

"God, you have no idea, do you?"

"No idea, what?"

"How beautiful you are. How *intimidatingly* beautiful you are."

"Oh." I flushed, tipped my head down to sip from my drink.

"I'm out of practice here." Joel fumbled with his drink napkin.

"I hope so, for your wife's sake." I was trying to be funny.

"Let me start over. First, we meet in the bar, then you end up on my flight, next to me no less, and then you're moving out here, and it seemed like… fate. This sounds so cheesy, but meeting you feels like a chance, something I shouldn't ignore."

I was halfway through my vodka tonic and had eaten all three lime slices and a skewer of olives.

"You fascinate me. I've never met anyone so independent. And then, when the turbulence hit, it was like the gods had the plane in their fist, like 'wake up, man!' Don't laugh," he said, laughing at himself, which was fairly adorable. His voice turned serious. "But I had an epiphany. Do you know how you can live a long time, going through the motions, not realizing you're unhappy, doing it because it's what you've always done?" Joel swallowed. "And then something happens, and it feels like it *might* change the entire course of your life?"

I thought of sprinting down the jetway, kissing while the overhead luggage rained down around us, claiming Vader from the metal table.

"Yes," I said, but wondered, did he mean meeting me was changing the course of his life?

"I like this feeling, fresh eyes, like I'm seeing things clearly. I need more of this—you—in my life."

"What about——" I wanted to say, *your wife, your daughter*, but I didn't.

I fished an ice cube out of my drink, crunching it so hard I accidentally cut my lip.

"I don't think you're meant to eat that." Joel leaned to me, moving the cocktail napkin away from my mouth. Then, glancing around, he kissed me, took my lower lip between his and sucked gently until the bleeding stopped. When he pulled away, I took a deep, shivering breath. My mouth felt like I'd licked a nine-volt battery. I stood up, dizzy, the pull from my body to his.

This was going to be different from anything I'd ever done.

"Let's go," I said.

"Where's your coat?"

"In the room," I lied, weaving deliberately toward his car. I assumed we were going to Flagstaff House. Food would be a good idea.

"Why don't we go up and get it?"

I shook my head, opening the back door of his Audi for Vader; the car seat was gone. I lowered myself into the front, trying not to think, this is where the wife sat.

Joel put the car in gear and turned the heater on. Freezing, I folded my hands in my lap to keep from pressing them to the whooshing vents like a homeless person.

When I glanced over, I noticed Joel had a very sharp profile, like a bird of prey. I'd never been with a man this grown-up, this good-looking.

"Drive."

CHAPTER FOURTEEN

Carolyn

S ome newlyweds we were: our first summer in Boulder, when we lived in the townhouse, Joel and I made love exactly twice.

It was the stress, the transition, work. I had missed the registration for the second year of law school, and partway through July, Joel confessed to me that he had exaggerated some of his capabilities and command of certain applications during the interview process at Yakimori, so at night he was trying to learn what they assumed he already knew. Plus housebreaking Ben was challenging; we worried about our security deposit.

I often found Joel up at night browsing real estate—he wanted to move closer to town, or into the mountains, wanted a more authentic Boulder experience. He was enamored with the progressive green movement, the idea that we could bike to work and walk to the organic grocery store.

"What's the point of living out here if we can't enjoy the lifestyle?" he said. "We might as well be in some slapped-together development in Hackensack."

Joel ate lunch with three single guys at work who drove Jeeps, who went hiking and camping, off-roading on old mining trails in the mountains on the weekends. They were working their way through the Fourteeners, hikes of mountains over fourteen thousand feet.

But our weekends were spent house hunting. Everything we looked at was triple what we could afford, from log cabins off Sunshine Canyon to lofts that overlooked

Pearl Street. Even the ugliest fifties split-level in town was out of our range. Our realtor stopped taking Joel's calls.

In the fall, I audited a second year class, Advanced Appellate Advocacy, and was terrified at the way my thoughts drifted, the terms, once familiar, difficult to wrap my mind around as the professor zipped on in a lilting Indian accent. I wasn't eating anything but honeycrisp apples then, and with the thinner air, I felt too much space in my head, a strange, dizzy hollowness. When the professor called on me, I stammered through an excuse of being a first year auditing, but he persisted, insisting I could form an opinion until the whole room was squirming with me.

"Come now." His voice was surprisingly gentle. "If you cannot handle the classroom, how do you expect to fare in the courtroom?"

I picked up my bag, apologized to him, the rest of the room, and left.

"I should get a job," I suggested that night when Joel came home. His bangs were long, no time for a trim, and sticking straight up, meaning he had been running sweaty hands through his hair a lot that day.

"What? Why? Things are about to turn around. You're going to be a lawyer and I'm going to be making plenty of money soon. Lee said as much in my review. Would we be going to look at houses this weekend if I weren't?"

Joel had found a new realtor and resigned himself to the fact that we were priced out of Boulder proper. We found our current house, a stucco 3-bedroom 2.5 bath in a new subdivision farther East, former farmland, with a strangely green lawn (sprinkler systems), a fenced yard for Ben and a garage.

"A starter house," Joel said. "When you're pulling in those big lawyer fees, we'll move into town."

I was supposed to be studying, prepping for second year law, but I got claustrophobic in the taupe and beige spare room. I bought glossy, colorful magazines—*Parents, Fit Pregnancy*—and stashed them like teenage boy's porn between the mattress and box spring of our bed. Ever since the accident, I'd always been aware of babies, but now it was bellies. Women leaving the gym in yoga pants and sports bras with naked watermelon bellies or pushing their carts through Sprouts with that age-old arch to their backs, panting behind jog strollers with bowl-cut toddlers inside, everywhere, their perfectly rounded abdomens. *Why not me?*

I ran miles every day, to a new Pier 1 on Arapahoe. I also started shopping. That was something else.

Then right before Christmas, Joel got called into the CEO's office.

He told me the news over dinner at Flagstaff House, a four and a half star restaurant overlooking Boulder Valley. "Lee is raising my salary, closer to the original offer."

"Oh honey, that's great!" I said, and meant it.

"So we can start to relax, enjoy things here, each other, more. Lee says we're welcome to use his condo in Breckenridge this weekend, get some skiing in."

He clinked his wine glass against mine and we both sipped. His eyes drifted out to the valley that swept down from the plate glass window, all the lights of town twinkling.

"I feel like we're finally where we are supposed to be. My resolution, the job, the money, Boulder, us. It's all coming together."

What Joel didn't know on that night six and a half years ago: in the linty bottom of my purse, there were a dozen tiny white and pale blue pills. The month before that, I'd thrown the whole prescription out the window on a bus ride home from Pier 1 along Baseline—littering! In Boulder!

This means it was my fault: I deserved what happened later, those bloody hours in the cramped airplane bathroom over the Pacific.

Our first year in Boulder, without consulting Joel, I'd started playing Russian roulette with my birth control pack.

CHAPTER FIFTEEN

Maia

In his car, in the dark parking lot outside Wine Merchant, I was wondering when (if?) we were ever going to Flagstaff House. We took turns swigging from the heavy neck of the champagne bottle Joel had bought, Vader's head nudging between us like a bossy chaperone.

"This is crazy." Joel ran his hand up over his face, but he was smiling. He glanced back at the dog. "I still can't believe you rescued a dog."

"It was more the other way around," I said, but I was thinking about how Vader had bolted when things got dicey with Homer. "How come you weren't at the shelter?"

And though he said it was a work thing, I could tell that it was his family.

"What's in the bag?" he asked.

At my feet was the plastic one from Buffalo Exchange, which I'd been trying to carry like an intentional purse, stuffed with my old clothes, Scarlett's flats, and my empty wallet. I appreciated why homeless people used shopping carts.

"I'm a woman of mystery," I said, picturing something smoky-dark, reds and purples, to go with the dragons on my platform shoes. I tried out a line I'd been tossing around since the plane, a mantra of the new Maia, "I never say no to an opportunity."

"Or stray dogs, apparently." Joel shook his head. "So, what have my woman of mystery and Marmaduke been up to in Boulder?"

I told him about wandering downtown. I described the creek trail, the scene on Pearl Street, saving Vader. I left out the part about Homer and the juice bar. "You were right; I'm falling in love with Boulder."

"I want you to fall in love with me." Joel was pouty and, I realized, drunk.

I looked out the window. In the distance, I could just make out the silhouette of the mountains against the night sky. Now that I had Vader, going back to Philly was significantly trickier. Joel followed my gaze.

"Amazing, aren't they? You know, living here, a place like Boulder, watching everyone get the most out of life, it makes you extra sensitive to all the things you might be missing."

"FOMO," I said.

"What?"

He really hadn't heard of FOMO? Exactly how old was he?

"It means Fear of Missing Out."

"Oh." Joel nodded. "Right, okay. Yeah, so if you pick backyard BBQ suburbia, what they don't tell you, if you pick married-with-children, is that everything changes. Your wife. Your life. Your mobility. You become tethered. Nobody warns you about the paraphernalia, all the stuff that comes along with kids! We travel to Florida every Christmas, to see the in-laws. It's a nightmare. I love Sasha; I'd do a hundred doctor's appointments, preschool interviews, carry a thousand suitcases of G-diapers through airports for her but… Hashtag FOMO."

I glugged from the bottle, bubbles making my eyes water.

"Sorry to dump all this on you. I sound like a jerk, like saying the trouble with marriage is all the closet space your wife takes up."

He was waiting for me to say something; I was waiting for him to tell me if the problem with marriage really was all the closet space a wife takes up.

Bold with the champagne, I asked, "And what happens if you pick me?"

He turned with purpose, and just like the plane, and the bar, I knew what would happen next, his lips finding mine. He pressed me against the passenger window, kissing, and I grabbed his shoulders, dizzy with champagne, altitude and hunger. I wanted this.

In the backseat, Vader growled.

"I want to make love to you. Tonight. Now." Joel's breath was hot in my ear.

He wore that dopy-desperate face that Janelle calls "grotesque display of male li-bi-do."

"Wait, we can't…" I turned my head, "go to the Boulderado." I whispered, his lips against my throat.

"Why not?" he pulled back, reluctant, his hand on the ignition.

"The dog," I mumbled. "We got… kicked out."

So instead he drove us out of town to the Boulder Adventure Lodge Motel with its sad, flickering security lights and peeling red paint railings and if there's anything more depressing and cliché than that, I don't know what it is.

In the room, Vader growled at Joel, but he was all bluff. I dragged him with me into the narrow bathroom, closing the door.

"It's fine." I patted my dog's head while I peed, but he gave me this big-eyed, disappointed look down his long black nose.

Come on, I haven't even done anything yet!

When I came out, Joel was sitting on the bed. I leaned against the closed bathroom door, wondering what would happen next. Vader scratched the door behind me.

I was having a hard time placing myself in this moment. I forced the narrowed, hazel eyes of his little girl—*how come, exactly, are you here?* —out of my mind. I was on the climb from giddy-drunk to the first glimmers of sober. Too bad we'd left the champagne in the car.

Joel stood up and crossed the room to me, with intention.

"You," he stroked my neck, "strike me as an incredibly strong, independent woman. Traveling across the country solo, rescuing needy dogs." He smiled his crooked smile, trailing the tips of his fingers up my cheek. "But you don't have to be, all the time. Let me be there for you. Let me…"

Inside me, something came undone, the breath I had been holding since I ran after him down the jetway.

I knew then we were going to finish this. I exhaled. Joel's fingers slipped under the floss-thin straps of my dress, snapping them. He worked lower. The tiniest moan came out of my mouth. Behind me, on the other side of the bathroom door, Vader whined.

I kissed Joel hard on the mouth. I pushed him backwards by walking forward. When I kicked off my heels, we were the exact same height. He stumbled, shuffling, until his calves hit the edge of the bed. I placed both palms on his chest and pushed, and his knees buckled. He lay beneath me, breathing hard, watching to see what would happen next.

The cut on my lip reopened and I licked it, tasting saltiness. Joel groaned. I pulled the dress up over my head, nothing between us now but the new black G-string. Before this, it had only been Mark. I looked down. He wanted me-me-me. Crawling over him on the bed, I straddled his thighs and worked on his shirt buttons, my fingers thick from the alcohol.

What did it matter? It wasn't like I *was married.*

After, I collapsed on top of him, hyper-aware that his arm did not wrap around my bare back to hold me the way Mark's always did.

Then Joel was sliding out from under me, letting my dog out of the bathroom, getting rid of the condom, running water, me watching the orange patterns of the flickering parking lot light on the ceiling. Vader paced the room, whining.

Joel pulled on his clothes. "It's late. I'm sorry. I've got to go."

I wondered where he'd told her he was. I couldn't talk because I felt like crying.

He crossed the room and Vader grumbled, scrambling on the bed. I wished I'd gotten under the covers. Lying there naked, him dressed, I felt vulnerable. He trailed his fingers down my bare thigh and sighed.

"God, you are so beautiful."

Joel brought his face down to mine and kissed me with fresh, minty lips, a brief goodbye peck. His clean mouth made me feel sour and gross.

Had he planned ahead? Brought a toothbrush?

"Ugh." I gulped on a sob.

"What's wrong?"

"Nothing. I just, I think, I've made a huge mistake."

He cupped my cheek and wiped at my tears with the pad of his thumb. "Shhh, it's okay," he whispered, and I could tell that he was a good dad to Sasha. My face was freezing where his warm hand had been.

"What's wrong?"

I blurted it all out. Well, not everything. I started with sitting in an airport watching peoples' lives take off.

"Wait, so you work... in the airport?"

"You bought the shoelaces from me!" I didn't add, *For your daughter!*

The Kardashian sister, bopping between first-class cities with her pedigreed pooch, slipped away into the night, leaving me and my booze-breath, and Vader, scratching himself so hard the motel bed shook.

I could feel Joel watching her go. With disappointment.

"That was you?"

I kept talking, not mentioning Mark, the legal trouble back in Philly or the part about stealing the kiosk cash from Ritchie. Instead, I told Joel how I got on the plane, following the question he still hadn't asked me, how at the moment, there didn't seem to be any other option, like adopting Vader. Like I had to do it. I ended up with us in the motel, after, with him leaving me.

When I finished, the corner of Joel's lip twitched.

"Wait a minute." He straightened up. "So you got on the plane, moved here, *because of me?*"

It was like he didn't know if he should be flattered or run for the rocky hills.

"It wasn't just you," I clarified. "It was my whole life, everything. And then you turned out to be…." I didn't even say the word. Never mind what our bodies had just done—awkwardness filled the room like smoke. He actually glanced at his watch.

"So, now." I took a deep breath, "I just need to know one thing."

Joel nodded.

"What did you want to ask me? At the airport, at the bar, in Philly, you told me all about Colorado and then you said, 'Can I ask you a question?'" I pushed myself up on my elbows, felt Joel's eyes taking in all seventy-two of my naked inches. "But you never did."

"Oh." I heard a jingle of change in his pocket, a shift. He looked at the door. "Nothing."

"What?"

"It's stupid, now, a line, trying to be charming. I was going to ask, 'What's a pretty girl like you doing in a place like this?'"

What does pretty get you?

It was one of my mom's favorite sayings.

I turned my face to the wall. "You should go."

"Will I see you again?"

"Maybe." I reached over and stroked Vader's silky ears, not sure how much longer I could keep my face neutral.

Vader threw Joel a look and growled.

"You know, a dog, any dog, is a big responsibility, but a dog like that—"

"Yeah, thanks, *Dad.*"

Joel winced, but kept going, the importance of consistency for dogs that have been abused, how he needed supplements for arthritis, lawsuits if he bit someone…

"We're fine. I have a job, at Vitality. Don't you have a family to get home to?"

He exhaled, a long sigh. He didn't kiss me. When he left, the door was on a hinge, swinging shut behind him.

Afterward, I filled the bath and folded myself in. At Mark's, there was only a shower. We'd had a tub back at my mom's, but she was the only one who ever used it, the ceramic stained brown along the edges from cigarettes she left burning. Vader waited right beside me on the bathroom floor, his chin on the edge, snoring, and I stayed in all night, one hand on his head, adding hot water every time the tank refilled, until the sun was shining fire on the mountains.

For the rest of April and the first week of May, I lived on bagels and smoothie pour-off and slept beside Vader on a futon in Jenn's apartment. I worked the unpopular split shift. I woke up at 4:45 and went in on Jenn's behalf to open up and work until eleven. She loaned me clothes, her jeans like capris, her shirts showing my bellybutton, until my two boxes arrived from Scarlett. I was happiest about seeing my six pairs of shoes. Walking everywhere in her flats, my feet were a mess of blisters and scabs.

Joel saw them one time, afterwards, when we were getting into the shower at the motel, and I lied, "They look worse than they feel."

That's the other thing. Starting that first Monday, Joel picked me up on his lunch hour, Mondays and Fridays, when he wasn't in Philly. We went back to the motel. Having sex with Joel was simply easier than… not. I was trying on 'never say no to an opportunity', like Buffalo Exchange dresses.

But the problem was, the more time that passed, the more I realized that Joel and I weren't building to anything, the less I liked what I was doing—putting Vader in the narrow motel bathroom with some dry food, sex, showering, and getting dropped back at work.

We did it exactly nine times, until the week everything changed.

It was the middle of May when my favorite Vitality regulars came in looking scruffy and cheerfully hung over. College boys, shaggy handsome and flirty—Jenn and I had nicknamed them the Three Amigos: RPB (Rich Pretty Boy) was Luke, Tall Stoner was Beau and Shy Guy was Will. It was Friday lunch; Joel would be there any minute.

"Hey, Maia, can we put this up in here?" Luke, who drove the Range Rover, waved a flyer. *Roommate wanted.* I told him I had to ask Jenn, carrying it into the back to read: Basement bedroom available in house off Iris, $650/month, plus utilities. Large backyard, hot tub, pets negotiable.

"Sorry, Jenn said no."

"What? Tell her to get her hot little ass out here. Jenn!" Luke was clearly used to getting his way.

"She said you can't advertise until you let me check it out. I think she'd be happy to have her futon back. My dog and I've been crashing there the last few weeks."

"What kind of dog?"

Vader sealed the deal. I took the guys around back and they fell in love with him; he gave them wary, tail-thumping tolerance. Will, the quiet one, rubbed his ears while Beau put 22 Juniper Court in my phone and Luke agreed to waive the last month's rent deposit if I could move in the next day.

"Hey, we're going biking, right now, if you want to ride with us? It could be your inaugural Club 22 outing."

They had their mountain bikes on the rack of Luke's Range Rover. They said Beau's girlfriend taught spinning every day and the thousand dollar mountain bike her parents had given her had been hanging, with the tag still on it, back in the garage.

"We could pick it up on the way."

"I never say no to an opportunity." I grinned. "But I have to warn you: I'm kind of a mountain biking virgin."

We were standing in the parking lot, arguing about where to ride, Meyers Homestead versus Rattlesnake Gulch, when Joel pulled in.

"The Gulch? We're not trying to kill her, dude."

Joel got out and stood there uncertainly in the parking lot, looking from me to the boys to Vitality, not going in, until they noticed him.

"It's open," Will called out helpfully.

It was hard to read Joel's eyes—he had his mirrored aviators on. Finally, he started for the door.

"Nice suit, dude," Beau called out. He'd told me once, at the motel, that Lee, his boss, was old school and insisted on full suit and tie.

"I'll be right back, I'm just going to fill my water bottle," I said, which was a big thing in Boulder.

Inside Vitality, Joel was carefully folding his sunglasses, placing them in the pocket of his suit jacket, pretending to scan the menu.

"Hey." I touched his arm.

He didn't say anything, then, "So what's good here?" Even though every week, I brought us a strawberry banana pour-off to share.

"Listen, I'm just going to ride bikes with these guys. They're my new house-mates—it's a house outing. Okay?"

Jenn came out.

"Can't stay away? Go take your break!" she laughed at me, and then a professional smile and "What can I getcha?" for Joel.

He stepped forward, away from me, to place his order. What was I supposed to do? So I left. But I felt Joel watching me through the glass the whole time.

CHAPTER SIXTEEN

Carolyn

Last February, Joel came home from his first trip to Philadelphia with what he thought was good news: a promotion, his salary increasing by seven percent, a two year contract this time. This was important; we'd been living beyond our means, still whittling away at student loans and the last of the debt from my shopping.

"The only downside is that I'll have to travel Tuesday to Thursday to the client in Philadelphia."

"*Every week?*"

"This is huge for us," he'd said, lifting the suitcase onto our bed and unzipping it.

"I don't want to be a single parent!" I howled, stomping around the bedroom, throwing clothes back in drawers. "I can't do it all by myself; she's so high energy. I cannot watch her every second! And now there are going to be two of them!" I blurted out the news; not the way I'd been planning to tell him.

"What?"

"I'm pregnant."

Joel got very quiet.

"Again? How?"

"Do you need a flip chart?"

"No, it's just…I wish I'd known. Before."

"Well, now you do."

Joel zipped his suitcase closed, lifting it up to the top shelf of the closet. "I'll be gone less than half the week. It'll be two nights, three at the most, and we'll have the weekends."

Now it was my turn to be quiet, but when I dumped his toiletries in the bathroom drawer, I slammed it closed.

"I thought you'd be glad," Joel said softly, and I realized that he had been so excited to tell me, so proud. Before I could say anything, the conversation took a hard turn. "I mean, you certainly won't mind spending the money!"

"With you traveling all the time, what if I have to go on bed rest again?" I stopped in front of him.

"Then we'll deal with that. We'll hire someone. God, I thought," he said, sounding bewildered and tired as he sat on our bed, "that this was going to be good news."

Exhausted from the burst of adrenaline when we argued, I sagged down next to Joel on the bed.

"Me too." I should have congratulated him, but instead I said, "How will I pay for anything, if you're not here to co-sign checks?"

His solution: the cash envelope.

It was early May, twenty-three weeks, almost viable, when I called him in Philadelphia to tell him I'd need more money in the envelope next week.

"How much do you need?" Joel asked, the line humming across the states between us. In the background of his hotel room, I heard the TV on, a basketball game.

"Four hundred," I said, wishing it sounded less like an apology.

It was actually $372, but I always rounded up.

"Jesus, for what?"

"A car seat."

"A four hundred dollar car seat?"

"This one is for Sasha. It's bigger, a five-point. She can pass hers down to the baby."

"Isn't she ready for those booster things yet?"

"The law says they have to ride in a full restraint until age 8. This is the best, the safest five-point on the market. The Isaksson-Hellman study showed that the maximum effect of a restraint system is not attained if the child is not using the optimal CRS for its age."

"You're not even speaking English, Car."

I sat there, breath coming in short bursts. How *dare* he question the choices I was making for the safety of our child? It wasn't like I was out buying shoes and purses. This was a car seat!

"Let's hold off before we blow that kind of money on a car seat for a baby that's not even here yet, okay?"

I couldn't answer.

Finally, trying to be funny, Joel said, "This baby must be another girl; she's costing me a fortune and she's not even out yet."

We hung up—hanging by a thread.

CHAPTER SEVENTEEN

Maia

22 Juniper Court was like a ski lodge, all wood and thick carpet and black-light fish tanks and stone fireplaces. Past the living room, dining room, kitchen, and breakfast area on the main floor was a theater room with a huge TV and speakers taller than Vader. He padded close behind me, anxious about Dakota, Luke's hyperactive Golden Retriever, barking and herding us both.

There were three bedrooms upstairs with views of the mountains. Luke had the master, with a king-size bed and a sunken Jacuzzi. Beau had the one next to his and another giant fish tank. The last one was nothing but mirrors and racks of clothes, their girlfriends' shared walk-in closet. Monique and Nikki spent the night a few times a week, Luke said, but both had dorm rooms on campus. My first impression was that the place was incredibly clean for a bunch of college guys. I found out later that we all chipped in a hundred and fifty bucks a month for a maid service that came in and turned the ends of the toilet paper into roses and origami birds.

"So it's your house, then?" I asked Luke.

"Technically, my stepdad bought the house sophomore year. I'll be a senior in the fall. I know Beau and Will from the ski team. Will graduated last year but he works in town for Spyder, you know, the company that does the Olympic team's clothes?"

I didn't, but I nodded, rubbing the short hair between Vader's eyes as he followed me down to the basement room for rent.

"So you and Will are sharing a bathroom down here, but he's totally a neat-freak and nine-to-five, so it's cool."

The basement had a disco ball, reclining leather movie theater chairs, and another giant flat screen with game controllers snaking out. Behind the bar were all the guys' snowboards and skis standing like soldiers, and a set of DJ turntables and milk crates full of records. Next to a plug-in Budweiser neon sign was one that announced *DJ EPOCH in da HOUSE!*

"I'm DJ Epoch," Luke explained. "We have some wild after hours down here at Club 22. I also spin at a few places in town. You should come—my friends get free pitchers. That's Will's room," he gestured to a closed door. "And this is the bathroom."

"Nice." I pointed to a tile seat in the shower.

"Yeah, but if you're like most girls and want a good bubble bath, you're welcome to use my Jacuzzi. With me. Kidding, of course." He smiled, flashing the whitest of teeth. "Here you are."

Vader and I followed him into the room, which was clearly never meant to be a bedroom. It was tiny, half the size of the girlfriends' dressing room upstairs, with three closets, one of which had a bare double mattress nestled into it, two walls of floor-to-ceiling shelves and another wall with a built-in desk, three spaces for office chairs and long plug strips.

"We call it the Trifecta. Three desks, three closets."

"One window." It was dirty, spattered with reddish mud from the yard, long and thin, at ground level, letting in a sliver of light.

The room was nothing special, but the rest of the house and the boys were. Though there really wasn't much to move, I texted Joel:

Busy Monday. Moving.

But then Tuesday, Scarlett called, saying she needed me to pay back the money she'd loaned me, which wasn't like her at all.

"What?" I joked, anxious. "You need an abortion or something?"

She didn't laugh. I told her I'd get it to her as soon as possible. I'd just given Luke the first-month deposit on the room at Juniper Court; I had thirty-four bucks to last me two weeks to the next payday.

Then Joel called me from Philly to say he was flying back early and would pick me up after my evening shift on Wednesday, a surprise. I was secretly hoping it was something I could sell.

Instead, he drove us to the Boulderado for real, and he'd put some thought into it, lighting candles and everything. He ran a bath in the fancy claw-foot tub and washed my hair.

I wondered how to tell him this was ending.

"It's our anniversary; one month, tomorrow."

"Seriously?" I stepped out, wrapped in a towel. Everything that had happened in a month—Vader, Homer, Jenn and Vitality, now Juniper Court and my boys, and through it all, the only constant had been Joel, and the mountains outside the window.

"You forgot?" Joel pretended to sulk, pulling me by the arms to the bed.

"It's been a crazy month." Which was not a lie. I told him about how the guys and I had been going mountain biking on my lunch breaks now.

"We should go mountain biking, or rock climbing, or for a hike, without the dogs this time."

Once, on a lunch break, we had tried to do something other than sex. Joel brought his dog—we'd planned to take them out to hike at Chautauqua but ended up having to hold their collars to keep them from killing each other, though Joel swore Ben had never been dog-aggressive. He hinted the fight was Vader's fault. I couldn't argue.

He said in the winter, he had a friend's condo in Breckenridge where we could ski for the weekend.

I showed him some mountain biking badges of honor, bruises on my shins, and laughing, I said, "I'm not the most coordinated."

His head was on my chest, fingertips tracing up and down the length of my stomach.

"What happened to 'never say no to an opportunity'?" Joel teased, but the truth was, I had no idea where I'd be that winter.

"I don't know if that motto has turned out so well."

And the saddest expression passed over his face, like he was realizing what I already had: we had no future.

"Hey," I said. I hadn't meant to hurt him; I honestly didn't mean to hurt any of them.

I wanted to live in the new house with my boys, pay off my sister, my Philly debt and stay in Boulder, but it was starting to feel like Colorado had an expiration date.

"Here." He handed me a package, a crinkly bundle of tissue paper. I opened it, and out slipped a short, gold choker necklace with a huge diamond. I'm more of a silver person, but it was the most expensive thing I'd ever been given.

"Happy anniversary." He fastened it around my neck, where it barely closed, the diamond settling in the space between my collarbones. I could feel it when I swallowed. He'd bought me an outfit, too, black lace with thigh highs and a G-string; only it was hilariously short.

"A small? You bought me a *small*?" I giggled as I tried to pull the stockings up past my knees. "I'm six feet tall!"

"But you're so thin," he faltered, embarrassed. "I didn't want to upset you." And I wondered if he was thinking of his pregnant wife.

"It's fine." I tried to buckle the bottoms of the merry widow to the stockings. "I mean, so long as I don't stand up," and I laughed, hobbling over to the bed. The garter straps came undone, the elastic snapping my thighs.

Then he laid me out flat, and sighed, his fingers working down the length of me, nylon, lace and skin.

"God," he said reverently. "You have the body men leave their wives for."

The body, he said.

What does pretty get you?

I turned and grabbed the phone off the nightstand.

"Let's order champagne."

Joel did, a magnum, and we drank it, and while I kept waiting for us to have sex, we didn't. Instead, he held me, his fingers running up and down the length of my back until they stopped, and I realized he was asleep.

I'll admit it was my favorite part of everything, because of the way he breathed. Lying awake next to Mark the last few years had never been relaxing. He breathed like a pissed off, wheezy cat—asthma and allergies, and a tendency to smoke whenever he got drunk. But listening to Joel, there was this peaceful, soft sigh, so predictable and comforting. I could have ridden the rhythm of his exhales like the late night R3.

In the morning, we hadn't moved. Joel still curled with his arm draped over my waist, his face in my hair. The necklace felt tight, the diamond pressing against my windpipe. I needed to end things. But then he rolled me over and we did it, finally. Slowly. Sweetly. His hands in my hair, our faces inches apart. I ran my fingertips over his morning stubble; I'd never seen it before.

"I like this," he said, catching my fingers and holding them against his cheek. "Wait, I have something else for you." Joel rolled over and slipped it out of his jacket pocket.

"A plane ticket? To Puerto Rico?"

"I have a business trip next month. It's just the Philly group, nobody there knows anyone out here. We'll have a suite. You can lounge on the beach with umbrella drinks all day; I'll be free at night. I want to do this, fall asleep with you," Joel said. "I want to hold this," he cupped his hand over me, "all night."

I read the name on the ticket, "Maia J. Kramer."

"I saw your real license, last week, when you were in the shower. You're not even twenty?"

"End of the month. Sheila McHugh's just my bar ID." Which wasn't really a lie; it was why Mark had originally bought it off Nick when he found it in a condo he was painting.

"Ugh, I feel like a dirty old man. And for the record, I really thought you were older than nineteen. I can't figure out, what age is it, when women want to start being told they look younger, not older?"

"Probably right around whatever age your wife is," I said.

"Ouch." His hand stopped moving on my back. "Anyway, will you come? Puerto Rico?"

"I don't know." I slithered out from under him. "I just…" I tried. "I wonder, sometimes, why we're doing this." Sitting up, meeting his eyes in the mirror, I held my breath.

It was almost a turning point.

He sat up next to me, but he didn't say anything.

"Listen, Joel. Why don't we tell each other every horrible thing about ourselves, come clean, make it easier to end this?"

I shuffled through the list in my head, wondering which one I'd offer up.

Joel dug his forehead into my shoulder. "I don't want to end this. I care about you. It's complicated."

"My life's not exactly simple either." I was thinking about money, of course.

"You work at a juice bar and live with a bunch of rich frat boys with nobody but your dog to worry about! I've got this huge presentation, this bitch of a boss, and my wife, she doesn't—"

Joel's cell rang then, buzzing on the cherry nightstand.

"Hello? What? My flight's at three." The wife, obviously. I reached for my clothes. Whatever.

"When? Oh my god, where are you? Okay, call Jackie, or an Uber. I'll meet you at the hospital—" he stammered. "A-as soon as I can, I'll get on a flight. Okay. Okay. It'll be okay. Love you too."

Joel sank to the bed, burying his face in his hands.

"Carolyn's bleeding," he said, not looking up. "She's going to the hospital. It's too early."

But he couldn't go to her, because he was pretending to be in Philadelphia.

"We lost a baby. Before Sasha," he continued, jumping to his feet and pacing, jerking on his clothes. "That's part of why Carolyn's so…" He stopped. "We weren't planning to have a baby, when she got pregnant the first time. I didn't know what I was missing, but—" His voice broke. "It was a boy."

I tried to sneak a look at his watch, praying one of the guys would let Vader out to pee back at the house. I had to get to work.

"Terrible," I mumbled, but I didn't really want to hear about his wife or their dead baby after he'd just kissed my cheeks raw with his morning stubble. I yanked on my yoga pants, twisting my hair up off my neck. The necklace was definitely too tight; I couldn't wait to take it off.

"You know, all of this," I waved my arm at the fancy room, the underwear, and the necklace, "including the trip to Puerto Rico, might be better spent on your wife."

He sat on the bed now, fully dressed.

"You," he said suddenly.

"What?" I didn't understand.

"You said we should tell each other the worst things we've done, to end things. You, Maia. You're the worst thing I've done."

CHAPTER EIGHTEEN

Carolyn

Here is the truth about infidelity: you imagine you want to know, but you don't, because once you know, everything has to change, and by virtue of knowing, it becomes your job to change it.

It was a Thursday morning in May, Joel supposedly still in Philly, when I woke up to blood, twenty-four weeks and six days pregnant.

Not again! I thought. Haven't I paid enough?

I didn't even try Jackie—while we'd seen each other at Friday playgroup, there'd been no more BBQs. I called an Uber and Dr. Michaels met me at the hospital, where he confirmed that I was three centimeters dilated. He ordered the steroid for the baby's lungs, in case, and a shot of terbutaline which made me shake so badly I had to hold on to the side rails. Poor Sasha was perched on the rattling foot of the bed, her face pinched as she stared pointedly at the tiny ER TV.

Dr. Michaels came back in after four brutal hours, eight cartoons of *My Little Pony*, and studied the monitor strip. "Good. Looking better. We'll want her to stay put," he patted my feet under the sheet, "couple more weeks, months really..." he mumbled, scanning.

"Her?" Was he talking about me, or the baby?

"What?" He looked up over his glasses. "Oh, yes, I see here, fetus, male." And he frowned, because everyone who has had a premature birth knows the truth: girls do better than boys. "So your husband must be excited that it's a boy?" Dr. Michaels was being irritatingly casual when I wanted medical facts, statistics, instructions.

Promises.

"Yes," I lied, because I had no intention of telling Joel. He'd called me again while the terbutaline sent shocks through my body, saying he'd caught an earlier flight and was on his way up from Denver. I did the math; it was impossible for him to have traveled from Philadelphia to Denver, unless Yakimori was now booking their employees on rocket ships.

Sasha and I were discharged with instructions for me to go straight home on bed rest. Instead, I gave the driver directions to Vitality with the hazy outlines of a plan, a thin envelope of household money in one hand, and my daughter's sweaty fingers clutched in the other.

Inside the juice bar, I spotted her right away—her long coltish neck, flawless face, arresting height. I had guessed right. When our eyes met over the whirring of the steel blender blades, I smelled something distinctly metallic mingling with the fruit scents in the air: fear.

Sasha recognized her immediately, tugging on the sleeve of my wrinkled maternity blouse.

"Look, Mama, we know that girl with the yellow hair. We know her! From the airport!"

Here is the truth about infidelity: it creates a dance between suspicions and confirmations. I suspected Joel was having an affair, sadly because of his recent level of cheerful solicitousness at home. But the biggest clue of all had come from my pregnancy-induced hyperosmia: my nose had led me to multiple Vitality cups buried in our garage trash reeking of banana, a fruit so high in net carbs Joel would never touch it.

"Hello!" I pushed my belly out extra far as I approached the counter. "Aren't you the girl my husband and I gave a ride up from Denver? What was it, about a month ago?"

Maia raised her hands and placed them both in plain view on the counter, like she was poised to play the piano. Like the rest of her, they were long, slim and lovely.

"Um, yeah. Right. Are you *okay*? I mean, how are you?"

"Still pregnant!" I laughed, high and shrill.

"Right! Good. Well, um, here's the menu," Maia pointed over her head.

A pack of mountain bikers carried their smoothies out into the blinding Boulder sunshine, so it was just the three of us, me, Maia, and Sasha, alone in the juice bar.

"So, what can I get you?" Maia's accent was stronger than I remembered; East Coast, nostalgic. I ordered a strawberry yogurt smoothie for Sasha. Seeing the mangos behind the glass reminded me of my babycenter.com email alert that morning: *At 24 weeks, your baby is about the size of a large mango. It now weighs just over a pound and is more than 11 inches long—and if you turn on some tunes and sway to the music, he can feel you dance.*

I needed to get home, horizontal, quickly. I leaned in.

"So, Maia, right?" Of course I knew her name. "How are you enjoying Boulder?"

"Um, great. It's good. I love it out here. I have this, um, this great place, with these great housemates, and I've got a great dog, and everything." She checked over her shoulder, then mine, but there was nobody coming to rescue her. I continued.

"Wonderful." That was all any of us wanted—to feel safe, a semblance of control over our lives. Nobody knew that better than me. "What kind of dog?"

"Um, he's a Great Dane."

"Really? A black or brindle, or what's that other color? Harlequin?" I didn't have time for chitchat, but I needed to know. I selected one of their dine-in stainless-steel straws in Sasha's drink and handed it to her—we'd stay there long enough for her to finish.

"Black. He's black."

Of course. That explained the short hairs, like dozens of fake eyelashes, I'd found when I buckled Sasha into the backseat of Joel's Audi.

I leaned closer; she took a step back from the counter.

"Listen," I told her, my voice low. "I'm actually looking for a mother's helper. I've just come from the hospital. I'm supposed to be on bed rest for the next eight to twelve weeks. My husband...of course, you've met him." I smiled carefully, gauging her reaction. "He travels a lot."

Friends close, enemies closer. It was the perfect solution. How many other women, I wondered, how many wives, would kill to be in my situation? The idea fairly shimmered with genius: If Maia was with me all day, she couldn't be meeting my husband on his lunch hour.

"Um, okay. I can ask my manager if we could put up a notice on the board or—"

I pressed my belly against the glass. "May I ask how much you're making here?" Maia swallowed.

"Eight ten, hourly. And we split tips, when they come."

"Really?" I made my mouth a shocked O. "You can't live on that in this town!"

"Believe me!" Maia rolled her eyes and she looked so young and fresh, so straight off Instagram, that I almost didn't go on. I wasn't sure I could stand to look at her creamy skin and willowy limbs while I melted into the family room couch for the next three months.

"Actually, I'd prefer it to be someone we're already familiar with. The doctor says I'll need someone with me at all times, either you or my husband, to help with Sasha. Are you interested?"

"Wait, you're asking *me* if I want to come work for you, in your house? Like a babysitter?" She glanced at Sasha, who was sucking down the smoothie in deliberate gulps.

I hesitated. What had seemed like a brilliant idea, to gather information, to keep tabs on my husband's mistress, shifted like a fun house image, macabre and crazy.

What was I doing?

A contraction built in my lower back, a weightlifter's belt wrapping its constricted warning, adding to my sense of desperation.

I took out the cash envelope Joel left me every Monday and counted out the singles for the smoothie. I wondered if Joel would react when he went through it Friday night—a receipt from Vitality!

"I know this sounds sudden," I began, "but I should have been in bed half an hour ago." I glanced over my shoulder to the Uber that idled, fingering my cash envelope. "We'd double your salary, under the table."

It wasn't my nose this time, but I could smell Maia's financial need. I sensed her hunger, in the same way I knew when she had the flu that Sasha would vomit, seconds before she actually did.

"Wh-what would the hours be?"

"Mondays and Fridays, it would be after my husband goes to work, eight thirty to maybe five forty-five or six, earlier and later on the nights he's in Philadelphia. The work's tedious, but not hard. Basically, you would be, well," I smiled again, "you'd be playing me."

Maia's fingers drifted to her long neck and she rubbed her throat, then up under her blond hair, sending it tumbling out of her twist like a perfect rippled waterfall.

"Where do you live?" Maia asked.

And I smiled, knowing I had her. After that, I sat back and reeled her in.

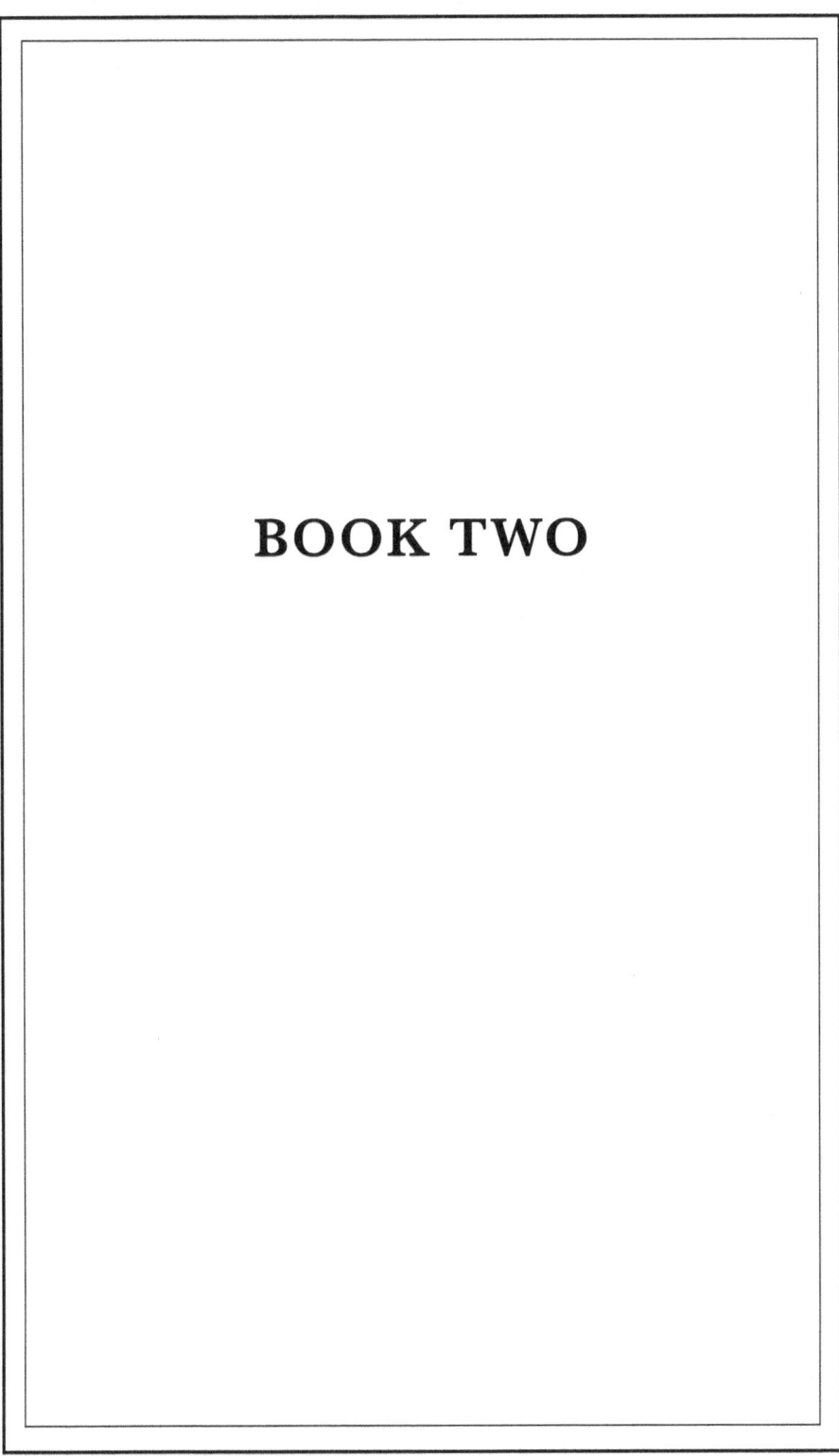

BOOK TWO

CHAPTER NINETEEN

Maia

I get that it was a little insane, accepting a job with my married ex-lover's wife. Honestly, when she offered me all that money and eight to twelve more weeks in Boulder, she could have said the job was hand-slaughtering horses for a dog food factory and I might have taken it. I needed to pay back Scarlett, and I still owed Ritchie, and I loved living at Juniper Court with the boys, but it was even more expensive than I thought. First there was the maid service, then Luke went to Costco for 'household essentials' and while it was great to know we would never run out of ketchup, garbage bags or powdered Gatorade, that was another forty-three bucks each. Then Vader developed this monster appetite and refused to eat the day-old bagels from work. He'd wolf down a huge mound of Gravy Train and start in on Luke's dog's expensive Blue Buffalo.

My first week at the new house was a constant party—the guys' friends and girlfriends flowing in and out, and cases of liquor and take-out food with receipts highlighted and divided by four taped to them. Friday night, Beau hosted a roll-your-own sushi party, and we all went to shoot pool at the Foundry. Beau's girlfriend Nikki said I could use her bike whenever, so Will and I'd single-tracked, me scream-laughing, down Rattlesnake Gulch. In the afternoon we went for a house hike at Hayden Lake, then the Foundry again. Sunday night Luke was spinning at Juanita's where I drank so much free margarita I could only piece together patchy bits of the afterhours back at the house before Vader and I crawled onto our bare mattress. We woke up under a sleeping bag Will admitted he'd spread over me.

"I promise I'm not a creep, but your door was open, and you two looked cold."

I didn't talk to Joel all weekend. He didn't call or text either. After the morning at the Boulderado, when he told me about their dead baby and gave me the diamond necklace and the plane ticket, and then said I was the worst thing he'd ever done, I'd decided to stop having sex with him. So in my mind, by the time his wife walked into Vitality, we were broken up anyways.

The Carters house was in this complicated cookie-cutter development a few miles out off Baseline with all these variations on Birch: Birch Way, Birch Park, Birch Circle, Birch Court. I made three wrong guesses and thank god Joel's car was already gone by the time I got there on Nikki's mountain bike.

I scratched my neck and knocked. The neighborhood was dead quiet; it could have been suburbia anywhere, except for the white-capped mountains looming like judgy old men. I was about to bail when Sasha answered the door wearing a nightgown, ropes of Mardi Gras beads, and sparkly Mary Janes.

"Hi." She smiled shyly. My first impression: she was smaller/friendlier/cuter than I remembered. "Are you my Fairy Godmother?"

"Come in!" Carolyn called over the sound of the television. I followed Sasha to find my new boss—Joel's wife! —reclined on the couch of a totally destroyed family room.

"You're late. I hope that's not going to be a regular thing." Her voice was cool.

My cheeks flared hot, a queasy spasm in my throat that tasted like leftover tequila. I opened my mouth to tell Carolyn—Joel's wife!!!!! —I was sorry, this had been a mistake, but before I could get the words out, she plowed on.

"My husband, Joel, needs to be off to work no later than eight-thirty Mondays and Fridays. I'll need you here promptly. Sasha is too active for there to be gaps in coverage. And when he's on the East Coast, Tuesday through Thursday, I'll need you here at least seven to seven, possibly later, depending on how she's settling for the night."

I nodded, staring at a spot of wall three inches above the wife's head, simulating eye contact. Twelve-hour shifts, maybe more. Fine. How hard could it be, right? I'd do it for a week. If I avoided Joel, I could work here a few days, pay back Scarlett, and quit. Fine.

"Sasha's doing the Cinderella routine because I'm making her pick up her toys. It's not usually like this," she said. "Obviously my husband isn't much of a domestic."

I stood there, a smile frozen on my face—was she apologizing to *me?*

"I've stationed myself on the couch for the morning because it's central and I can direct you easily. I might go upstairs later for a nap but for now I'm supervising Cinderella. Sash, TV off, *now.*"

The little girl ignored her, standing so close to the screen she could touch it with the tip of her cute nose, her back to us.

I shifted my weight, wondering if I was supposed to step in like The Babysitter. It was absurd to be in her domain, and still, *his* house. There was so much to look at: the wedding photo in the front entry, the aggressively rust color of the wall—his choice or hers?—the titles of books stacked by the couch. Joel beamed out at me from the top of a mountain in a frame on their bookshelf, eight inches from my right eye, and I swallowed. Fine, I'd do it for one day.

"So, um, where do you want me to start?" Thinking, *Please, God, somewhere else.*

"The kitchen. Joel handled the meals this weekend, but I'm sure he didn't clean up."

Relieved, I mumbled something about getting right to it. I found old grease from eggs and bacon, piles of dirty dishes towering in the sink, a saucepan with dried red sauce on the stove, and a fat fly buzzing around a half-empty pot of coffee, a burn circle under it on the butcher-block counter, tufts of golden dog hair everywhere. This was a project I could get lost in.

As I cleaned, I realized I didn't even know how Joel took his coffee. Was he obsessed with sushi like my housemate, Beau? Did he leave the toilet seat up? I knew more about Will, who shared my bathroom (green tea instead of coffee, no on the sushi, and toilet seat down, lid closed), than I did about the guy I'd sat astride at the motel two days a week, nine times total if you counted the Boulderado, in the last month. I thought of how Beau and his girlfriend, Nikki, cooked together in the kitchen at Juniper Court, their unspoken dance, the way she knew to hand him a spatula before he even asked. I wondered if Joel and his wife cooked together; if they had, back in their early days.

I moved canisters and dug into the grime behind them with an SOS pad. I got down on my hands and knees and scoured the Spanish tile with a bleach solution.

"You must be doing a really thorough job in there!" Carolyn called.

"Yeah." I opened the door between the kitchen and family room again. "My mom used to clean for some ladies on the Main Line; I'd help her out on school breaks and stuff. Some of the houses were so boring, cleaning where it wasn't even dirty. But this is great!"

In the silence that followed, my broom swishing against the floor, I realized Carolyn might be insulted, but I hadn't meant it that way. I moved the pile, mostly

Ben's hairs, into the foyer where I could see into the playroom, about to apologize when she said, "We've fallen into a fairly traditional assumption of gender roles."

"What?" She picked the most complicated way to say basic things.

"Joel brings home the bacon, and before, I'd cook it." Her tone was a little testy.

"You usually clean up after too, I guess?"

She didn't say anything for a minute. "Right. Until...." By which I guess she meant that it was my job now.

"Sounds like he's getting the better part of that deal," I said.

"Sorry?" She cocked her head to the side, her blond hair falling out of her bun, right around rosy cheeks, and I saw again how pretty she was.

"Nothing," I mumbled. "Just, your two jobs, to his one. That's all." I turned to the little girl, anxious to end this stupid conversation. I'd leave at the end of the day. Neither of them knew where I lived. I'd ask for cash. I just had to get through one day.

"So, um, Cinderella, did you get all those chores done?"

"Yes," Sasha sighed and wilted dramatically across an ottoman. "It took for-ever."

"That means you get to go to the big dance tonight?"

"What?" She perked up.

"I mean, if you're done, and you're Cinderella, you get to go to the ball."

"Where's the ball?" She narrowed her hazel eyes at me, like she had in the backseat the first day.

"Uh, it's at the prince's castle?" I had no idea where this came from, but she was into it.

"Where's that?"

"Well," I thought, stalling. Panicking. I had no idea how to play with this kid. Growing up, some girls I knew said babysitting was easy money. I was never one of them. "I guess we have to um, make a castle."

"Come on!" Sasha grabbed my hand and pulled hard. "We'll play in my room! My room will be the castle!"

I paused and glanced at Joel's wife. She used her finger to mark her place in *Hypnobirthing the Easy Way.*

"I suppose you should take a break from cleaning, and play with Sasha for a while."

But she still sounded a little frosty and I was happy to follow the hand tugging mine up the beige carpeted stairs, past the blown-up wedding photo on the landing. It took me a minute to recognize them; they looked like the fake insert that comes with the frame. Joel looked so young, like my boys at Juniper Court, but there they were, those crinkly blue eyes that had lured me out here. Carolyn was like a model, a Barbie doll with big shiny hair, tiny-tiny waist, lots of lace and blush. Beautiful. Happy.

I hurried after Sasha, swallowing my guilt. Thinking, *the best I could do was work hard for them. For her. One day!*

"Come on!" Sasha was waiting for me. Her room was a kid's dream. It was painted like the sky with big puffy clouds, shades of blue and purple, and I wondered, was Carolyn the artist, or did they hire someone to come do the butterflies in the corners? Joel? She had a white frilly canopy bed that was at least a queen and carpeting thick enough to curl my toes so they disappeared.

"The castle! Come on!"

So I got some sheets from the endless stacks in the linen closet across the hall—how many beds did these people have?—and hung them down the sides of her canopy. Inside, she pulled my hand until we were lying on our stomachs and I wondered *what next?*

That was the last time I ever had to worry that I wouldn't know how to play with Sasha. The kid's imagination was like a ticker tape, spinning out never-ending ideas and scenarios, and my only job was to follow along. Sasha put her face so close to mine I could smell the bacon on her breath.

"Hi," she whispered. "My name's Maggie, and you're my widow aunt, and this is our tent. There are animals outside, and they are not our pets. Hide!" She yelped and dove under her fluffy comforter. I crawled after her. In the shadowy light from the purple sheets, Sasha laid both hands on either side of my face. "I like you, Maia-Papaya," she told me seriously, and I hadn't realized I wanted her to, until she said she did.

Lunch was surprisingly nice. Beau had gotten me addicted to veggie sushi, so I biked to the grocery and picked us up a few packs. Carolyn offered to pay me for her sushi roll, but I waved it off. Checking the clock, I'd already made $68, and anyway I owed her way more than a twelve-dollar lunch. I cooked Sasha a grilled soy cheese sandwich and some tomato soup and while our sushi chilled in their freezer, I laid a little table for us next to the couch in the family room. Sasha got into it, bringing a cup from her tiny tea set, folding the napkins into sloppy triangles.

Turned out Carolyn loved the cucumber roll so I gave her all mine out of the veggie pack and she gave me her avocado, which were my favorite. With Sasha there, clinking mugs with us and endlessly toasting, it was going okay. Peaceful, domestic. I certainly didn't miss the midday rush at Vitality, or Joel showing up—I thought suddenly, *would he show up?*

What would Jenn say? I'd given her no real notice on Friday, just told her I had to quit because of the phone call the week before at Vitality, a guy with a 215 number trying to track me down.

"How would anyone know where I was?" I'd said, worried it was Ritchie, or the police, but she pointed out my sister had shipped those boxes of clothes, so maybe it was just Mark. I told Jenn I had to move on, that I was afraid my past was catching up with me. But then I felt bad, because she gave me the number of a women's shelter in Boulder and told me how an ex-boyfriend broke three of her ribs with the butt of a loaded gun before she left him. It hadn't been a total lie, my past catching up with me, but still.

Jenn would probably just tell Joel I'd quit, and I'd try to be gone before he got home. And then?

I'd ended it, hadn't I?

But then Carolyn sent Sasha to her room for quiet time (twenty-minute freak-out; she wanted me to read her ten books, I said one, we compromised on three) and called me upstairs to the master bedroom where she was resting while, according to a list she was making, I was supposed to run the laundry and the vacuum cleaner.

"Here." She reclined on top of the straightened bedspread, a rose print, with a book titled *Passionate Marriage: Keeping Love and Intimacy Alive in Committed Relationships* open across her mounded stomach. I wondered if I was supposed to sit, or what? I could tell which side of the bed was his, from the sparseness of the nightstand: a phone charger, a box of mint floss, a nasal allergy spray, a glasses case. Her side was piled with books, hand lotion, candles and mauve nail polish.

"I wanted to have a talk with you. Establish the rules."

"Right," I said, and cleared my throat. "Great." I pressed my hands together, sweat squelching out.

No more sex with the husband.

She knew everything. Should I confess, deny, apologize, or just bolt? The muscles of my thighs twitched. Run.

"First things first," she began, and I calculated my escape route, down the stairs, right at the front door. I could be back at Juniper Court in less than half an hour, if I pedaled like crazy. "Under no circumstances do you take Sasha out in the car."

What? I blinked. How could she know what had happened, about my license? My hand flitted to my chest, checking for the hard edges of plastic tucked into my bra. It was still there, just in case.

"There may be times when we need you to run errands, groceries, dry cleaning—"

"Oh, sure," I said, but I hadn't seen a car in the driveway and when I'd carried the garbage out to the garage, it was crammed with boxes and sports clutter. Also, these sounded like instructions for someone who was going to keep coming back. "Is your car…"

"We're a one-car family; I don't drive. I can have Joel take the shuttle and leave you his car mid-week as needed in the future, but you are never to take Sasha with you. Understood?"

I nodded, waiting. Wondering. She didn't go on.

"You don't drive, now, because of the…" I circled my stomach with my hand, "or ever?"

"Ever."

"Wow, that's got to be hard, living all the way out here. Not being able to get into town and stuff. How do you buy groceries?"

Why had I said that? Their life was none of my business.

"Joel and I used to go together, on Saturday nights. It was sort of like a date. When we first moved out here, before there was delivery, before Sasha. We used to go on our way back from skiing Eldora…"

She trailed off, a hint of a smile.

I felt extremely dirty.

"Anyway," she started again. "There's a playground at the end of the cul-de-sac. If it's nice, you can walk her there some days."

Right, Sasha. I thought of the way she already plunked her head down on my chest, right over my heart, her holding my arm while I'd read the three books to her at quiet time, her fingers tickling and closing around my wrist like a handcuff.

"There's sunscreen in the downstairs bathroom, and a separate stick for faces. Her skin is sensitive—and you have to do the part of her hair, and the tips of her ears, and if she's wearing her Keens, don't forget the tops of her feet, between the straps."

I nodded again, keeping my focus on the rim of the headboard behind her. I caught sight of a familiar shirt hanging in their open closet, the one he'd worn the day we tried to take the dogs to Chautauqua. Next to it was the striped, blue one he'd worn that Friday we did it twice, him bending me over the wonky motel table, my underwear shoved to the side, his khakis barely unzipped. My face burned.

Had that been worth it, to him?

"Also, we suspect she's allergic to dairy. We're in the process of removing dairy from the house. Joel would be happier if we were all Paleo, but I need to do a little more research before I'm convinced it's healthy for children."

Carolyn kept talking, rules, safety, panda bike helmet, hand gel, cleaning cabinet lock, no monkey bars, trampolines, swimming pools, watch out for bears, coyotes, mountain lions, eagles, and I just kept nodding, willing my eyes not to wander around their bedroom, not to picture them in here.

After he left me at lunchtime, he slept here beside her. She was the one who got to listen to his beautiful, even breathing every night. Did their bodies touch when they slept? I thought of Mark, how, in the winter, he insisted I tuck my cold feet between his calves to warm them. Did Joel curl up behind his wife, his hand over her waist, the place where their baby was? I wondered then if the baby would be a boy or a girl. I didn't think I'd be there long enough to find out.

"I realize I never got a chance to get any references from you," Carolyn was saying.

"I'll bring them in tomorrow," I mumbled. Honestly, I wasn't coming back. I checked the clock; I'd made eighty dollars. Easy money, sure, but being there was even weirder than I thought it would be.

Moving on, Maia.

"Great. Now, the laundry. There should be a pile of Joel's dirty clothes on the floor in the bathroom. I have a trisected hamper set up inside the door to the left. I don't know why he can't put his stuff in there; I've explained it a hundred times. Darks, then dry cleaning, then whites. Alphabetical, left to right, just like you read." She was smiling at me, and I realized I was supposed to compliment her on her system.

"Makes sense," I mumbled, wondering how bored this poor woman had to be.

Down the hall, I heard Sasha's door open.

"Papaya!"

It was a relief to get out of their bedroom, to have someone calling who needed me.

CHAPTER TWENTY

Carolyn

At first, I imagined I had the upper hand with Maia, that she had no idea what I knew about her and Joel.

"I'd like you to smoke outside," I'd said in the morning, anticipating the surprise on her face. *How do you know I smoke?* she'd gasp, and I would smile knowingly, thinking of the smell of Joel's hair on Mondays and Fridays for the last month, cheap, follicle-drying shampoo, not the kind I packed in his travel kit, and stale cigarette smoke. I wanted her to worry.

"Oh, I don't smoke," Maia said blandly, her eyes scanning the titles of the bookshelves in the family room, cruising over Joel's face in the framed photos without a hint of emotion. My sense of smell had failed me—how could I not have realized that the smoke was not ashy and fresh, but years old, saturating the wallpaper and polyester bedding of some disgusting motel?

As I rummaged around in my kitchen candy stash, I heard them upstairs, Sasha and Maia, shrieking with laughter, romping up and down the hall, Ben barking as he followed. I replayed my morning with Sasha, a bitter mix of snapping orders from the couch for her to pick up toys, anxious after Maia's comment, about her impression of our chaotic home. Then a mother-daughter scramble over the remote, and guilty peace as she zoned out with **PBS Kids** while I inhaled a few chapters of *Coach Yourself Thin*. The girl I suspected of having an affair with my husband was playing with my daughter, in my home. I was *paying* her to. And they were having fun. When was the last time I had been fun? I'd let her go at the end of the day, find someone from a nanny agency or Joel had even hinted he'd be willing to have my mom come out, since it would be cheaper. Financially, anyway.

My parents had flown out after Sasha was born, my mother her usual hundred and two self-righteous pounds. She took one look at me in the airport and burst into tears. It turns out a cousin of hers had "let herself go this way" and her husband left her—for another man, I might add.

"Lay off her, Judith!" My father squeezed me to his side.

"She just had a baby." Joel tried to direct my mother's attention to Sasha in the car seat over his arm. Joel actually lost weight during my pregnancy, running around for me; he's also blessed with a metabolism most women would sacrifice a small, unimportant finger for.

"I was on bed rest; I could only get up to pee!"

"That was weeks ago! In my day, doctors advised not putting on more than ten pounds during pregnancy. Do you know you weren't even five pounds when you were born, the cutest little thing."

"And I had to stay in the hospital for two weeks! Times have changed, Mom. Smoking is no longer recommended as a way to have smaller babies and easier births."

"Still, this is a sin. What kind of a role model are you to your daughter?" I'd secretly loved that Sasha would wail every time my mother bounced her over her bony shoulder.

I could not have my mother out again. I was in the middle of thinking up a better plan when Maia caught me, off the couch, literally with my hand in my hidden chocolate supply, a Twix half-chewed and three mini-Snickers wrappers on her newly cleaned counters. All the carpeting, and Sasha still jumping on her bed upstairs, I hadn't heard her coming.

"Ah, I wondered if those were yours or your husband's," she said easily, smiling.

Had she planned, practiced this, not using his first name, a fake formality? What was stranger—she wasn't reacting to me and the candy. Couldn't she see I clearly had no business eating anything other than salad, fruit, lean protein?

"Can I?" She reached in and pulled out a miniature Butterfinger.

"May I," I corrected, a habit from Sasha.

"Right, thanks. Wow, I haven't had a Butterfinger in forever! But are you allowed to be up? What can I get you? We should have a system, a bell or something."

"I…I was just using the bathroom, and my blood sugar was getting low." I made a slinking move back toward the couch.

"You should have called me. Sash and I were playing, but you're the priority here. I lost track of time." She took her candy wrapper and all of mine, balled them up and threw them on top of the trash. I made a mental note to bury them before Joel got home that night.

The phone rang; Joel saying he would be home at six, how was Sash liking the sitter, was there anything I wanted for dinner?

"Would you mind picking me up a vegetable sushi pack? The sitter and I had them for lunch—delicious." If this meant anything to him, he gave no hint of it. I wondered if he knew how to get right to the sushi section in Sprouts, if it was on the menu for their lunchtime rendezvous.

I turned to Maia. Suddenly, I wanted her gone. I could survive seven weeks with my mother, who used to creep into our bedroom at night and pull Sasha right off my breast, and deny sneaking formula into her, passive-aggressively leaving the dirty Dr. Browns bottles in the sink.

"Joel's on his way, I'll be fine until he gets here."

"Oh, okay, do you need anything else?" Was it me, or did she seem equally eager to go?

"No, he'll be here any minute. He's picking us up dinner. Isn't that wonderful?" I chattered. *Go*, I thought.

Maia stopped, her purse over her shoulder. Sasha took both of Maia's hands in hers—I saw a tantrum brewing. Maia twirled her on the linoleum while Sasha sang, "Someday my Prince will come."

"I guess," she said.

"What?"

"I don't know." Maia shrugged. "I guess it's wonderful. I mean, you are growing his kid. It kind of seems, like, the least he could do is bring you dinner. And then," she gave a half-smile, "you know, would it kill him to clean up a little after?"

"That's not how things work," I said, but wondered, *wait, why not?*

That night last February, when Joel told me about the new commute, when he proposed the cash envelope to keep me from overspending, I'd exploded.

"That's not fair!" My temper surged, and I could have left him, right then, just taken Sasha and gone, if I could have driven. I felt the baby, no bigger than a Jujube back then, like a stone in the stomach of Little Red Riding Hood's wolf, sinking me in the river of this life. "You have to let that go! You cannot bring that up every time we fight!"

Joel's solution meant, like a teenager, I received an allowance envelope of cash each Monday morning and was expected to return it to Joel with receipts on Fridays. It had been five years since my mistake, and still he treated me like this.

—

"Anyway," Maia said, "it doesn't really matter if he doesn't clean up tonight, since I guess I'll be back here in the morning…" There was a long pause. "I mean, right?"

Sasha had both of her arms wrapped around Maia's leg, while Maia thunked around pretending she couldn't figure out what was impeding her.

"Right." I looked at the clock. I called for Sasha to fetch my purse from the front hall table.

"Can you remind me what we agreed on for salary?"

"Um, you said you'd double my old paycheck, so seventeen per hour?" She shifted her weight and I swear she checked the clock on the cable box. My head throbbed. I should have asked her to pour me a glass of water; dehydration is a classic culprit in premature labor. I would keep her until the end of the week, no longer, buy myself a little time.

I did the math on the outside of the envelope: $145. I counted out the sum, down to the singles, doing more fast calculations. Her midweek twelve-hour shifts would run nearly $200/day. My hands shaking, I redid the balance on the outside of the envelope, anticipating the confrontation with Joel. After Maia accepted a swinging hug from Sasha and the cash, I watched through the front hall window as she pedaled away. I felt the slim nothing of my cash envelope as I placed it back in my purse, wondering exactly who this arrangement was supposed to be punishing.

When Joel got home with the sushi, I told him we'd need more money in the envelope for the week.

"How much?" He flipped the TV on, a basketball game.

"Eight hundred." I gulped, swallowing the end of the sentence.

"Each week?"

"Yes," I said, wishing my affirmation sounded less like an apology. Maia was right, I was growing his child, for the *third time*! I waited.

"Okay."

Okay? I tried to breathe normally. Okay to give Maia eight hundred dollars a week?

"Kitchen looks nice," he said, sitting down in front of the game with three sliders wrapped in lettuce, bacon and avocado. My mouth watered. I watched him eat with a mix of envy and loathing.

"And you said Sash liked her. New nanny seems like a keeper."

In the morning, I pretended to be asleep while he zipped the suitcase closed. Sasha had come into our bed in the night. I kept my eyes closed and he pecked both our foreheads. He smelled the same, like our shared shampoo from the shower. He was gone before Maia arrived.

She stood in the front hall, flushed with sweat at her temples from biking, a hot pink tank top hugging her chest, a brightly-embroidered canvas bag over her shoulder—hints of a life that existed beyond my stucco walls. In our house, she felt like a door left open, the outside world seeping in. Sunshine.

"How was your night?" she asked, dropping her bag on the front hall table.

"Fine. I think Sasha's Pull-Up leaked. Her nightie's still damp, but I'm letting her sleep. Joel left her sheets in the front hall."

Maia nodded.

I lay on the playroom couch. I heard her go into the kitchen, rattle around. A few minutes later, she came in with two mugs of tea and the honey jar.

"I don't know if you want any, but…" She put it down on the coffee table next to me. "My housemate, Will, he got me hooked on this tea. There's not much caffeine or anything, if you're worried."

"I smell… flowers… jasmine?"

"Wow, you're good."

"Unfortunately, I've been cursed with the nose of a bloodhound again this pregnancy."

"That's crazy," Maia said, like *go on*. She was picking up the toys scattered like buckshot on the floor. She slid another toy bin back on the shelf, and I bit my tongue—she'd put a Littlest Pet Shop kitten in the Princesses bin.

"It's called hyperosmia. I can almost smell color, if that makes sense."

"Wow, wait." Maia disappeared into the kitchen. She stood outside the family room door, just out of sight. "What am I doing, right now?"

"Peeling a clementine?"

"You're good! Here." Maia put it in front of me on a plate, the slices fanned out. "And you only get this when you're pregnant?"

"Well, once before. Right after I was in an accident, my junior year of high school." I had no idea why I'd told her that; it just slipped out.

"A car accident?" I felt her looking my body over for physical scars.

"Yes."

"Oh, so is that why you don't …" She jerked her head toward the driveway.

"Why I don't what?" I wondered if we were still talking about my driving.

"Why you don't drive? Or don't want me to drive Sasha? You seemed pretty serious about that yesterday, the rules and everything."

"I am serious!" My voice was high, and it cracked when I said, "*I* don't even drive Sasha! Ever!"

"Right." She turned to put a stack of foam puzzles back on the shelf. "It must have been a really bad accident."

I'd torn my ACL and suffered a concussion, but that was nothing, comparatively.

Sometimes, I wondered at who I might have been if the accident had never happened, if I hadn't lost everything—my two best friends, my boyfriend, my sense of self—in that one tragic, stagnant summer.

The summer I was seventeen…

"I don't drive at all, since." I spoke softly, carefully, thinking of the face of the other driver, blood running down his forehead, his van's grill in my passenger seat, the windshield smashed out and draped like a lacy skirt over the hood, his moan when he looked into the silence of the backseat.

"Did you ever try to learn again?"

"Twice, before we were married," I told her, "Joel tried to teach me. He even bought me driving lessons for my twenty-fourth birthday."

It caused one of the larger fights in our relationship.

I didn't tell her I'd screamed, "If you love me, you love all of me!" Far easier to demand back at 108 pounds.

Maia talked about the ease of navigating East Coast cities, one of the things she missed about Philadelphia. "I mean, there's public transportation in Boulder? I didn't even notice," she joked.

"You don't drive either?"

"No." She laughed, picking up the wet sheets on the way to the washer. "I mean, I can, I had—have—my license. Here, I just can't afford the wheels."

Sasha stumbled into the playroom, her hair standing out from her head like a dandelion in the dry air. Barely awake, she wrapped her arms around Maia's tiny waist.

"Papaya," she murmured. "You came back."

The night before, Maia had slipped a hair band from her ponytail around Sasha's wrist like a princess bracelet. Even so, Sasha had asked me anxiously if I was sure Maia was coming back in the morning. Funny how in a four-year-old's world, it only takes a day to establish an expected routine. I hoped I'd been right when I told her yes.

"Good morning, Sweet Girl!" Maia said.

"I'm not Sweet Girl," Sasha snapped. "I'm Maggie. I'm a alicorn!"

Maia waited in silence. Sasha's tantrums could stop an avalanche.

"You know what that is—a alicorn? From *MyLittlePonyFriendshipIsMagic*? It's a unicorn with wings."

"Right, okay, Maggie," Maia said carefully. "Let's go get you a magical bubble bath, okay? And then we'll polish your hooves with some sparkle?"

"It has to be rainbow and golden!" Sasha scampered after her, leaving the faint sweet scent of urine in her wake.

With them out of the room, my heart rate went back to normal, the baby settling into his favorite position, feet pressing up between my ribs. I had almost told Maia more than anyone knew about me, including my husband. Of course Joel knew I'd been in a car accident before we met, that it was why I didn't drive, but I imagine he'd filed it away with other marginally significant parts of my history, like the fact I'd made varsity volleyball in ninth grade, and for a time in middle school, I'd played the flute and piano.

The truth was, Joel didn't really know anything.

CHAPTER TWENTY-ONE

Maia

Back home at Juniper Court, Will was in the kitchen heating up chicken patties for dinner.

"So how many kiwis and dragon fruits gave their lives for the thirsty hipsters of our fair mountain town today?"

"Oh, I quit Vitality."

He muted SportsCenter and sat down at the dining room table next to me. "Seriously?"

"Yeah. This lady came in and offered me a job as a mother's helper for double the salary, no taxes. I kind of needed the money." I thought about Scarlett, ran my tally in my head.

"No kidding. Boulder is the greatest place in the world, but you pay for it. Guys like Luke, doesn't matter. I've seen him drop three hundred bucks on a bar tab, throw his credit card statements in the trash, without even opening them. Trust fund manager pays them."

Will glanced over our heads, where a headboard thumped against the wall—Luke's bedroom. He lowered his voice. "I don't want to badmouth, but sometimes I think he just got Dakota to pick up chicks. He doesn't take proper care of that dog."

It was Will who brought Dakota along on my nightly neighborhood walks with Vader when I got home, entertaining each other by making up stories about the people inside the yellow windows of the houses on our street.

"But why would Luke be picking up chicks? Aren't he and Monique pretty serious?" We were both pretending his girlfriend wasn't yipping like a Chihuahua right above us.

"You don't have a thing for Luke, do you?" Will asked.

"No!" I felt the blood hot in my cheeks. Honestly, the air had an electric charge whenever Luke was in the room, different from when it was just me and Will and Beau and Nikki.

"Lots of girls do," Will said sadly, like it was a sickness. "Speaking of…" He pulled one of the candles out of the holder, shaving the wax off in curls with the blade of his thumbnail. "You don't have to say. It's just, you know we all feel like your big brothers around here, so it's our job to give you a brotherly hard time. You, um, the other night…last week you weren't here. I let Vader out, it's fine, but you have a guy, right?"

I had a flash of the Boulderado, thighs wrapped around Joel in the tangle of the ivory sheets. It felt like weeks ago, not just last Wednesday.

"I was sort of," I waved my hand, "seeing someone. But not really."

"Really?" Will pinched the pile of crumbly wax into careful little towers. "For, um, how long?"

"About a month."

"Wait. I thought you said you'd only been living in Boulder a month."

"Actually, I met him on the plane out."

"Oh, really?" Will physically startled, which was pretty cute. Sometimes, you could see exactly what kind of boy he was, one who collects frogs and knows their scientific names, so earnest you just want to take *him* home in a shoebox and keep him safe.

The front door opened; Beau and Nikki. Dakota and Vader leapt off the family room couch and bounded to meet them, barking and whapping tails.

Beau winked at me, hefting shopping bags on to the counter. "I hope you didn't eat," he said. "I see Will had the usual patties *de poulet*. Dude, we'd have the most boring fridge if it weren't for me. Look, I picked up another case of vino."

I saw the receipt taped to the box, knowing I'd get a bill for a quarter of it, quickly adjusting my tally.

"Maia was just telling me she's been secretly seeing some guy she met on her flight out here." Will filled our wineglasses.

"Yeah, Nikki figured you had to have a guy. You're fucking gorgeous, dude. Bring him over here to shoot hoops after hours or something."

97

"Yeah, it's not like that…" I tried.

"How'd you meet on the plane? I never sit next to anyone good. It's always the crying babies or the manspreaders." Nikki opened a pomegranate. There were never more than eighteen inches between her and Beau, their elbows touching as they assembled a salad.

You could set your clocks by them: 6 am to the gym for her spin class, CU summer classes, a run in the Flatirons, and then home with Whole Foods bags, gourmet dinner, snuggling on the couch with Netflix and wine, like they were forty, not twenty.

"It's not really like you guys think. It's not that romantic or anything." I gulped my wine, thinking if I was paying for it, I might as well drink it.

"Sounds romantic to me," Nikki said.

"Actually, he's older."

"Older sounds interesting!" Nikki insisted. "What's he do?"

"He's the chief of something at a tech company in Niwot."

They all looked at me, like I'd said the wrong thing. I plowed on, "And he's married."

The whole room went dead except for Beau exhaling a long, somber, "Duuuuuuuuude." If I thought Will had startled before, it was nothing. He fumbled the mangled candle back into the holder.

"She's kidding," he said quickly. Then, "Or, okay, you're not?"

"Hey, it's all good," Beau said. "I mean, my dad cheated on all his wives, and he's still a cool guy."

I kept my back to them as I refilled my wine glass. I said softly, "For the record, I didn't exactly know, when we first started, you know, that he was married." Which wasn't entirely true.

"But then you keep seeing him anyway?" Will was incredulous and I wished I could evaporate. I was thinking about just taking my dog quietly down to the Trifecta to bed, but then Monique and Luke came down the stairs, her riding on his back, his jeans half-undone, both of their eyes too bright, and announced we were going out.

"House party! To celebrate Maia!" Luke winked at me.

"Jesus, it's Tuesday." Will sighed, but he shuffled into his Sambas and we piled into Luke's Range Rover, Monique up front in her high-heeled cowboy boots and her fur jacket. Nikki and I were crammed in the back seat, hugging the doors to make room for Beau's long legs, and poor Will folded in the way back next to Luke's subwoofer. Luke blared music and drove too fast while Monique sucked on her vape and squealed "Sweetie!" whenever he took a turn hard.

"So, when do you graduate?" Nikki leaned over Beau to yell in my ear.

"What?" Stalling.

"You already graduated?"

I shook my head, realizing too late that was the wrong answer.

"Oh. Are you on a gap year?"

I had no idea what she was talking about, but I nodded and she gushed how jealous she was.

We pulled up at the Foundry and Luke ordered the first round of shots, dropping his credit card to start a tab, but I imagined we'd be splitting that too, somehow, on an invoice with the rent.

"Can I see some IDs?" the bartender asked, and I fumbled in my purse before I handed Luke Sheila McHugh.

"That's not bad," he laughed, throwing an arm over my shoulder to pull me closer, like he was inspecting my face. "Sheila, the bartender here is a bro, Sigma Nu. You can give me the real one. He just has to ask. Anyway, nobody over the age of twenty-five hangs here."

"I don't have it on me," I lied, because it was tucked, as always, into my bra, opposite my heart. Just in case.

Luke narrowed his eyes. "Really?"

I had filled out my real name on our lease, Maia Jane Kramer.

Luckily, a friend of Will's came over to the pool table and I was introduced as the new roommate, which Monique had to clarify.

"*House*mate! Lukey and I are the only ones who share a room." She sucked a deep hickey into his neck before staggering to the bathroom, sniffling.

"As if she needs to snort any more of that shit, dude," Beau said to Luke. "Check your girl, Bro."

Nikki pulled me aside. "Don't let her bug you," she yelled over the noise. "She's still doing it to me. She's freaked out because you're new and like, completely gorgeous."

"She can keep her Trustafarian," I snorted, repeating what Jenn called Luke, and Nikki laughed and laughed, her hand on my arm.

"Trustafarian! Funny! You're so funny!"

Will turned to me, close to my ear over the noise. "I'm sorry, about before, if I sounded like a jerk. I guess I'm more traditional than I think. My parents," he continued, "are small-town Ohio. They were going to be a priest and a nun, fell in love on a missionary thing. Moved out here to Golden. They're teachers. My brother and I joke that the only times they had sex were to make me and him. My mom is so proper, you can't imagine."

"Is your Dad like that too?" We had to practically push our heads together to hear each other over the thump of the music, so close I could see how long his eyelashes were—*hanba*, a shame, on a boy!—Mark's Babçi would say.

"Nah, Dad would've been a terrible priest. He's crazy for old sports cars. We've got this 1972 Porsche that we've been restoring in the barn behind the house. We basically rebuilt the engine from nothing. He says when we have her in mint condition, he wants to take my mom for one ride, and then she's all mine. I go home sometimes, to help out on the weekends. It's nice, quiet, different from here. They've got chickens and stuff…"

"So they're still in love, your parents?" I didn't know anyone whose parents were still in love. I thought about Joel and Carolyn, his comment about the trouble with marriage being closet space; her talking about their romantic early grocery store dates.

"Yeah. But it's not like," he gestured at the other couples around the bar. "With my parents it's quiet, understood. He introduces her as 'my bride.' If me or David ever got mouthy to our mom he'd say, 'Nobody treats the woman I love like that.' They garden, since they're off all summer. My mom makes a mean stuffed squash. In the evening, he brews iced tea and they sit outside. They um, they're really into watching bats."

"Wow." I smiled at him. *I'd like to meet these people, Will's parents.*

Then Luke grabbed my arm, embarrassing Will by calling us "lovebirds." It was my shot, which I aced because I play pool better when I'm drunk.

"Winner!" Luke hauled me into a hug, since we were on the same team, whispered in my ear, all hot and breathy as one hand passed over my right breast, where my license was nestled. "Ahh, there's the real. You know, fake's not bad, but Maia Kramer's a hell of a lot more fuckable than Sheila McHugh."

I pushed away, shakily. Monique would be coming back any second.

"Okay." Luke, who had done three more shots, stepped into center stage, resting his pool cue on the table. "It's time we tell Maia the cautionary tale of Stan, the most recent resident of the Trifecta."

I waited. Monique was back, glassy-eyed, and sat on the edge of the pool table, her legs around Luke's waist.

"So I advertised the room on campus, and we got this guy, Stan. We all met him, he seemed normal enough, no more whacked out than our buddy Will here, so we rented him the room. And then we found out—"

"He drove a fucking maroon Chrysler Le Baron convertible, with cream pleather seats," Monique slurred, as if that sealed the deal.

"Wait, you gotta let me tell," Luke moved her to the side. "So he was in the house about a month, and it was okay, but everything we did, Stan did times ten. If we got a hold of some 'shrooms, he'd be tripping his balls off for *days*."

"I don't think the kid ever went to class," Will added.

"The dude was a slob. Fucking Stroh's cans all over the TV room, and then he'd break into our IPA, and replace it with his poor man's beer." Beau complained, "I can't drink that shit, dude. Heartburn City!"

"The last straw was a few weeks ago, when Stan had been on a bender for days. He wasn't going into work—"

"He had a job at the *fucking mall food court*," Monique leaned in, one hand clutching at Luke for balance.

"Right and like Will said, I don't think he'd been to class since Spring Break. So I come home, these guys were up at A-Basin doing some back bowls, and I'm the only one home, and the next thing I know, it's four in the morning and there's this horrible smell, and the smoke detector's going off and Dakota's freaking out, barking, and I go downstairs and the kitchen's full of smoke, right? It reeks of burning plastic and there's Stan, laid out, just passed out, face down on the kitchen floor, and there's a huge fucking fire in the toaster oven."

"Stanley got the munchies," Beau sniggered, and they all looked to Luke for the punchline.

"Tried to make himself a snack, only what he put in the toaster oven, still inside their plastic baggie, was the fucking frozen brine shrimp for Beau's fish!"

"You're kidding!" I laughed.

"Dead serious. So I put out the fire, and I grabbed a handful of his hair—"

"You should have let him burn," Monique interrupted.

"I grabbed a handful of his hair like this, and I picked up his head and I said, 'You have until the end of the week to get out of here.'"

"And it was a Thursday!" Monique crowed. "Bottom line, he couldn't hang with us."

"If you can't run with the big dogs..." Luke began.

"We're not running a halfway house for freaks and fish addicts, dude. Like, Maia, if you keep grooving on that sushi I make, that's cool, and if you need to dip into my fish's shrimp supply, be my guest, but," Beau pointed the pool cue at me, "just don't be cooking it in the brandy-new toaster oven."

"You don't have to worry," I said, "I don't even like cocktail shrimp."

They laughed and laughed and Luke yanked me to his side. Then he spun me to face the group, one hand clutching my shoulder.

"It's official. Everyone!" he yelled, keeping me pinned along the length of him. "Everyone: Maia's in!"

I hadn't even realized that was in question but squinting carefully around the circle of faces, Luke's arm slung heavy over me, I saw it had been. I exhaled, let the warmth flood my chest. Maybe it was tequila, but it felt like belonging.

The rest of the week, I worked hard for Joel's wife. Being in their house, I could see all the things Carolyn did. I felt more than a little horrible for rolling around on scratchy motel sheets with Joel nine times. I had this sickening sense that before, I'd been banging around where I didn't belong. Sleeping with a married man wasn't just a little tacky, an "I Never" or a rite of passage, like admitting to a threesome. This was something bigger I'd been messing with.

Worse, Joel kept calling me from Philly, leaving messages like he was thinking about me, or he'd driven around the city, wondering where I used to live, stuff like that, to the point where the guys were pissed about my phone going off every fifteen minutes while we were trying to watch the Stanley Cup playoffs.

It was just the four of us housemates and the dogs in the family room, eating edamame and drinking beer, me cross-legged on the couch between Will and Beau like I'd always been there, Vader and Dakota at our feet.

They wanted to know how I knew so much about hockey, why I trash-talked Crosby so hard.

"Turnpike rivalry—we hate the Penguins," I said, but of course 'we' meant me and Mark, who blew a ridiculous amount of his warehouse salary on nosebleed season tickets with his idiot friend, Nick.

My phone dinged again: Joel.

"You've seriously got to break up with him, dude," Beau said.

I turned my ringer off. How could Joel not realize that I was shedding him, like snakeskin, like Mark, and Philly before him?

"Don't you think I sort of have?" I asked. "If I don't talk to him, and I don't have sex with him anymore, he'll get the message, right?"

And every one of the guys in my new house looked at me like, *Wrong*.

"Don't take this the wrong way, dude, because you know I'm all in for Nikki," Beau said. "But guys don't let girls that look like you get away that easy."

Every morning at the Carters', it was a new disaster, no matter how I'd left it the night before, how few waking hours they had while I was gone, a never-ending parade I called *laundishes*. Carolyn wrote me numbered To Do lists and I was lucky if I got through half of it by the end of the day, partially because Sasha was tailing me around with her endless questions, staying just enough ahead of or behind me to create more work. "Helping," pouring her own cereal, pouring her own anything, making me an "art creation," or searching for a missing piece of Polly Pockets clothing or dress-up accessory, all ended in disaster. Carolyn had this whole system of storage baskets, labeled, but seriously, the person who was meant to be using them couldn't read.

We were having our usual sushi lunch, and I was cutting up reheated organic chicken fingers for Sash, when she flopped over into my lap, and said, out of nowhere, "You're so pretty, Papaya. What's your last name?"

"Uh, Kramer, McHugh." It came out, a fast lie.

"Papaya-Kramer-McHugh-I-love-you. I rhyme!"

I laughed; my face hot. "Well, thanks."

She jumped up and smiled shyly over her shoulder, calling, "You're prettier than Cinderella!" before she ran up the stairs.

"Yeah, well, what does pretty get you?" I tried to make a joke, but the only people who would get it, Scarlett and Mark, were thousands of miles away.

"Pardon?" Carolyn held her chopsticks in midair.

"Oh, nothing. It's just my mom's famous saying."

"What was it?"

With Sasha out of the room, and an afternoon to kill, I told Carolyn where it came from, about my dance recital in third grade, when Ms. Honeycutt had put blue eye shadow on me with the soft pads of her thumbs, and how I'd stepped out under the tangerine lights to take my bow and seen him standing in the back under the glowing red EXIT sign.

"Who?" Carolyn asked.

"My dad. That was the last time, before he left for good. He almost never came home back then, sometimes sneaking in when my mom was out cleaning to get fresh undershirts. But he showed up at my recital. I had to curtsy, and I was already pretty tall. I bent so low I fell, right in front of everyone. Totally awkward.

"Afterwards, there was the usual, you know, everyone shoving around for Hawaiian punch and brownies. When I saw him, I got shy."

Carolyn nodded. "Sasha's like that too, sometimes, when Joel's been gone."

"My dad was a quiet guy, normally, but he said, loud enough so people turned to look, 'Sweetheart, you looked so pretty up there.'

"And then there was my mom and I was so embarrassed, because she'd stopped.... trying. You know, stains all over her coat, hadn't changed out of her house shoes, all treaded down the back, and she's got my little sister by the arm, and her hair's not brushed—Scarlett used to hate to have her hair brushed—"

"Like Sasha," Carolyn and I said at the exact same time.

"So, what happened? When your parents saw each other?"

"Right, so my mom hears my dad and she yells, right in front of everyone, 'Don't tell her that! Never tell her that! What does pretty get you?'" I made my voice all nasty, how Scarlett and I do when we imitate her.

"What does pretty get you?" Carolyn nodded, like she was taking notes. "Okay."

"After that, he left for good. Now my mom's line, it's what my sister and I joke, whenever things go wrong for me: *that's what pretty gets you.*"

"Oh, Maia," and Carolyn had the saddest look on her face, like pity. I jumped up to clear our lunch away. I'd said too much, considering who she was, and that of course, I was quitting as soon as I had enough money.

My fourth night there, Thursday, Carolyn was in her usual spot on the couch, talking me through prepping coconut chicken.

"Joel will be exhausted after his flight," she said, and I hoped my face didn't show my panic. I'd been so busy trying to do a good job, to impress her, to make up for Before, I'd sort of forgotten it was Joel's house, that he was coming home.

"I thought it might be nice to have a special dinner ready. You know," she marked her place in *Your Strong-Willed Child* with her finger, "it's the little things that make the difference in a marriage. Thoughtful gestures. Love languages. Passion only goes so far."

I didn't say anything; it felt like a dangerous conversation. I thought about Will's parents, sitting out on the porch watching bats. Sasha wandered in and flopped at her mom's feet, sighing that she was bor-ed. This was the kid's pop song chorus, ninety percent of the day. You couldn't really blame her. If I hadn't been so busy running around for Carolyn, I'd have been out of my gourd, stuck in this house too.

"With a lot of men," Carolyn continued, "the passion goes away too. Lots of fireworks, and then, one-trick pony."

Was she trying to tell me something?

"I'm getting started on dinner," I said, glancing at the door.

We were yelling back and forth over the annoying jangle of a show Sasha wasn't even watching, running between the rooms hassling us both, like she could sense something about to happen. I was starting to feel like I might not have to fake a stomach thing to get out of there before Joel got home.

"Sash, you have to look out here, I'm right in the middle of—ow!"

Sasha stomped on my bare foot in her treaded purple hiking boots as she raced around the island whooping about Clifford the big red dog. She had a jar of finger paint in her hand, eying Ben, who was underfoot hoping I'd drop some food.

"Okay," Carolyn called, "now add half a stick of butter to the pan."

"Papaya? Is Ben a big, yellow dog?"

"You cannot put that on the dog." I snatched the paint out of her hand.

"Did you know," Sasha wriggled between the counter and me, yanking painfully on my arm, "there is only one queen bee and all the other bees work for her?"

"Watch out, Sash, it's hot here." I hip-checked her away from the stove, too hard.

"Ouch!" she pouted. "My Mama is the queen bee. You're a drone!"

"Sorry, did you say half a cup or one cup of butter?" I yelled. I'd been cooking with Nikki and Beau, learning, but my brain was scrambled.

"Neither; half a stick!"

"She said half a stick!" Sasha butted my hip bone with her skull, hard.

"Yeah, I heard." I threw butter into the pan that had been sitting over the flame for too long. The butter hissed and spat, turning brown and sending up a geyser of smoke.

"Ow-ow-ow!" Sasha jumped away from the range, rubbing her cheeks.

"Did some get on you?" I asked, but she ran to the TV room, crying that I'd burned her.

"You what?" Carolyn shrieked. "Let me see."

"Not on purpose!" Why was she acting like this? I wanted to hurry, get this stupid dinner on the table and pedal away, home to Juniper Court, my dog, my boys, another night of the Stanley Cup.

"Now add the chicken?" I yelled back, just as the smoke detector went off and Ben threw back his head to howl with it.

"What's burning?"

I'd thought it was just the butter, but glancing over my shoulder I saw the blackened flakes of coconut in the oven, smoke flowing like a backwards waterfall.

"I want chicken nuggets! I hate coconut chicken and I hate that no-oise!" Sasha joined in, wailing with Ben and the smoke detector. I imagined the baby inside Carolyn, crouched up against her spine with a "no freaking way am I going out there" look on its face. Sasha punched me in the thigh as she passed, yelling, "Why do you have to leave! I hate it when you go!"

I was teetering barefoot on a stool to knock the cover off the smoke detector with a broom when the front door opened: Joel. My heart lurched into my throat.

Too late.

"What is going on in here?" I could hear him in the front hall, the door slamming behind him. "Sasha, stop that! What's burning?" He appeared in the kitchen doorway just as I nailed the nine-volt with the broom handle. It skittered across the kitchen floor and Ben stopped howling to pad after it, sniffing.

Dead quiet.

He looked older than I remembered, the wrinkle between his eyes so different from the babyfaces of my boys at Juniper Court. Joel belonged here, in this kitchen, this life.

I did not.

I hoped this meant it would be clear to him that my new role was just maid/nanny.

"Hi," I said in the blaring silence that followed. I was hyperaware of Carolyn in the other room, the TV muted. "I'm Maia. Remember, from the plane?" I climbed down off the stool and offered him my hand. "You guys gave me a ride home?" *And eight days ago, you held me all night and gave me a diamond necklace, and then told me I was the worst thing you'd ever done?*

I didn't let my face show anything with Sasha skulking in the doorway—she was that kind of smart. She'd dragged the stool to climb onto the counter where I'd put the paint. I gave her a hard look and she snarled on her way back to the TV room. Joel and I were alone, for a moment.

"Right." He walked past my hand, eyes trained on the kitchen door, his face white and unreadable, yanking it open to let Ben and the smoke out. "Nice to see you again." I could have cut the raw celery with the edges of his words.

⌒

I turned back to the range and added strips of chicken to the pan. I stirred them, watching the pink flesh go white, then darken to dirty black in the burnt butter.

"I ran into Maia at Vitality. She agreed to help us out while I'm stuck on the couch," Carolyn called out. "Remember, the sitter I told you about?"

"Mom, it's *Paw Patrol*, turn it up!"

Joel grabbed my free wrist under the counter, squeezed it hard, hissed, "What the hell are you doing here?" Urgent, pissed off. I shook my arm free and made a face like, whatever.

A teeny tiny part of me was enjoying this.

"Well, if you're home, it's time for me to go." I gave the pan a little shake, turning the handle towards him, not even letting him take off his tie. "You'll have to start the coconut over." I nodded at the cookie sheet covered in what looked like black toenail clippings.

"Daddy, I want to watch *Paw Patrol* and Mommy is sitting on the remote!"

"Come on, Caro!" Joel snapped like she was another one of his children.

I wanted to slap him for her.

CHAPTER TWENTY-TWO

Carolyn

Friday morning, I called Maia into the family room.

"Yeah?" She arrived in the doorway, cheeks flushed, looking too lovely for words, her creamy skin glowing with the effort of tackling our messy life.

"'Yes,'" I corrected.

"What?"

"I was not allowed to say 'yeah' growing up. Judith, my mother, considered it as bad as cursing. She always told me, 'Yeah is for Valley Girls; a crisp, clean 'yes' serves you better.'"

"Oh. Okay, yessssss," Maia stressed, laughing, pushing the wisps of her hair back into her ponytail, and I couldn't help but smile.

"I guess that was my mother's, 'what does pretty get you?'"

Maia gave me a tolerant look, like she didn't think our childhoods could have had anything in common.

"Guess the scent?" she had a tray with tea and mugs, and I closed my eyes.

"Hibiscus?" It reminded me of Jamaica, our honeymoon.

"Dang, you're good. Sorry it's taken me forever to make tea. The kitchen was a holy disaster."

She bent over to put the mugs down between us, and I could see the hollows of her collarbones, the lace of a bra, a perfectly flat stomach down the neck of her shirt. I looked away.

"It's not like this when I'm able to get off the couch," I said, defensive.

"Oh, I didn't mean you! It's not your job. Anyway, I've seen way worse, cleaning with my mom. Rich people can be so filthy, you have no idea. One family just let their cats go to the bathroom all over the basement floor so even though we cleaned it every week, with their snow shovel, whenever their furnace blew…."

"Usually, though," I couldn't stop myself, "my house is very organized. I have a system."

"Oh, don't worry, I can tell," Maia smiled at me over her mug. "Did you always want to do this?"

"What, lie on a couch and gestate?"

"No, I meant, be just a wife, a mom. Run a house. No offense, but you seem really smart. You love to read," she nodded towards the tower of books. "You could be doing anything. This thing, it's a great job, but it's kind of tedious; laundishes, peed-on sheets, temper tantrums. I mean, I love your kid, but I'm getting paid good money, and normally you, you do it, all the time, for nothing. Was this what you wanted to be when you grew up?"

I shook my head, wondering how I could tell her that for me motherhood was a tangle of compulsion and terror, the fiercest love, the biggest test.

"Like in your wedding picture." She gestured towards the front hall. "You look like a model."

Funny, I thought, this gorgeous young girl telling me, nearly two hundred pounds, thirty years old, that I could have been something based on my looks. A few years ago, I'd stopped telling people I met that before I followed Joel to Colorado, back in New York, I'd been in law school. With little intention of returning, it didn't feel relevant. So much had changed.

"In that picture, you look… really happy."

I'd been afraid she was going to say "less fat."

"It was the happiest day of my life," I told her, honestly. Judith had organized everything—the buffet and tented reception in my childhood backyard before my parents sold their Cherry Hill house. It wasn't a huge wedding; sixty-five people, because of tent capacity and my father stressing about what it would do to the lawn, for the property value. When I think about it now, there were more of my parents' friends as our wedding reception was their going-away party.

Appearances mattered. My mother was especially concerned about the lack of bridesmaids. In the end she asked my only girl cousin on her side to stand up with us. After the accident, I'd lost Holly—she just disappeared—the girl I grew up playing

Wedding and Family with, who knew the first and middle names of my seven future imaginary children.

"That picture is gorgeous. Sash's going to look just like you," Maia gushed. "Did you ever get scouted?"

"Actually," I told her, "the photographer asked to use our wedding photos as the signature in his advertising." Flattered and surprised, I'd said yes, though later I realized should have at least asked for a discount on our album. When I look at the photo now, I can see objectively that we made a striking couple. Joel—handsome as always—and in the photo, he'd just swooped me up like the swarthy hero on the cover of a bodice-ripper novel, my waist so tiny and deep hollows under my clavicles, a hint of shadow in my cheeks. This photo was everyone's favorite, except mine.

The one I love is candid. We were taking pictures before the ceremony, and lost track of time. My mother was screeching for us to hurry up, the quartet was starting "Minuet in G," and Joel was running down the street of my childhood home, the background as familiar to me as my father singing show tunes in the morning while he ground coffee. In my favorite shot, I'm hurrying after Joel, slower with all my underskirts, and he is turning to me, waiting, his body pointed west, towards the setting sun and our future across the country in Colorado, but he is holding out his hand to me. I'm following him, my own hand reaching out, our fingertips almost touching. I had the strangest urge to get out the album, to show Maia our beginnings, to say, *things weren't always like this.*

"Yeah, you look really happy," Maia said thoughtfully. "Way too skinny, but happy."

"I weighed 108 pounds on our wedding day."

"Yikes. Also how do you even remember that?"

"I used to eat nothing but fruit." I remembered the discipline, the zippered plastic bags of concord grapes the weeks leading up to the wedding.

"What do you mean, nothing but fruit? Like, literally?"

"Literally." It had started the summer after the accident. "Back in New York, before we got married, I was training for a marathon."

"You look better now," she insisted. "Healthy. Where I come from, girls who look like that, that kind of skinny, it means somebody's not taking care of them. It means they're hungry," Maia laughed.

I almost forgot who she was, why she was in my home, almost told her about the five-pound bags of mail-order pistachios and salted almonds that I shoveled in to stave off the loneliness my first year here, the beginning of my undoing, before Pier l opened, and I moved on to shopping and chocolate.

Thankfully, Sasha arrived in the doorway.

"I painted my own nails!" she crowed.

"Wow, among other things," Maia laughed, picking up her empty mug. "I've got this. Come on, Miss." She led Sasha out of the room, holding her red-smeared hand by the wrist.

When they were gone and I was left alone with the silence, replaying our conversation in my head, I realized I almost wanted her to come back, to keep talking.

"Should I … do you want me to get started on dinner?" Maia called. "I might need to leave a little early, today, if that's okay." Of course, I assumed this meant she didn't want to see Joel. Or that she did? Five days with her in our house, and I didn't know anything.

They intersected out in the driveway, where I'd sent her out to tackle the front garden beds. Joel came home from work before five o'clock for the first time in seven years.

"Carolyn, look at this girl! It's nearly a hundred degrees and you've got her weeding outside?" He had his hand under her elbow. "She could have heatstroke."

"I'm okay." Maia was smiling in a way that managed to appear wan and vulnerable and feminine. There was a smudge of dirt across her cheek like a line of poetry.

"You could file a suit against us for poor workplace conditions." He took her arm again. "Come into the kitchen. I'll pour you a glass of juice."

"I'm fine." She jerked her arm free of Joel. "There's an eggplant lasagna in the oven, and I told my housemates I'd be home early to help prep for this BBQ thing we're having this weekend. Sorry."

"Why don't I take you and Sasha out? It's too hot for that. We could go to Juanita's, or Panda Express. We can bring something back for Mommy."

"Panda Express—dumplings!" Sasha shrieked. I felt how quickly she abandoned me for Maia deep in the space where my sternum met my windpipe.

"Oh, thanks," Maia said. "But I really can't."

"It's the least I can do, after my wife ran you into the ground today."

"Come!" Sasha wailed. *Traitor.* What had I done? Orchestrated it so that the three of them would go out, while I was pinned to the couch by two pounds of fragile fetus?

"I've got to get going."

"She said she has something going on at her house, Joel!" I yelled from the couch. When had I inherited Judith's bellow?

"At least let me drive you home then."

I was embarrassed for him, really. It was a little pathetic.

"No, but thanks," Maia came into the entry to pick up her purse. "Riding my bike is the only exercise I get."

I looked up from a book I'd barely grabbed in time. I called Joel to pay her, thinking of the extra money I'd get to keep in my envelope.

"Yeah." Maia leaned against the wall, patting the back of Sasha who was clutching her leg. She was a mess—green hands and stains on her shirt from their Play-Doh (point five on the To Do list), oven cleaning grease on her forehead and shorts (point seven), red dirt ground into her bare knees and along her cheek. And yet, somehow, she looked like she had stepped out of an absurd, high-fashion model shoot. "I mean, yesss." She corrected herself, smiling at me. I didn't return it.

"Hey." Joel frowned at me, wallet out, thick with cash. "We're paying her what?"

"Seventeen an hour."

"Do you think that's enough? She works really hard. Let's make it twenty?"

A surge of hot rage washed over me. Works really hard, doing everything I usually do for nothing! For a cash envelope you check against my receipts?

"It's fine." Maia took the cash, and I noticed she didn't meet his eyes when their fingers touched. "Seventeen's great."

"Still seems low." Joel's eyes drifted to where Maia was trying to negotiate untangling from Sasha. Even if I had been wrong, if nothing had ever happened between them, if all of it was pure paranoia, he was acting like an idiot. I almost felt sorry for him, for all men, how little control they had over themselves around the Maia McHugh's of the world.

After she left, Joel stood in the doorway. "What do you want to do for dinner?"

I shrugged, though I was thinking about cool, clean vegetable sushi again, Maia's thin, honeyed jasmine tea over ice.

"A BBQ's a nice idea. It's summer." He looked out the window. "Wouldn't that be fun? We could invite Russ and Jackie, maybe that new couple—you know the ones, the guy's a cop? Some guys from work?"

"Tonight?" I panicked; we couldn't have Jackie and Russ here, tonight! It took me two days to prep the house for playgroup. I was already making Maia's lists for the one I was hosting the following week.

"No, just… sometime. I actually had a decent time at their place that other night."

I didn't point out that it had been more than a month ago, and Jackie had made no move to invite us again, hadn't even texted to see why I wasn't at playgroup this week.

Joel sat down near my swollen feet on the couch. "It might be fun. Don't you think? We should be having more fun."

It was true—we were not having much fun.

"Maybe," I said, "this isn't the time of life when we go for ski weekends in Breck or hike the Fourteeners for fun."

"Okay," he said slowly. "Maybe right now, we have to find it in other ways?"

I could have thrown my arms around him. "Let's host something next weekend.""

"Next weekend I'm in Puerto Rico, remember?"

I made a mental note to ask Maia if she was available to come for fourteen hours, Saturday and Sunday. What if she said no, because she had plans?

What if her plans were with Joel?

I'd also have to ask Joel for more money to pay her. I wasn't sure which thought was responsible for the clutch of anxiety in my chest.

"Maybe the weekend after that? Or the one before the Fourth of July?" Joel was still talking.

"You'd have to be in charge of most of it. There's not much I can do from the couch."

"Fine!" Joel looked genuinely thrilled. "I'll get a big thing of ribs from Costco, hot dogs for the kids, watermelon, everything. It'll be a huge party."

"Okay." I smiled back at him tentatively. I was almost liking the way things were going until he said, "Great, I'll work it out with the new nanny. What's her name? Maia? She can help me put it all together."

CHAPTER TWENTY-THREE

Maia

Friday, after I ran ragged for Carolyn all day, Joel stopped me in the driveway. "What kind of game is this?"

I told him I wasn't playing any game, it was just a job, and by the way, I definitely wasn't coming to Puerto Rico. I wanted him to realize things were over, but he'd hauled me toward the house, threatening to make me tell Carolyn the truth.

Bluffer, or maybe that was me, pretending to faint on their front steps.

Anyway, he didn't, I got paid and pedaled to the bank and made a cash deposit, $670, and for the first time ever, my bank account hit four digits. First thing, I transferred cash to my sister, $180, PAID. After all this, I should have felt great, but I didn't. My head throbbed. I kept thinking about Sasha, wailing she loved me and freaking out about not seeing me for two whole days, and I felt about as big as the ants I was avoiding coming up the sidewalk to Juniper.

Inside, even Vader's kisses didn't help, and the guys had gotten some new video game right outside my bedroom where I shivered under Will's sleeping bag. The last thing I wanted to hear was *"Battle one—fight!"* and the nonstop clang-clang of video-game swords clashing.

I stomped past and gave the boys Janelle's mom's best Evil Eye, hissing, "It's Friday night—don't you guys want to go out somewhere?"

"Why, do you?" Beau asked without even looking up. The girlfriends had abandoned them to their new obsession, probably been through this before. I kicked through containers of leftover chicken wing bones and soggy celery.

After I slammed my door, I heard Will say, "Go to Menu, turn it down."

Saturday, I slept in, rolling back into my sleeping bag until I couldn't ignore Vader's whining anymore. Upstairs, it was gloriously sunny, and the mountains outside the kitchen window nodded at me like loving aunties. Beau and Will came home with coffee, shaking a box of pastries at me like a peace offering and the three of us loaded the dogs in Beau's Bronco and headed out to Lichen Loop.

When we got home, sun-warmed and laughing, we found Luke alone down in the dark basement, trying to get ahead of the other two in the game.

"Dude, it's a stupid game. You missed an epic hike—we just saw a fucking mountain lion!"

"It was a bobcat," Will said.

"Dude, get your eyes checked."

"Bobcat," Will coughed softly.

"Nice to see you all feeling the love again." Luke looked right at me.

"Hey, I was tired last night. I work hard."

"Babysitting?" Luke scoffed. "Twelve-year-old girls do it. How hard can it be?"

I didn't touch that one, but I felt sorry for Monique if their condom ever failed. I thought of Carolyn, how hard she worked for Joel, for nothing.

Luke paused the video game. "Even the queen of the door slam will be feeling the love soon. By the way, you can thank me later. I tightened your hinges. That's not code, though I'd be happy to do that too." He reached behind me and opened and closed my bedroom door smoothly. "No charge. I did the whole trifecta." He tucked his head into the space between my neck and shoulder, whispering, "Maia Jane Kramer, 962 Shackamaxon St—"

I froze. He'd been in my room? I whirled around, and he smiled like he was full of secrets and something dangerous. My neck itched, a bloom of hives, where his breath had passed over it. What had he done with my license, which I hid in the door frame of one of the closets, and the necklace?

"Speaking of feeling the love…" Luke produced a three-inch square gold envelope from his pocket and shook eight beige pills into his hand. They looked like multivitamins, except they were stamped with a butterfly. "While you were all out in the foothills stalking someone's domestic shorthair, Hammer, our friendly local pharmacist, paid a house call."

"Duuuuuude," Beau exhaled, smiling. "Nikki's gonna kill me."

"Two for you." Luke dropped them into his hand. "Two for you," to Will, who sighed, "Just one. I have to function on Monday."

"When was the last time you did X?" Luke asked me and I shook my head—never. "*One* for you, then, and more for me! Shall I fire up the blender?"

He did, making strong margaritas, and we took our pills.

Why not? I'd worked hard for the Carters all week, and I deserved to have some fun. We sat out on the patio watching the dogs circle the yard. Luke had his speakers facing the open windows, playing Bob Marley. I closed my eyes and tilted my head back.

"I think it's already hitting Maia," Will said.

"God, it'd be nice to be an X virgin again, wouldn't it?" Luke said.

"We should go out dancing or something," I said, my eyes still closed. Warmth spread, flooding out from my breastbone up my neck, and lower. Their voices washed over me, like cherry Kool-aid, sweet and red.

"If Boulder had any good clubs…"

"We could go to Denver…"

"What about Catacombs?"

"I don't want to hear that shit depressing music."

"Let's just go to the Foundry."

"I'm not going to the fucking Foundry again."

"Boys…" I said, watching fireworks on the backs of my eyelids. "I thought X was supposed to make you act loving. While you guys figure it out, I'm going to shower."

In the shower, under the hot spray, I ran my hands all over myself. God, what a drug. I sat down on the shower bench and suddenly realized the water wasn't running hot anymore, and I was shivering.

I got out and stared at myself in the mirror. I'd never been fat in Philly, but I hadn't been sculpted like this. My legs looked runway ready, my stomach didn't move a bit, not even when I jumped up and down. I turned to check out my ass. Bike riding had been good to me, I thought, giving my cheeks a loving smack. Hello, cute perky buns!

And that's when I realized that:

1) I was out of my gourd

2) Will and I we were out of towels

I thought of making a dash for my bedroom, but I could hear them outside the door, playing their stupid game again.

"Battle two—fight!"

"Hey!" I stuck my head around the door. "Will!" It was our bathroom, after all. "I need a towel."

They all turned, and their eyes looked like giant black holes, six hungry black holes. Luke smiled, his teeth white and square like a skeleton's.

"Oh, I'll get you one."

Luke came back with something that was definitely not a towel. He put his hand around the door, "Not peeking," he said as he pulled it open and stared, handing me a silky pink bathrobe, size small. I yanked the door closed and slipped it on, and while I was plenty skinny, Monique was at least six inches shorter than me. It barely covered anything and stuck to my wet skin; my nipples poked through the fabric when I cinched the tie around my waist.

I opened the door and tried to walk casually to the bedroom, but three heads swiveled over the back of the couch.

"Battle two—defeat!"

"Me likey," Beau whispered.

"I should definitely dress you more often," Luke said, getting up and following me to the bedroom. "May I?"

I fell onto my bed, my face a thousand degrees. *Why not?*

Luke came back with a pair of skimpy red panties, matching push-up bra, and a tiny black Lycra halter dress covered in orange and fuchsia poppies.

I went into one of my three closets to put on the bra and panties, while Luke took my place on the bed. I struggled into my dragon heels from Buffalo Exchange, holding the wall for balance. I was flying, so it didn't bother me in the least when Luke threw open the closet door before I had the dress on. Thinking, bra and underwear weren't that different from a bathing suit.

"Need any help?" he asked, and he put his finger to his lips as he pulled the slatted door closed behind us. He pressed against me in the dark, so close I could smell the delicious spearmint of his gum.

"Steady now." He grabbed me by my arms, and I had another realization: none of them was as far gone as I was. Time to act more sober.

"Oh-kay," I whispered, and his hands grazed my sides, my hips as he pulled the dress over my head.

"I never thought dressing anyone could be so hot," Luke whispered, an inch away from my neck, his breath fire and ice. He slipped something hard and plastic down inside the front of my bra. "Returning a little something that fell while I was doing my landlordly duties."

I didn't have to take it out to know that it was my real driver's license, that for whatever reason he had been looking at it, he was now returning it. He was trying to fasten the too-tight necklace around my neck when the closet doors flew open, exposing us to my bedroom's glaring bright lights—Will and Beau.

"Well, well, seven minutes in heaven," Beau sniggered.

"Time to go bowling." Will yanked me out of Luke's arms. Even through my haze, I could sense Will's disappointment in me.

Upstairs, we filled up our drinks and drank fast, daring a brain freeze to ruin our buzz. In Luke's car I was aware of three things:

1) the colors—after the sunset everything was jewel-toned, deep purple sky, and the ruby-red of the cars' brake-lights as we wound down Iris.

2 how much I loved these boys, with their abrasively loud music, their yelling, their macho. I tried to explain to them how they were all connected to primitive man, and I could see the vulnerability in them of having to hunt or be hunted, and how they walked waving their sticks, clanging their video game swords, but the music was really loud and Beau leaned through the seats and said, "What are you MUMBLING about up there, dude?"

3) Luke's right hand clamped high on my thigh.

"Are we picking up the girls?" I asked, just to be cute, because I knew-knew-knew I was the only girl on any of their minds.

Beau said, "Nikki doesn't even like me to eat processed carbs. She'd fucking freak if she knew I took X again."

Luke didn't answer, but then again, I was wearing Monique's dress and panties.

At the bowling alley parking lot, I could feel the cold night air blowing up under the short dress. I shivered, and Will put his arm around my shoulders to warm me. It was a curious shake, all in my face and jaw. Luke pulled a flask from his hip pocket before we went in.

"This will heat you up."

"Augh!" I sipped and spat. "What is that, freaking Drano?" I wiped my mouth with the back of my hand, wondering if I had ever put on lipstick, and if I'd just smeared it across my face.

They laughed and laughed.

"Everclear. Try again, Maia Jane."

So I did and kept it down but my throat felt like I'd gargled fire.

Inside, they made a case for me keeping my dragon platforms on. The pimply guy working the counter had me stand out from it and twirl around, bend over and do a mock bowling run. I did, trying to keep from showing my entire ass, to much whooping.

"Yes, yes, she can."

The boys teased me about how picky I was selecting my ball, getting the fit and heft just right.

"My Aunt Rainy used to be in a bowling league," I said.

"Really?" Will's eyebrows went up, his interested-earnest look, but I realized from Luke's expression that I'd said the wrong thing. Nobody they knew bowled for real, sober.

"Where are you from again?" Beau asked, like maybe bowling was regional.

"It's big in Philly," I said, teetering away from them with my ball cradled in my arms like a puppy.

The bowling was silly fun. Just like shooting pool, turns out I bowl better when I'm wasted.

"If there were drunk Olympics," I yelled to the boys over the thumping of the bass and clatter of the falling pins, "I would be a freaking gold medalist." I lined it up and wham, a strike! I threw my arms over my head and the boys went wild. Luke pulled me onto his lap and kept me there until it was his turn. When he stood up, Will pulled me down to his, keeping his hands lightly on either side of my waist, like we were riding a motorcycle.

"Are you okay?" he asked, his mouth near my ear and I turned so our black-hole eyes could connect like laser beams, grinning.

Oh-kay.

Luke hit a strike and loped over and kissed me, hard on the lips, "for being my lucky charm."

"You're up, Will." He yanked me off Will's lap. "You can kiss her, for luck."

Will shook his head, pretending to inspect his bowling ball.

"What, you don't want to kiss her? Here!" Luke was half-holding me up by both shoulders, my head bobbling like Babci's dolls with the broken elastic, shoving me towards Will.

"It has nothing to do with not wanting to," Will said so quietly, but even with all the noise, I heard.

Then it was Beau's turn, and he came over "for my lucky smooch" and dipped me comically, pressing our closed lips together and twisting his head back and forth like Sasha pretending to make out with her gigantic Hello Kitty.

After that, I was kissed by Luke and Beau at every turn, in different ways. Luke kept taking it too far, sticking his tongue in my mouth, and once he sipped from his flask to transfer the burning liquor in, but I clamped my lips, let it dribble down my chin and chest, where he licked it off. But I saw out of the corner of my eye Will's expression before he shoved Luke on the shoulder, away.

"You're up," Will growled.

It was black-light bowling, dark, loud-loud-loud and I was hitting it like a pro and loving the kisses and glow of attention from everyone around us, all eyes on me, but then suddenly, I really-really-really had to pee.

Holding on to the wall, I weaved and slipped in my platforms to the bathroom and peed for about an hour. It took so long I folded over on the toilet and rested my cheek on my bare knees, closing my eyes. I might have fallen asleep for a few minutes. Stumbling out, I held on to the sink so I could get a good long look at myself in the mirror again. I decided it was time to put on some makeup. My eyes were black holes too, and my hands shook as I applied thick coat after coat of mascara, so it came out sexy-smeary. I pursed my lips at my beautiful self. I could definitely still be scouted, I thought, for real this time. Never mind what Mark said—maybe it's time to find a new dream. It wasn't too late.

On the way back from the bathroom, the guys at the shoe counter called me over.

"Yeah-yesssss?" I was careful not to slur. Getting us kicked out would hoover the fun right out of the evening.

"So we just want to know," he indicated his friend behind the counter, sucking down sweating cold fountain soda—god I was thirsty!—"which one of them it is?"

"Which one of them what?" I waved my hand. "C'mere!" at the kid with the soda. I grabbed the cup from him and sucked at the straw until there was nothing left, my eyes watering from the sting of the bubbles. "Thanks. Which one of them what?"

"Which one of those guys you're going home with?"

I dropped his empty cup on the counter and walked back to where my boys were waiting, all three of them. Six black eyes had been watching me at the counter, waiting for me to kiss, to sit on their laps, to be their lucky charm—

"It's been your turn," Beau said, maybe a little annoyed.

"Hey!" I called to the shoe counter and the guys looked up. "Hey, you wanted to know which of these boys I'm going home with?" Now I had the attention of every man in the place who could hear me over the pulse of the music, the rumble of the falling pins. I felt all their eyes, the hot glow of their hungry attention. *They all want you.*

"Yeah?" Shoe Guy called back, grinning.

"All of them!" And I tipped backwards until I fell into their waiting laps, hands clutching at me, holding me there, so I didn't fall. "I'm going home with all of them!"

The bowlers around us erupted into a roar of cheering; women turning away—jealous!—and in some tiny sober corner of my mind, I realized that those were Will's hands gently tugging the hem of my dress down to cover me up when I'd fallen over.

After bowling, we went somewhere for food, a diner-type place with breakfast all the time. Someone ordered for me. I lay down in our booth, using Will's thighs as a pillow, and this was the nicest part of the night, his hand cupping my bare shoulder, their still drunk-happy conversation, what sounded like boring ski team talk, bouncing above me.

My eggs came, done the way Sasha likes me to make them, over medium, and when I pierced the yolk with my fork, the golden liquid spilled over the white onto the chipped plate, and my heart ached, a throbbing right under my breast.

"That's…. the saddest thing I've ever seen," I whispered.

"What?" Will tipped his head toward me, ever polite.

"This," I gestured to my plate. "It's the saddest…" I couldn't even finish my sentence.

"Do you want mine?" he offered his blueberry pancakes.

"No," I turned my face into his shoulder so they wouldn't see me cry. "It was a baby chicken," I whispered. A baby chicken died, for me to eat it with no thought for who it might have been…Tears ran down my cheeks. What was I doing here? In this diner, in this city, in this life?

"Already?" Luke looked at his watch. "Five hours?" he said testily. "Fuck. I should've given her two. She's skinny, but she's tall."

They ignored me, eating while I sniffled into Will's shoulder. He said something about the eggs we eat having no chance of becoming chickens, and I thought of the baby Joel told me about, who would have been Sasha's big brother. The more I wanted to stop, the more sad things piled up, the worse I felt, the harder I cried. Round and round.

I missed Scarlett. I wanted to be home in our room with the sirens and hissing buses every sixteen minutes and her conning me into doing some crazy art project, like gluing bottlecaps to the trash can or painting the lampshades with paisley swirls. I wanted to go shopping under the El train shadow, where you could buy a turquoise polyester club shirt and three unlabeled cans of food for a dollar. We'd put on our hoochie halter tops, whose hems would fall out by midnight, try to make our six cans of mystery foods into something like dinner, and maybe go dancing at Delaware Ave. With my sister, I didn't have to be anyone. Out here, I was so tired of … trying.

Then there was Mark who, for all his flaws, had grown up with me, looking out for me, more like a bossy brother than anything else. I thought of how he liked to sleep curled around my back, how he used to spell out LUV U with Alpha-Bits on the counter before he left for work.

And at the Carters, there was Sasha, the way she'd hang around my neck, smelling like baby shampoo and crayons, begging me not to leave her every night. God, you'd think her dad was the one who left with the parakeets and the blue suitcase and the Heidi book…

And Carolyn.

Joel wasn't just another something I probably shouldn't have done, like stealing the money from Ritchie. It wasn't just me flirting with different ways I might want to be—I'd been banging around in something sacred: someone's family.

At the car, Beau got in up front next to Luke.

"Let Will babysit her," Luke snipped, and he didn't call me Maia Jane.

I tipped my head against the cool glass of the window and bawled, sick to my stomach over all the lies and secrets in my wake.

"What is it? Are you really upset about something? I mean, other than the baby chickens?" Will asked with a tolerant smile.

"I've made a mess of my life," I howled. "And I'm dragging them through it, too, and she doesn't deserve this! They're a nice family."

"Who?" Beau asked from up front at the same time Will said, "You're not still seeing that married guy, are you?"

I just cried harder. Will stopped patting my thigh.

"Well, *this* was fun," Luke said.

We drove by the university and let Beau out at Nikki's dorm and when we got home, Luke didn't say anything. I careened through the living room alone, using the wall to hold me up down the stairs. I flopped onto my bed and buried my face in Vader's bristly neck. At least he was glad to see me. I didn't deserve him.

"Hey, you want water or anything?" Will was standing in my doorway. I rolled over, tugged the dress down over my ass cheeks. I couldn't tell from the bed, but his eyes looked less black-holish.

I shook my head, and my real driver's license, where Luke had tucked it, poked my boob. I pulled it out and studied it, squinting my eyes at my sixteen-year-old smile, my high ponytail, so young and dumb. I should never have left.

Will crossed the room and sat at the foot of my bed, carefully unbuckling my platforms.

"Listen, you're probably going to feel worse in the morning, but it doesn't mean anything. It's just chemical, your body's inability to process any more serotonin. It's why I usually don't do the stuff, the way I feel the day after."

I nodded. He slipped my shoes off and for the briefest of seconds, he cupped one of my heels in his palm.

"Wow, you, you even have beautiful feet," Will murmured. "Sorry," he stood up abruptly, his cheeks bright red. He ruffled Vader's ears before he lined my shoes up neatly by my closet. "Good night, you two," he said, turned out the light and shut my door gently.

Of course, he was right. I woke up to the smell of shit and found a steaming pile of it on the carpet, and poor Vader cowering by the closed bedroom door where his nails had scratched deep grooves in the wood, and when I got up to let him out, I realized I'd gotten my period in the night, in Monique's dress and underwear, staining my sheets. And even worse, I couldn't even get to the bathroom because guess what? The three boys were all back in position, playing their stupid video game again.

Battle three—defeat.

CHAPTER TWENTY-FOUR

Carolyn

Friday night, I was surprised when I heard Joel clinking around in the kitchen after dinner. He appeared in Sasha's doorway, smiling expectantly.

"I did the dishes. What are you ladies up to?" He shifted his weight from leg to leg.

"I'm reading to Sasha; it's what we do around here in the evenings." Sometimes, solicitousness was more irritating than tension.

He ignored my snarky comment. "Can a Daddy come in?"

"Sash, here," I gripped her shoulders, pulling her with me. "Come here, move closer."

She was tired and uncooperative, pushing back against my belly.

"Careful, watch the baby. Make room for Daddy."

"No!"

I caught Joel's eye in the second before he put on a nonchalant expression. He looked like he was waiting for an invite to the prom.

"Huh, Sash? You sure there's no room for your old dad in there?" Joel asked with a forced cheerfulness.

"Sure there is!" I tugged Sasha over hard and she sat straight up, folding her wiry arms across her chest.

"Ow!" she said, too loud, too late. "No. I want Papaya! How many more sleeps?"

"Three, love." I kissed the top of her head. I wanted for Joel to get in with us, to smell how, under the apple shampoo scent, there was the lingering, vulnerable whiff of humanity if you pressed your nose to her scalp. I imagined this smell was what animals detected, what meant *human* to them. I wanted Sasha to bridge the gap between us like she had in Jackie and Russ' chairs, on my lap, her feet in Joel's.

Now Joel perched next to her, trying to fit his long legs in, his size-twelve dress shoes pointing up at her cloud-covered ceiling.

"Dad," she shook her head. "No shoes in the bed."

"Oh, right, okay." Joel tugged them off and I could smell the tang of leather and thin dress socks.

"PU, your feet stink!" Sasha pinched her nose, shrieking into a giggle and I recognized this hysterical pitch; we were moments away from a meltdown.

"Okay." Joel stood up, his fingers hooked through the heels of his shoes. "I can see I'm not welcome here." He waited in the doorway for her to contradict him. Instead, she pressed her face into my armpit, her face scrunched.

"Good night, Cinderelly."

"Good night, Smelly Feet!" she called, her eyes squeezed shut. Joel left.

"You're being rude, Sash." I folded the book closed with my finger marking the place.

She ducked her head into my armpit again and popped her fingers out of her mouth. "Read?"

"I don't know that I feel like reading to someone who was so rude to her daddy."

"Read?" Sasha repeated like a toddler, her eyes shiny with tears. I opened the book again, emotion flooding the small space left under my heart. She was just a tired little girl, scrambling to understand all the changes in her life.

In the doorway of our bedroom, I stretched, trying to redirect the throbbing in my lower back. Joel was on our bed with a glass of Scotch balanced on his chest, basketball on the TV.

"Has she had any dairy recently? She seemed really wound up."

I shook my head.

"Who's Papaya, a new character?"

"It's Maia, the babysitter." *Your mistress.* I watched his face for a reaction. None.

"So…" he said, a poor imitation of casual, "What made you hire *her*?"

"Why wouldn't I? I ran into her at the juice bar on the way home from the hospital. I was short on options. I'm pretty isolated out here." It was an old point, a verbal poke in his chest.

"Whose idea was it?"

"What do you mean, whose idea? Like, she saw me and asked if *I* needed a babysitter?" I laughed, meanly. "I was desperate; you weren't here." Jab.

"It just seems a little out of character for you."

"What do you mean by that?"

"Jackie said it the other night, at the BBQ, everyone in playgroup calls you the Safety Queen." Kick. "And then you hire someone we barely know to care for the most important thing in our life? She worked at a juice bar before this! I mean, what experience does she have with children?"

"Sasha adores her!" Block. "She's wonderful with her."

"Did you check out her references? She probably lives with a bunch of commune hippies, or partiers, or drug addicts or—!"

"Actually, Beau and Will and Luke sound lovely."

"You know their names?"

"Her housemates? Of course. We talk, about all kinds of things." Throat punch.

His reply was to use the remote to turn up the volume on the basketball game.

I went to the closet and closed the door to block his view of me while I put on my maternity leggings and a T-shirt.

"Wow," he said when I came out of the bathroom. He checked his watch, "Seven forty and you're ready for bed. Awesome Friday night."

"I'm on bed rest. What did you have in mind?"

"Never mind," Joel said.

"What?"

"I've been gone for three days and you're ready to go to sleep."

"What do you want to do?" Though I suspected I knew, and Dr. Michaels had said absolutely not.

"I don't know! Talk, get naked, smoke a joint! Something!"

"*Smoke a joint?* You're asking me to smoke pot? I mean, since when do we smoke pot?"

"We don't. That's the point. But I got some today… and I thought we could. Some guys at work were talking about it." He sipped off the watery remains of his Scotch, the alcohol fumes so strong in our bedroom I wondered if I should open a window. "A lot of them do it—pot, hash, X—with their significant others, to take it to the next level."

"Take what to the next level? Are you talking about making love?"

"Or whatever. Even just talking. They say X makes you feel so much love for each other, makes it easier to talk about things. Express yourselves. One guy said his therapist prescribed it for him and his wife when she had breast cancer, so they could cope. Forget it."

"What kind of things do you want to talk about?" I realized I was holding my breath, forming his answer for him, *about what's happening to our marriage.*

"I don't know! Forget it. I thought it would make for an interesting night. Whatever."

Whatever? I thought. It was a Maia word.

Instead, I said, "Why would I want to chemically sabotage the future of our baby? Why would I take any risks?"

"Fine. I didn't mean you, necessarily. Forget it." Joel sat up on the edge of the bed, peeled off his socks and threw them in the direction of the hamper. They left an arc of aroma like a comet trail. He got up and, ignoring the socks, opened the briefcase on the dresser and pulled out another airplane bottle of Scotch. He broke the seal and refilled his watery glass.

"What?" He met my eyes, a challenge.

"Nothing. Just, you're acting strange," I said quietly. I wondered if it could be true, if he had forgotten about our baby—and would it be different if I'd told him the truth about the ultrasound? It made me sad, this giant chasm in our inner thoughts. I spent every second being aware of this pregnancy, constant reminders in our son's movements, in my frequent trips to the bathroom, every moment focused on the well-being of our children. Joel, off in the world, commuting, his head full of his work thoughts and god knows what else… could it be that us having a baby in a few weeks had slipped his mind like a missed dental appointment?

"Forgive me for trying to unwind. The guy at work, who had the weed, had X too, but I knew you wouldn't go for it, because of the chemicals. Marijuana's natural, but God forbid we do anything to make you uninhibited."

"But you are remembering that I'm pregnant," I said coldly, folding my hands over my belly. "And they can lace those drugs with anything, heroin even. You don't know what you're getting. How were you going to smoke it anyway?"

A look of consternation passed over his face, as though he had just realized he'd misplaced his keys. He slammed into the bathroom and turned on the shower. I saw it on the bedside table, a little bag, the kind spare buttons come in attached to a sweater, filled with something that looked remarkably like dried thyme.

I carried it with me when I went down to the kitchen to refill my water bottle, touched to see he had cleaned everything, leaving Maia's lasagna pan to soak in the sink. While I ran the filtered water, I looked out towards the lights of Boulder, the town lights twinkling. I imagined Maia under the strobe of a nightclub, the center of everyone's attention, living in a body that was lithe and unencumbered, free. Did I want that? Would I even know what to do with myself in a world outside this dark kitchen, this house surrounded by tumbleweeds?

I took a Granny Smith apple from the ceramic bowl on the island and washed and cored it. Then I poked a small hole in the side with a skewer from the BBQ set. I took a tiny square of tin foil and perforated it several times with the pointy end of the skewer and laid it on the cored top of the apple, where the stem had come out. I nestled a little bundle of marijuana on top, a perfect fit.

Joel was back on the bed, shirtless, in a pair of boxer shorts, still like the college boy he had been when we met, glaring at the basketball game. The light from the screen cast shadows over his face, making his nose look even more like an eagle's beak, leaving a dark shadow in the crease of his frown line.

"Honey," I sat down as gently as I could on the edge of the bed, cupping under my stomach with my free hand. "Do you want an apple?"

He turned to me, and his eyes focused, lit up. The line smoothed, as though we were just the same two kids we had been in the dorm at NYU, as though I was a girl who could sit on a bed without feeling the folds of my skin everywhere. As though we weren't parents in a stucco house with faux brass locking door handles on the master suite. The lock I turned.

"I can't do this, obviously, but I can be with you."

"Wow," he beamed, turning the fruit. "Did you come up with this?"

"No. When I was going out with Alex, his older brother showed us how."

Joel's face clouded as it did whenever I mentioned my first boyfriend. "So you smoked pot with him?"

"No." It was the truth. I'd pretended to once at a party, before the accident, but that was it.

Joel found some matches in the bathroom and I watched as he sucked on the hole in the side of the apple, and the spicy-sweet smoke curled out of the apple and drifted around the room. I worried about Sasha coming down the hall, and I waited for it to hit him, for him to unwind, for the ancient remedy to bring about the change he obviously wanted.

"Shall I open a window or something?"

"Honey," he coughed, resting his head lightly on my belly, "I wish you could try a little." But his request was resigned, mellow.

"I know."

"I can feel it in there," he said dreamily. "It's kicking my cheek."

I was desperate to talk about the baby with Joel, to connect the three of us, and I almost told him, right then, about it being our son, but I didn't.

He sat up, took another hit from the apple. My stomach was warm where his head had been and I wondered if our baby could sense the change in temperature, the presence and absence of his father. I guided Joel's head back down to me, stroking his cheek.

"Honey," he reached up and sweetly cupped my breast, dopey-eyed, "you know I love you."

"I know." I smoothed the hair off his forehead.

"I just, I feel so much love for you, and Sasha, and then..."

I waited.

"Sometimes I'm afraid of her."

I burst out laughing, "Oh, we're all afraid of Sash." I thought of Maia, our shared looks when a tantrum was brewing.

Joel's eyes narrowed. "All of you women, with your agendas and your secrets... terrifying."

All of what women?

"I feel like sometimes, I'm not what you want me to be. I'm not ready to be who you want. God, this stuff must be hitting me now."

"It's okay," I said softly. I picked up the remote and turned off the chatter of the basketball game, our room dark.

"I feel like you're so far ahead of me. So much more settled than I am. Content."

I wanted to laugh. Waddling around at nearly two hundred pounds in my subdivision life with no friends? Content to watch this marriage, the foundation of the only thing I had accomplished in my adult life, slipping through my fingers? Frantically stuffing chocolate into my mouth so that I could continue to hate who I had become? Now we were getting somewhere.

"Nobody is ever content. Everyone has a few back-up plans up their sleeve, but you can't admit them to each other." I was thinking about Jackie, how the week she asked Russ to move out, she ordered a credit card in her maiden name and paid $80 for internet searches of all her ex-boyfriends, just in case...

Maybe I hadn't said that out loud, because he continued like he hadn't heard me.

"I think I'm having a hard time being grown up." Joel rolled off my belly. "I see these guys in town, these college frat brats, no responsibilities, everything a possibility, can go anywhere and do anything, and I just think, they have no idea how good they have it. They're having the Boulder experience we're missing."

"But this is what you wanted to do. You picked Colorado, and you wanted this job at Yakimori, remember?" I was thinking of the day he proposed.

We were happy, back then. I remember long winter nights on the futon at the apartment, my books and a bottle of wine open, which inevitably led to him folding over the corner of my law text and closing it, distracting me with kisses at the nape of my neck. I remember running together, before he blew out his knee, Central Park, long routes on the weekend, which made up for the occasional pizza or Chinese food I'd sometimes let myself enjoy. He used to take all the nectarines in our ceramic fruit bowl and mark them with tiny dotted lines, guide maps, for the way I loved to cut them with a paring knife, a sliver at a time, making one piece of fruit last a whole afternoon.

"You were the one who wanted to move to Colorado," I said again. And you wanted me, I thought but didn't say, as he lay with his head on our unborn son.

"Yes," he said, sounding unconvinced. "But we don't do any of the things we used to do. You don't run anymore, and I thought we'd be skiing more, or…. Our snowshoes still have the tags on them."

When I tried to laugh, it sounded like a cat getting sick. "People change, Joel. They evolve. They grow up. Life, things happen!"

"This stuff is wild. Everything's out of whack. Except," he touched my face, "we're still real, right? We're okay?"

"We are," I whispered, and I grabbed for this truth. All that had gone before, Maia, my suspicions of infidelity, were the overworked, paranoid mind of pregnancy. Right? We were fine. This was real life, married life. The constant, the everyday, this man I closed my eyes beside at night.

"Am I freaking you out?" he asked, and his breath smelled of hash and sweet apple.

"No," I lied, trying to match his gaze, his intensity.

"I've made mistakes," he looked away.

"Everyone has," I said quickly. Please, I thought, don't say anything you can't take back.

"Not you." But he said it sourly, without a trace of admiration.

I could have told him about the moment I would never get over.

The summer I was seventeen...

How this created an anxiety in me so deep and howling hungry, I sometimes had to shovel handfuls of chocolate or salty nuts from the stash just to keep it quiet. I could have told him that most nights when I couldn't sleep, before the bed rest, I ate so much that I went to bed with my ribs aching, hating myself.

I didn't.

"There was the credit card thing…" I said, but Joel waved me off. Old news. I raised an eyebrow. Were we past that? And the cash envelopes?

He sat up, turned on his bedside table lamp, surveying our bedroom like he'd never seen it before.

"Some people say it's a bad idea to get married in your twenties," he said slowly, tasting his words. "Because you still have so much evolving to do."

There was a long silence and tears squeezed out, rolled down my cheeks. I sat up and wrapped my arms around his back, pressing the baby into him. I willed our son to wake up and wriggle, to remind Joel of the threads that connected us, but he was still.

"You could look at it this way: that you have a best friend to make mistakes, to change and grow up with," I finally choked out.

"You would," he said, matter-of-factly, all of the warmth gone. "You would look at it that way."

Maia showed up late Monday morning, and I would have been irritated if I weren't so surprised to notice that I'd missed her company in the two long days. Joel had tried to engage in our routine in spurts, but there wasn't the same easy assimilation of Sasha and her imagination into the daily routine. Maybe men aren't as intuitively good at that, or as Rachel from Friday group says, men can't multitask. Or perhaps it was because he wasn't getting paid? He seemed distracted, retreating for hours on his laptop, working on the presentation for Puerto Rico, two long hikes with Ben, and he came home smelling like fresh air and dirt and pine trees, and I hated him a little for being able to do these things, or at the very least, for not taking Sasha.

When I reminded him early Monday morning I needed a ride to my checkup with Dr. Michaels, he looked surprised.

"Sorry, I have a think session at work at 11:00. It's about the presentation. The boss lady put it on my calendar." Code for command attendance.

"Can you rideshare with Dave and leave me the car, then?"

And such a look of hopefulness passed over Joel's face, as though all these years of me not driving were just an affected adherence, like gluten-free people who hork down the dry turkey on wheat sandwiches and the complimentary cookies when stuck on a grounded airplane. Like when push came to shove, I would just get behind the wheel and drive myself to the doctor.

Instead, I enjoyed the look on his face when I said, "Maia can take me."

It had been seventeen days since I'd left the house, and I squinted around, pointing out the signs of summer, flowers in our yard, as Maia and I walked to the car, her with a hand under my elbow like it was icy. I'd called and asked Jackie to take Sasha to the playground, so for the first time, it was just the two of us. It felt funny, strangely proper, like we were on a blind date.

"Are you sure you wouldn't rather go with Jackie? I could watch all the girls," Maia paused as she opened the door so I could lower myself into the passenger seat.

I assured her I didn't. The last thing I needed was Jackie letting my weigh-in number slip to the Friday group, with a 'poor thing' murmur and her big sheep eyes.

Maia took a long time adjusting the mirrors, her visor, squinting, first with her sunglasses up on her head, then over her eyes as she decided which was better. She mumbled how long it had been since she'd driven, narrating the route and repeating all my directions out loud. Then she fell into a jittery silence, punctuated by the turn indicator she left on for three blocks.

"So how was your weekend?" I asked, to make conversation.

"Ugh," she answered ruefully. "Too crazy. I'm done with all that."

Done with all what? I wondered.

In the waiting room, the nurse gestured for us both to come on back.

"Oh, no, I can wait," Maia faltered, "here." But the nurse encouraged her, assuming she was my reluctant partner.

"Come," I urged, suddenly afraid of being alone with the tech if the machine turned on to nothing but white noise and having to meet her eyes over a dead baby.

So Maia followed us down the frigid hall. At the scale, I second-guessed my decision. *Why had I invited her, of all people, here?* But as I took off my shoes and stepped on the scale, Maia politely distracted herself, playing with a due date wheel, studying a poster for warning signs of overactive bladder.

"You've actually lost three pounds," the nurse chirped, "but you're still in a good range, and that's normal with bed rest."

In the darkened ultrasound room, Maia took the chair by the bed, looking away when I tugged down my maternity waistband, exposing angry red stretch marks and the old scar, silent as we both waited while a new tech squirted warm goo on my belly.

"I've never, you know, seen one of these. I keep waiting for my sister to get knocked up, but…" Maia chattered, filling the quiet.

I could barely breathe with anticipation.

"Dr. Michaels ordered a 3D this time, so we can get a more detailed view of the baby's anatomy and more accurate cervical measurements," the tech narrated, swabbing around my stomach.

"I can step out, if you want," Maia offered again, but we both ignored her.

"And there's the heartbeat," the tech said, as the comforting thrum of my baby's life force filled the room. "Pulsing at 172, lovely. Now baby's finally waking up, maybe you'll be lucky enough to get a good sleeper." She moved the wand and then suddenly, beside me, Maia gasped.

"What?" I swiveled to her, away from the screen, as if she would see something, know something, I didn't.

"It's…" She put a hand up to cover her mouth. A smile peeked out from the corners behind her fingers. "It's Sash!"

She was right; the view of his scowl looked just like his big sister, right before a tantrum.

"Grouchy Sash!" I laughed, relieved to have seen him pouting, waving tiny clenched fists through fluid. *Relax*, I reminded myself. It's better for the baby.

"Looks like this one's got a temper," the tech chuckled, moving the wand down my stomach, lower on his body.

"We want to keep the gender a surprise," I said quickly. She was not the same one I'd had before.

"No problem. I just have to take a few measurements here. Oh look, baby's trying to find a thumb."

Snuggling into the pillowy placenta, his expression changed from Sasha's pre-freak-out frown, to pure, adorable bliss.

Maia reached out for my hand; maybe because it's what people do when one is in a hospital bed. She squeezed and when I turned, I saw a shine to her eyes.

"It's…Carolyn, I mean, my god!" she whispered, self-consciously dropping my hand to swipe at her eyes, staring at the screen. "Sorry, I just didn't expect it to be so clear. I never really realized… there's a tiny person in there, right there!"

"3D's pretty vivid." The tech had a smile in her voice.

"Amazing," Maia murmured. "Thank you, for letting me come in."

Afterwards, she drove me home, grandma slow, braking long before we reached intersections, her hands gripping the wheel at 10 and 2. As we merged on to Baseline, she pulled off to the shoulder to let an SUV loaded with kayaks and cute boys fly past us, muttering at their rush.

When I teased her about it, she said, "Are you kidding me? Not only is your husband's car probably worth more than my mom's house, I've just seen that I am carrying the world's tiniest, most precious cargo. I feel so protective. Is it weird…? I don't know how to say, without sounding crazy, but when the face looked just like Sash… I just, I don't even know him or her, but I feel like… I already love it a little. Is that ridiculous?"

"No." I smiled at her over Joel's gearshift. "I know just what you mean."

"Do you think…" she started and stopped, pumping the brakes as she eased us into a red light.

"What?"

"Hear me out, but I think you would feel better about everything, a little more relaxed, if you knew you could drive the car if you had to. Like, if I wasn't here, in case of an emergency."

The old prickle of defensiveness made the hairs on my arms stand stiff. I opened my mouth to speak, but she cut me off.

"Maybe sometime we could do a little—"

"No!" I could still hear the shriek of brakes, the rain of glass on the pavement, the crows screeching overhead on the wire out my open sunroof.

The summer I was seventeen, my boyfriend was a lifeguard at the local pool and I…

"I just meant—"

"I am on bed rest! What is with all of you people not respecting a doctor's orders?"

"Sorry. Sorry." Maia inched the car up the short distance of the driveway. "Sorry."

She settled me on the couch, and then fussed in the kitchen.

"Here." She brought me a tray, a large square of her reheated eggplant lasagna, and a crisp kale salad with toasted quinoa, flecks of white cheese and slabs of avocado.

"So," her tone was purposefully light, "it looks like nobody was a fan of my lasagna. I won't tell Beau; his recipes are like his babies."

"It's the paleo thing. Joel's not doing dairy." I picked up my fork.

"Yeah, well, I put some goat cheese on your salad. It's better with that, and the avocado's meant to be really good for the baby, you know, the good kind of fat. I'd have put some chocolates out too, for dessert, but I think we're running low. I can run out and get some …"

"It's fine." I held up my hand. I hadn't purchased any in weeks, was thinking I might not. "Thank you."

She poured us two tall glasses of iced jasmine tea.

"Joel used to eat lasagna. He ordered it for us, in fact, on our first date, in New York. It was my junior year of college; we met in a literature class. He passed me a note, like grade school, asking me to dinner."

I remember I weighed 115 pounds. I'd exercised in the NYU fitness center for two hours and was so hungry it felt like my brain was being sawed in half with a dull knife.

"We went to Giovanelli's, this lovely place on Seventeenth, and he ordered me the house special—triple-cheese lasagna."

It was a food I would never have let myself eat, though I'd loved my father's once, before the accident.

"That sounds delicious," Maia said, dribbling fig balsamic over our salads. "Growing up, my mom always warned me and my sister if we ever wanted to eat a piece of cheese, we should slap it on our thighs, since that's where it was ending up." She laughed, eating her lasagna in efficiently-stacked, ample bites. "So was it good, this triple-cheese lasagna?"

I pushed it around, inhaling the smells of spices and tomatoes, telling myself that had to be enough when Joel said frankly, "You're not one of those eating-disorder girls, are you?"

"What?" I dropped my fork like he'd accused me of something sordid.

"You've cut that into about a thousand pieces but you haven't eaten a bite."

"Oh, no," I said, bringing a mouthful to my lips, pretending to blow on it.

"My buddy went out with a girl like that in high school. She was a sweet girl, but batty as a

bedbug. Wouldn't eat anything that wasn't the color white, had to sniff everything first, I mean really sniff it, like a dog. She also had this thing about asbestos, wouldn't even say it—called it the A-word. She was terrified of it; researched all the buildings in town and made us drive these ridiculous routes to avoid them, or she'd hold her breath as we went by, put up all the windows.

"Then she got so skinny she grew this funky fur all over her arms and her parents had to send her away. The sad thing was, when they put her in a hospital, she was most freaked out by the fact that the building was old construction, that they hadn't been listening to her. She still calls my buddy sometimes; breaks his heart. Anyway," Joel said decisively. "I'm glad you're not one of those. I wouldn't sign on for that."

"No," I said, looking down, and gratefully scooping up a bite of lasagna, so glad that he was showing me a way out, that he was signing on for me. "I just like really small bites."

"Good," Joel said, beaming as I ate. "Want to split some tiramisu? It's amazing here."

The only problem was after—how to eat and still punish myself? Perhaps it was the weight of the secret; not telling Joel about the accident, for fear he would leave me.

At first, I didn't tell him, because I didn't tell anyone. Then too much time had gone by, and it felt even more significant that I hadn't told him, like I'd tricked him into falling in love with me. And then there were all the accoutrements of the accident's aftermath that clung to me like dust and dog hair to broom bristles—the fear of driving, the obsessive anxiety about safety, the need to research everything, then the spending and regrets, and the eating and exercising loop-de-loops...

I looked up. Maia was still waiting for an answer—had the lasagna on our first date been good?

"It was the best lasagna I ever had," I told her, cutting myself a huge bite and smiling, "until yours."

CHAPTER TWENTY-FIVE

Maia

Joel called eleven times over the weekend, twice on Monday night. He left messages about the plane ticket, a direct flight for the coming Saturday, Denver to Puerto Rico. I didn't answer because I'd told him I had no intention of going with him. Then, while Nikki and Beau were making kombucha, Luke made this announcement that we all needed to silence cell phones "for the endless personal calls," which was obnoxious since I was obviously the person he meant. He'd been a jerk to me ever since the X night.

Will and I had walked Vader and Dakota around the neighborhood. We were watching an Animal Planet on gorillas when Luke plopped down on the couch too close, his thigh mashed into mine. Right in front of everyone, he made a big deal about asking me for the rest of my rent deposit.

"Did you hear me?" Luke said, his hand massaging my shoulder. On my other side, Will stared straight ahead. "I need your last month's rent. I know when you moved in, I waived it, but everyone else paid first and last when they came. I want to be fair, and I'm in kind of a bind with Visa."

I froze. He kept pinching the skin on my shoulder, squelching it against the bone under his palm. I'd gotten sunburnt out on the patio doing chalk drawings with Sash. I tried to shrug him off.

"You know, Maia Jane, if you can't run with the big dogs…" he said.

I was supposed to finish it for him, "Stay on the porch.'" I didn't.

"You feel me? I'm in a little cash deficit myself."

"I don't have it," I said flatly. "I mean, I have some, but not all, right now." I tried to joke, "That wine split last week did me in."

He finally took his hand off my shoulder but moved it to the zipper of his khaki shorts.

"Sure it's the wine split that's the trouble? Sure it's not something back home? My father's company has an office there, City of Brotherly Love, did I ever tell you that? He says Philly's a real hole. I mean, that's why you're here? Mountain views prettier than skyscrapers, right?"

I didn't answer. On the flat screen, oily-skinned poachers were sneaking up behind a female gorilla with a baby dangling from a water balloon breast while she blinked and casually brushed a fly off her face, unaware.

"Are you any good at this?" Luke cupped his crotch. "I'd take a down payment."

He was joking, right? But I heard the distinct parting of metal teeth and felt Luke's hand clamp down on the back of my neck, a firm pressure.

Will jumped up beside me, muting the screams of the baby gorilla as his mother was dragged away by a foot, her eyes vacant and glazed, blood trickling from her open mouth.

I shot up too, shrugging off Luke's arm.

"Kidding," Luke said, tilting his head to follow me, in slow motion, a jester's smile on his face. "Cash. Only. By Friday."

Working for Carolyn Tuesday through Thursday was extra-exhausting, a long list of playgroup prep. Weeding their backyard and shopping for snacks, the organic fruit, Annie's Cheddar Bunnies—overpriced Cheezits! —new essential oil air fresheners in all the plug-ins, baking blueberry scones and spinach-cheese beggars' purses (all of which would have been easier without Sasha's 'help'), not to mention sorting and organizing the labeled bins of Sasha's toys.

"How many kids are coming?" I asked after she had corrected me a third time, pointing out the difference between a Polly Pocket and a Littlest Pet Shop.

"Seven. Why?"

"Nothing, I'm just thinking, why are we sorting these and getting everything so clean in here for a playgroup? Aren't the kids just going to dump them all out and make a holy mess playing?"

"That's not the point," Carolyn said. That's when I realized playgroup was not really about the kids.

⟋⟍

I took her list and tackled it like a penance for those nine stupid times I was with her husband. And honestly, I really liked the tone of our days, our quiet conversations and tea, so different from Juniper Court. I'd vowed never to touch X again, to rein in the drinking and going out, especially on weeknights. I couldn't afford it, on so many levels.

"So it seems like, what you said before… you're finding your social life easily?" Carolyn asked from her bed Tuesday afternoon while I was putting away their laundry, finally caught up from the weekend.

"Boys, yes," I said, thinking of Beau and Will, how good they were to me. "Beau's girlfriend Nikki, who loaned me her bike, she's super nice, but this other guy's girlfriend, Monique, is pretty cold. I have a hard time making girlfriends." I told her about ninth grade, how I grew seven inches, and then all the St. Mary's cardigan girls decided I was "out." I'd saved to buy a sweatshirt from Hollister, trying to find a niche with another group.

"My first day wearing it to school, the cardigan girls jacked my locker and destroyed it. They wrote STORK DORK and GIRAFFE GEEK all over it in Sharpie and shredded the sleeves."

"They were probably just jealous of your looks," she said, the same thing Mark used to tell me.

"Maybe."

"There's no maybe about it. You don't know you're beautiful? I imagine with your height, *you* could model," Carolyn said.

I shrugged, tucking a stack of Joel's T-shirts into his top drawer. The idea was starting to feel like leaving cookies out for Santa every year when your house doesn't have a chimney and there's nothing in your stocking except a bag of Rite-Aid ninety-nine-cent starlight mints.

"It was my dream for a while. I don't really know how to let it go." I thought of Mark, that last night in Philly—*you're almost twenty-fucking-years-old.*

"Did you try?"

For no good reason, I told Carolyn about it, this thing I'd never even told my sister.

"I did get scouted once, when I was fifteen. I had a fast-food job at Wendy's, and I had to wear my hair in braids, and this blue jumper, and I was supposed to draw on freckles, like Wendy had on TV? That was the year my legs grew, so I'd been getting some attention, not all of it good, you know? This guy stopped me after work, said he was a scout, wanted to take my picture, made an appointment for nine o'clock. At night."

Carolyn's eyes went wide with worry. "Oh, dear," she murmured.

"Yeah. He had a business card and everything, Mike's Models, I still remember the name. Like, how generic is that? I should have seen it coming. Anyway, my boyfriend wouldn't let me go alone." I remembered riding the bus there, looking at us in the reflection against the black night, the skinniness of Mark's neck, his hollow cheeks, and I had a flash of how young we were. Babçi was healthy back then, made us a pot roast every Sunday and sent us home with leftovers in tinfoil, and sometimes she boiled water and did Mark's wash in her tub, but other than that, we were totally on our own. In the bus window, we'd looked like two little kids out after dark. I remember wishing we were back in the apartment, eating mac and cheese and watching *Full House* on the rabbit-ear TV.

"Where was your mother?"

I waved a hand to show that she didn't figure into the story, that I'd already moved out.

"Of course, this supposed modeling scout turned out to be a Chester. He paid me and my boyfriend some money to take photos of us." I remembered the heat of the lights, like being onstage at my first and only dance recital, the one where my father told me I was pretty.

"Chester?"

"Oh, that's what me and my sister call them. Rhymes with 'molester.' He was just some perv in a crap apartment in Kensington. The whole time me and Mark were doing it, the guy's Sloppy Joes were burning on the stove. I can't eat Sloppy Joes to this day." I tried to laugh, but Carolyn didn't.

"Doing what?"

"You know." I wished there was more laundry, but the basket was empty. I remembered looking down between my legs at Mark, how shiny his forehead was, sweaty under the white lights, and him whispering, *sorry* before he closed his eyes. "It."

"Oh."

"Anyway, we used the money for a deposit on a one-bedroom, and a PlayStation, and I got to go shopping. I got some clothes at TJMaxx. That's it, my entire modeling career. That was the only time I've ever been scouted."

I was surprised, when I looked up, to see Carolyn blinking back tears.

"See, that's what pretty gets you," I repeated my mom's line, trying to be ironic, funny.

"Maia," Carolyn said, so earnestly, patting the space beside her like she wanted me to sit down on the bed.

"What?" I took a step back, holding the empty laundry basket against my stomach, between us. "What?"

"You were fifteen? That never should have happened to you."

"What?" I paced their bedroom, straightening their duvet, wiping down the windowsills with a spare sock, anything to keep my hands active.

"What that man, that pedophile, did, that wasn't right. That predator took advantage of you. He could, he *should* go to jail."

I shrugged to show her it was no big deal, but I heard Mike's voice:

"I'm thinking I could use the two of yous like this: I could paint a story, through the eye of the camera, young love. I'm going to write down a figure here. I want you to look at it first, and then hear me out, but it would be for the two of yous, here, in a shoot tonight. And if you test out well, if I can find that beauty through the eye of the camera, I'm saying there might be the possibility for more work down the road? All I'm asking is you two do what you two lovebirds do in the backseat anyways. It will be classy."

I stood up, looking at Mark.

"How do you pay?"

"Right here, tonight. Cash."

Mark put the paper in his hip pocket, not meeting my eyes.

"Anyway, it doesn't matter. We were stupid. It was a long time ago," I told Carolyn, but I remembered how Mark and I didn't say anything to each other the whole bus ride home, how it was months before we had sex again.

"Your parents, someone, should have protected you, told you that was not your fault," she repeated, her eyes shining. "This should not have happened."

Nobody ever said that before. It was the craziest thing, but I had to leave the room or I would have started crying.

⟋

Wednesday night at Juniper Court, we were all home in the kitchen, bumping around, Beau and Nikki prepping kebabs for the grill when my phone rang.

"Let me guess," Luke sneered.

Only this time, it wasn't Joel; it was my sister. I took the call in the backyard and sat in the evening light, watching the flames from the grill. Vader had followed me, his head lolling in my lap as I scratched his ears.

"Maia?" Scarlett's voice was tight. "When are you coming home?"

"I don't know. Why? Hey, did you get the money?"

"Things are getting serious! The cops were by, looking for you. Mark said they'd come by his place too."

"When did you talk to Mark?" I asked, but she ignored my question.

"They know you're not here anymore."

"What?!"

"Mom told them she hadn't seen you in months, that you broke your parole. She told them about Ritchie, and the money, too."

"What? Why would she do that?" My heartbeat thudded in my ears.

"Things aren't good around here," Scarlett said softly. Whenever she'd said this before, calling me across town at Mark's after I'd moved out because of creepy Ed, the original Chester, it had been a gross understatement. "You really need to come back."

"I don't think I can."

"Why not?" She was angry and I had to swallow. Nothing turned my stomach like arguing with my sister.

I thought about Sasha, how I still had to leave my hair band around her wrist every night, "so you have to come back and see me in the morning." I pictured the baby inside Carolyn, sucking its thumb. And of course, there was my sweet Vader, licking my palm in complete adoration, rolling on his back so I could rub his ribs.

"I'm sorry. I can't. They—" I paused, not sure how to put into words how good, important it felt. "I can't leave. I think, I hope, they need me here."

⟋

Before I'd left the Carters on Thursday, I'd come into the playroom to clear away our afternoon tea. Carolyn was finishing an exhaustive Q&A with Sasha on how babies were made, complete with all the technical terms like ovary and uterus. The crazy thing was it didn't seem that far over the kid's head.

"Mom." Sasha looked up from where she was making beds for the Barbies out of all the dish towels I'd just folded, "when the baby comes out of your 'china, who will take care of it, you or Maia?"

"I will, of course."

Sasha looked skeptically at Carolyn, half-reclined on the couch.

"Then will Maia take care of me?" She crawled over to rub her face against my shin like a cocker spaniel. I scratched her behind the ears and she sniffed my bare knee, barking.

"No, Sweetie, I'll take care of you both," Carolyn said, and I remembered how little job security I had. My mind raced to the balance in my bank account, Luke's demands that I was hundreds short of meeting.

"How?" Sasha wanted to know, and I waited to hear what things would be like after the baby came.

"I think I can handle two children." Carolyn laughed. "Did you know I was going to be a lawyer, before—" She was talking to Sasha but her words were obviously meant for me.

"A lawyer?" I said, shifting the basket to my other hip. "What happened?"

"Life. Marriage. Moving. Babies. Money. Not all of it was easy for us," she said, and I wasn't sure which part she meant.

"You should go back and finish!" I urged. "You really should. You should be doing something! Look at all these books! You're so smart—"

"It's an interesting idea, in theory, but who would raise the children?"

"I would!" I piped up, thinking how she had stood up for me when I told her about the modeling thing. "I mean, I'd be happy to keep helping out here with the kids." Suddenly, I had a flash of our future: I would be the clean-cheeked nanny to the Boulder family who said things like, "We don't know what we'd do without Maia," and took me along on their vacations. Carolyn and I would be friends, go clothes shopping together, over-analyzing my relationship with some boy, and we'd pass our days at Chautauqua Park hiking in the wildflowers, the baby draped over my shoulder, the little girl running back to show me ladybugs…

For the millionth time, I was so glad she never knew what had happened with me and Joel.

Please let me be a part of this. Please tell me I'm good at something that has nothing to do with my outsides.

Instead of answering, she sent Sasha for her purse and counted out my money from the envelope, and even though I really needed it, I didn't have the heart to tell her she'd shorted me twenty bucks.

CHAPTER TWENTY-SIX

Carolyn

Friday morning, my day to host playgroup, Joel left before sunrise and I'd barely finished writing my list for the day. In a stroke of genius, I'd had Sasha bring me the dry-erase board from Joel's home office, and I scribbled furiously with my three color-coded markers:

8:00 – Maia arrive, touch base

8:10 – feed Sasha/clean kitchen/start laundry. Carolyn: write grocery list

8:20 –

"What have we got here?" Maia looked over my shoulder at the white board. "Wow."

"What? It's better than my paper lists. This way, if things change or take longer or shorter than expected, it's erasable. We can be flexible! Go with the flow. And better, for the environment—Are you laughing at me?"

Maia went into the kitchen to start the tea, the rumble of water in the kettle. Teatime was an understood now.

"Not at all. It's just, you're so far from flexible." When she put the tray down, she paused like she might say something more.

"What?"

"Nothing." She poured us each a cup.

"I've been flexible in my life!"

She didn't answer.

"I'd say it was pretty flexible, spontaneous, of me to move across the country, with Joel, sight unseen. Do you know I'd never even been to Colorado before? Not even a visit? We just got in a U-Haul and that was it."

"What, seven years ago? Okay. I stand corrected, Elastigirl."

"I used to be more flexible, impulsive even." I gripped my steaming mug, cradled it in two hands. "Before, before Sasha and everything," I said, meaning what happened, our baby boy, in the bathroom on the plane back from Japan. "I was extremely impulsive. I shopped, all the time. Pier 1. I went every day, shopped us thousands of dollars into debt."

"What?" Maia's eyes flew wide. "Why would you do that?"

The narrowness of my life had been suffocating, and the ladies at the Pier 1 that opened on Arapahoe loved to show me new stock, even take me in the back. It had made me feel special, like I belonged somewhere.

By Halloween, the account was over six thousand dollars. I threw out the statements and collection notices until someone called during dinner. After insisting it was the wrong number three times, Joel got very quiet.

He hung up, carried his dinner plate to the kitchen sink. As he washed it, he turned it over; *Pier 1* was stamped on the back. "I just don't get it. We got boxes of china for our wedding! I remember loading them in the U-Haul."

"But not *everyday* china." The china from our registry was Wedgwood, picked out by my mother at Bloomingdale's, fussily East Coast, wrong for Boulder. These were modern, earthy colors, contemporary. "Isn't this nice?" I ran my hand over the smoothness of the stoneware glaze, caressing my soup bowl. I'd imagined we would use them for dinner parties, people from his office, friends. Soon.

The look on Joel's face scared me, like he didn't know me, which was the razor's edge of truth.

"I don't know why," I told Maia, honestly.

"What happened?" Maia asked.

Joel accused me of sabotaging our future, threatened to leave me if it ever happened again, I remembered, the air catching in my ribcage, a pain like heartburn. I slid a hand over my unborn son.

"The cash envelope happened," I said, explaining it. "Joel makes me pay for my mistake, every day."

Her eyes filled with sympathy, as she lifted her mug to check the bottom for the incriminating stamp. "Do you think he'll ever forgive you?"

"Oh," I waved my hand, keeping it light. "My dad paid the debt." In Florida over Christmas, before the pregnancy test came up positive the first time, my father took me for a walk on the beach, his arm heavy on my shoulder, loving and furry and stern, warning me how I couldn't do this.

"Well, that was good of him," Maia said, and her tone was a little snarky, and she gave a "must-be-nice" sniff before adding, "Anyway, that shopping thing sounds more compulsive than impulsive. I just meant, with Sash, maybe you could be spontaneous like, hey, let's go to Boulder Creek and turn over rocks and look for crawdads today, or let's have pancakes for dinner! Let's not schedule everything down to fifteen-minute increments. Let's have some *fun!*"

"Those are unfair things to say to a woman on bed rest about to host fifteen people," I said sharply. I thought of Joel the other night, accusing us of not having enough fun.

Was this something she and Joel joked about behind my back? Once, early in our relationship, Joel found one of my TO DO lists and edited it, adding in his distinctive block script, *Go to bathroom. Wipe. Flush. Go downstairs: first left foot, then right.* When we'd first moved into this house, he'd brought me the kitchen box, saying he knew I wouldn't be able to sleep until the spice rack was alphabetized. In the argument about whether or not I'd come with him on a last-minute business trip to Japan, he'd snapped, "You couldn't be spontaneous if you scheduled it!"

To be fair about why I hadn't wanted to go: I'd been four and a half months pregnant with our first baby.

"I'm just saying, for Sasha's sake, maybe you need to lighten up, learn to let go a little?" Maia's tone was softer, backpedaling, twisting her hair up off her reddening neck. She couldn't possibly understand everything I did to keep the ship on course, the passengers safe.

The summer I was seventeen, my boyfriend was a lifeguard at the local pool, and I was responsible for...

"It's easy to be impulsive when you're you—young, beautiful, no responsibilities, no regrets!" I was thinking what I wouldn't give to rewind several key points in my life. "I'd love to have your problems!"

"No," Maia stood up abruptly, "I bet you wouldn't." She picked up the tray and left and didn't come back until after the first playgroup guests arrived.

⸻

Of course Maia was right. Playgroup hadn't been in session ten minutes when Allison's twins yanked the organized bins off the shelves and upended my careful systems, chucking plastic animals at each other and tearing heads off Barbies while Ella and Sasha screamed. I was sitting on the couch, flanked by Jackie and on the other side, the newest member of playgroup, Rachel, breastfeeding her infant daughter, Cedar.

Maia came around and topped off everyone's coffee mugs, Sasha acting as her pint-sized waitress with the cream-and-sugar tray.

"I'll be right back out with the snacks," Maia said, and her eyes drifted to the dumped bins. She looked meaningfully at me, and her eyebrows said, *See?* I couldn't help laughing a little and offered her a smile of reconciliation before she disappeared into the kitchen. I was looking forward to our tea and digesting the day with her afterwards, hearing her impressions of my friends.

"So since when do you have a nanny?" Jackie asked. "Is she a live-in?"

"Oh, no, she's just helping out…while I'm on bed rest."

"Bed rest!" All four women's eyes darted to me. "Since when? Why didn't you tell us?"

"Is that why you weren't at playgroup the last few weeks? We were wondering," said Rachel, barely there two months. I envied the way she'd so easily inserted herself into the group, made herself part of the "we."

"You should have told us!" Jackie scolded, but it felt nice, big-sisterly. "We should be helping out more with Sasha."

"Or bringing you meals, anything," Rachel added, switching the baby to her other breast. "Dean always overcooks."

Allison proclaimed how grateful she'd be for a bed rest sentence, so she could learn a third language.

"I took French in high school! Who knew Spanish would become our country's first language? I never get time to get on Duolingo. I swear my cleaning ladies are talking about me right in front of my face."

Yasha sighed, "I *wish* I had doctor's orders to stay in bed all day! I bet you're all caught up on current events and book club reading."

I didn't bother to explain the challenges of bed rest, or that I didn't have a book club.

I watched the kids through the open doorway. The little girls were playing with the fresh tins of Play-Doh I'd had Maia pick up and arrange in a perfect pyramid on Sasha's table under the sunny window.

"Honestly, Carolyn," Allison continued, "nobody can help you if you don't share what's going on. You have to let us help."

With Maia handling the kids, I was able to relax, and have an uninterrupted conversation, tell them about my placenta previa and bed rest with Sasha and even participate in the latest round of the vaccine debate with Rachel and Yasha (con) and Allison and Jackie (pro).

"We'll just have to agree to disagree," Rachel said cheerfully, but Jackie was riled, looking for the next drama to pounce on and pull the stuffing out of.

Maia came in and stood next to me, leaning on the couch arm, sipping her own cup of jasmine tea. It was the morning lull between snack and lunch where we had fallen into a routine of having a second cup of tea, when we usually chatted.

"The kids look really happy," she said. "I had to break up one little thing between Sasha and that girl with the pretty eyes, Ella. *Someone* didn't want to share her toys," she raised an eyebrow of emphasis at me.

"It's always hard for the junior hosts at playgroup," Rachel noted, smiling up at Maia.

"Now they're playing Unicorns and Alicorns. Guess which one has to be the queen?"

I noticed Jackie staring at Maia's legs, stretched long and crossed at the ankle. Maia was wearing jean shorts, barefoot, toes painted bright flame, not a spider vein or fat dimple anywhere in the landscape.

"Who's Ella's mom?" Maia asked and I nodded to Jackie. "Oh my god, she's gorgeous. Those eyes, wow."

Jackie didn't say anything. She looked pointedly to the door of the playroom, nostrils flaring.

"She gets them from you, I guess," Maia kept trying. "Yours are the exact same color, really pretty. I bet people fuss over her all the time."

"Actually, we make a point not to focus on the physical. Russell and I don't tell our daughters they're pretty. Society does enough of that. We focus on their other, more important qualities, like intellect." Jackie drank long and slow from her mug. "Excellent coffee, Carolyn. Is it free-trade?"

"I don't know. Maia picked it up at Whole Foods this week."

"You do errands too? I want a Maia!" Rachel smiled.

Jackie stared at the door, where there was a loud squeal. "Looks like *someone* needs to mediate again," she said meaningfully.

I should have said something to defend Maia's right to a five-minute break, relaxing in the living room with us, but I didn't.

"Right, okay." Maia pushed off. "That's me. You ladies chat. I'll take the kids outside with the bubble stuff."

We watched her go, the muscles in her calves moving under skin like a racehorse's.

"Well, you've hit the jackpot," Rachel said as she popped a steaming beggar's purse in her mouth, nodding towards the backyard window where Maia was blowing streams of bubbles. "She's amazing with the kids. It will be great for Sasha to have someone to entertain her when the baby gets here."

I didn't bother to correct her, but I wondered, what exactly *was* my plan for after the baby?

"Well," Allison declared, "I consider anyone who can tame my twins and make these snacks worth her weight in gold." She helped herself to a beggar's purse.

"Not much weight on that one," Yasha noted and Jackie snorted.

"I'm going to have double up on my Zumba this week."

"Seems a little dangerous to have someone around whose 'girls' don't need the help of underwire to look that perky," Jackie looked to the other ladies for approval.

"Dean would love it if we got a nanny who looked like that."

"If we get someone to speak Spanish to the boys, I'm looking for the homeliest old Five Points *abuelita* I can find."

"Yeah, I don't know about Joel, but Russell could not control himself with that right under his nose."

"But Joel's not around that much, right?" Allison said a little smugly; her husband worked from home.

"Where's Maia from?" Rachel asked diplomatically.

"Philadelphia," I said, but I realized I didn't know this for sure. Funny—I knew that she had been conned into posing for juvenile pornography, but I still hadn't gotten her professional references.

"Her accent; it's like 'oh my gawd,' you can't believe anyone really talks like that," Jackie laughed, "I mean, it's so bad."

"When she asked if she could pour Oliver a drink of 'wudder,' I thought it was some new brand of kombucha," Allison chimed in.

"You're from New Jersey, though, aren't you?" Rachel said. "You don't have the same… inflections."

"Different areas," I said carefully. "And her mother is a cleaning lady." I thought of all she'd told me, about the modeling scout, her father leaving, her life before.

Immediately, the tone shifted to the appropriate embarrassment of the privileged.

"Well, she's wonderful with the kids and she can cook. You're lucky," Rachel said, crumbs dropping off her scone onto the head of her sleeping baby.

At the end of playgroup, Maia's enthusiasm hadn't wilted. She was helping match children with their Keens and Lifefactory water bottles, plying them with organic juice boxes on their way out the door. Finally, only Jackie and Rachel were left.

Maia looked at me as she pulled Sasha's sweaty hair back into a ponytail, my girl leaning against Maia's willowy legs. Maia's eyes said to me, *Success, yes?*

"Hey, isn't Joel going to Puerto Rico this weekend?" Jackie finished up the strap on Gracey's pink overalls and wrapped her soiled G-diaper insert in a plastic bag.

I was touched that she'd remembered.

"Russ said something about it, that Joel had asked if we might be able to help out with you, since he'll be away. Since nobody realized you were on full bed rest," she scolded.

"Oh, I'll be around to help," Maia offered. "I'm totally free this weekend." She had both Sasha's hands in hers, letting her walk up her body and flip over backwards, right over the tile in the front hall. A few weeks ago, I would have freaked out, demanded that she do that over the carpet, fretted over dislocated shoulders. What had Joel said they called me—*Safety Queen?* Instead, I plastered on a smile.

"Why don't you let us pitch in?" Rachel asked, buckling Cedar into her car seat.

"No, I really don't have any plans," Maia insisted. "I miss my monkey girl on weekends anyway."

"Oohahh, Monkey wants Papaya!" Sasha chattered animal noises, throwing her arms around her Maia's neck in their chimpanzee hug.

"Really, what time do you need me?" Maia asked. "I could be here all day, or nights, whatever."

"Not necessary," Jackie said firmly. "We can take care of it. I mean, it might not be as clean as now, Miss Maia will have her work cut out for her Monday, but we girls will have a proper party."

"Really?" I looked at her hopefully.

"Of course. Girls' weekend." To Maia, Rachel said, "You go be young and crazy, dance the night away with the boys of Boulder."

"No, I'd be happy to come this weekend, really."

"No need," I said, the tight space under my heart flooding with gratitude, "It looks like I won't need you at all."

I was surprised to see the hurt in Maia's face before she turned away, but I'd never promised her anything long term.

CHAPTER TWENTY-SEVEN

Maia

My chest ached, a throbbing hurt. The scene on replay was me standing there, waiting, beside the couch, while Carolyn's bitchy friend ignored me, and then later, her saying, so coldly, dismissing me, "We don't need you at all."

I wanted to help Carolyn, to be good at this! I wanted—what does anyone want?—recognition. And I guess, after everything, I'd made the mistake of considering us friends.

Or, worse, my stomach clenched, maybe it was something else.

As I was cleaning up the playgroup mess, Sasha came and hung off my arm, complaining that she was bored.

"If you're bored, you're being boring," I said. "That's what my mom always told me and my sister."

"You have a sister?" Sasha asked, her hazel eyes glowing with interest. "I might have a sister. Can I see your sister?"

And I felt Carolyn watching my face as I hurried to erase all my ache, my worry about Scarlett and why she'd suddenly called in a debt. "My sister lives far away."

"Will she come here to play with us? I'd like to play with your sister."

"No," I said, too sharply. Sasha turned away, confused and hurt, and I was immediately sorry.

"I have a dog, here, though," I told her. "A really big one."

"Can I see him? Can you bring him here?"

"Oh, no, Sweetie, our dogs don't get along—" I stopped.

Above Carolyn's head, a fat housefly threw itself against the dusty window screen. I twisted my hair up off my flaming neck as it buzzed and flailed.

"What?" Sasha prompted. I felt Carolyn's eyes boring into my soul.

"I mean, I don't think our dogs would get along, Sash, because, well, they're both boys, and sometimes, in the animal world…"

Joel's wife closed her book sharply.

"Maia's worked a long day. Why don't we let her go a little early and you and I will play Candyland, sweetheart?"

I was afraid to meet her eyes. I carefully wound the vacuum cord in a perfect figure eight.

"Enjoy the weekend off, and now with my friends chipping in," Carolyn said, as I tucked the cash in my purse, "I'm realizing if we need any help after the baby, they will be here, or we could always just hire someone from a service."

I still felt her words on my hot face like a blast of deep freeze.

Everyone is right; the weather in Boulder can be so variable.

Back at Juniper Court, smoke curled from the backyard, and I hoped it was Beau and Will, making brisket, but it was Luke, topless Monique on his lap in the hot tub, their two sad vegan sausages burning on the grill.

"Hey," I waved, watching Vader and Dakota circle the backyard and pee on the bushes from the garden center Will had planted. I'd put the rest of the rent money for Luke in an envelope on the fridge that morning; I'd noticed it was gone. "How's it going?"

They didn't answer; Luke pulled on the vape and passed it to Monique.

"Do you remember that loser who used to live in the basement, Stan? With his fucking maroon Chrysler LeBaron?"

Will had told me on a night dog walk about how, after the brine shrimp incident, after Luke kicked him out, Stan's Dad had to come up from Denver to help him pack up with his mason's truck. "I was helping, carrying stuff out to the truck. He told me Stan had been the first one in their family to get into college, and now here he was, failing out. It was a bad scene."

Now Monique said shrilly, "And who was the next one, that tall girl, with the fucking accent and the ugly black dog?"

"I can't remember her name," Luke looked right through me, "but that ass was slapping."

Monique narrowed her glassy eyes. "Too bad she couldn't hang."

⟜

Downstairs with Vader, I threw all my things to the center of my room. I kept the door closed so nobody would talk to me and did my usual inventory. After I'd paid the rest of the rent money to Luke, I still owed Ritchie the $350, and with the $50 airport shuttle to Denver in the morning, I'd be left with a whopping $13.

I borrowed a camping backpack from Will, stuffing it with clothes and my fake ID. This was more than I had when I arrived in Boulder, I reasoned. If only I didn't have to leave Sasha, and of course Vader, behind.

It was still dark outside when my alarm went off. Last things: I reached up to my top shelf and grabbed the diamond necklace, stuffing it in the bottom of the pack. It was my second most valuable possession, monetarily speaking. Having it with me made me feel the way I did when I rubbed the hair between Vader's eyes—safe. I could sell it at any moment, a thousand, maybe fifteen hundred. Finally, most important of all, the slim plastic that would get me on the plane, tucked inside my bra, my true identity.

I imagined I wouldn't come back. *Moving on.* It would be better, for everyone, except Vader. But this didn't have the heady promise of my last flight. I wasn't chasing a future. This time, I was just running. I put a mountain of dry food in Vader's bowl and left a note for Will and Beau, thanking them.

⟜

Joel was already at the gate, reading his phone in a shaft of sunlight, his Colorado mountains a sparkling postcard-perfect backdrop behind him. I dug around inside myself for the hopeful feeling that had inspired me to board that first flight with him, two months earlier. Instead, I found a familiar tingle in the back of my neck, the hives warning that I was headed for a point of no return.

"Hey," I said, flipping my hair over my shoulders, suddenly unsure. "This seat taken?"

I towered over him in my heels, and his eyes traveled the length of me. If he was mad, it was hidden behind the basic male reaction to a woman in a short skirt and high heels inches away.

"Well." He glanced around. "I'll be honest: You are the last person I expected to see here."

I sat down next to him, crossed my legs, tugged my skirt to cover my thighs. I swallowed and tried to smile but I felt pretty close to vomiting.

"This is becoming a habit, following me on to airplanes," he said. "Might need to get you some professional help. Boulder's got to have a twelve-step program or something." I was glad to see it then, thank god, the hint of his old crinkly smile. "I assumed you'd be playing house with my wife all weekend."

My feelings were still pretty raw from constantly replaying me standing there, being dismissed by Carolyn.

"Oh, no. Her friends are helping out." I tried not to sound like a pouty Sash when I added, "She said they didn't need me. At all."

He nodded, looking out into the sun glinting off the plane at the neighboring gate. "I haven't seen her so excited about anything as this weekend. I always thought she was pretty independent. That's how she was when I met her at school. I guess I didn't realize how much she needed girlfriends out here."

She had me! I thought, but didn't say.

"So you want to tell me what the hell's been going on?" He jerked his head behind him, towards Boulder. "You took a job with *my wife*? And you didn't tell me? I mean, I should be flattered, right, that you wanted to be closer to me, but then you don't take my calls for the last three weeks? And I'm thinking, why else would she do this? Are we going to open a pot and find a rabbit cooking?"

"What?"

"*Fatal Attraction,* that movie where the mistress goes psycho and cooks the little girl's pet rabbit?"

I shook my head; I'd never seen it. I was still stuck on his choice of words, *mistress.* It sounded dangerously long-term.

"It was just money. Story of my life. I needed money and Carolyn walked into work at the right time and offered to double my salary. That's all. I wasn't trying to freak you out."

"I'll give you money," he said, which was funny, because technically he already was, just not the way he meant. "I have to admit, that was my first thought," he laughed at himself. "I was worried you were going to try and blackmail me."

I tried to laugh, but it came out high and yelpy like Vader's bark when Dakota had him pinned in the backyard. I swallowed, thinking how much I already missed my dog. I'd asked Beau to feed him, since I didn't want another interrogation from Will. He'd already grilled me about borrowing the backpack—where are you going, how long, with who? Questions I couldn't answer. If I didn't come back, I hoped Will would step up to care for him.

"Anyway," Joel interrupted, "let's settle this. End this nonsense. I'll find someone else to help Carolyn, you go back to your old schedule at the juice bar or whatever, and then if you still need money, you come to me. Okay?"

Didn't he know me well enough to know that I never moved in reverse?

"I think your wife needs me more than you do right now," I said. He didn't agree with me, and I was suddenly near tears. I exhaled, a shaky breath.

"What's wrong?" he asked, in the gentlest daddy voice. I shook my head, tears in my eyes. I pictured him with Sasha, swooping her up when he came in the tiled foyer. I didn't want to be here.

I didn't know what else to do.

"Hello, Joel." The woman who came up behind us was severe-looking, striking. On me, her hairstyle would've looked like an institutional buzz cut. On her it read smart and polished. With her tailored pants and diamond studs, she was the picture of corporate competence.

"Liddy," Joel stood up. "I-I didn't expect to see you on this trip. Dave said it was just the Philly contingent?"

"Last-minute decision from on high. Mr. Lee asked me to come and oversee your presentation." She turned to me and said in a voice that could stop boiling water, "I don't believe we've met: Liddy Harbor."

"Hi." I was in awe of the way words marched out of her mouth, scrubbed clean and precise. I smiled, tried to neutralize my accent. "I'm Maia."

She tilted her head to the side and then looked away. I was glad she didn't want to shake hands since mine felt all-day-at-the-Grange-fair sticky.

"I should go. Sam is with me and he's at that age where if I leave him alone too long. . . I'm looking forward to an update on your presentation, Joel—we'll find a time to talk at the hotel." And the way she said it, you could tell Joel worked for her.

She had the headed-somewhere-important walk I'd seen at my cart, the way Joel used to move past me, the kind I dreamed of having one day.

"She seems," I struggled for the right word, "cool."

"Angry divorcée, ditched for the younger model, who takes out her misery on the rest of us? Fuck," he hissed, and though my Juniper Court boys tossed that word around like nothing, I'd only ever heard Joel use it right in the thick of things, a moan, back at the motel, *fuck me.*

I watched her sit down next to a slouchy red-headed boy playing on an iPad. He slid away when she stretched her arm over the back of his seat, the muscle of her triceps popping.

"You might have told me, yesterday, you were coming," he said.

Yesterday, I thought, *I was planning to surprise your wife and daughter with a weekend of Disney Princess movies—Will had a box set, all three Little Mermaids.* I was definitely about to throw up.

"Can I borrow some money, for food?"

Joel slid his wallet out of his pocket, his expression unreadable.

He was the one who invited me! How was this my fault?

He handed me a twenty.

"Do you want anything?" I asked and he shook his head sharply.

Maybe I should go, I thought while I ordered a double cheeseburger and large fries at the food court. But even with the change, I couldn't get the next shuttle, and if I did, I'd just be back in Boulder, flat broke, flaming bridges everywhere.

I sat down next to Joel again with my burger and fries, a huge Coke. I offered him a sip. He shook his head.

"I can go," I said quietly. "If it's a problem."

"Too late. It's already a problem."

My face burned. I'd get to Puerto Rico, and there might be a job, I thought, at a hotel, and didn't everyone always say how living there was so cheap? I definitely couldn't go back to Philly. I'd figure out a plan, I'd meet someone, a door would open.

Right?

On the plane, I could tell Joel was faking sleep because that breathing I loved to listen to, his regular, even rhythm, was gone. His breath came out in sharp, short exhales like a cartoon bull.

This time, one of the flight attendants was a guy. He kept offering me things, a pillow, a blanket, asking if I was comfortable. When they brought the drinks, his female coworker accidentally sloshed a tiny bit of Sprite onto my tray, no big deal, but he freaked out.

"Please, can I get you something? More napkins? A glass of wine, on me?"

I took him up on the wine—I'd assumed drinks were free and was surprised to see people around us paying for them. I guess it depends where your seats are.

After the cart moved on, Joel spoke matter-of-factly, his eyes still closed.

"This happens to you everywhere you go, doesn't it?"

"What?"

"Men, you; the way you look." He said it like a revelation.

I didn't answer. Using the cap of a pen, I shaved all of Sasha's red fingernail polish off, crimson shards littering my damp tray table.

Joel was right—it did happen. In fact, my pretty was the only reason I had a real license to fly to Puerto Rico. Last February, back in Philly, me, Mark and his buddy Nick had stopped at WaWa, late night. The boys were just coming off a Flyers loss, pissy-drunk. I was tired from a beer at the game, so I stayed in Mark's truck while they went in. According to Mark, Nick was just messing with the clerk, but apparently he stuck his finger in his jacket pocket like a gun and pretended they wanted the smokes for free. The guy panicked and hit the button under the counter, and Mark and Nick ran out, jumped in the truck yelling, "Drive, drive!"

So I did.

Unfortunately, I hit a curb and sort of side-swiped a parked car with an old lady in it, who ended being taken to the hospital. The guys were still yelling at me to go, so I went another two blocks before slamming Mark's truck into a pole, which made it a hit-and-run. Mark posted my bail, and my court-appointed lawyer was this tiny guy who looked about twelve and came up to my armpit. He was waiting for me with a bag of my things in the lobby at the police station—my Flyers hat, my wallet, my shoelaces. He was too shy to even look up into my eyes, holding out one more thing, glancing around before saying, "You're not even supposed to have this, you understand? Your driver's license is suspended. This shouldn't be a big deal, hopefully the victim will be released this weekend, and drop the charges, so I'm giving it back to you, but you are not to drive a vehicle or leave the jurisdiction until we get a court date, do you understand?"

And I'd hugged him to thank him, accidentally-on-purpose pressing him into my chest while I cried grateful tears on the top of his head and he turned even pinker, mumbling how he could get into so much trouble.

The part about not leaving the jurisdiction had honestly sort of slipped my mind until I was next to Joel on the plane from Philly, flying over the patchwork quilt of Ohio, and he was going on about the amazing view from the top of Mt. Sanitas.

In the San Juan airport, Joel steered clear of Liddy, hooking us up with the Philly group. He introduced me to Matt and Steve. Their wives seemed nice; one was an assistant manager at Target, the other a nurse at Einstein. I liked their obvious East Coast-ness, the familiar way they dressed and spoke, and the fact that none of them knew or mentioned Joel's wife and family.

"Have you seen the Partner Itinerary and the fifty dollar spa credit?" Steve's wife asked me. "I think tomorrow's the El Yunque forest, and I hear there's amazing shopping in Old San Juan."

On the bus to the hotel, the mood shifted. A Philly guy in a dorky Hawaiian shirt had obviously had too much to drink; he took the mike from the tour guide and sang a dirty version of *La Cucaracha*. Soon everyone was bopping between seats like we were on a field trip.

Joel bent his head to my ear, speaking to me for the first time in hours. "This is how it is. People will have a few cocktails, loosen up." I'd noticed he'd had two of the rum punches the guide passed out, tossing them back like shots. "Maybe we'll have a good time."

The Camino Real Hotel was like a movie set, like nothing I'd ever seen. After Joel checked in, we walked the blue-tiled pathways under palm trees, past the shimmering pool where people were sitting on underwater stools sipping umbrella drinks. To get to our rooms, we crossed a bridge over a lagoon with colorful fish and sea turtles the size of the new baby's bathtub Carolyn had had me pick up at Target.

I wondered what they were doing, Carolyn and her friends, but then I looked past the hotel to the white lounge chairs and the sparkling ocean, and thought, who cared? Not me.

Our hotel room was three times the size of mine at Juniper Court, nicer than the Boulderado. I went right into the bathroom with my backpack, feeling frizzy-haired and wrinkled. I'd spent the whole bus ride looking at the other women's shoes. All

I had brought were my dollar flip-flops and my Chinese dragon heels. I slipped the diamond necklace around my neck; at least I had that.

Before I showered, I locked the door. Honestly, I needed some privacy, and I hadn't told Joel I wasn't sure if I was having sex with him on this trip.

I chose another short black skirt I'd had to wear when I was (briefly) a waitress at TGIFridays. When I threw it on the bed, Joel looked up from the TV.

"Is that what you're wearing to dinner?"

"Well, I was thinking I'd put a shirt on too."

Joel didn't laugh. "It looks really short."

I turned my back and pulled on a ribbed tank top. It was more faded than I remembered, so the blacks were off. I slipped back into my platform heels, cursing myself for not bringing the broken-strap Buffalo Exchange dress too; I could have worn it strapless.

"Is that the door?" Joel called from the bed and I clip-clopped across the tile in my microskirt and heels.

"Hello, Maia, is Joel in?" It was Liddy, looking flawless in an ivory linen sheath dress and leather gladiator sandals.

"Yeah," I gestured toward the room. "Yes." I corrected myself, like Carolyn said, a nice crisp yes. "He is. Right this way."

"Liddy!" Joel struggled to sit upright on the bed. "I was just about to call the front desk for your room number."

"But here I am. Maia, why don't you have a seat? We can do this right here."

I sat on the other bed, pulling down my skirt to cover more of my thighs when I crossed my legs. Liddy sat in one of the wicker chairs under the window, her legs perfectly waxed and smooth without a bruise or a scar. I wondered how fun *her* childhood could have been. Behind her, I could see the sunset, flaming orange on the ocean. If only I could dive in and swim away…

"The first is personal and unfortunately, unpleasant. I don't like what your bringing a mistress on a partner-plus trip says about your regard for me, or for this company."

There was that word again.

"I bought her ticket. The time I spend with her will be outside of the conference—technically, my private time!" Joel exhaled, an irritated sound.

Liddy just let her pinched-mouth-wine-lipstick expression be her answer.

"I'm sorry," I said, to break the silence.

Liddy stood, smoothing her dress. "Your apology doesn't really mean anything to me. Joel, I have some critical corrections for your presentation. I'll leave them at the front desk, and you can pick them up after dinner."

As soon as she was gone, I flopped back on the bed and pulled a pillow over my flaming face; the fabric was deliciously cool from the air conditioning.

I hated her, him.

Me.

"Who does she think she is?" Joel paced. "Lee doesn't care if you're here. Men don't care. You notice she didn't even say you had to leave. She was just here to 'express her feelings.'"

She was right; I had no business being here. My head stayed under the pillow.

"Come on. Let's forget about all this, go have a nice dinner, a bottle of wine."

Carolyn cannot find out about this.

"Alright," he said, in an entirely different Dad voice, "when you decide to stop acting like a three-year-old, you can come find me at the bar."

As soon as he left, I went through Will's entire backpack of my belongings. There was nothing I had brought that worked for me in this place, this life, this moment.

I sat on the balcony, watching the kitchen staff in food-spattered whites feed the barracudas in the lagoon with scraps from the kitchen, no idea what to do next. Finally, I took off my dragon shoes and slipped between the cool sheets and cried myself to sleep.

When I woke up, the clock on the nightstand said it was after midnight. Joel was undressing in the light from the bathroom and I watched him through the fan of my eyelashes. He peeled back the covers beside me.

"Are you awake?"

I didn't answer.

If he dared try to touch me…

But he didn't.

Instead, he said, staring up at the ceiling, "I figured it out. You're running away, aren't you? That's why you're here. Which means before, Philly, you were too. This all has nothing to do with me."

He kept going, his voice a little slurry, hard. "You're dangerous, a train wreck, out of control. And my family almost got hit. I won't let you hurt us."

When I thought I couldn't cry anymore, a tear leaked out of the corner of my eye and slid down to my pillow. I sniffed. *I loved his family; didn't he know that?*

"I cannot believe," Joel said, colder than the air conditioning, "I ever found you attractive."

I remembered what he had said, the night at the Boulderado, *you have the body men leave their wives for.* I was thinking how insignificant the *me* in me was to Joel: I could have been anyone.

Then he rolled over, his back to me. I could smell gin wafting from his pores. In the moonlight, there was a large mole by his left shoulder blade I'd never noticed before. With it, his whole back looked different and I had a flash of panic then: here I was, stuck on a foreign island with a man I barely recognized.

I would leave before sunrise, I decided, but I had no idea where I was going. I wished for Vader at the foot of my bed, silky ears to rub, boys to make chicken patties with, hazel-eyed girls who wanted to play imaginary games.

For the first time since I left Philly, I was scared.

CHAPTER TWENTY-EIGHT

Carolyn

Rachel called me first thing Saturday morning, before Sasha woke up.

"I'm coming over in ten minutes. I've got croissants and fruit and decaf and I'll dress Sasha and take her to Jackie's, and then after you lounge and relax all day, I'm picking you up at four. You realize what this means."

No hello: I only knew it was her from Caller ID.

"Hi, Rachel." I couldn't keep the smile off my face. It was happening—my Boulder life was beginning.

"What it means is, this evening I got Dean's nieces to come over and watch the kids at our place while you and me and Jackie have a spa evening. I'm making sangria—I heard it's as good as beer for milk production—and for you, Mama, the best horizontal spot in the house: Dean's automated Barcalounger!"

Per Jackie and Rachel's instructions in the dozen phone calls throughout the afternoon, we arrived with Sasha's pajamas, two different kinds of mud masks, three nail polishes, and the remainder of my chocolate stash.

"I made a trough of salad!" Jackie was already in her bathrobe, her face smothered in a green mud mask.

Dean's nieces, adolescents wearing what I hoped was experimental eye shadow, whisked Sasha away with Jackie's girls to a full-service princess party set up in the dining room, complete with tiaras and face painting.

"Don't worry; Dean's on duty until eleven and I've made enough sangria to drown us all. What can I get you?"

Rachel's windows were open and the smell of her potted star jasmine and orange trees wafted in from the backyard. The jasmine made me think of Maia, and our tea, but Rachel had the Beatles on low and goose-down pillows fluffed up for me on the prettiest slip-covered chaise longue in a corner of her kitchen.

"We couldn't carry the Barca in here, I hope this is good. Did I tell you we're quitting playgroup?" Rachel said as I settled into the softness of the pillows. "Jackie and I decided that it's too stuffy. Nice ladies for a book club or something, but we need a sisterhood. We're starting our own thing; are you in?"

"Of course," I whispered, thinking, this is how it happened, this whoosh of belonging. Why had it taken so long?

While the girls laughed in the next room, my peach-painted nails dried, and my mud mask cracked. The salad was replaced by a baked brie Rachel found in the back of the freezer, but we were still hungry. I ordered us three trays from Whole Foods delivery—a Mediterranean sampler and baklava dessert assortments, and a sandwich platter for the girls.

The two women oohed and ahhed when my contribution arrived, and I was glad I had spent the money on them. The night went on, the Beatles blended into Van Morrison, and with Rachel's gentle coaxing and a few sips of watered-down sangria, I told them everything, about the last six weeks with Joel, and Maia. Rachel asked all the right questions, genuine and gentle, her reactions honest.

"So, wait, you don't know for sure if anything ever happened between them?" Rachel called from where she was washing off her mud mask at the kitchen sink.

"I don't. But remember she accidentally said something about Ben and her dog not getting along."

"Only in Boulder does a man cheat on you by dog-walking in the Flatirons with another woman!" Jackie tried to joke, but it wasn't really funny.

"Jack," Rachel murmured, a warm hand squeezing my knee.

"Ok fine, too soon. But you said the second night after she shows up in Boulder, he's out late and comes home smelling like wine?" Jackie said, like we were playing a game of *Clue*. "This was the night after you came to dinner at our place? And then he lied about his whereabouts?"

"She said it might be a lie. Remember he told her he had to entertain clients in Denver," Rachel pointed out; she seemed to be on Joel's side. "Though what I still don't understand is why you hired her to be your nanny?"

"Well," Jackie answered for me, swiping a cracker through a garlicky hummus so strong I could smell little else, "she was in a childcare crisis!"

"But why Maia, of all people?"

"No, it's clever." Jackie tilted her fourth glass of sangria in my direction, clicked in the back of her cheek like a camera shutter. "Brilliant, really. I told you Carolyn was smart, Rach—a little quiet, a little neurotic, but smart! Think of it: when Joel's not in Philly, he or Maia has to be with her all the time. It's genius!"

"Except right now, when he's in Puerto Rico. Where's she now?"

I followed their conversation like a tennis match, back and forth, honored that they were giving my situation so much attention, flattered that Jackie thought my original plan—that *I* was clever.

But then my stomach turned, remembering how cold I had been on Thursday, the way I'd hinted to Maia that she was insignificant—replaceable.

"True, she might have gone with him," Jackie waggled a finger, and then turned her hand to inspect. "Darn, I've ruined my mani!"

"But didn't she offer to come help out this weekend, when we were there for playgroup?" Rachel fished in the bottom of her sangria glass for the smooshed straw-berries.

Jackie made a noise of assent, wiping off blood-red polish by the sink.

"Let's back up. You'd never had any suspicions, never heard of her before she stepped off the plane with Joel in Denver? What about her references? Did they check out?"

I flushed hot under my green clay face. "She's never actually brought any. She always forgets them."

"Forgets them," Jackie harrumphed. This, I thought, was how it felt to be a grown woman with sisters. It was something I'd never had, this bossy, loving analysis, this protective cocoon of food and wine and beauty product. I nibbled at a cracker.

"But Carolyn's on bed rest," Rachel defended me. "It's not like she leaves Sasha alone with her. Of all people, Carolyn would never. And Maia was really good with the kids this week." She added, "I mean, we can't crucify the girl just because she's young and gorgeous."

"Why not?" Jackie smirked.

"And honestly, she's been pretty great to have around," I admitted, adding, "Better than Joel, sometimes."

"The deck is stacked against dads," Rachel mused, shifting in her chair. "Dads go to this controlled, completely adult environment all day, while we're home building up our immunity to the meltdowns. Dad comes home, trying to shift gears, when the kids are at their worst. He isn't equipped to handle the misery, he blows his top, he feels guilty that his only interaction with the kids is negative. Everyone loses." She gulped from her drink. "Maybe men are like toddlers, bad with transitions. Maybe that's all it is."

But Jackie would not let it go. "I've got it! You just gave me the best idea, Rach. We should get Dean to run her nanny through his computer at work!"

Rachel's husband was a cop with Boulder County. Jackie raised her eyebrows to me.

Things were moving too fast. I thought of how Maia carried Sasha on her back, neighing like a pony whenever they came galloping back from the mailbox, how Sasha let Maia sift her fingers through her dandelion hair, French braiding it into two perfect balls just above her tiny ears.

"She wouldn't even have to know we did it. What's the problem?"

"How do you spell her name?" Rachel asked, reaching for her phone, and I paused. What was I afraid of? "Or I'll just Google her."

"What?" Jackie asked. "We're doing this now. Why not? How do you spell her name?"

"I'm not actually sure. I think I know. M-a-y-a and then her last name is Cramer, or Cramer-McHugh. I'm not sure."

"You don't write her checks?"

I shook my head; too embarrassed to tell them about our financial arrangement at home, my slim cash envelope, Joel's iron-fisted control of our finances. Revealing suspected infidelity was one thing; my compulsive shopping was another.

"Wait a minute—you've never seen her driver's license? You got no references?" Jackie couldn't keep her mouth from hanging open. Everything in her expression said I was the Safety Queen, the mother who was supposed to be so careful!

But I knew Maia... didn't I?

"I-I," I faltered. "I'm always with her." I thought about our afternoons, the easy peace, the honeyed jasmine tea, the conversations.

"We could have him check multiple spellings," Rachel suggested. "I'm sure she's clean, and then at least then you'd know she wasn't a thief or a criminal or anything."

I shook my head, no.

Enough. I felt strangely protective of Maia. There were things a girl like this might have had to do that these women had never encountered.

⌐

"You're a good mom," Maia had said during our tea on Monday, the week before playgroup. "Sasha's lucky. My mom? One time, I told her if she didn't break up with her creepy Chester boy-friend, I was moving out. She called my bluff; had my bags packed and outside the door by the time I got home from school."

"What? Your mother kicked you out? How old were you?"

"Fourteen."

"Why?!"

"Because I tried to tell her about Ed."

"I thought you said his name was Chester."

"No, that's sister code, remember? What me and my sister call anyone who's creepy?"

"And he was?" Of course, I wished he wasn't.

She nodded. "I woke up to Ed, the Chester, peeling my covers off me one night, with it out of his pants. That's when my boyfriend, Mark, dropped out of school and got a place, so I could move in with him, somewhere safe. And you know what last words my mom said to me when I left?"

"That's what pretty gets you?"

"Yep." Maia tried to laugh, but I didn't join in.

I sipped her tea, grasping for words. "That sounds like bad parenting to me. Really, really bad parenting. And your dad was gone by then?"

She nodded, a sad attempt at a light shrug.

"You've been through so much," I murmured. "Amazing, that you are as together as you are."

"Well, before you have me sainted, you should know I've done some pretty terrible things."

"Like what?" My heart pounded.

"Oh." She drew the word out long, looking up to the ceiling like she was trying to decide which one of a long laundry list to tell me.

"Well, for one I stole Mark's grandma's ashes."

"What? From whom?"

"His horrible aunt. Total holier-than-thou-bronze-minivan-driving, pretzel-peddling bitch."

"Wow, you lost me. Pretzel-what?"

"She and Mark's uncle run a soft-pretzel chain."

"And why is she a bitch?" I remember we both laughed, hearing that word come out of my mouth.

"She sicced Child Protective Services on me and Mark because we were living together underage. How ridiculous is that? I tell them everything, about my Mom's Chester boyfriend, and my sister *stuck still living there with him, god knows what happening, and they try to send me back there!"*

"It's a flawed system." I shook my head. "Part of why I was going to law school…" I trailed off. It didn't matter what my good intentions had been.

"So when his grandma passed, I was over at the horrible aunt's house, and I couldn't help it; I stole Babçi's ashes."

"His aunt didn't find out?"

"No." Maia giggled nervously, as if daring herself to tell the whole story. "We, I, replaced them with a substitute."

"Whaaaaat?" I asked.

"After CPS, she sicced her priest on us too, for living in sin." She stood up, starting to clear the cups, and I was afraid she wouldn't finish. "He lectured us for an hour, then left stacks of pamphlets behind, Chastity and You, The Hundred Ways You Will Burn in Hell for 'Doing It.' You know," she rolled her eyes, and I was struck, as often happened, by how unassumingly beautiful she was. "So me and Mark burned them, to replace the ashes. The pamphlets, and…" she cringed, "well, the Bible too."

"Oh."

"I know," Maia ducked her head.

"Well, Babçi must have been a very small woman," I said.

"Oh, she was! Tiny! And it helped that the priest gave us the King James plus New King James versions, combined."

We burst out laughing.

"I know, I'm a terrible person," Maia gasped, her hand over her mouth.

"So where are her real ashes now?" I asked, wiping at my eyes.

"Me and Mark took them, scattered them in the Schuylkill, right down under the art museum, where the river does this pretty little waterfall over the rocks. She liked to walk down there, when the weather was nice."

"And you were only fourteen?"

"Oh, no, I was older, almost seventeen when Babçi passed."

"So the modeling thing had happened already?"

She nodded.

"It seems like, before you even got a chance to choose, lots of people made choices, took advantage of you and very few of them really looked out for your well-being."

Maia shrugged, shifting the tea tray on to her hip and deadpanned, "That is what pretty gets you."

"Don't!" I told Rachel and Jackie, surprising myself with my own vehemence. "I," I faltered, looking down into my glass, "I get the sense Maia's been through a lot."

"Okay, it's your decision." Rachel put her phone down. "She is great with Sasha, and let's be honest, right now, you DO need her."

Jackie stood up, bored with us, irritated to see the potential drama pass her by.

"Did I tell you our business got access to the top-secret mailing list for the second largest national scrapbooking group? We're planning a total blitzkrieg marketing campaign that will take us all to Disney. Who wants more sangria?"

Sunday was hard. Rachel and Jackie were hung over, Rachel had Zumba and Jackie had to teach Sunday school at the Unitarian church. They promised to come by around noon, but each thought the other had. When Rachel called after three and realized I was still on my own, she was tripping over herself with apologies—Cedar was sick; Dean had to work a double shift; her nieces had a soccer game. She promised to send Jackie. I'd talked Sasha through getting herself breakfast, and then we'd spent most of the day on the couch, coloring and watching TV.

"I'm bored," Sasha told me, dropping a bruised clementine in my lap to be peeled. "I want Maia!"

I did too.

I realized with a shock that I hadn't thought about food, hadn't eaten anything all day, and when I sent Sasha for my candy stash it was gone, taken to Rachel's the night before.

That's when I knew: I was done building layers of unhappiness with guilty mouthfuls of nuts and chocolate and cookies. I wanted to reinvent myself, to start fresh. Of course it was Maia. With her in the house, I hadn't been gorging, but watching the casual, comfortable way she treated food, I was learning. She ate when she was hungry, stopped when she was full. She declared the edges of a brownie burnt and put it aside. She could eat a few handfuls of Sasha's afternoon TV popcorn without having to pop herself a second bag and cram it in so fast the kernels cut and salt stung her lips.

I admit there were times I stared at her perfect body while she worked. I was shocked by how strongly I reacted to the visual—the long legs, her breasts, the taut skin. My hands would tingle, and I wondered if this was an erotic response, tried to picture myself doing sexual things to her. The hungry feeling stopped.

I realized it was the same way I ended up returning everything I ordered from Athleta and Victoria's Secret after Sasha was born; because it was not the clothes I was trying to buy.

My longing was not sexual, to do things to the body; it was envy, to be the person *in* that body.

⌣⟶

"Hellooo?" Jackie let herself in. "Rachel was up all night with Cedar," she said, dropping a bag of food on the bed beside me. "I've left the girls in the car. Where's your nanny, anyway?" Her eyes drifted to the mess that had accumulated, and I dared her to judge me because there was a Littlest Pet Shop emergency vet clinic set up on the coffee table.

I explained it was Sunday, that Maia didn't work on the weekends anyway. I didn't add that she and Rachel had promised they would do everything, and that when I had called Maia earlier that morning, her phone had gone straight to voicemail. Perhaps another "crazy" night with her boys.

"Well," Jackie glanced at Sasha, "if Joel's not due back until Tuesday, the real test will be if she shows up tomorrow morning."

"I'm sure she will." I realized I was hoping this was true. I missed Maia. I felt sorry for the way I had treated her.

"And just because you're not interested in digging around her history doesn't mean I'm not. Girls like that, who look like her, they have stories; trust me." As if she was familiar with looking the way Maia did. "You may not be worried about protecting your family, or our daughters, from her type, but I am."

I opened the reusable plastic bag Jackie had brought—a completely resistible homemade warm tuna fish on seedy bread (a pregnancy no-no), a small, browning banana and one of my own mini chocolate bars. Nothing to drink.

Jackie stopped, one hand on the door. "Do you have any idea how many Maya McHugh's there are? It might take a bit; it would be easier if I knew how to spell her name. But if there is dirt to find on that girl, trust me, I will."

CHAPTER TWENTY-NINE

Maia

"Hey *gringa*, you lost, little girl?" he called out in drawling American English and waved me over to the van. His smile was friendly and wide and he reminded me a little of Beau. He had the same U.S. surf logos on the side window of his van that Beau had on his Bronco back at Juniper Court. On the rooftop, a cracked plastic sign said, TAXI.

"Not lost," I said. "Just waiting for a ride." I was working on a plan; but it was as slow as the sun coming up over the palm trees. "I…I have a flight to catch. At the airport."

It was too hot already, the air heavy. A lizard ran over my sandal and I jumped. The guy in the van laughed at me.

"Hop in, no worries. I'm headed that way." He reached behind him to yank open the long door, revealing the metal shell of a stripped-down van, racks of surfboards, assorted hand tools and trash.

I swallowed; hungry and thirsty. I'd helped myself to a Coke and a pack of nuts out of the minibar while Joel was out the night before. Over by the dumpsters, four guys watched us. They were using machetes to hack dead fronds off a short, fat palm tree. One of them called to me in Spanish again.

"Come on, name's Maurice."

"How much to the airport?" I only had the change from Joel's twenty.

"For you?" he looked me up and down. "*Nada*. I already told ya I'm headed that way. Hop in."

I pictured the airport restaurant, and my last nine dollars turning into a huge plate of eggs and bacon, a chilled orange juice. Why not? Things were going to be okay.

I glanced behind me at the hotel. White curtains billowed out over a fancy balcony, and I wanted to be back in the beautiful room with the ocean views, only I knew for sure I didn't want to be there with Joel.

I got in the van.

"Eventually, *chica*," Maurice laughed as he accelerated, gravel and broken shells spraying.

"What?" I could barely hear him over the music, Soundgarden rattling on blown speakers. I'd thought that he was younger but as the van sped along the nearly empty waterfront road, I could see that he was thick and middle-aged, the hair across the backs of his bare shoulders flecked with silver. There was a glint in his eyes, sand wedged in the cracks of his leathery face. The van smelled like mildew and the sour burn of hash. My hand drifted to the necklace. Quietly, I moved the diamond back and forth on the chain. He watched me out of the corner of his eye. I wished I'd followed my original plan of leaving a note for Joel. Nobody knew where I was.

"I said, eventually I'll take you by way of where you were intending to go, but right now, I gotta ride some curlers."

He pulled off the highway and veered onto a rutted sand road.

"I need to get to the airport," I said, fingering the reassuring hard edges of my license tucked inside my bra.

"Yeah? What time's your flight?" He drove, jerking around potholes.

"Um, I'm going stand-by," I said. "Family emergency. My sister, she's pregnant, on bed rest. She needs me to watch her daughter."

It should have told me something that just mentioning Sasha around Maurice felt wrong,

He talked as he drove over bumpy terrain, meandering, contradictory stories of his past. He was a surf champion in Maui, he was from California, his parents were Austrian diplomats, but then later his mother was addicted to drugs, he was divorced three times, he had never gotten married, he was putting together a big deal with capital from his rich fiancée, a beach resort, on the property we were headed to.

"But Maurice don't believe in love," he told me when he pulled the van to a stop outside a shack on the corner of a pebbled parking area surrounded by rusted trailers. "This'll be your place," he nodded over by the dunes. "The best hut for our top chef."

"Chef? I can barely make dairy-free macaroni and cheese." I was trying to be funny, as if by not showing fear, there would be no reason for it.

"Have to earn your keep somehow."

"I'm not staying in Puerto Rico," I said. "I told you, I have a plane to catch. My sister, her little girl, they need me."

"You got to go with the flow more, *senorita*. You been in the Mainland US of A too long. Re-lax. You wanna smoke?"

I waited, one hand on the van door handle.

How long had we been driving, how far were we from the hotel? Five minutes, ten? I should just get out. I could hear the roar of the ocean. If I followed it to the beach, walked back in the direction we'd come, eventually I'd end up at the hotel, right?

I looked around the sandy lot for signs of life. The two rusted trailers had sheets covering the windows. A radio inside one played staticky pop music and a mutt lay under the other, licking its balls. No other people. Still thinking I was in control of the situation, I opened the door of the van.

"Where do you think you're going?"

"To the airport." I heard something in one of the trailers, wondered if it was better for me to have other people around, or not. My neck itched. I needed to get away from here.

I stepped out of the van.

"You got to chill, right here, right now, *chica*. I said I'd take you out by the airport." In a second he was beside me, grabbing my wrist, hard enough to snap the bones.

"But I'll miss my plane." His fingers were locked around my arm. He stared at my necklace, tight around my hot skin.

"Planes come and go. You got any smokes on you?"

I shook my head, squinting out towards where the water was. It was getting hotter; I could feel a sunburn in my scalp, and it made me think of Carolyn–her list of instructions, about sun-screening the part of Sasha's hair. I heard her words again.

Your parents, someone, should have protected you, told you that was not your fault. You know that, don't you?

I blinked into the sun, guessing it was maybe eight thirty or nine in the morning. Joel might just be noticing I was gone. I hoped, anyway.

"I'm going to bum a few *dollares* for a pack," Maurice said and he dropped my wrist. My hands flew to my neck, itching. Before I knew it, he was standing at the side of the van, digging through my backpack.

"Hey!" I snatched my bag away from him and hitched it up over my shoulders, slogging through the loose sand in the direction of the ocean. When I stopped to take off my Chinese dragon shoes, I heard huffing behind me—Maurice.

"I mean, where are you going?" he grinned, all stained teeth. Maurice watched me take stock of my options with an amused look on his creased face. How could a beach be so deserted in June? "Come on," he laughed. "You want to go, okay, let's go to the van. I'll take you out by the airport. Jeezus," he muttered. "American psycho-bitch." He held my wrist, too hard, and I struggled to keep my feet under me.

Back at the sandy lot, I was relieved to see two brown-skinned men and a pregnant woman about my age crouched outside the trailers. The men were under the shade of an awning off the side of the trailer in frayed nylon beach chairs; the woman stirred something on the smoking fire pit.

They exchanged a handful of words in Spanish with Maurice. I eyed his van, anxious, but he squatted by the men.

The woman brought three plates over, one balanced on her upper arm like she was used to working in a restaurant. Eggs, over a tortilla, with a steaming pile of scorched rice and refried beans. On the side of each plate there was a charred, smoking pepper. Maurice popped his into his mouth, chewed with it open to let the heat out.

"Makes you shit fire," he grinned at me, tilted his plate my way, like he was offering me some. I shook my head.

There were warm beers floating in the cracked cooler. I drank one, only because I was so thirsty. The woman kept meeting my eyes and once she subtly shook her head at me. When I got up to go to the outhouse, a breath-holding, fly-infested affair, she followed me.

With a glance over her shoulder, she grabbed my arm and whisper-hissed a string of sentences to me, in Spanish. We were horribly outnumbered. I didn't know who she was trying to help, her or me, so I could only shrug. *No comprendo.*

"What're you girls gossiping about over there?" Maurice hollered, and she hurried back to the camp.

The sun was climbing, the men's plates clean, the radio playing Ricky Martin's "Cup of Life" and Celine Dion wailing that her heart would go on.

"Siesta!" Maurice said, standing up and stretching. "Somebody's sleepy." He looked right at me. "You need a nap before the airport."

"You know what?" I backed towards the dunes, keeping my eyes on him. "I'm just going to walk out to the road and catch a cab." The men under the awning watched our exchange like a dogfight, wide grins showing gaps in their teeth. The woman looked down, picking up empty plates.

"You don't got no money," Maurice laughed, and I realized I'd stupidly left my backpack while I'd gone to the outhouse. I had my license. I could leave it here, run. "You're stuck with me. Don't worry," he smiled, the exact same words as Joel on the first airplane, "I'm harmless."

Maurice closed the distance between us in five strides, clamping his hand around my upper arm. Despite the physical pain of what came next, the worst part of it was before, the moment when I realized what was going to happen inside. My feet skittered on the broken shells like Vader, being dragged down the long hallway at the Humane Society.

I let him, a split-second decision.

If I play along, don't fight back, maybe he won't kill me too.

Inside his shack, he tossed me to a mattress and used his teeth to tear a condom wrapper.

"Never play without my raincoat in sunny Spain!" he cried, yanking up my skirt. He used a dirty thumb to tug my G-string aside and split my legs like a wishbone.

I didn't say no.

It's not rape if you don't say no.

I watched a roach going in and out of a hole in his tin wall, and I gritted my teeth, while he sawed in and out of me. It didn't last long.

But afterwards, when he reached for the necklace, his hands on my throat, I wedged my knee up between us and twisted out from under him. He grabbed for my arm, but I jerked free and ran, bare feet on the broken glass and cracked shells, cutting the soles of my feet open, ran and ran.

I almost made it to the main road.

"Help," I panted, breathless, but the only truck, a dented green pick-up full of hollow-faced workers, was driving fast, too far away.

I heard them coming, Maurice and the van–where was Vader-Will-Beau-Joel-Mark-Daddy? He jumped out, crushing me to him, pinning my arms to my sides. My feet were sliced open, bleeding. I couldn't have run any more anyway.

"Help." It came out pathetic and raspy, the dream-scream with no sound.

"Get in the fucking van, ya dumb bitch," he laughed, tossing me to the metal floor, slamming the door shut behind me. "Jesuschrist."

He pulled on to the main road, tires sending up sand, driving fast. I curled up in a ball on the floor, arms wrapped around my knees, panting. Inside, I burned, and I could feel throbbing pain, bloody wetness oozing all over the soles of my feet.

He kept the music on, thumping his palm on the steering wheel, flicking his fingers like drumsticks against the dashboard.

"I was a back-up drummer for these assholes, Smashing Pumpkins," he told me. "I tell ya that? Billy Corrigan and me, we're like this." He twined his fingers together, the ones that had ripped my underpants. "Are you fucking listening to Maurice?"

Minutes passed, and I lifted my head, looked around the back of the van for a weapon, anything. That's when I saw it, outside the dirty side window, a yellow sign in the scrub grass with the word: AEROPUERTO. I started crying, quietly, relief and exhaustion. Maybe my plan had worked, he was going to let me go?

"Christonacross, I told you," he said irritably. "What, you think you're so pretty every guy wants to fuck you, so then you think they gotta kill you? Just because I fucked you?" He laughed and laughed as he pulled up to the curb at the Departure gate. "Maurice ain't stupid. You just go home and tell mommy and daddy how much fun you had on spring break."

I reached for my shoes, and Will's pack with my wallet, my phone, but he snatched it back out of my hands.

"Uh-uh-uh," he shook his head. "Javiera needs some new clothes and you need to thank her, pay for that beer you drunk. Remember what I said about earning your keep."

"Please…" I wiped furiously at my face. "My wallet, my phone, so I can…." Out of the corner of my eye, I saw a valet watching us. Maurice noticed him too, which meant I really might get away. He flipped through my wallet, flicked Sheila McHugh out to the sidewalk. When he reached over the passenger seat for my throat, my necklace, I bit his hand, hard, like Vader—he tasted like dirty, smoky salt.

"Fucking bitch," Maurice pushed me out the door, leaving me on the curb with nothing but the license in my bra, Sheila McHugh, and the yellow flip-flops for my bare, bleeding feet.

BOOK THREE

BOOK THREE

CHAPTER THIRTY

Maia

The truth is, it isn't expensive to take a taxi from the Denver airport to Boulder. All you have to do is get yourself a cabbie with rheumy eyes and photos of his grandkids in the visor and wait until you're outside the city limits to whisper through chattering teeth in a voice you don't recognize that you don't have any money on you, exactly.

"You want me to take you by the police?" At first, I thought he was threatening me, but then I met his eyes in the rearview mirror. "The hospital?"

"No." I wrapped my arms tighter around my folded knees, brushed the salt-sticky hair from my face. I had been shaking since I got on the plane, my teeth chattering like they had the X night with the boys. My jaw throbbed from clenching them. The whole flight, I'd been thinking about how enough was enough. How I wasn't going to let anyone think they could just do what they wanted anymore.

"You've got a look like my Penny, after they got ahold of her," the cabbie told me. "It wasn't her fault, sneaking into a bar. They took her out and did those things to her, like got-damn men got to do to you girls, and then ran her over with their van, threw her in a ditch."

I looked out the window at the now-familiar landscape, rust brown and sage green. It was okay, I told myself.

I hadn't said no. It wasn't rape.

It was just using what I had, the best way out of a bad situation.

This is what you get, Maia Jane Kramer!

My fingers went to my necklace, singing the diamond along the chain. At least he hadn't taken that, and in my bra, just next to my heart, the voice in my head was wrong: Maia Jane Kramer was still alive.

"Van broke Penny's legs so the bone was sticking through, where they drove over them. Good thing was, it was winter here. Doc said she would've bled to death except the cold froze her blood. Colorado winter saved my Penny's life."

I just needed to get home and get a shower, forget about what happened.

I never said no.

"I know someone got ahold of you. You have that look, like my Penny, after. Let me take you by Avista?"

My feet had finally stopped bleeding; I'd wrapped them in paper towel from the bathroom at the airport in San Juan, held it on with two hair bands under my yellow flips.

"I'll turn off the AC, if you're cold."

I nodded and he smiled at me in the rearview mirror. For a second, I panicked—I was alone in a car with a strange man, and just because he was old didn't mean I was safe...

It was just a bad situation.

I peeled back the paper towels, their dried blood, to inspect the damage in the fading light. The cabbie turned off the AC and I didn't say anything more until we were into Boulder, and I had to give him directions. I wanted to go to the place I felt safest—Carolyn's family room, to the sunny quiet times in the afternoon playing Maggie and Her Widow Aunt under the sheet tent, where the thick pillows on the family room couch, the deep pile carpet were padded buffers between the hard realities of all the secrets and shame.

But I couldn't.

"My cousin's kid's a cop up here. You sure you don't want me to take you by the station?"

I shook my head. "L-l-l-eft here, Juniper Court."

Outside the house, I saw rows of familiar cars, Sunday night, another party. I tilted my head against the cab window, bone-tired.

"I knowed you didn't have the money, when I first picked you up."

I nodded.

"You don't have to pay me, but you promise me something. You promise me you'll go inside and tell your folks what happened to you, tell them to call Dean White,

Boulder County Police. He's the one to talk to. You tell him you rode with Mickey. Don't matter where it happened to you—Dean'll help you out."

He took a card out of the visor, scrawled *Dean White* on the back of it, pressed it into my hand.

Mentally, I was already inside the house, under a hot shower, curling up under my covers with Vader. At least I still had Vader.

"Don't keep it inside, like my Penny did, okay? It'll eat you alive. You call Dean."

I waited until the taillights disappeared before facing the house, cars parked all up the street. With a party, it would be impossible for me to go through the front door without running the gauntlet of Monique and the sorority smokers, so I limped around to the side gate, arms wrapped around my waist, shivering in the night air.

Vader bounded to meet me, whacking my thighs with his whip-tail and I let my knees buckle, going down to the ground like a prisoner of war returning to American soil.

"Baby, baby." Vader licked all over my face and I wrapped my arms around his neck, instead of holding on to myself, feeling the knots in shoulders releasing. He woofed, deep happy barks, and soon Dakota was there too, leaping up on us both. I struggled to my feet, tears on my cheeks.

"Dude?" It was Beau, squinting from over by the keg into the dark corner of the yard. "Dude, Maia, oh my god, Dude, you're alive!" He loped across the lawn in three strides and crushed me in his arms. "What happened to you?"

"We were so worried!" It was Will, shyly sidling up, lifting his arms like he might hug me, then dropping them, unsure.

"W-what are you talking about?"

"Your psycho boyfriend has been calling here, the house phone, like every half hour, looking for you."

Psycho, he'd said, and I thought first, Maurice, but then boyfriend—Mark?

"He said you left the hotel, but when we told him you weren't here either, he freaked."

Oh. Joel.

"Where were you?"

I shook my head.

"How did you get home?"

"Cab."

"You should have called me, Dude. I would've come for you."

"I lost my phone," I said, my voice sounding like a robot. As if that was the worst of it.

"Where are your things?" Will asked, staring at the bloody paper towels flaring out around my flip-flops.

"Stolen," I mumbled. "Sorry about your pack."

"What?" It was Nikki. "Did you tell the airline? You should write a complaint, or Twitter-shame them! I had that happen once, they lost my whole set of luggage and I was at the counter for like an hour, crying, like how do you lose an entire set of luggage?"

"You need a beer," Beau kept an arm around me, guiding me toward the keg.

I shook my head. I'd thrown up my one beer in the airport bathroom, reliving it. What I wanted was a toothbrush, a hot shower, Vader, my bed. To feel safe.

"What happened to your feet?" Will's eyebrows were a mountain range of worry.

"Are you okay?" Nikki asked. "I mean, you look gorgeous, as usual, but..."

"I'm g-going to t-take a shower," I said ducking under Beau's arm. I walked away from them but Vader and Will followed me down the steps to the basement.

"I get that your bag got lost, but your feet? What happened?" Will stopped at the bathroom door, one hand on Vader's head. Their matching expressions broke my heart a little. I shook my head. I wanted to say I was fine, but my voice wouldn't work.

"I'll be right outside the bathroom, okay?" Will moved to the couch, Vader padding after him. "I'm going to be sitting here, okay? If you need me."

On Monday morning, at 7:32 am, I walked carefully into Carolyn's front hall, wearing socks with sneakers over my bandages. She was coming down the stairs in nothing but one of Joel's old shirts like a tent over her belly, and underpants. She startled, like she hadn't expected me.

"I know I'm early. Did you try to call me?" I asked, afraid maybe she had, that she had told me not to come back. "Because I lost my phone, and my ... wallet, this weekend." I hung back in the doorway like Vader whenever new people showed up at Juniper Court.

"No," Carolyn grinned; she looked so excited to see me, everything in me relaxed. What I really needed was Sasha's chimpanzee hug. Like she could sense what I was thinking, Carolyn nodded behind her. "Upstairs, still sleeping. She is going to freak when she wakes up. Oh, I'm so happy you're here; you have no idea!"

"Where else would I be?" I asked, my arms hanging empty at my sides.

Out of nowhere, Carolyn threw hers around me. I felt a cracking inside me, like I was made of nothing but brittle, broken shells. When she let go, I felt abandoned and empty. She tugged my hand towards the downy pillows of the couch, saying she had to get horizontal.

"Come, sit! I'm just so glad. My friends turned out to be a little…" she kept her head down, settling into her usual spot, "busier than I thought they'd be. I'm so glad you're back. We missed you."

"I missed you too, and Sash, so much."

"Are you limping?" And the way her eyebrows shot up, her caring almost undid me. I made up a story—tipped over recycling at a party, broken glass—but I couldn't look at her while I lied.

After, I let myself fall into the busywork of getting their house back and, most important, Carolyn fed. Turns out her friends were more than busy—they'd forgotten to bring her dinner at all! I cooked thick butcher-cut bacon and mango and Greek yogurt crepes drizzled with honey. Every familiar action was another layer between me and Puerto Rico, as though I'd never been, a bad dream. The three of us ate and ate in the family room, Sasha and Carolyn toasting my return, and the warmth in me was more than tea.

Then there was getting her house under control and of course, playing with Sasha. My feet were killing so we lay on our bellies on Sash's lavender carpet and used her Barbies in this complicated game of Animal Rescue Fairy Princess. Later, I was changing the bandages in the upstairs bathroom and she barged right in on me.

"What happened?!" Sasha stared. One of my cuts was still weeping. Before I could stop her, Sasha bent her head and kissed my feet, right on top of the cuts. Carolyn would have freaked. "That will make you feel better, Papaya." And then she rested her head against my side like Vader, and it was all I could do not to burst into tears.

God, I loved that kid.

When I showed up Tuesday morning, there was the whiteboard on the front-hall table, but the timeline was broader, nothing in ten-minute increments. My feet still hurt, and one of the cuts was looking like it might be getting infected. I'd had Will pour hydrogen peroxide over it in our bathroom that morning while I bit my lip and

Vader paced, his toenails clicking, making his soft, pathetic whine.

I took Sasha to the park at the end of the cul de sac for the morning, and when we got home, I saw that before going upstairs for her afternoon rest Carolyn had edited the schedule.

2:00 – Sasha: bedroom toys in bins, ONE story, quiet time, (nap???) C & M: TEA and TALK. IMPORTANT. Upstairs.

I wrapped my arms around my waist, pacing the landing, afraid.

CHAPTER THIRTY-ONE

Carolyn

W hen Maia walked back into our life Monday morning, the tensions raised by Jackie's insinuations unfurled, like a spring leaf, where my shoulders met my neck. Of course she wasn't with Joel! I let go of the suspicions, replacing them with gratitude for her return.

But my nose was picking up something, a scent on her. Something had happened.

Her usually flawless face carried a vulnerable tenderness I'd never seen before. I thought about her playing with the due date wheel at Dr. Michaels. About her "crazy nights."

"Is there any chance you're pregnant?" I blurted, when we sat down to tea on Joel's side of the bed Tuesday afternoon.

She burst into the strangest, barking laughter.

"Oh no," she said ruefully. "Not a chance."

"You're sure?"

"Safe sex, only. Plus I just got my period the other weekend, in my housemate's girlfriend's underpants."

"What?" I nearly dropped the cup.

Maia stared up at the ceiling, shaking her head. "Long story. So many long stories."

"Oh. Are you, *dating* one of them?"

"My housemates? No."

"It's none of my business," I said, but I hoped she would go on. There was a world I imagined she occupied, one I had never been a part of, even before. I was curious about erotic youth, promiscuity, the body given freely, the soul kept close, like Julia Roberts as the prostitute in *Pretty Woman*, not kissing her tricks on the lips. Going straight from Alex to the accident, losing him, then college, then Joel, this had never been a part of my life.

"Things got a little wild the other night, at the house. Before. That's all."

"So you're just sleeping with one of them?"

"It's no big deal." She looked away from me, out the Palladian window to the aspen leaves, and I wondered, did she mean sex was no big deal, or something else?

"Making love, sex, is always a big deal. An intimate act, two partners…" I fumbled, feeling like a joke, the dorky sorority sister in the movie. Where were my horn-rimmed glasses, my milkmaid braids?

"Not always," Maia said. "Sometimes, when you come from where I come from, you realize it's an advantage, an asset. Things happen, and you realize, it's not you, it's just your outside! Good ol' mom tried to warn me." I waited for her to go on. She looked back at me. "Pretty gets you places. It's, like, currency. It's okay. It means, as long as I look like this, someone will always want me. I'll be taken care of!"

"No," I said. "That's not the way it should be. Thinking like that, living like that, it makes you a—"

"It makes me smart!" Maia interrupted, her voice a sharp slap. She choked back a sob. "That's all. It makes me smart."

What was wrong? I studied Maia's face, the ugly contortions, the hardness.

"It's not like that," I continued lamely. My back hurt, a steady throb, not like the ebb and flow of labor. I moved to my side of the bed and lay down, crossed my ankles carefully. "At least, not for me."

"Yeah, well, you probably never had to worry," Maia said. "Right from your daddy to your husband, someone was always going to bail you out. Just like the guys at my house. All of you people out here, living this golden life, you don't get it. You don't have to worry about anything."

I remembered how Joel had threatened to leave me if I took us into debt again. I swallowed.

"It wasn't just my father to Joel. There was someone else," I said, changing the subject.

"What?" Maia's hands were shaking with the weight of the half-full mug. Her long neck was bright red, and she scratched it.

"What you said, about going from my dad to my husband. Joel wasn't my only boyfriend. I've had other… men. Singular. Man."

I thought of Alex, a body memory of us in the front seat of my Accord, before the accident, when I had picked him up from basketball practice, steaming up the front seat of my car. I could feel everything again, every detail, the parking brake between us pushed into my thigh, the slippery mesh of his still-damp jersey under my hands, the burn of his cinnamon gum on my lips. How I wanted him.

"I even liked the way he smelled," I confessed.

"You what?" Maia put her mug on the windowsill.

"Alex. My first boyfriend." My cheeks burned. "He smelled… even his sweat smelled good to me."

"Umhmm." Maia looked out the window.

"It was different then," I continued. "I was, thinner and everything was… better. I actually wanted him to touch me, all the time."

"Right…" Maia said, but in the drawn-out way that means, that's normal and anything else isn't.

"It was the same with Joel too, in the beginning," I said, meaning when I was skinny, when I hadn't lost things like the baby, or worse, my willpower.

"What happened to him?"

"Who? Alex? It wasn't his fault. Just… something bigger than either of us were prepared to handle."

The summer I was seventeen, my boyfriend was a lifeguard at the local pool, and I was responsible, for a baby…

Maia waited for me to continue and I knew what she was thinking—an abortion, a suicide, I saw her mind scrambling to fill in the blank.

I jumped up. "Hang on."

I checked on Sasha, zoned out in front of the iPad, her thumb pulling down her lip like a fishhook. On the bookshelf, next to the coffee-table books of the Rockies, I found our ivory-and-gold wedding album.

I suddenly felt bashful. What did I want her to see? Me, skinny? Him? Us, young and hopeful? What did any of it matter?

"Here," I said, simply and opened it in front of her. "This was me, us…. before."

I turned the pages for her, and she looked at every photo. A flick of her finger told me when she was ready to turn.

"Nice," she said finally, and it didn't sound insincere, just distant. "Your flowers, are those Gerbera daisies?"

"And delphiniums. You see," I continued, trying to make my case. "It was... we were..."

"You told me, before; it was the happiest day of your life."

"Yes! I felt fortunate. Everyone told me how lucky I was. To have Joel."

"You both are," she said flatly.

"What do you mean?"

"He's lucky too. Everything you do. You run ragged here; I know, I've been doing it. He should respect, appreciate, you more. How much you care. What a good mom you are, the way you look after Sasha. That's like ... gold."

Something in me soared. She saw exactly what I did. She appreciated my careful attention to the everyday.

"And before, you said the sex was good?" Maia asked, as frankly as if we were talking about food at a restaurant she wanted to go to.

"Y-yeah," I stammered, following her lead, cheeks on fire. It had been a long time since I'd had anyone to discuss this sort of thing with.

"A nice crisp 'yes' serves you better," Maia smiled, and I could feel, smell, her coming back to us in small increments. A hint of jasmine, with the tea.

I nodded.

"So what happened?"

"Well, then...now...I mean, after Sasha, I don't really want to do it, as much, anymore. It's not that uncommon." I thought of the ladies at playgroup, how some complained of this, decreased libido, their fantasies more about going to bed alone: deep, uninterrupted sleep.

Others were still hungry for their husbands. Allison, who did co-sleeping with her twin boys talked about how adventurous this sleeping arrangement forced them to be: a blanket in the backyard under the stars, baby monitor humming, while the twins slept in their bed, or incredible shower sex, her legs wrapped around his runner's trim waist. Sandra said they got a sitter twice a week, but the kids went to the sitter's house.

"We tell her we're refinishing our basement. But we usually just have hot sex, and then order in Chinese," Sandra laughed. "The basement still looks like a bomb went off."

"We lock the door and tell the kids we're 'talking about Christmas presents' and they can't come in," Yasha added. "That can start as early as October. After that, there's 'on a conference call with the Easter Bunny'... Summer's harder. We need another holiday in there."

I realized it was mostly Jackie, when she was separated from Russ—and me—

united in miserable silence.

"But isn't that sort of part of the whole marriage thing?" Maia was saying. "Aren't you basically saying, when you get married to someone, 'I want to do this, be close with you, in every way?' Don't you sort of, I don't know, *sign on* for sex with your husband?"

"What about 'in sickness and in health?'" I snapped.

"But you're pregnant, not sick."

"That's not what I meant!"

"Sorry," Maia said. "I guess I don't understand—"

"I got fat!" I blurted, and I confessed to her my second-most hideous secret, something only Joel and I knew, and him only because he had been in the nurse's room, jiggling a screaming, colicky Sasha at my first post-partum appointment. "After Sasha, and the bed rest," I whispered, "I weighed two hundred pounds."

Maia didn't say anything, waiting for me to finish.

"Joel gave me this necklace afterwards, a 'pushing present' the guys at his work called it. Isn't that a vulgar name? It was lovely, but I couldn't fasten it. Even my neck had gotten fatter."

Since then, I'd felt like an invalid, like something disgusting and foreign was in my body, like my very cells, my fat was tumorous and repugnant.

"*That's it?* That's what this is all about? You don't want to have sex because you feel out of shape?" Maia sounded so incredulous, I turned away, tears stinging at my eyes. I folded my arms protectively over my stomach mound. How could she understand the layers of self-loathing that I had accumulated over the years, everything that had come with the loss of willpower?

"Sasha wasn't an easy baby. It was more important for me to care for her than get on a treadmill." I'd relished the challenge of her, the enormous responsibility of keeping her safe and happy. Patience and nurturing were my new shroud, layered with my newly-thickened skin. Sometimes I wished I could recall more distinct memories of that time, but so much of her babyhood was tainted by the irritable constant of my self-loathing, the prickles of my anxiety about the insides of my upper arms catching on my bra strap bulge, my thigh fat chafing when I walked her around the nursery in the middle of the night. Waking up with my stomach stretched out on the bed beside me like a sleeping tomcat, I was claustrophobic inside my own skin.

"Okay, so what?" Maia continued gently. "Okay. No worries. So after you have the baby, we'll start exercising. We'll get a bike, the kind with a trailer for the kids. We'll take turns towing them around. It will be fun. Would that be okay?"

I didn't answer, swiping at my tears. I wanted it all to be that easy.

"This was nice," I said carefully. "We should make a habit of this. Confessional tea. Therapy. Every day."

"Put it on the whiteboard," Maia said, a smirk tilting her lips, and when she carried our mugs down to the kitchen, I was glad to see a little of the light back in her eyes.

⌐⌐

Then Joel got back from Puerto Rico Tuesday night, looking like he'd been dragged the whole way, dropping his bag in the front hall with a heavy sigh.

"How was it?" I asked.

"Hot," he said, as if I cared about the weather.

"No, your presentation?"

"Oh, that," he sighed. "Fine, I guess. Liddy made a bunch of last-minute changes, so I looked like an idiot during the Q & A." He sank into the couch at my feet. "It could have gone better."

"I'm sorry."

"You have a nice time with the girls?"

Honestly, that Saturday night in Rachel's kitchen felt like weeks ago. I nodded.

"Did they just leave?" He looked around, at the cleaned playroom, Maia's vacuum lines still in the carpet.

"Jackie and Rachel? That was back on Saturday. We went to Rachel's."

"Oh. What about the rest of the time?"

"Oh, Maia's been here."

"Maia?" he said, like he'd never heard of her.

"Our nanny? I'll need you to leave some more cash, and maybe leave your car, so she can run some errands, if you're flying to Philadelphia tomorrow."

When I went up to bed, there were six empty mini bottles of Scotch on his nightstand, the basketball game on the TV, and he was snoring uncharacteristically.

⌐⌐

On Thursday, Jackie and Rachel stopped by while Maia was out picking up the healthy groceries from my list. They had brought me a thick brick of pumpkin bread from playgroup, slathered in icing, enough for two. I put it aside to share with Maia during our afternoon tea.

Sasha was playing Barbies under the table, and Ella and Gracey campaigned for her to come up the street on a playdate.

"Um," I paused and Jackie rolled her eyes.

"She can ride in El's booster. I don't even make her ride in it half the time. Good god, we all survived the nineties!"

I was thinking it would be better if she rode in her own. It was only a few blocks. Safety Queen, indeed.

"So…" Jackie prompted, her voice low.

"What?"

"Have you asked her? References? Her driver's license?"

"Oh, no. We've been busy. Maia thought up this brilliant system of taping photos to my storage bins, to make it easier for Sasha to put away her own toys. You've got to see it."

Rachel glanced politely at the shelves on the playroom wall, asking, "Do you still want Dean to run her through the computer, though, for peace of mind?"

"I don't actually think she's a criminal! We came up with a fun, vegetarian menu plan for the week. She's becoming a great cook! And the other…" I trailed off. "I was wrong. Paranoid. Silly. I don't worry about it anymore."

They both looked a little deflated, frustrated.

"You've got to do more digging!" Jackie insisted, and I wondered if I was their guilty pleasure, my life a midday soap opera. Catering to the three-foot dictators all day could get dull. "Nobody invites a stranger into her home without precautions! In the name of responsible parenting!"

Just then Maia walked in, arms full of Alfalfa's bags, stalks of Brussels sprouts and scallions sticking out the tops.

"Papaya! You're back!" Sasha scrambled out from under the table and shoved past Rachel and Jackie to throw her arms around Maia's perfect, narrow hips. Maia twirled Sasha's ponytail around her finger, oblivious to the other women's intense stares.

"Call me," Jackie raised her eyebrows, making the sign of a telephone with her fingers, before they let themselves out.

"Listen, I had a thought," Maia said. The groceries were put away and she was clearing our lunch of salad and iced herbal tea into the kitchen. "Please don't get angry, again, but I think this is important."

I knew what she was going to say.

"You wouldn't even have to ever do it, or tell anyone that you could, but later, after," and the way she left it open, I assumed she meant, when she was gone, "when it's just you and the kids, and Joel's traveling, and maybe Jackie's got her phone turned off at Goddess Yoga, but you need to get somewhere, for one of the kids…"

She was right. I had played out a hundred emergency scenarios—wildfires, high fevers—horrible outcomes because I had no way to get my children to safety.

"Let me just give you a little lesson? A refresher?"

"But…" I waved my hand down my horizontal body, calculating in my head. I was thirty weeks pregnant. Devyn, who used to come to playgroup, had the twins at twenty-nine; they wore tiny glasses but were otherwise okay. I hadn't felt anything like a contraction in days.

"It wouldn't even take that long. Hardly longer than a pee break. And you drove when you were younger—"

"Thirteen years ago!" I could tick off a long list of things that were different thirteen years ago.

"Like riding a bicycle." Maia grinned, jingling Joel's keys in her hand like a dinner bell. "Now's the perfect opportunity. Sasha's at a playdate, it's just you and me…"

She held out her hand to me on the couch. Someday, I thought, I might need this. So I followed her, heart pounding, out into the afternoon sunshine.

CHAPTER THIRTY-TWO

Maia

My plan was to keep her actual time at the wheel short and sweet, praising her for the tiniest accomplishments, like I'd seen her do with Sasha trying something new. It seemed to be coming back to her as she puttered super slowly around their tree-name subdivision, turning careful circles in the cul-de-sacs.

"I kind of want to go somewhere," Carolyn giggled, "but I'm afraid."

"Like where?" I asked her.

"I don't know. Somewhere. Anywhere." When I glanced over, Carolyn was breathing hard, her teeth pinning her lower lip as she hunched over the wheel. Her baby belly bumped the horn and we both burst out laughing. She pumped the brakes and put down Joel's driver side window, drinking in the dry air. "Anywhere. Out of here. Can you drive for a little?"

"Okay." We switched, I got behind the wheel and waited to merge out of their subdivision. "Where do you want to go?"

"Somewhere, new, different. I think," she laughed at herself, "I'm going a little stir crazy. Just drive!"

A horn blasted behind me, a Subaru loaded with bikes, so I pulled out slowly, headed towards town and beyond it, the mountains. I stayed in the right lane and let a line of cars pass us.

"You know, you're really no better," Carolyn teased as I edged along, one set of tires on the shoulder.

"Hey, precious cargo!" I laughed back, and then the lights came on behind me. "Shit."

I pulled over, hives running up under my hair like my skin was made of snakes.

"What's wrong?" Carolyn asked, as in the rearview mirror I watched his deliberate approach. "Relax," she told me. "We're not doing anything wrong."

She had no idea. I put down the window.

"Do you know why I pulled you over?"

"No, sir." I kept my eyes on his belt buckle until he leaned down to put his meaty face closer to the window, mirrored shades showing nothing but the blue sky behind us.

"You were driving erratically, and about twelve miles an hour under the speed limit."

A panicky tear slipped out from under my glasses.

"Which isn't illegal," he smiled. "It just gets my attention. I need to see your license and registration."

With a shaking hand, I passed him the rectangle of plastic.

"Take your sunglasses off, please?" he asked, holding it out.

Cinderella's midnight; my pumpkin carriage smashed on the side of the road.

"You're twenty-seven?"

"Yessir."

"Huh. You look much younger. My sister's twenty-seven, kids ruined her, though. Gray hairs, fat. I mean, sorry." He nodded at Carolyn's obvious belly. "You're here from New York?"

"Yes, just… visiting."

"I know what they say, about the DMV being criminally bad at photography, but this photo is a sin… Anyone ever tell you, you could be a model?"

By accident, I burst into nervous giggles, and Carolyn joined in, muttering under her breath, "What does pretty get you?"

Unbelievably, the cop smiled into the car, like he was getting somewhere.

"So then, who is Joel Carter?" He flicked the registration Carolyn had produced from the glove compartment. "Who owns this car?"

"It's my husband," Carolyn piped up, leaning over my body to beam up at him. "Hi!"

"Then I'm going to need your license."

"I don't drive—" Carolyn said at the same time I said,

"She doesn't drive."

"Oh-kay."

"Which is why I'm driving," I said.

"You're…." He left it open.

"Sisters," Carolyn interjected.

"Okay. Sisters. You must be the younger one," he smiled at me. "So I assume your brother-in-law knows you're running around in his A6?"

"He's traveling, out of town, for business," Carolyn explained, flitting her hands to show he didn't matter.

"Ladies, this is a very confusing scenario." But the cop pushed his glasses up on his head, and rocked back on his heels, obviously enjoying himself. "I'm going to go run this," he held up Sheila, "and I'll be right back."

"Holyshitholyshitholyshit," I gasped, pressing my lips over my fingers gripping the steering wheel. I opened my eyes to glance at the terrain, open and flat, some bored cows munching brownish grass on the other side of barbed wire. Nowhere to run.

"Okay, what's wrong?" Carolyn turned, her hand over one of mine.

"Nothing," I gasped, scratching my neck. "Nothing, except that I can't really breathe."

"When he comes back, let me talk, okay? It's Joel's car, and I was the one who told you to drive. I've got this. It's fine. Nobody has done anything wrong, except, well, me earlier, driving without a license."

"Right." I nodded. In the rearview mirror, I watched him approach. Fuck-fuck-fuck.

"Okay, Sheila?"

"Mmhmm?" I braced myself, pressing my lips together, feeling Carolyn staring at me.

"Okay, we've got a problem, Miss McHugh."

I opened my mouth, but Carolyn jumped in.

"Oh my god!"

I stared blankly at Carolyn, as she slipped into a long, low groan and slouched in her seat, squinching her eyes together.

I opened my mouth again and she cut me off, blinking up at the cop.

"Just give me a second." Carolyn held up a hand. "Can I say what happened? This is all my fault."

The cop furrowed his eyebrows at her huffing breathing, but continued, "This license, here, is coming up as a registered driver in the state of New York, but you have several unpaid parking tickets."

Parking tickets? I could have cried.

"Oh my god," Carolyn bellowed. "You never paid those? I can explain. I called Sheila, my sister, this morning, SOS, because I'm in early labor and Joel is of course Mr. Busy-Beaver-Businessman, doing a presentation. His company's going public," Carolyn held a finger to her lips, her eyes wide and gorgeous, her voice slipping into a slight, bizarre drawl. "My sister, bless her heart, she leaves a fashion shoot, for Cosmo! Hops a flight from JFK, zooms out here, because she knows I can't face natural childbirth without my number one hypnobirthing coach! While she may be drop-dead gorgeous," Carolyn clapped a hand on my shoulder, "this girl is the most scatterbrained seabird you'll ever meet. Guys forgive her, looking like she does, you can imagine, but she has the tickets, keeps them up on top of her dresser, with all her incense and tarot cards and jewelry and guys' phone numbers, you can't imagine how many, and dear lord, the rest of the holy clutter...."

This, I thought, this is where Sash's tickertape imagination comes from.

"Sheila's the worst kind of slob, but guys forgive that too. I'm the organized one! I've tried to teach her my systems but, ack!" Carolyn winced again, throwing herself back against her seat, continuing with her eyes closed. The cop startled. "She just hasn't gotten to paying them yet. I am amazed they even let you on the airplane with that license this morning!"

"Well, if you're just traveling domestically, they only use it for photo ID," the officer explained, leaning in to squint at Carolyn. "Ma'am, are you alright?"

Carolyn nodded, huff-huffing like one of the cows beside the car.

"We're fine," she said through gritted teeth. "It's my third, I can feel it's not fully engaged in the vaginal canal. Number two was over forty hours in the chute."

The cop straightened, fiddling with his radio, another transmission.

"But you, Miss McHugh, should not be driving with those unpaid parking tickets."

I shook my head, serious, NO.

"Technically speaking, I should confiscate this and—"

"Can we get to the reason of why she's here?" Carolyn waved a hand over her giant belly, "and why she's driving like a nervous granny, and I'm over here, moaning and groaning? We need to get going." She snapped. "Baby time. Pronto."

I loved her. With all my heart.

"Can I offer you an escort to Avista?"

"Oh no, I'm doing a waterbirth at my midwife's cabin up the canyon! And we still have to pick up my doula and the drummer and the sage smoker guy, and didn't Willow say she's coming to get the placenta? I hope she pickles it again, that tasted so much better than the stew."

"There's a lot of humming and drumming to happen yet," I said, trying to keep a straight face. Unbelievable.

The cop put his pen back in his shirt pocket.

"Listen, Miss McHugh, Sheila, I don't want to hear of you driving again out here while you're visiting Boulder, until you take care of those tickets."

"No, sir. I won't. Promise." I saluted and held up two fingers, smiling wide. Amazingly, my hives were gone.

"Okay, I'm going to let you two cowgirls get going, to whatever it is you're up to, but uh, if you ever have some free time, Sheila, while you're out here, um, after the baby," he scribbled, "here's my card, if you want a break from babysitting, or whatever, I like to uh, do some top roping, and a little paragliding, when I'm off, if you're interested."

"Thank you," I told him. "That sounds like a lot of fun."

We held it together until he was back in his car and I'd gotten Joel's window up. Then we exploded, laughing until tears ran down our cheeks, Carolyn gasping that she might have just peed a little.

"'If you're ever interested in uh, top-roping?' What the hell is that?"

"Rock climbing. Boulder flirting. He's trying to impress you with his mountain manliness."

"Well, I never have tried rock climbing," I said, which made Carolyn laugh even harder.

"Two cowgirls," she choked, wiping under her eyes for smudges of mascara.

"You are nothing short of amazing." I stared at her, and she sighed. "That story, that accent? A drummer and sage smoker? Wait, you're not really in labor, right?" I asked suddenly.

"No more than you're a twenty-seven-year-old named Sheila McHugh."

"Bar ID." I twisted my hair out of my face and turned back to the road, putting Joel's car in drive. "My boyfriend's friend got it for me, back home, so I could get into bars with them."

"But you do truly have your driver's license, right?" Carolyn asked as we eased back on to the highway.

"Not on me," I said, which for once was not a lie. I had left it, permanently, with the necklace, behind a piece of loose trim at Juniper Court.

Carolyn put her window down, a pleased cat's smile with the sun on her face, as I drove us carefully back home.

"Sss," she giggled and made a scoffing noise in her teeth, tipped her face into the wind like Vader. "And my husband says we're not having enough fun!"

⌣⟶

After Carolyn's first driving lesson, we picked up an early sushi dinner. When I suggested a reward destination, she managed a merge and three lefts to get to Moon Gate, and then hopped gratefully into the reclined passenger seat, sending me in with a credit card to pick up our sushi. I carried it tightly in my palm.

Inside, I ordered us a bunch of rolls we'd never tried before, including spicy tuna, since they were out of avocado, and pork- fried rice for Sasha. Turned out Carolyn couldn't eat the raw fish, so I gagged down both the tuna rolls. It was super-fishy, and it reminded me of the smell in Maurice's yard, drying seaweed. A few minutes later, I felt really sick. Not just queasy, but the kind where I broke out in a sweat on my upper lip.

"I think I need to go home," I called to Carolyn as I ran past her in the family room, doubled over in cramps, to throw up into their front-hall toilet. Sometimes, barfing makes you feel better afterwards. This wasn't one of them. I leaned against the bowl, cheek to cool porcelain, panting, waiting for the next round. It came.

At Carolyn's suggestion, I crawled up the carpeted stairs to the guest bathroom. She had a little silver trash can I could barf in while I was folded in half on the toilet with fire-hose diarrhea. When I leaned against the wall to dump it down the toilet, I noticed on the bottom: Pier 1, from her crazy shopping days.

It was so strange to think of her, years ago, alone all day, crazy-shopping them into debt, when she knew it was wrong. It was hard to imagine that Carolyn as the same one who'd called me her scatterbrained little sister, put on that hilarious accent and conned a cop, who sent her daughter to lie outside the locked door to be with me.

Sasha told me stories about Maggie and the widow aunt. Between my sweats and vomits, I touched my fingertips to her tiny ones poking under the door.

Carolyn knocked and I crawled over to let her in. I could tell by the way the light slanted across the spare room that it was evening, huge thunderclouds boiling along the sunset.

"You're staying here tonight," she insisted. It was Wednesday, which meant Joel was in Philly. "I'll call your housemates, make sure your dog is okay."

"But you're meant to be the one on bed rest!" I croaked. "I'm meant to be taking care of you!" She had already been up too much because I'd nearly gotten us arrested during a driving lesson.

"I feel fine," she insisted. "Better than fine. Thank you, for today."

Behind her, the creamy white sheets spread taut on the mattress looked like heaven.

In the sweating darkness, fever dreams swirled. I was back in Puerto Rico, in Maurice's shack, only he was not human but a giant cockroach. When I screamed, Carolyn was sleeping beside me, smoothing my sweaty hair off my neck, whispering, "Shhh, shhh, it was just a bad dream."

In the morning, I got one more chance to go back to Philly and make things right. It was late June, Thursday after the driving lesson. My guts had stopped trying to leave my body, and we were folding a mountain of laundry and drinking coconut water Carolyn had ordered from Whole Foods delivery.

"You need electrolytes!" Carolyn had just thanked me for the hundredth time for the driving lesson. "I feel so different, like a world of possibility has opened for me again! Not that I'd even need to do it, but Maia, just knowing I can—"

We were interrupted by the doorbell. She stopped and looked at me. Most of her packages, I noticed, arrived on Tuesdays, and UPS usually didn't ring the bell.

"I guess I should go check? Though I don't know if I could keep down Girl Scout cookies," I joked, opening the front door, and there, in his faded black jeans, was Mark Duncheski. My Mark.

"Hey," he grinned, peering over my shoulder into the TV room at Carolyn and Sasha. "What's up?"

"My god, Mark, what are you doing here?" I kept my voice low. Worlds colliding; I wanted to shove him out the door and lock it.

"I got in town around noon, and some guy at your place said this was where you worked. That is one sweet pad. Yo, I been trying to call."

"My phone's lost."

"Yeah, I figured," and relief passed over his face. "Anyways, it took me for-fuck-ing-ever to find this place. It's like, every street out here is Birch something or Raven this or Aspen that, you know?" I was hyper-aware of his language, his Philly accent right then, of Carolyn listening. "But hey," he grinned. "I mean, I finally found you, right?" He ducked forward, bumping my cheekbone with his jaw when he kissed me. I took a step backward.

"Why did you, what are you, what are you doing in Boulder? Why are you here?"

"I believe that's my line," he said.

"Everything okay?" Carolyn called out and Mark looked over my shoulder, waiting to be invited in. "A friend of yours?"

"Sorry, it'll just take a sec. Listen, Mark—"

"Yeah, your sister's fat-ass boyfriend gave me the address. I wasn't even threatening him or nothing. Maybe a little, but not, like, you know, for real, and then he starts blubbering and shoving papers at me and shit. All I was doing was asking where you were, if you were okay. Shit's going down at home," he said darkly, and added, "Plus, I missed you, Babe."

"Listen, Mark, there's kids around. And I'm working."

"Yeah, yeah." He was still trying to see past me, more of their house. "What time you off?"

"Seven, maybe?" I'd been planning to leave before Joel got home. I looked over my shoulder where Carolyn and Sasha were pretending not to listen.

"You want me to scoop you?"

"No, I've got a bike."

He raised his eyebrows at that, underlining how much I'd changed.

"Cool. I'll just go hang back at your place then."

"Wait, no. Do you know where my room is? Downstairs? I only rent the room, not the house." I was desperate to keep him from Beau and Will and Luke, especially Luke, who I'd been avoiding.

"It's cool. I'll see you when you get home, Babe." He kissed me again, this time finding my lips, and there was the familiar bristle of his goatee scraping me.

I closed the door, dreading my return to the family room.

"'See you when you get home, Babe,'" Sasha said in a deep voice, butting her Ken doll's head against Barbie's with a crash of plastic.

"Well," I said, moving the laundry basket aside so I could sit down on the couch. "It wasn't Girl Scout cookies."

Carolyn had turned off Nat Geo; things were more interesting in her own TV room. She did a terrible job of acting uninterested as she exhaled a leading, "So...."

"Sorry. Totally unprofessional. He's," I considered launching into a lie, but

WHAT PRETTY GETS YOU

changed my mind. "That's my old boyfriend, from Philly. God," I realized I was still holding Joel's old NYU T-shirt, unfolded. "Ex-boyfriend. I think I'm still in shock."

"He cursed four times." Sasha's tone was grave. "And you kissed!" she shrieked, falling off my lap. She dove under an empty laundry basket, crawling with it on her back like a turtle.

"So this is the one from the story, with the grandmother...." Carolyn said.

"Yeah. Babçi, his grandma, brought him over from Poland when he was a baby."

"What happened to his parents?"

I pointed with my head toward Sasha and shook it; not a story for kids.

"Anyway. That's Mark. What he's doing here, I have no idea." I rested the heavy laundry basket on my hip. This was a tiny bit of a lie, because I knew in spite of everything, Mark loved me, imagined a future for us. Not to mention, of course, the legal thing.

CHAPTER THIRTY-THREE

Carolyn

Thursday night, after I let Maia go early, I heated up the dinner she'd made for Sasha. I was too antsy to eat. Afterward, I put on a full-length movie, *Lady and the Tramp*, upstairs in our bedroom, hoping Sasha would fall asleep to it. My mind was humming; I needed to think.

We'd never used the garage for Joel's car. It became a catchall for things we didn't use much but hoped to sometime, like my old exercise bike, our snowshoes and skis. Farther back, past the trash can where I first smelled the banana in his buried Vitality cups, past the things Joel knew about, were the UPS boxes that Maia sometimes carried out for me.

Like most people, we kept our clutter closed up in our garage, out of the scope of the life we presented. I was breaking bed rest to move it all around, pondering a new use for the space, when headlights surprised me. A door slammed, and there was my husband. I quickly draped a beach blanket over boxes I'd ordered.

"What are you doing up?" Joel waded through the waist-high boxes to me, to take my elbow. "You're not supposed to be out of bed."

I was not far from the prenatal appointment when Dr. Michaels had said he might release me from bed rest.

"I'm looking for the crib," I lied. Ever since my conversation with Maia that afternoon, I'd been thinking of another use for the space. "We've got to clean this out," I told Joel. "Get rid of this junk. Animals could be living out here."

It had moved from weekend to-do list to to-do list for years—ORGANIZE GARAGE.

"Yes," Joel agreed, like he always did. "But not you, not tonight. You're meant to be horizontal."

I didn't move.

"You must be nesting," he tried again.

Inside me, the baby moved, and I did an unconscious kick count; all was well.

"Caro, please. Come inside. Lie down."

I let him lead me to the familiar, family-room couch. Neither of us turned on the light switch—the foyer light I'd left on was enough, and the night sky was glowing an eerie orange from a semi-contained forest fire burning out near Loveland.

He filled us both glasses of ice water and we sat down, our pairs of feet propped on the coffee table. Our shoulders touched, side by side.

"So the weather's looking a little ominous for Saturday night," he said. "There's potential for a thunderstorm."

"What's Saturday?"

"For our party."

"Oh!" I couldn't believe I had forgotten. "I suppose we need the rain." Boulder County had been on a HIGH forest-fire warning for days. If heat lightning came first, it could be dangerous.

"Yes." Joel looked at me curiously. "Are you alright?"

I nodded, slowly.

"I'll head out tomorrow night after work and get all the supplies. One of the Philly guys gave me a great rib-rub recipe, and I'll get some corn and watermelon, and some beers. If it doesn't rain Saturday, I can get the yard in shape. And I guess even if we don't clean the garage, we should probably at least dig out that crib and get it set up."

I was wondering, if Dr. Michaels would let me get out of bed next week, whether or not I could put a Dumpster on my credit card. It would only take Maia and me a few days next week to empty the space.

"I've been thinking, recently." Joel's tone shifted, his voice sober. "I want to make this, us, our family, a priority. I need to help you out, to be here for you more. I'm really hoping this Philly merger happens; I'd like to stop this crazy commute, get our old lives back."

I didn't answer right away and he continued.

"I want to get things on track, with us," he said, softly. "I've felt a distance, for a while."

"Yes…" I said carefully, wondering. I remembered what it was like to run up the stairs to our apartment, and see the light shining under the door, and how my heart would stutter-stop, because it meant Joel was home, waiting for me.

"I had an idea," Joel said slowly. "Maybe, if we tell each other the worst things we've ever done, we can move on, move forward?"

I put a hand over my stomach instinctively, swallowing. The only sentence that I could form was the one I had started, but never spoken to him, a thousand times.

The summer I was seventeen, my boyfriend was a lifeguard at the local pool, and I was responsible for a baby, a little boy. His name was—

"It's a boy," I blurted instead.

"What?" Joel pulled away from me so our shoulders weren't touching anymore. His face split in the bittersweet way I knew it would. A boy, like the one we'd lost the first time over the Pacific. His hands traveled to mine over my stomach, curled possessively around him.

"I had an ultrasound. I meant to tell you, before." *Would it have made any difference if I had told him the day he walked off the plane with Maia?* Our foreheads tilted until they touched, and he whispered,

"I…." But he left the sentence unfinished, and I could feel by the shudder against my chest, that he was quietly crying.

Later, I was in the master bedroom, tapping back to the baby's kicks, and eavesdropping as Joel took care of the bedtime routine. Sasha was in the bath and he was doing this thing with her water dolphins he used to do when she was younger, using different squeaky voices. There was lots of splashing and her shrieks of laughter.

I thought of Joel sneaking into the church to hide a love note inside my wedding dress, surprising me with the prick of a straight pin, and then the rawness of his scrawled emotions. I remembered him crying over Sasha's crib one night, confessing his fear that he wouldn't be everything she deserved.

Some women, I thought, had this every day of their lives. A man who cherished them, a life without secrets, easy children. And I didn't envy them, because unlike me, they would never know the rush of gratitude for a moment like this.

They were on to stories now, Joel reading in her bed, Sasha's tone drifting down from its hysterical bathtub pitch. I could picture them under her canopy, Sasha tucked in the crook of his arm, sucking on her fingers.

And then it was quiet, and Joel came and stood in the doorway, a satisfied smile on his face.

"Lights out—success. This was nice, being home in time to put her to bed," he said, watching my son and I do our Morse-code communication. "How's my boy, huh?"

"Good," I smiled at him, thrilling with possibility, a new future.

"I can't wait until the commute is over, and it's just our family again, little man on the outside, the four of us...."

"Mmhmm." I was thinking in a few minutes, if he initiated anything intimate, I might even be willing.

"You know what I really look forward to?" he added, stretching in the doorframe, and I admired the lines of his abdominal muscles, same as ever, when his shirt rode up. Remembering my conversation in this very bed with Maia, about Alex, sex, I thought, I might even initiate something myself. He was still an incredibly attractive man.

"What?" A million things spun through my mind, all the possible answers, something to do with the baby, a trip, undressing me...

"Getting rid of Maia."

CHAPTER THIRTY-FOUR

Maia

When I got to Juniper Court, my stomach sank. Mark's truck, the yellow YO Toyota with the dented half-bed, was in the driveway, blocking Luke's sacred garage spot. I was thinking, *thank god he's not home yet.* Then I looked over my shoulder and saw Luke's Range Rover parked on the street. Shit.

Mark was on my bed with Vader, flipping through a *People* magazine Carolyn had passed on to me. He still had his work boots on, feet crossed at the ankle.

"Hey," he said. "Did you know this is the town where that little beauty queen kid was killed?"

"Yeah." Joel had pointed out the Ramsey house to me, the day we tried to drive the dogs to Chautauqua Park.

"Why would you come all the way across the country to live in a place like this?"

"Kids get killed in Philly every day. Every hour! You haven't seen the mountains? You don't think it's beautiful here?" I closed my bedroom door. One thing that was not up for debate in this house: the ultimate coolness of Boulder.

"Your view is especially nice." Mark chucked the magazine. He got up and went to my skinny ground-level window, poked around at my flower sprouts on the ledge. "What kind of weed is this?"

"They're going to be cosmos and black-eyed Susans."

Will and I had bought the seeds and on the windowsill in the kitchen, tomatoes and basil. We were planning to plant them outside in the backyard beds when they were tall enough.

"Looky Martha Stewart," he said, pacing the room, jingling the keys clipped with a carabiner to the belt loop of his jeans. I knew for a fact these were the jeans Babçi got him for his seventeenth birthday—it had been a point of pride that he still wore the same 30-inch waist.

"Mark, what are you doing here?"

"I told you, that's my line."

I didn't say anything.

"God, it's summer and it's fucking freezing down here." He rubbed the goose pimples on his bare arms.

"Here." I handed him a sweatshirt to put on over his ratty Killers T-shirt. No matter how many times I'd told him to throw it out, he kept it because we first met sneaking into their concert years ago, probably why he was wearing it now. It was both touching and irritating, Mark in a nutshell.

"I got all these calls from Ritchie about you ripping off your register or some bullshit. And then me and Nick had the lawyer all down our throats about the trial, trying to cover for you. It's postponed, and I paid him, anyways."

"Paid who?" I looked up.

"Ritchie. Told him it didn't sound like you, stealing. But I paid him anyways, so there won't be trouble when we get back."

"Thanks."

"*You took it?*" he seemed so genuinely surprised I thought about lying, but that's not how things were with me and Mark.

"It's a little more complicated than that," I said.

"Don't sound too complicated to me."

When I didn't answer, he asked, "So, what, you fucking someone out here, is that it? One of those pussies upstairs?"

"I just needed a change." I was naively hoping, if he really loved me, he could see how much better things were for me here. "Let's go; we've got to move your truck."

Upstairs, people were showing up, cars in the driveway, Monique's ice-blue BMW parked behind Luke's Rover, and cars all up our street, another party at Club 22. We moved Mark's truck and headed to the backyard.

Outside, Monique was pouting prettily on the edge of the hot tub in her string bikini.

"It's such a drag to date the DJ."

"Who's that?" Mark was tit-staring.

"The girlfriend of the guy who owns the house."

Mark snorted. "One of those pussies? Get outta here, what is he, a Mainliner or a dealer or what?"

"He's a fratbrat with rich parents."

Mark whistled through his teeth.

"Hey." Will walked over to us in soccer shorts and flip flops, a Spyder sweatshirt. "There's a keg over by the gate. Hammer just tapped it."

"Okay, thanks." But my heart sank, because every time Hammer showed up, the parties got chemically silly.

Will stood around expectantly for an introduction to Mark, but I didn't feel up to it. Honestly, I just wanted to find my dog, and hide the two of them down in my room until I could convince him to go.

"Hey, Maia," Beau called from over by the grill, "I picked up some of that Pinot you liked last week, if you're interested."

"Pinot?" Mark sneered. "I'm getting myself a beer." And he disappeared.

"So, uh, has he been married long?" Will asked politely, his eyebrows raised.

"Oh, god, no! That's not him. He's from Philly. High school thing. Junior high, really. Long story."

"You keep saying that," Will said, "and I've got nothing but time." His expression was so earnest, like his face had been carefully molded from soft clay.

"Thanks, maybe later. I want to find Vader. I should be doing some kind of damage control or something. I think Luke's still pissed."

Will did not disagree.

"Hey, I have something for you." Nikki grabbed my hand to follow her up to her dressing room. It turned out to be a bikini she'd bought for herself from Hollister.

"If you like it, you can have it, save me the hassle of returning it." She bent her head closer. "So that guy, is he the married one from the plane?"

"Mark? No, he's just an old friend from Philly."

"Oh!" Nikki burst out laughing. "Beau thought," she tried to catch her breath, "sorry, for some reason, Beau thought you were going out with him. I told him that guy was way beneath you. I mean," she caught herself, "I'm sure he's a good friend or whatever, but that hair! What color is that? It's like Missouri Compromise mulletville."

"Yeah," I said evenly, correcting myself. "Yes. He's just a friend."

But I thought about how he had given the money to Ritchie, no questions asked, and for a guy like Mark, three hundred and fifty bucks meant a lot. Nikki, who'd just given me a ninety-dollar bathing suit because she didn't want the hassle of returning it, would never understand.

Vader and Mark were alone on a lawn chair under the dogwood tree, more people spilling out the sliding door, clustering around the keg and hot tub and grill. Luke had the outdoor lights on and the bass cranked too loud for a weeknight.

"Hey." I sat down at Mark's feet, rubbing Vader's head.

"Truth time: What are you doing out here?"

Knowing Mark so long, this was his *I've had a few and I'm spoiling for a fight* mode.

"Obviously taking care of the best dog in the world." I ruffled Vader's ears. "What, you don't see this? Who wouldn't want to live here?" I gestured at the mountains past the redwood fence.

"For real, Maia." Mark was not buying it.

We sat in miserable silence—nobody came to talk to us.

"Damn!" Mark said, too loud, throwing his plastic cup on the ground. Heads swiveled.

"Um, recycling!" A sorority chick sing-songed.

"You'd think with all this fucking money they could've at least got some decent beer!" Mark said, standing up to go get another. I didn't follow.

Will pulled me into the kitchen, his face anxious.

"That was the Dennenbergs, from next door, on the phone. They've called the police, but they wanted to give us a chance to get any illegal substances put away."

"Did you tell Luke?" I asked.

"He's all coked up. They all are. But I think I've got things pretty much out of sight. I'm going to bed, unless you need me."

"No, thanks."

"Okay, good night."

I was dying to follow him downstairs, to my own bed with my dog, but I had to find Mark first.

I got to the yard just in time to hear Monique's distinctive shriek. She was scrambling out of the hot tub, one raspberry-colored nipple hanging out of her bathing suit, slurring, "I said, get your fugging white-trash hands off me!"

Mark.

Luke was right behind me—the rapping stopped and the record just spun the same bass beat, over and over. Beau intercepted Luke, towering over him by half a foot.

"Easy, relax, dude's just drunk. Not even worth your time." To me, "Maia…"

with a hard, warning look.

I was ahead of him though, hustling Mark out of the hot tub. He was wearing nothing but grey underwear, and I hauled him up by his armpits like a kid.

"I didn't touch her! I swear she was all-fucking-over-me—"

"I want that douchebag out of my house!" Luke put up a show of a struggle against Beau's chest. "Tonight, Maia!"

I held on to the fact that he wasn't acting like I was invisible, that he didn't say I should leave with Mark.

The bass beat spun over the pall in the yard. In the distance, I could hear sirens.

"I swear to you, baby, she was all-fucking-over-me. She said her rich boyfriend had a pencil dick. Would I make that up, a dumbass dropout like me? No, you ask her. She called it a pencil dick, or maybe a pencil prick to be more poetic or something."

"Come on, Mark." I led him toward the house. "You're shaking."

In bed, even under my blankets, he didn't stop shivering. I took all the clothes I had on my shelf and piled them on top of him.

"G-g-g-g-od, b-b-b-b-aby, I'm so c-c-c-c-old," he chattered. "This w-w-w-asn't meant to turn out l-l-l-ike this. I j-j-j-just wanted you to c-c-c-ome home with m-m-m-me."

"Shhh."

There was a soft knock at my door.

"Hey." It was Will, handing me Mark's clothes from out by the hot tub. "The cops are here, so things are thinning out. How's he?" He nodded at Mark. We could both see the bed vibrating with his chills. "I've got another sleeping bag in my trunk. I'll go get it."

Will and I spread it over Mark, tucking the edges in around him. I went to the bathroom to brush my teeth and Will followed.

"Listen, while you and Nikki were inside, your friend was doing lines with Hammer, and you know his shit is rarely pure, so you probably want to keep an eye on him tonight."

I spat, wiped my mouth with the back of my wrist.

"Thanks."

"Maia," Will started to say something, but I cut him off.

"This," I nodded to our toilet paper roll, which he'd turned into a swan. "Some of your best work yet."

When the cleaning ladies came, they made the toilet paper ends in the house into roses. If Will used the bathroom first, he'd recreate it for me, getting more and more intricate. I'd found the slim book under the counter, *Origami Folding for Beginners*. He blushed.

"Thanks, Will. Really. And for watching Vader the other night while I was sick."

"I would have come and gotten you, just so you know."

"I was really, really sick." I wanted it to be clear, that I wasn't with Joel.

"I know. I would have taken care of you." Will looked down, dispensing toothpaste in a perfect curl on his bamboo brush.

"Thanks." I opened the bathroom door to go back to Mark.

"Anytime," he said quietly, shutting the door behind me.

Vader got up on the bed on one side of Mark, molding himself into the curve of Mark's stomach. Then I took the other side, wrapping around him from the back, my face against his chlorine-wet hair. I didn't let go until his breathing settled into its familiar rattle. Nikki was right; Mark didn't fit into the picture. But they thought I did, and I held on to that.

⌣⟶

"Maia, where's the john? I gotta piss like you wouldn't believe." The bed was soaked in cold sweat. Mark scrambled out from under the tangles of my clothes. I checked my watch. Even if I skipped a shower and Mark drove me, I'd be late for work.

"So, you workin' again today?"

"Yeah. I've gotta hurry."

This conversation, our shorthand, could be happening back at his place, could be us starting any morning together for the past six years, but it was like a chapter from a story I didn't want to read anymore.

"You want, I give you a lift on my way out?"

"That'd be good." I smiled, a thank you for the ride, for understanding he should leave, grateful for not making me say it.

I put Vader out in the backyard, no time for our morning walk, while Mark lifted Nikki's bike into the back of his truck.

We were quiet. It was strange seeing his profile against the mountains, like running into your kindergarten teacher in the grocery store. I gave him the barest of directions.

"So, the old Toyota's running pretty good. I mean, she made it all the ways out here."

I nodded, watching the brown landscape, the scrubby pasture, the poky heads of prairie dogs and the big black cows, go by.

"Not too bad for a truck you plowed into a telephone pole. You'd better not be driving on your suspended license or nothing."

I didn't answer.

"Court date's rescheduled. Twelfth of July."

Two weeks away.

"Okay."

"You need money, for a plane ticket or anything?"

"I owe you already, for paying back Ritchie."

"Fuhgeddaboutit," Mark said like a mobster. "Hey, remember that time we were driving the Toyota up to Times Square for New Year's Eve cause you wanted to see the ball drop and it was that huge fucking snowstorm, and I was just passing all the semis doing like ninety, and you…" He trailed off.

"Yeah, I remember. Yes," I corrected myself.

"Come home with me, Babe," Mark blurted.

"I can't. Not now."

"Why the hell not?"

"Can't you just be happy for me? If you loved me, you'd be happy for me."

"You're seriously trying to tell me you're happy here?"

In the driveway, we passed Joel leaving. Mark had to back up so he could pull out of the skinny driveway, the two staring at each other like Vader and Ben right before they lunged. Joel tried to flag us down, rolling down his window, but I hissed, "Ignore him. Just drive."

There was a long silence, and then Mark said, "It's him, isn't it."

"Him what?" I reached up to itch the back of my neck.

"You're fucking the husband." Mark slammed the dash of his truck for emphasis. This was not intuitive genius; Mark accused me of sleeping with pretty much every guy who looked at me twice.

"No!" I said. Not recently anyway.

"You're lying. Your cheeks always get red when you lie. I bet your hives are back too."

"They're not!" I could feel them creeping up my neck.

"Can't believe I drove two thousand miles for this bullshit. I could lose my job."

"Nobody asked you to come!"

"I'm sick of covering for you. Nick says we should put the whole thing on you if you don't show up for the trial. Make it like the whole thing was your idea. The reason

I came out here, for your information, was to bring you home to clear all this up."

"Me? You two were the idiots pretending to rob the guy!" I felt it inside my throat, the itchy panic I got whenever I thought about my legal problems. I swallowed. Mark was pissed—now he probably wouldn't drive me back to Philly if I got on my knees and begged. That's another thing about him: stubborn.

I reached for the door handle and Mark grabbed my wrist. The bruise from Maurice had faded, but my skin still held the memory. I lunged away from him, wanting to run inside, to Carolyn. To safety.

"You know who I feel sorry for? That dickhead's fat wife, and his kid."

"She's not fat; she's pregnant!"

"God, that's even worse! You're not who you used to be, Maia."

"I'll take that as a compliment." I twisted my arm away from him, opened the door and got out, straightening my shaking shoulders. I hauled Nikki's bike out of the back. In a minute, I'd be inside, safe.

"You know what? You're nothing but a poser now, Maia." Mark reached over, grabbed the door handle. Here it comes, I knew from years of fighting with him: the name-calling.

"A fucking poser-whore, out here trying to use your pretty to fit in with these people, bootlicking and cocksucking the rich!"

With that, he slammed my door, raced down the driveway and peeled out of the cul-de-sac.

Knowing Mark, he repeated that last line out loud to himself all the way to Kansas.

CHAPTER THIRTY-FIVE

Carolyn

Maia arrived shortly after Joel left for work Friday morning, and I showed her the tablet I had been working on for the BBQ, complete with menu, decorations, shopping lists from three different stores, recipes from magazines, Pinterest boards, I'd saved over the years.

"I want to make it classy," I told her. "Not your average Boulder backyard thing. Like an event in the Hamptons, like you'd see in an aspirational lifestyle shoot. Joel's getting ribs and doing his mango guac, and beer, but for hors oeuvres, I've got a menu from an old Martha Stewart entertaining cookbook—I hope there's fresh lobster. Rachel says you can borrow her minivan. I told her what a good driver you are," I paused. "You do have your real license on you today?" Maia nodded, a hand passing across her heart like a pledge, and we shared a smile.

"Good. Then, I need you to go to Sturtz & Copeland. I want to do planters filled with sage and lavender to line the patio, and centerpieces." I showed her the inspiration image. "The works."

"Oh, I could do this with just the stuff in the yard," she leaned in, and I smelled a sourness on her. Weren't those yesterday's clothes? Had she had another crazy night? "Can't we just raid the garage?" she protested, but I insisted, ushering her toward Rachel's van with the credit card from the zippered compartment of my purse.

When Maia came home bearing packages and plants, she found me dusting eighteen barely used ivory pillar candles from our wedding reception. This party would be a celebration, something old and something new.

"What are you doing up? Rearranging the garage? Get back on the couch!"

"I have an appointment with Dr. Michaels on Tuesday," I told her. "I might be allowed to get out of bed. The baby's fine."

We compromised; I sat at the kitchen table with my legs on another chair, peeling shrimp while she worked on the centerpieces. I had given her a list with all native Colorado flowers, golden blanket flower, and the deep violet Rocky Mountain penstemon, spiderwort, harebells, windflower and of course, Columbine.

"And I could trim some of the living sage from the planter boxes for greens," Maia was saying as she arranged them in Mason jars. "And these weren't on the list," she pulled out bunches of Oriental poppies, "but I thought, with the Fourth of July coming, they could be really pretty, add some color?"

"Beautiful!" I agreed; it was just what the arrangements needed. "You know, you're very good at this."

"Will and I've been starting to garden in the backyard. I've been growing some perennials from seeds. I'm sort of blown away by nature. Before this, here, I never really grew anything."

"Where are you, in college?" I asked, realizing I had no idea how old she actually was.

"I'm on a gap year," she said breezily.

"What does that mean for you?" I asked.

Maia's hands were deftly trimming stems and pinching off dead leaves, the kitchen filled with the pungence of sage.

"I have no idea," she confessed, laughing. "But it seems to make everyone out here feel better when I say it. In my old life," she said, "college wasn't really an option."

"You should look into it, horticulture, floral design. You have a gift, and there's lots of money in it, if you do weddings." I wasn't sure why I was encouraging her; the night before I had imagined her staying on, taking care of the children so I could find *my* dreams. Now, something different was taking shape, like cloud patterns: A new dream.

"Well, you're the natural event planner. Look at this." She nodded her head; the lists, the bags of foods waiting to be prepared, the flowers, the planter boxes, and the candles I was tying in trios with raffia. "You could put those whiteboard skills to use."

"My dad says the same thing. Last year he secretly sent me an application to an event planning school near them in Florida."

Maia made a face. "Florida! So many old people!"

"Well, back then, I think he was thinking, if it was ever just me and the kids. In case. He didn't realize there was going to be a Maia."

We both paused what we were doing. I smiled shyly at her. Because of her, I could dream.

"Where should we go?"

"How about California? I've never seen the Pacific Ocean."

"Never?"

Maia shook her head. "This is the farthest west I've been."

"Do you like to road trip?"

"Never really tried one." Maia's head bent over the flowers.

"We drove out here, right after we were married in the U-haul. Joel downloaded the audios of *What Color is Your Parachute* and *The Seven Habits of Highly Effective People.*" I giggled, adding, "Unabridged."

Maia rolled her eyes. "Yeah, if I'd gone back home with Mark, it would have been endless Howard Stern."

"What?" I stopped, my hands in the ice-water bath of shrimp. "You were going to go back with him?"

"Oh, no," she said quickly. "I mean, that's why he was here. He wanted me to. But I'd never leave you in the lurch like that, with the baby coming. I was saying 'if.' Anyway, sure, I'd like to run naked into the Pacific before I die."

"California it is, then." I settled back in my chair.

"California," Maia said, playing along as she tried different placements of the plants for the teak boxes.

"We could grow our own avocadoes and cucumbers for our sushi rolls. And then, we could expand to catering, full-service weddings to the stars."

"And hike up and take pictures of Sasha at the Hollywood sign, with giant sunglasses." Maia went on.

"I hear they have excellent public schools."

Maia looked up and said, "You sound serious."

"Forget public! We'd be making enough with our catering business she could go private, with all the stars' kids! And forget having to be scouted—you'd be spotted at one of our parties, go straight to the big screen, the next Taylor Swift… can you sing?"

"No," Maia's tone downshifted to sober and she focused on her hands. "No more of that."

218

"No more of what?"

"I'm not really interested in that, in modeling, anymore," she said quietly.

The air in the kitchen sparkled, dust particles from the planter dirt, and the rich scents of earth, lavender and sage were swirling around us.

"I—" She took a deep breath. "I'm ready for people to think of me as something more than just the outside."

We looked across the counter at each other, waiting for the other to wave it off, to say we were only joking about the rest.

Maia moved first, picking up the planter boxes to carry them out to the yard. I stopped her.

"Wait," I told her. "I'm serious. This is what I've been thinking," I rushed, "what I wanted to talk to you about. You and me, and this business, flowers and weddings. We could really do it."

"What, seriously? Florida or California?" Maia laughed it off, still not understanding.

"Eventually? Maybe? But to start, you could move in here," I said, softly, so that Sasha wouldn't hear in the next room. I didn't want to get her hopes up; mine were already teetering at the top of the high dive.

Maia put the sage and lavender on the counter.

"Come here." I stood up, motioned for her to follow me, and I threw open the door to the garage. "I know it's nothing to look at now, but it does have two windows, behind all those boxes, and we could insulate it, get some drywall put in, a proper floor, and you could pick any color of paint. I was thinking a celery green would make it seem really light, cheerful."

Maia still hadn't said anything.

"Obviously," I continued, "we'd get rid of all this junk. We've been meaning to anyway, and all that baby stuff in the corner will be coming out any day now."

"I, I have a dog," she said, and my heart soared—she was thinking about it. "A really big dog and—"

"Excellent! I have a fenced yard! Really, you could be a huge help to me, with the kids, with Sasha." I threw a look over my shoulder towards the family room. "You know she adores you, and you're so good with her, you know all the tricks, when to divert, or be stern or tickle and laugh it off. You have no idea how unique that is." I thought of Joel the night before, how listening to him in his trying-hard mode had underscored the easy way Maia was with her.

"I could take a class or two, get out more. Maybe event planning, or interior design, or home staging. And exercise! We could take up Goddess yoga! In the evenings, you could study floral design, or college, or you could work part time at Longs Gardens, or they have that wildflower center at Chautauqua. We could make a list, a five-year plan, with personal and professional goals…."

I trailed off, but she was smiling, I noticed.

"Look." I tugged her hand.

I opened the box from Kemo Sabe I'd hidden from Joel under a Christmas garland, and showed them to her. I'd checked the size of her shoes when she'd left them by the door and ordered us matching pairs from the store in Aspen, the day after the driving lesson: cherry red elk-skin boots, extra tall for her, with fine-contrast turquoise stitching.

"Wow," she breathed. The elk skin was soft, like a baby's cheek, and she stroked it with the backs of her knuckles. "They're beautiful."

"Just a thank you, a little something I ordered the other day," I murmured, leaving out the extra seventy dollars for rush shipping, and then blurted. "I got myself a pair, too; they're upstairs, under the bed. I even got a pair for Sash. But I was thinking, we could call our future business: Two Cowgirls."

"Two Cowgirls," she drawled. "I like it. How about Just Two Cowgirls?"

"And the red boot could be our logo, with some daisies peeking out!"

"You know—" She surveyed the garage. "Celery green might have too much yellow. I'm not a big fan of yellow." She pushed the garage-door opener, flooding the space with natural light. "What would you think about a blue? Do you think a Colorado Columbine blue would be too dark?"

That's where Joel found us, the garage door open to let in the last of the day's sun, six garbage bags already out on the curb, and Maia hauling the baby things into the house.

"You need to be lying down! Sitting on the steps is not bed rest. You can't keep getting up!" he scolded. "You should not let her get up!" He glared at Maia. "What are you two doing out here anyway?"

Maia and I said in unison, "Reorganizing."

"Scheming," Maia added, picking up the bassinet. Joel followed my gaze to where she was carrying the baby bed into the house, her ponytail bouncing, the tiniest smile twisting the corners of her mouth.

"Put that down," he said, too sharply. Adding, to me, "I've got it; I told you I'd take care of everything this weekend. Get back in bed. Maia is going to run an errand with me."

Before they left to buy ribs and drinks from Costco, Maia came back inside to transfer Sasha from her usual clinging hug.

"You'll consider what we talked about?" I asked, a hopeful smile splitting my cheeks.

"As if I could think about anything else."

When she followed Joel out to his car, I was picturing us walking briskly along Pearl Street mall, headed for an important meeting in our matching red cowgirl boots.

CHAPTER THIRTY-SIX

Maia

We weren't even out of the cul-de-sac, our first time alone since I had slipped out from between the white sheets of the hotel bed in Puerto Rico, when Joel started in on me.

"We need to talk."

"Yeah," I agreed. "Yes."

"They say, guys who do this, they say not to get involved with someone who doesn't have at least as much at stake as you do."

I looked out the window to the East where the haze of the wildfire in another town burned, dark gray smoke on the horizon. Joel kept going.

"I thought, in the beginning, those rules didn't apply to us, that we were above all that. I thought we were doing a good job of things, before. Being careful. I remembered to celebrate our anniversary, gave you the necklace, I got the room at the Boulderado, and-and-and then practically the next goddamn day," he slammed his palm into the steering wheel, but not that hard, and I thought of Mark, that morning, their matching little-boy tantrums, "you take a job working for my wife! I mean, what is wrong with this picture?"

It occurred to me then that he might be enjoying all of this, the dramatic scene, and I wondered if the whole reason he'd initiated things had nothing to do with me, and everything to do with the way Joel's boss, his subdivision life, whittled away at him. This realization made me able to sit through his rant without punching his obnoxious, chiseled jaw.

"You're always running away," he continued. "You don't return my calls, you're hanging around with your sporty little mountain biker CU boyfriends who happen to live closer to Boulder than we do, while meanwhile, I'm sweating bullets, wondering what you and she have been doing, talking about all day, worrying about what she knows—"

"What I've been doing all day?" I sputtered. "Exactly what I'm paid to. Picking up your shit. Literally! Washing your dishes and dirty underwear and socks and your dog, doing for your family what you should be doing, pulling your weight! You expect too much of Carolyn! You take her for granted—"

Joel kept going like I hadn't said anything. "So then not only do you put my marriage in jeopardy, but then you show up in the airport and threaten my job."

I took a deep breath and spoke to him like I did to Sasha when she was on the verge of a meltdown. "I don't want to hurt anyone. I would never want to hurt you." There was a long pause, the shh-ing of the tires against the road. I kept going. "When I got on that plane in Philly, it had way more to do with the circumstances of my life than you. I didn't go looking for this."

"You say you didn't want all this, but you never said no."

I never said no. The shaking started in my hands, remembering, *it's not rape, if you don't say no.*

That's when I realized we had missed the turn for Costco.

Where he was taking me?

"You never said no. Not to me, the motel, or the Boulderado, not the necklace or Puerto Rico or all those lunch hours. It sounded more like yes-yes-yes!" He mocked me in bed.

We were on Iris, doing thirty-eight. I put a hand on the door handle, thighs tensed, ready to open it and run at the next light.

It was getting darker, the blue-green glow of the dashboard lights highlighting his profile as he stared straight ahead and said, "I don't want to see you anymore."

I laughed out loud, mostly relief, because he was turning right, towards Juniper Court.

"What's funny?"

"Nothing, just, I'm sorry; are you seriously trying to break up with me?"

He looked flustered, and then in a flash, angry, pulling the car up to the curb behind Beau's Bronco.

"Carolyn goes to the doctor next week, to find out if she can go off bed rest. If he says yes, you're fired. I want you out of our lives, Maia. Gone. Forever."

I got out, slammed the door with a sound that I hoped rang with finality. The sky was metallic gray, and the wind turned the leaves of the tree in the front yard over, showing their yellow undersides.

Inside, I ran downstairs, desperate for a steaming hot shower.

"Hey."

I jumped a mile, surprised to find Will and Beau sitting in the shadows of the TV room, the video game on pause.

"Your phone must be out of battery?" Will said. He and Beau glanced at each other.

"What?" My phone was still back in Puerto Rico, no money to replace it. The shaking in my hands that had started in the car was getting worse. I clamped my arms over each other, clutching at my ribs.

"We've been trying to reach you for an hour, Dude. Will called the place where you babysit, everywhere. Bad news."

"What? Why?" I glanced around, looking for Luke to deliver the final blow, that, like Stan, I was out.

"Okay." To brace myself, I sat down on the arm of the couch, worried about my face, how to arrange it.

"Your sister called. Your mom, she... she tried to commit suicide."

Tried, he had said, and I grabbed on to the one word because I was falling-falling-falling.

"How?" was the first question that came out. I knew when, and I knew why. I wasn't surprised, really. She'd threatened it a thousand times— "I'll end it all! You girls don't care!"

"Overdose, your sister said. Alcohol and pills. She's in a coma."

"And," Beau pulled me into one of his hugs, crushing me against his chest. *Jesus, there's more?* "They think she was without oxygen for a long time, Dude. They don't really expect her, to... make it, or be... normal, or anything, really. If there's anything we can do...." I sunk into him.

Will was right there too, rubbing my back. "I have frequent-flier miles. I can get you a ticket, you can be home tonight."

I shook my head, no, no thanks, as I stumbled toward my room.

For the last few hours, I'd been thinking about a different future, being a part of something good, useful. I had let myself dream of one last new start, California, Carolyn. I couldn't go back.

This is what you get, Maia.

CHAPTER THIRTY-SEVEN

Carolyn

Joel and Maia had just left for the store and I was back on the couch, as though horizontal time was a bankable commodity, something I could make up. In our excitement, I had been up too much that day and it was hard to tell if the pains in my back were dangerous, or the usual aches of the third trimester. Tuesday loomed, my appointment with Dr. Michaels, and his decision. Lots of babies born at thirty-four weeks were just fine. But then, of course, some were not. I ran my hand over the tight mound of my stomach.

The phone rang, Will, one of Maia's housemates, looking for her. An emergency. I said out loud to him, "She's not here. She's out helping my husband pick up some groceries. She should be home in about an hour."

I realized I'd sent the woman I'd originally hired to keep away from my husband because I once suspected an affair, on an errand alone with him, an hour or more unaccounted for. I smiled, noticing it didn't bother me at all, until the doorbell rang.

"Sash," I yelled, hoping she would come down and answer it.

On the third ring, I got off the couch to answer it myself, stunned to see Joel's impeccably groomed boss.

"Carolyn," she said coolly. "Liddy Harbor."

"I know," I said, straightening the maternity top, horrified to notice it sent up little whiffs of garage dust from my scheming with Maia. "We met on the Tokyo trip."

"That's right. It's been a long time." She looked at my belly.

"Joel's out," I said carefully.

"I'm actually not here for Joel. I came to talk to you."

I wrapped my arms around my stomach; I needed something to hold onto.

"Can I come in for a moment? We have a gift, for the baby." We, I wondered, as she glanced back at the open window of her car, where a red-haired boy slouched. "Sam, the present."

"Don't take forever!" he yelled and stuck his arm out the window, dangling a lime-green gift bag.

"Sam," her tone was familiar, warning, Mom voice, but he turned up the volume on the car's radio.

"Come in," I said, pushing the sweat-damp hair off my temples. "Sorry about the mess." I regretted that this would be the one time she would form an impression of my domestic abilities —piles of party prep debris, and all the Rubbermaid baby boxes from the garage spilling out into the foyer. "Tomorrow night, we're hosting a party and my nanny, my helper," I never knew what to call Maia, "is out helping Joel shop."

She cut right to the chase, an unpleasant turn of her mouth before we'd both even sat down on the family room couch.

"I apologize that it has taken such unfortunate circumstances for us to get together, Carolyn."

I knew then that it had nothing to do with the baby gift, the bag still looped over her thin forearm.

"Yakimori doesn't make a habit of interfering in employees' lives. However, on a personal level, Joel's recent error in judgment regarding the conference couldn't be ignored."

Liddy leaned in and laid a hand on my knee. I could smell her stinging perfume prickling my nostrils and making my eyes water.

Still, she said nothing. I was conscious of the spread of my thighs on the couch, the way my belly rested on top of them. I tried to sit up straighter, to erase any wrinkles, create an illusion of togetherness.

"I attended the conference in Puerto Rico with Joel," she said and for a moment, my stomach went into free fall—I thought *she* was confessing an affair, confirming infidelity.

"For the presentation," I said, not understanding. "Didn't everyone?"

"No. It was meant to be the Philadelphia contingent and Joel, but I attended at a last-minute request from upper-level management. Something unfortunate happened, which, as a woman, I couldn't let go." She grimaced earnestly and I could see white in the creases of her crow's-feet—evidence of age, recent sun exposure.

"I'm afraid I don't know what to say." I didn't want to be in my skin at that moment, wondered if we could stop this conversation, an excuse—where was Sasha?—if I could see her to the door before she said any more and it was too late.

"Would it come as a surprise if Joel had shared a room with someone else at the conference? A female companion?"

The apricot and chia granola Maia had made for our breakfast leapt into my throat. I gulped quickly, blinking back tears, face burning.

I shook my head, and she inched closer. I was afraid she was going to try and hug me.

"Let me guess: You thought it was a one-time thing. You thought it wouldn't happen again, am I right?" she said gently.

"Oh," I exhaled, and a tear squeezed out. "I had suspicions, a few months ago, before, but then I was sure I was wrong. I didn't think there were more, another, others...."

Liddy nodded. "There always are," she said, reaching out to rub my shoulder sympathetically. I jerked away.

"Was she—" I started, and then stopped. What did it matter who it was, when at least it wasn't Maia?

Just Two Cowgirls, I thought, picturing us walking in our red boots down a street, this time lined with palm trees, the sun setting over the ocean.

"Tall, thin, blond? They all are," Liddy said. "I'm so sorry," she stood up, handing me the gift bag. "For the baby."

I thanked her but made no attempt to open it in front of her. I didn't want to prolong her presence in my house. I couldn't deny it—Joel had cheated/was cheating on me. Still, I grabbed on to the fact that it wasn't Maia. Maia, who had offered to spend the weekend with me, who had shown up for work that Monday morning Joel was in Puerto Rico. Who was quickly becoming the most integral part of my back-up plan.

I walked Liddy to the door, her heels clicking on our tiled foyer floor, her slacks swishing, and I had a terrifying flash-forward of what my life could be like, juggling resentful children as I re-entered the workforce, alone.

Outside, Liddy's son was shooting glares through the car window, arms crossed, and I saw her deflate, a tiny leak of self-assuredness, a crack in her veneer.

The weather had shifted. It had been dark, threatening a storm when Maia left with Joel. But now a flashbulb-bright sun stabbed through the clouds, painting our suburbia in surreal chrome filter colors.

"Carolyn," Liddy turned to me.

"What?" I said, too sharply, eager for her to leave.

"Nothing, only, if you think, this might be something you could live with, if you love Joel, you might try…" she faltered.

"Might try what?"

"I had to leave the trip early," Liddy's tone shifted to confessional again. "I had taken Sam with me, thinking he, *we* might have fun. But my ex made trouble, with the lawyers, allegations about me taking him without his consent. He doesn't care that Sam and I were starting to have a nice time, that this was an excellent opportunity for him to use some of his Spanish and see his mom as something other than exhausted and overworked. My ex and his girlfriend, they live to make my life miserable. My lawyer told me it would be better to come back, take him to his father's. I've just picked him up from there."

"So he's mad at his dad?"

"Oh, no," Liddy shook her head sadly. "Sam's mad at the whole world."

She paused, glanced at the car again.

"When Rob cheated on me, I thought it was the worst thing that could ever happen."

"What are you saying?"

"I'm saying there are worse things than cheating. There's this," she waved her arm to indicate her hurt, angry son, the closed car vibrating with blaring music. "And there's starting over alone."

BOOK FOUR

CHAPTER THIRTY-EIGHT

Carolyn

The morning of our BBQ dawned gray, with the ashy smell of the distant forest fire. I lay in bed, watching the weather report, and listening to my family. Joel was up with Sasha, still trying hard. Too hard, I thought angrily. The night before, he'd stayed up late, watching a baseball game, and when he came to bed, I'd played my part, feigning sleep, rolling toward the wall. I wasn't ready for the conversation; there was so much more I needed to do first, stacks of lists to write, plans to be made.

I listened as he navigated Sasha through her myriad outfit changes, including her insistence that nothing was allowed to have cap or three-quarter sleeves, contain even label threads with the colors black, brown, green, navy or brick red, and under no circumstances could shirts be "flippy-floppy" or bottoms "slouchy." He fared at least as well as Maia or I could, and I lay there, my stomach sour, wishing that I could unhear what Liddy Harbor had told me the evening before.

Kate, a mother who used to come to our playgroup once talked about how, after Ethan's diagnosis with autism, she'd struggled for months to fall in love with him again, to see him as anything but AUTISM.

"It wasn't anything either of us hadn't known, on a gut level, but now, our son's behavior had a name, this label," she'd said. "I had to learn to love him all over again."

Since Liddy had come to the house, I looked at Joel and saw only, UNFAITH-FUL in such glaring neon that I had to avert my eyes when he brought me toast and strawberries and lukewarm tea with almond milk on a tray in bed.

Then my phone rang, after Joel had disappeared down the hall with the arm-loads of baby items, whistling, jumping into the nursery and party-prep projects with cheery zeal.

"It's me."

"Maia?"

"I can't find anyone," she was saying, high and tinny. "I woke up, and my house is empty, I'm sure they're all just out to breakfast or a bike ride or something, but there's nobody here, and I'm home alone, and—" her voice broke.

"Maia, what's wrong?"

"I don't want to be alone. I'm," she sniffed, a strangled half-laugh. "I'm afraid, of being alone."

"What's happened? Maia? You don't sound like yourself."

Joel appeared in the doorway threading a belt through the loops of his jeans, concern creasing his face and something else: *fear.*

"What's wrong?" I asked her.

"My mom tried to kill herself."

I gasped and Joel practically lunged on top of me.

"I mean, it's not a shock," she sniffed. "She wasn't the healthiest. And we defi-nitely weren't close—" her voice broke again. "The doctors don't think there's any-thing they can do."

"What can I do? Do you need a ride to the airport?"

"No…" her answer answered nothing.

"Do you need money, sweetheart?" I asked her, my eyes hard on Joel's.

"What?" he hissed. "Is that Maia? Give me the phone!"

"No. I'm not going."

"What?"

"I can't," she sobbed, breath catching, so I could barely understand her. "I can't go back."

"You shouldn't be alone. I'm sending Joel over to get you, right now."

"No! Please, no, I'm fine. They should be home soon. Will and Beau know what happened. They were the ones who told me—"

"Joel will be there in ten minutes. We could really use you here; we're getting the nursery ready for the baby, and there's the BBQ tonight, if the weather cooperates. Sasha misses you. Just hang in there ten minutes. He'll be there."

"No! Please."

"You're coming here. You shouldn't be alone right now."

"Well," there was a sniff. "If you think I can be useful to you, if I'm not in the way, I'll just come on my bike, so I can leave, whenever. It would be nice to be busy, with you, and Sash, to take my mind off...." Her voice was smaller than Sasha's. She thanked me and hung up.

Joel waited, hands hanging down his sides, like a man about to be sentenced.

"Maia's mother tried to kill herself. The doctors don't think she'll make it."

"Oh," he sagged against the doorjamb, mumbling, "Awful."

"She shouldn't be alone; she's coming right over."

"She's coming here." He repeated like an idiot. "To our house."

Now, instead of UNFAITHFUL, in the light of day, when I looked at Joel, I saw IT'S OVER. The phrase ran through my head like memorized play lines, a Sunday School recitation. Over and over.

"That's the idea," I said coolly.

Now that I knew, I'd wait for the right moment to let him know that I knew. Soon, not yet. The chilly detachment coursing through me felt like Maia's iced jasmine tea. It smelled like a match-strike, powdered glass and power.

"I talked to my sister again this morning." Maia was peeling potatoes for the rosemary and cucumber potato salad and I sat in the kitchen chair. Her face was blotchy and puffy, her hair in tangles at the back of her neck and her eyes meaty slits; not a pretty crier. There were welts dotting her neck, and red streaks where she had scratched them raw. It was exactly how, back in the early days, I'd wanted her to appear in front of Joel. But he'd barely looked at her, passing through for more bins of baby items, then retreated to Home Depot. I knew, from the weeks of crying after the miscarriage, that women in distress made him uncomfortable.

"Scarlett said there's no brain activity, that doctors say it would be a blessing," Maia's voice cracked. "If she just... went."

I wanted to make Maia a cool compress for her neck, lay some of the crisp cucumbers I was slicing over her swollen eyes, but she was anxious to move, keep busy.

"It's not like we didn't expect it." Maia sniffed a sob. "But it's still hard. She's only forty."

I nearly dropped my knife; her mother was only forty? Nine years away. I wanted to hold her, like Sasha, on my lap.

"You should be there, for your sister, at least." I inhaled the distinctive scent of fresh cucumbers. It smelled like spring, rain, possibility. She shook her head.

"There's nothing I can do. And I feel like, anyway, maybe you need me here more?"

I didn't disagree. My mind flitted back to Liddy Harbor's news, the confrontation with Joel brewing along with the thunderstorm. But was it fair? Could I keep her, tether our lives together, simply because my world was about to collapse?

"God," Maia looked out the window. "It's so cloudy out, a bad storm. It doesn't feel like summer at all."

"The sky looks like pewter, doesn't it?"

"That's Boulder weather; unpredictable."

"You're starting to talk like one of us," I teased, and she tried to smile.

The thunk of my chef's knife on the cutting board was a heavy metronome keeping time to her sniffs.

"After the guys told me, I just fell asleep, like I'd been hit in the head. There's been a lot, going on, recently, and I haven't been sleeping that well, but last night…" Maia rinsed the peeled potatoes in a bowl of water, sliding them around with her hands like a slippery bath baby. Inside me, my unborn son mimicked their motion, rolling, and I had a surge of love and protectiveness for him, for her. "I slept like a rock, no bad dreams, nothing, until this morning. First, I called Scarlett. Then, next, I called you. Thank you, for answering. For letting me come here."

"Of course. When will you go?" I pictured her staying in Philadelphia, swept up in the arranging of things, emptying a house, erasing a life. Nobody to help me after I told Joel that I knew, and everything dissolved. The inevitable—*it's over.*

"I don't know. How could I?"

"What do you mean?"

"You! The baby… You need me here," she said again, and I saw us, loading the car, buckling Sasha in, driving toward the setting sun. "I mean, I hope you do?"

"Of course I do! I want you to stay, but what about your family?"

Maia wiped her nose on her bare wrist. "My Aunt Rainy's driving down from Buffalo, but that's pretty much it, for our family. My sister will stay in the house, after… There's not really anything to do."

"But wouldn't you regret not going?" I couldn't imagine a family without the net of support my parents had always been, no matter what. Even for all of Judith's prickliness and hard edges, my parents loved and supported me. I hadn't realized exactly how isolated Maia was.

"I won't leave you in the lurch that way, with the baby coming." She lifted the hem of her baggy T-shirt to wipe her face, and I saw again those beautiful planes of her stomach, the perfect, taut oval of her bellybutton, like a bathing-suit ad. I looked away, more concerned about the ache inside her than the body that housed it. "Besides, I can't exactly go back to Philly. Not right now."

"What do you mean?"

"It's… complicated." Maia's lips were a tight, sour line.

Upstairs, Joel and Sasha had emptied the spare bedroom, relocating our home office to a corner of the family room, filling garbage bags on the curb, folding the futon back into a couch.

"We should have a baby more often," Joel said cheerfully as Maia and I surveyed the room. "We never throw this much stuff out." As he passed with the last bag of trash, he tapped me gently on the bottom and I jerked away. His mood and enthusiasm for the nursery was all very touching and it would have been lovely, if it hadn't felt staged, so over-the-top, if Liddy Harbor hadn't come by the day before. I could hardly stand to look at him.

It's over.

Maia walked the perimeter of the room with Sasha on her back. The clouds were still hanging heavy and pendulous with rain, making the corners of the room shadowy at midday.

"Honey," Joel stuck his head around the corner. "It's looking pretty questionable for tonight."

I shrugged; Jackie and Rachel coming over was so far down on my list of concerns.

"Oh, and I can't find the baby swing."

"It's in the corner of the garage, behind the Christmas boxes. The hardware should be taped to one of the handles in a Ziploc bag."

Joel shook his head. "How do you remember things like that?"

"It's my job," I said, without irony. I was off balance with Joel's new warmth, his affection. Too late, I thought.

Sasha turned to Maia and put her hands very solemnly on either side of her cheeks. "I know you're sad today, but I want you to be happy, even though I'm downstairs helping my Daddy."

"Okay. Thank you." Maia smiled, her eyes shining after her as she left. "She's amazing," she whispered. "How does she know that? Like how can she see straight into my heart?"

I lay down on the carpet while Maia unpacked newborn baby clothes from bins and hung them in the closet.

"Of course she's learned her kindness from you. It must make you really proud to be such a good mom."

"It's the thing I am most afraid to fail at."

"Yeah." Maia held up the tiniest onesie, shook her head over the size. She heaved a shaky sigh. "I mean, yes. I'm never having kids."

"I thought that once too. Things change." We sat side by side in the darkening room as clouds rolled in, folding tiny undershirts and matching rolls of socks the size of fat strawberries. How could I explain the obsession that had grown from a murmur to a roar, that had made me throw whole prescriptions of birth control out the window?

"What do you mean?"

"The summer I was seventeen, my boyfriend, Alex, was a lifeguard at the local pool and I was responsible for a baby, a little boy. His name was Matthew. He died."

I couldn't believe I'd said it. All those years of imagining I'd tell someone—Joel, of course—the secret lodged in my throat like a sharp, quartered apple. Now it slipped out easily. I had thought the first time I said it out loud there would be thunder and horror, that the truth would balloon up like a mushroom cloud and fill the room. But there wasn't.

"What?" Maia's eyes widened so I could see the whites clearly in the ominous gray light. But her one gentle word carried no judgment.

I kept going. "I was babysitting, a summer job, a cautious older couple's only child. It was an accident. Stupid—I was worried Alex was flirting with this sophomore from the pool's snack bar. So I badgered them into letting me take the baby. I told them how much he'd love it, how important socialization was. I reminded them how much he loved his bath. Finally, they agreed. We stayed the whole day, and we were late, leaving the pool."

We'd spent the day in the shade of Alex's lifeguard stand. I had to hurry, throwing all the piles of baby stuff into the bag Mrs. Stein had packed, rolling up the towel while Alex held Matty and let him drool all over the whistle hanging around his neck.

"This was fun," I said.

"Yeah. So you think they'll let you come again tomorrow?" he said.

The Steins, Matthew's parents, were my best friend Holly's aunt and uncle. She'd gotten me the job watching her little cousin, easy summer work, if a little boring.

"I'll tell them what a great day we had." I checked my watch. "Shoot. There's no way I'm going to beat Mrs. Stein home, and I haven't done any of the housecleaning on her list."

Alex handed me back the baby. "I'll walk you out."

I loved the way the sophomores who worked the snack bar looked at the three of us, me and Alex and Matty. Geometry—drawing lines between the points of a triangle with their eyes, looking for answers to genetic questions. They whispered into each other's lemon-juiced hair, "Who's she? Is that his girlfriend? Is the baby theirs?"

All day, I had been playing grown-up house, thrilled at pretending Alex was Matty's father, I his flat-stomached young mother.

The parking lot reeked of baking tar, and Matty fussed while I buckled him in. Tired, too much sun, probably hungry.

"Come on, Buddy," I said, kissing his scalp, inhaling the scent of baby and sunscreen and chlorine. I was usually great at calming him down. "Hang in there." But he screamed louder. I fumbled for his pacifier.

"Ugh," Alex groaned. "Enjoy that the whole car ride. I've got to get back." I was still in my two-piece, no time to change, struggling to get the pacifier in, my butt and legs sticking out of the car. Alex snapped the waistband of my bikini bottom, slid his hand possessively over me.

"Quit!" I laughed, flushing.

"See you tonight, 'kay?"

We had plans, Alex, me, Holly, who we were trying to set up with another lifeguard from the pool.

"Okay." I got in and started the car, checking Alex walking away from me in the rearview mirror, worrying a little that he hadn't actually kissed me goodbye. The radio was blaring and poor Matty was screaming louder than I'd ever heard him—definitely too much sun.

I waved and honked as I passed the chain link fence around the swim club, trying to get Alex's attention. My head was pounding with the combined noise of screaming baby and the Wilson sisters. I reached for the radio volume, making a last-minute decision to take a shortcut on Lincoln, jerked the wheel to turn left across Water Street, and I heard, above Matty's wails, the screech of tires, before I felt the slam of impact.

My head cracked the side window, my right knee jammed into the steering column, the sickening sound of metal crunching and glass raining down on pavement.

I'm alive, I thought, because in the silence that followed, I could hear crows on the telephone wire directly above my open sunroof.

"Oh," there was a moan, too close, practically in my passenger seat, the grill of a van. The driver picked his head up off the steering wheel, blood running down his cheek. Our eyes met.

"I tried to stop," he said. "I couldn't stop—you turned right in front of me."

"I'm sorry," I started to cry.

"Are you hurt, Miss?"

"No. I'm okay," I sobbed, but my head and knee were on fire. I just meant that I wasn't dead. The air around us was strangely still, heavy with humidity and oil fumes. I wondered if Alex had heard the accident, if he'd come running. I wanted him, someone, to come and lift me up, get me out of this. Alex, or my father.

"I'm sorry," I sobbed harder, because I knew. It was too quiet.

Another car stopped and a man ran to us, leaving his door gaping open in the middle of the street. He stuck himself into the tangle between me and the other driver, breaking the intimate space with his barking words.

"What happened? Is everyone okay? My wife is calling for help."

Relief passed over his face when the van driver, dabbing at the cut on his forehead, answered for us, a tentative, grandfatherly smile at my sobs.

"Shook up, bruised, but I think we're both going to be okay."

Then the man went white, backing away from the car, one hand snaking to cover his mouth three seconds before he vomited.

"Oh, God," he whispered. "Oh, God, there was a baby in the back."

"It was one hundred percent my fault. Matthew was in the back, in his car seat. His neck snapped." I spared her describing the visual I would never be able to unsee, that no amount of punishing running miles or fistfuls of chocolate would erase. "He died on impact."

"Oh!" Maia gasped. "How awful!" She reached across to lay her hand on my knee. "Oh, Carolyn, I mean, how awful for you."

"For me? For them! They never had another baby. He was their only…"

"Of course, how horrible for them. But, for you, the responsibility, the weight—" she seemed to think better of her choice of words, stopped. The weight. It was on me, all right. "But that was an accident. You didn't do it on purpose. You're the most careful, caring—"

"It was still my fault! Afterward, I was so afraid," I said, shakily, to drive, to eat, to love… "To become a mother. Everything that happened since then, it's been my punishment. I deserve all of it."

"You don't."

How were we both crying? She crawled across the floor and wrapped her arms around my shoulders.

"Shhh," she whispered. "You don't deserve anything bad. It wasn't your fault."

I tilted my face into her neck.

"Is that what happened, to Alex?"

I nodded. "I lost him, after that, and Holly, my best friend. Matty was her little cousin. It was more than any of us were prepared to deal with."

"Oh, Carolyn."

I'd said it out loud, and the phrase of the day came back to me again, in a new way, *it's over.*

Over.

Sasha appeared in the doorway then, her white-blond hair framing her elfin face, standing out with static from the coming storm. I felt a surge of love for her, held out my hand. What would happen if I confronted Joel, if everything changed? I pictured Liddy's sullen son, angry at the world. I needed to do better, be better. More energetic, more present, more fun, more like… Maia.

I wanted, I needed her to stay; I still had more to learn.

"Daddy says to ask should he wash the crib?"

Sasha wriggled her hand out of mine and folded herself into Maia's smooth, criss-crossed legs. Maia's hands twisted her wispy hair, making tiny braids down the side. Sasha batted her away, then gave her a quick kiss.

"Tell him it's his call, but I don't remember it being very dirty."

"Okay." Sasha's face pinched with the concentration of memorizing the message.

"And then, after all that," I told her when Sasha was gone, the secrets tumbling out. "I lost our first baby."

"A boy," she said, and I realized it wasn't a question.

Like she knew.

Like someone had told her?

I paused.

"Yes. I lost him in an airplane bathroom, flying back from Tokyo. I was almost five months along and we'd just had an ultrasound the week before, where we found out it was a boy. Joel was so excited. The baby, he must have died soon after." Dr. Michaels had told me this, since the baby was delivered not whole, but in crippling cramps and clots, flushed as nothing but heartbreaking pieces of grayish matter…

"It was my punishment, for Matty."

"Oh, Carolyn, no," she murmured. "It wasn't your fault."

"I was driving!" How could she forgive me, as quickly as one of the fast-moving silver clouds passed by the window behind her?

"So, were you relieved, then? When you had the miscarriage?"

"What?" I looked up, surprised.

"Weren't you? After what you said, your worries about being a good mom? Wasn't it like, a relief?"

"Oh. No," I said slowly, realizing the truth as I spoke it. "I never thought of it that way. Once I was pregnant, even the first time, I stopped worrying about whether or not I could be trusted with a child. Something changed, the Mother Switch. I knew I was going to do whatever it took to be the mother my child deserved. I'll do anything for my family. It's my job," I said again. "I didn't worry about me anymore; I worried, I suppose I still worry, about the *world*."

Maia knelt silent, the piles of folded baby laundry around her like a child's fortress.

"Thank you."

It was so quiet I barely heard her.

"Pardon me?"

"Thank you for telling me this, today. And for saying all that. You give me a tiny bit of hope." She was crying, her head bowed, her hands tucked between her knees like a little girl. "It gives me hope, maybe, someday, for me. Maybe one day, I could be a good mother too."

"I've come to realize," I told her, "that being still, being frozen by fear, it doesn't keep you safe."

Maia was quiet for a moment, then she said, "Neither does constantly moving."

On the floor between us, my phone rang. A male voice asked for Maia.

We shared a look as she took the phone from me, nodding. I reached for her hand and wrapped my fingers around it.

"I'm here," I mouthed.

"Okay, thank you for calling, for telling me," she repeated, robotic.

She pushed the phone against her breasts. "It's Will. My sister called him. She says they've unplugged the machine. They say it won't be long."

"It's a blessing," I told her. "I know you don't feel it now, but it's a blessing that it's going to be over soon."

Maia nodded, wiping the meaty crescents of her swollen eyes.

"Stay," I told her. "Please, tonight." *For good.*

"I…" Maia paused.

Jackie and Rachel would give me grief, treating Maia like a friend, inviting her to our party. I didn't care. I squeezed her hand.

"Please. For as long as you like."

"Will?" She tucked the phone back to her ear. "I'm staying here, for dinner, and a…a bit… I'll come home, get changed and let him out… Thank you, for everything." She looked at me thoughtfully after she hung up.

"You know how when you worry for a long time that something horrible is going to happen, when it finally does, the best part of the worst news is that you're not waiting for it anymore?"

I nodded; I did. Liddy Harbor had taken care of that.

CHAPTER THIRTY-NINE

Maia

Being at Carolyn's the day my mother died was the right place for me to be. I wanted to help her, in so many ways, especially after she told me about what happened when she was babysitting. It made so many things clear—and it made it that much more meaningful that she trusted me every day with Sasha.

I know she did it for me too, to take my mind off what was happening in Philadelphia.

Plus it was good to have the work of getting everything perfect. While I didn't really like her friends, this party was obviously important to her. We got the nursery mostly set up and the yard prepped, but the weather looked like it had other plans. I had to put the centerpieces out early to keep the tablecloths from blowing in the dusty wind that was screaming across the plains, clouds curling like a time-lapse video, coming our way. We kept the weather channel on all day; the local forecasters talked nonstop about lightning, the conditions perfect for another wildfire.

Please, I thought simply, looking up at the clouds' underbellies before I went inside. I'm not a pray-er, couldn't figure out how to put into words all the things I was asking for. An easy, painless passing for my mother; even after everything, she was still my mother. For Carolyn to forgive herself. For things to go well for her that night. I even prayed about red cowgirl boots, a new chapter: a better future for all of us.

At four-thirty, I was erasing heel marks from an old Sasha tantrum from the stairwell when Carolyn came out of their bedroom wearing a black cotton maxi-dress, barefoot, with her blond hair in a thick braid and simple turquoise beads around her neck.

"Is this too much, for a summer dinner party?"

"No! You look incredible. Sash, come see how gorgeous Mommy looks!"

"You're still cleaning?" Carolyn blushed, wrapping an arm around Sasha who came out stark naked to gawk at her mother. "Get out of here, go home, get dressed up. I have a no-sweatpants dress code. Put on something pretty. You can take Joel's car."

I took the keys, following Carolyn deeper into a game of make-believe that was feeling more hopeful and dangerous than anything I'd done yet.

Sasha whooped, "Cinderella's going to the ball!"

I had to park a block from the house. I could hear the pulse of the bass, the party noise all the way out at the street. Inside, I found Vader curled up on the living room sofa, his legs tucked under his body, hiding out from the chaos of the backyard. The heavy sky made it feel later than five o'clock, and I could tell that they'd started early.

He followed me downstairs, where I twisted my hair into a French knot and dressed in the only fancy things I owned: the now-strapless Buffalo Exchange dress, the Chinese dragon shoes, and finally, to top it off, the necklace with the diamond. My license wouldn't fit under the tight fabric of the dress, so I slipped it into my purse.

Upstairs, a red-eyed and bare-chested Luke was playing DJ, flipping through records with drunk-clumsy fingers, the headphones dangling around his neck. The speakers were against the screens, blasting Radiohead and Marley mixed to the backyard, where people clustered around the keg and soaked in the bubbling hot tub. Behind them, the clouds were so dark they were purple, blowing in swirls from the east.

"DJ EPOCH in da house!" he yelled when he saw me. I ignored him. For the first time since coming to Boulder, I wished I lived alone.

"Whazzup?" he yelled, a bad imitation of the boys who live in the kind of neighborhoods where he would lock the doors of his Range Rover if he accidentally ended up there trying to score coke. "Wildfire party—it's coming! Get out while you can!"

The TV was on the same as Carolyn's, The Weather Channel, but muted, constant coverage of a second wildfire burning in the foothills.

"What? Not talking to me?" He left his DJ station, coming toward me.

"No," I said neutrally, searching the fridge for one of Beau's kombucha brews.

"Not wanting me?" He was close enough the hairs on my arms stood up.

"You know what, Luke?" I straightened up, embarrassed by the way my voice shook. "Not everyone is charmed by you. Not every woman wants to have sex with you." I slammed the fridge door, shoving him with my shoulder to get past. Touching him made my hives prickle. How had I ever found him remotely attractive?

"Ooh! She likes it rough! Maybe you want to go back with your carpet-muncher from Vitality, is that it? You miss Jenn, all those things only a woman can do?"

Luke took his arm from the wall, sliding both around my waist, locking me in. I tensed, swallowing my panic.

"Luke." I tried to shrug him off. I could feel his beer breath against my neck. "Get off me."

"Come on, Maia." He slid one hand meaningfully up over my stomach, ground against me so that I could feel the growing bulge of him against me. "Look at you, looking like this, bam-pow, this dress, this body. Let's make up, okay? Kiss and make up." He tightened his arms around my waist.

"Luke, get off me!" I braced my hands against the door of the fridge and tried to buck him off. "Please, let me go."

"Maia," he crooned as I twisted inside his grip, "why you always so mean to me, huh?"

The hives were making my scalp crawl and my breath tight in my throat.

He wouldn't hurt me, right?

"Didn't I tell you my father has connections in Philadelphia, or how do you say it, Philly?" He mocked the accent, a bad cross between Jersey Shore reruns and Rocky. "It's not that hard, Maia Jane Kramer of 962 Shackamaxon, wanted in the state of Pennsylvania for hit and run, breaking parole—"

Panic, a sickening flutter in my stomach like the buzz of the fluorescent lights in the holding cell. Flashes of Ed, of Homer, of Maurice, of everyone who took what they wanted, who treated me like the outside, the body. He wasn't going to let me go. I pushed back against him.

"Maybe I'm not old enough for you, Maia, is that it? Not Joe Cubicle Corporate enough?"

I glanced around, everyone outside. I realized that before Luke left his turntables, he'd turned the music up extra loud to the outdoor speakers—the baseline hummed, trapped in my breastbone. Nobody in the yard would be able to hear me.

"It's not that hard, to find this sort of thing out. But this," Luke rotated his hips, grinding into me, "is hard. Whaddabout the closet? You liked me all up in here."

Against the thin fabric of the dress, he pushed his fingers against me, and slid them higher, groping my chest.

"Where is it? I know you've always got it tucked up in here—"

"Getoffme-getoffme-getoffme!"

Thank god Will appeared at the sliding glass door, a red Solo cup slipping from his hand. His beer bubbled as it soaked into the carpet and Will's empty hands closed into a fist.

"Will!" I called, hysteria rising in my throat. "Help! Please! Get him off me!"

Luke immediately dropped his arms, half-fell into the counter behind him, grinning. Wrapping my arms around my own waist to stop the shaking, I backed closer to Will.

"Get off me!" I screamed, my breath coming like torn sheets, ragged.

"He is," Will said, his hand light on my shoulder. "He is off you."

"GET OFF ME!" It was still coming out of me, a scream that raked open my throat, scaring us all. "GET OFF ME!"

"Maia," Will said gently.

"Asshole," I spat. "Drunk asshole."

"Always such a bitch," Luke chuckled. "Ain't she a lying, hiding, sneaky little bitch?"

"Shut up, man." Will bent to pick up his cup.

"Or is it that I'm not *married* enough for you? Or wait, I forgot, you like those skinny-ass hockey hair headbangers from Phil-lee too, don'tcha?"

Luke lurched towards the fridge, pulled out another beer.

Heading for the door, I held up one hand to show I wasn't talking to him, breath tight in my chest. I had to get out of there.

At the last minute, Luke lunged and caught me around the waist again, and I spun, arms flailing, hitting him anywhere I could.

"Hey!" Will yelled. Luke staggered back and I stopped. He stood there, a smirk on his face to show how little my fists had hurt him.

"Why don't you fuck off?" I screamed, but the way everyone abused that word in the house, it didn't have the weight I wanted.

"Hey, I was trying to!" Luke looked to Will for confirmation and got none.

I opened the door, so grateful Carolyn and I had a plan, that I had somewhere else to go.

I didn't get far. Will followed me out the front door, glancing up at the clouds over Juniper Court. In the distance, thunder rumbled.

"Maia, wait! I can give you a ride. You shouldn't ride your bike in—" He stopped and I wasn't sure if he meant the dress and heels, or the coming storm.

"I have their car." I stopped, my hand on the handle of Joel's Audi.

"I'm sorry." Will caught up with me. Behind him, the storm light was iridescent on the mountains. "For your mom, yesterday, for today, Luke… You deserve better, than all of this."

I sighed, sagged against the car, not sure how to answer him. Anxious, my fingers zinged the diamond around my neck along its chain.

"I'm so over the scene here," Will continued. "Beau told me Hammer's on his way over with a whole freaking pharmacy."

"Great," I said flatly. Across the street, the Dennenbergs were bringing in Shelby's tricycle. Sasha's age, she trailed behind them, carrying yard toys into the garage. The wind whistled, blowing tumbleweed down the cul-de-sac. They waved, Shelby calling out a high-pitched hello.

"Luke's getting in over his head; he doesn't know when to quit," Will said, waving back at Mr. Dennenberg. "It was like this here last summer too. Luke gets crazy when he can't ski, keeps upping the chemical ante. School starts up again, a little snow falls in A-basin, and things should settle down. Thank god Beau has Nikki, or he'd be up to his eyeballs like last year."

"What about you?"

"Me?" Will sputtered. "Are you kidding me? I can't waste my money on that junk. My dad's almost finished with the Porsche. You know much car insurance costs for a twenty-five-year-old single guy with two hundred and fifty ponies ready to run under the hood?"

I nodded, checked my phone. I needed to get back and help Carolyn move the party inside.

Will cleared his throat. "Maia, I have to tell you something."

I thought I knew what it was, that he was going to finally come out and say the unspoken.

"What?" I said softly, because it wasn't the time for this. Not now.

Will deserved better than me.

"Earlier, I was the only one home. A police officer came by, looking for you."

Oh. They came back in a flood, a hot bloom of neck hives.

"I told him you were out; he seemed nice enough, said he had some questions. He left me his card."

Will reached into his pocket, pressed it into my hand: Dean White.

"I've got to go," I told Will, and I drove too fast out of town, headed east, directly into the storm.

CHAPTER FORTY

Carolyn

In the sharp, ultraviolet evening light, before the first guests arrived—the calm before the storm—the backyard looked perfect: the distressed wood planter boxes of sage and lavender, the weeded and mulched perimeter beds with dahlias and marigolds to match the house trim, and the three covered tables with Maia's wildflower centerpieces all lit in finger-shafts of tangerine sunlight through the billowing clouds.

Joel came up behind me, his hands warm and cupping my shoulders. "We've pulled it off, Mrs. Carter; an amazing-looking party."

I stepped away.

It's over.

Later, after the party, I would tell him.

"It's a shame to bring it all inside but I think Mother Nature's going to have her way here in about twelve," he surveyed the coming storm, "fifteen minutes."

He went to put music on, a Miles Davis CD, instructing me to lie down and he'd get everything moved inside, wheel the grill under the overhang so the ribs could finish slow-cooking. I watched him, palming Sasha's head as she darted past in Mardi Gras beads and a feather boa. He had a faint smile on his face, whistling along with the music.

Rachel, Jackie and Russ arrived together; the girls squealing and disappearing with Sasha to the room Maia had cleaned in preparation for their play.

Rachel kissed me breezily, Cedar in the sling around her neck pressed between us, and I smelled the nostalgic perfume of milky baby breath, the familiar waxiness of nursing cream.

"Dean's on duty till nine, but he'll be here as soon as he can," she said.

"And he's bringing it," Jackie said, arching her painted dark eyebrows meaningfully.

"Bringing what?" Russ wanted to know as he set up their margarita machine on the counter.

"Nothing," Jackie assured him, "just some very interesting sleuthing."

I pretended not to hear her, headed for the couch. What did it matter? I knew Maia. I knew there were things that people had to do sometimes, when taken advantage of, that didn't have anything to do with who they were in their soul.

"As usual, your house looks amazing. I don't know how you do it, on bed rest no less."

"It's Maia," I said, but they drowned me out, gushing about the spread of food she'd laid out in the kitchen before heading home to change.

"Shouldn't you be lying down?" Rachel moved me toward the family room. "Let's let the boys take care of everything."

Joel uncorked wine and I saw their approving looks as he brushed their cheeks with his lips, imagined the honeysuckle smell, my shampoo, on his damp hair. They were talking weather, the potential for evacuation, if the lightning came before the rain.

He peeked into the sling at Cedar and said something that made Rachel beam.

I wondered if I had it in me to change the course of everything.

"Sooo," Jackie followed me to the family room, "Just out of curiosity, your Maia spells her name with an I, do you know that?"

"I think so? I don't know. What does it matter?"

"Where *is* the nanny tonight?"

"Actually, she's coming to the party. As a guest," I said carefully. "As my friend."

"Are you insane?" Jackie pounced. "Maia's coming here? As your friend? Before you've even looked at what Dean has? Her name's not Maia McHugh, but there is a M-A-I-A Kramer who looks exactly like her who has a criminal record in Philadelphia! You don't know anything about her!"

But I did. I knew I had barely slept the night before, Liddy's words, the open windows carrying the smell of Maia's lavender and sage arrangements, Joel's falsely innocent breathing beside me, the baby inside me. I'd been imagining options, a future for the four of us. Something different, something unique. California, Just Two Cowgirls. *Why not us?*

With that, the front door opened.

It was Maia, all six feet of her, in black platform heels embroidered with dragons, and a skin-tight strapless black dress. Behind her, I saw the first silver drops of rain, like pendulous pomegranate seeds.

"Whew," she said crossing toward us, her heels echoing on the tiled floor, shaking out her rain-sprinkled hair. "I just made it."

Then, in the light from the foyer chandelier, I saw it. Nestled just below the knobs of her perfectly angular collarbones, flanked by a cluster of red hives: what looked exactly like the gold choker with diamond solitaire Joel had tried to give me after Sasha was born, the one that wouldn't fasten around my thickened neck.

I jumped up so quickly my knees rattled the coffee table, jangling Jackie's margarita.

"What's wrong?" Maia was right there, concerned. "Are you okay?"

"Sit down," Rachel said, thinking I was worried about the weather. "The boys are handling it." Outside the family room picture window, we could see Joel and Russ dashing about in the pelting rain, wheeling the stainless-steel grill, hisses of steam coming off it.

"Typical cavemen," Rachel laughed. "Saving the meat first." As if I was still worried about a dinner party, a few drops of rain.

Behind them, Maia's centerpieces wilted in the rain and a whipping wind knocked two of them over.

"I—" I faltered. "I need to go upstairs."

I took the stairs faster than I had in nearly six months, two at a time, past Sasha's room where the three girls were huddled under the fresh lavender and ribbon sheet tent Sasha and Maia had made that afternoon. Nausea swirled in my stomach.

In the master bedroom, I dug through my jewelry box, trying to remember if I'd put it there, or in the fireproof safe box in our cluttered garage. It wasn't a necklace I'd even liked, a too-short gold chain with a gaudy diamond. I'd never worn it, never even tried it on again after it didn't fasten that first time, when I was so bloated from Sasha. But, I realized wherever it was, it wasn't here.

I stumbled backwards to the bed, one hand cradling the baby, trying to lift him up. I wanted to check the garage safe, desperate for an answer, but it was the middle of a BBQ being blown apart by an electrical storm. Now what?

At best, she was a thief. When had she taken it—the night of the food poisoning when I nursed her back to health? During our afternoon teas, when I was in the bathroom? But if she stole it, why would she wear it to our home?

The other possibility was a thousand times worse: *someone from this house had given it to her.*

Questions swirled, a rain bordering on hail pounded against the glass, and over it all, I heard a gentle knock on the door. I realized there was nobody in my house that I wanted to see right then.

"Hey." It was Maia. "Are you okay?"

I sank into the bed, gasping. It was definitely my necklace, glowing gold against her flaming neck.

"Is it the baby?" she asked, anxious.

I folded in half, wrapping my arms around the baby inside me, thinking the only thing I knew for sure is that I was here for him and Sasha.

The bedroom door whooshed opened again: Joel. His eyes met Maia's, traveled the length of her.

"What are you doing here?"

"Carolyn invited me. I think there's something wrong with her, maybe the baby."

I opened my mouth; no sound came out.

He shoved past her to the same dresser where I had just been rummaging.

"Where in god's name is it?" he yelled. By his side, I saw papers, a torn envelope in his hand. The earlier Joel—solicitous Joel—was gone.

"Where's what?" Maia asked, but he wasn't talking to her, and then I knew:

I knew exactly what he was looking for.

Joel was looking at me as though we were the only people in the room. Water dripped off his bangs, that sharply beautiful face I had once fallen in love with.

"Where is it?" He grabbed for my purse, sitting on the bedside table. He wasn't looking for the necklace.

In a matter of seconds, everything would be over. What had Maia said, about the best part of the worst things happening meaning you're not waiting for them anymore?

"Where is the goddamn Visa Platinum," Joel roared, "that you opened in MY NAME!"

My hands shook, but I thought: he's not going to find it there. Oh, no, he wouldn't.

It's over.

Joel shook the papers in his hand so hard they snapped. "I went in the garage to get a tarp, for the grill, and I find this in the trash," he read aloud. "Eight thousand dollars! What the hell is wrong with you? Again? Where is the goddamn card?"

The matching red elk-skin cowgirl boots from Kemo Sabe had been expensive, over a thousand dollars a pair, but I had planned for them to be our signature. I'd gotten little ones for Sasha, and a pair for the baby, too—a uniform for our new life.

But it was the three plane tickets to Los Angeles, for me and Sasha and Maia, purchased at two thirty that morning, that pushed it to the limit.

He dumped my purse on the bed. The card wasn't there.

CHAPTER FORTY-ONE

Maia

I watched them, Joel towering over her, screaming at his wife, and something in me shifted. Enough was enough.

I would not let him hurt her.

He pulled up the account on his phone and railed through the charges like a failing report card.

"April 17—$242 dollars at Target!" he raged. She said nothing.

I stepped closer to Joel. "I—" my voice broke, "I needed some clothes, when I first got here. I guess I went a little overboard."

He didn't even glance in my direction.

"April 19—$352 at Alfalfas—what is that?"

"I was hungry," I continued. "I'd just moved out here. Big grocery shop, for me and Jenn, and Rose, her girlfriend. You know."

Joel turned his head. I had his attention. The girls I used to talk about from Vitality, on our way to the motel.

"May 12, 15, 17, more in June—Moon Gate Sushi, there's a couple hundred dollars."

"I love their sushi rolls," I said evenly. "You know how I love my veggie sushi."

I watched tears running down Carolyn's face. She opened her mouth but still nothing came out.

"May 19—Target again for god knows what, $612."

It had been the new car seat for Sasha, for after the baby came. I'd teased her about it when Carolyn sent me to pick it up, that it cost more than my sister's boyfriend's car, a Barcalounger of a seat, big enough for me to ride in.

"May 31—another three hundred at Target, and Whole Foods."

It was the playgroup prep, groceries and juice boxes, sidewalk chalk and Play-Doh. I remembered Carolyn handing me the card, telling me to sign her name.

"I think me and the boys may have had a party that weekend. I might have gotten some patio furniture for the guys at Juniper Court. Me and Will have been trying to dress up the yard."

Joel finally turned to face me.

"You? You did this?"

I nodded, swallowing.

"You opened up a credit card, in my name, and ran up the balance?"

"I did."

His eyes scanned his phone.

"You ordered three hundred dollars from Whole Foods Delivery, on June 14?"

The day was burned into my brain—Puerto Rico, Maurice.

The day I didn't say no. The day I vowed would be the last time I let anyone use my body like nothing.

"Yes." I told him, tossing my chin in the air. Everything in me dared him to say more. He couldn't deny that I had done this, without admitting we had been together that day.

"But you were—" he faltered.

"June 14, best day of my life. We had a huge party, at Juniper Court. Beer pong, skinny dipping in the hot tub. I think maybe you were out of town, Puerto Rico or something?"

Carolyn said nothing. Joel turned back to his phone, but with less fire.

"And what the hell is Kemo Sabe? In Aspen? What did you buy there," his eyes scanned, "four days ago?"

"A dream catcher, for Sasha's nightmares."

"Made out of what, solid gold? For twenty-four-hundred bucks? And here's $213 at expressbusinesscards.com? This doesn't make any sense."

Outside, the rain pelted against their bedroom windows and I could see snakes of lightning in the distance.

"And in the middle of the night last night, over two grand on Delta Airlines? Where the hell are you going next? Fiji?"

"I'm leaving Boulder," I told them both. It was the first thing I said in their bedroom that wasn't a lie.

"Like hell you are!" Joel bellowed, and then he turned to Carolyn. "How could you bring this, this, *her* into our home? Of all people? How could you, the Safety Queen, hire a thief?" He spun back to me, laughing bitterly. "Of course, it was you, all along. Why wouldn't you steal from us too? You, who've got nothing to lose."

"Nothing to lose?" I gasped, hating him for his blind stupidity. "*You* are the one with everything," I waved my arm at Carolyn, the baby, the house, Sasha down the hall, "everything to lose."

I glanced at Carolyn, but she wouldn't meet my eyes.

I ran down the stairs through a blur of tears, sure only that once I got out of this house, I would never come back.

CHAPTER FORTY-TWO

Carolyn

"Well." I took a shaky breath, and pushed to stand, one hand holding my throbbing lower back. "I-I don't think, I don't know that it is worth it to press charges against her."

"No," Joel agreed, and a long look passed between us. He ran his hand down his face, and then up, pushing his bangs straight to the ceiling. "It's not that much money, in the grand scheme of things. I'd guess it's not worth it."

"Even though she's guilty of worse than credit-card fraud."

We stared at each other for one moment as heavy as the thunderclouds, and I knew that he knew, without me saying it.

"Yes." He looked away first. "Much worse."

"It's more the principle." I stood to leave the room, to extricate myself from the strange corners we had all backed ourselves into, only Joel was planted between me and the door.

"I guess we've all made mistakes," he said, evenly. He came to me. "I'm sorry," he whispered, and I thought I understood what he was apologizing for, what Liddy told me, until he added, "for assuming it could have been you again."

"I'm sorry, too."

The plane tickets were printed out, tucked in my nightstand drawer. I was going to show them to Maia after the party. I'd tear them up as soon as Joel left the room.

From downstairs, past the noise of the girls playing in Sasha's room, I heard

Maia scream.

I made it down to the kitchen in time to see the standoff, Maia shaking, her neck magenta, Jackie pinching something small and plastic between her mauve-manicured nails.

"What are you doing? Give me my purse!"

"It's her," Jackie said to me, holding up the driver's license. "M-a-I-a, Kramer with a K. It's her. Ask Dean. Your nanny has a criminal record in Philadelphia!"

Rachel clutched Cedar protectively to her chest, stepping back out of the kitchen, as though danger lurked in the room.

"I was leaving," Maia's breath was gaspy, the necklace glowing gold against the dark rose of her skin, "and I come in the kitchen, and I find *her*, going through my stuff!"

"But you say this like she's the one who has done something wrong," Rachel's voice was incredulous.

"What can she say? It looks like someone pretty's ugly past is catching up with her," Jackie sneered.

The sliding door opened with a howl of wind and rain, and in came Russ, dripping, carrying the smoking side of a pig in blackened tin foil.

"Whoa," he said, eyes raking over the spectacle of Maia appreciatively. "Didn't realize this was a schmancy dress-up party."

Maia snatched her purse back off the counter. She opened it and shook, until it fell to the counter: the card I'd given her to go shopping the day before, the Visa, in Joel's name. Her hands flew to her throat and she yanked until the chain popped, the diamond flying loose, skipping across the floor before it disappeared under the stove. She looked straight at Joel and pressed the broken chain into his palm.

Then she ran, her platforms echoing on the tile, the front door slamming behind her.

"Don't you think," Rachel said tentatively, "with the weather, maybe someone should go after her?"

Nobody answered. I checked: Joel's car keys were still in the dish on the counter, but she had her bike.

"Well, what the hell's going on in here?" Russ said on a loud guffaw, trying to lighten the silence that followed. "I leave you ladies alone for ten minutes and you can't play nice? Come on, man," he called to Joel, "this thing weighs as much as Gracey. Help me set this sow on the counter."

Joel and Russ slid the steaming meat onto my white Corian, leaving streaks of charcoal and grease. In the damp air, the kitchen reeked of roasting pig, chili powder and cumin. Joel's face was as pale as Maia's had been maroon.

"I think the meat's still good in here," Russ was saying, peeling back the foil, picking out a fingerful and popping it in his mouth. "And we've got margaritas. What more do we need?"

"It's like I'm back in the bayou, a hurricane party," Rachel chimed in. They were still trying to salvage things.

Beyond the steaming meat, I watched Joel's hand fold tentatively over his car keys in the dish.

"Well?" Jackie asked me, slapping Maia's driver's license onto the counter. Joel's eyes traveled to it, and the credit card. "She won't get far. She's not getting on any planes without this."

"Hey hey." The front door opened: Rachel's husband Dean, in full uniform, shaking the water from his hat onto the doormat and stomping. "It's getting ugly out there. Thought I'd swing by and check on everyone."

"Did you bring it?" Jackie asked Dean, waving the license. "It's her; Maia, the same spelling, from Philadelphia."

"Bring what?" Russ asked.

"The NCIS report? Yeah, it's out in the car. Accessory to armed robbery. Attempted hit-and-run. She's wanted in Pennsylvania. That was her I passed? The beauty, on the bike? In the dress? Day-umm."

Jackie and Rachel turned to me in unison.

"What are you going to do, Carolyn?" Rachel asked gently.

"Who's a criminal? What the hell is going on?" Russ wanted to know.

Joel reached for his keys; they clanked against the sides of the bowl.

"He's going after her," Jackie shrieked, and I both hated and envied the way she could scream truth, when I had been swallowing it for so long. Years, really. "I was right. He's been having an affair with her all along!"

"Who?" Russ boomed.

Joel didn't move. We were standing four feet apart, a world between us. His expression was a blank slate, with one small worry line between his eyebrows; the story of our past written there. I turned away.

"You go after her," I told Dean. It slipped out easily, like confessing everything to Maia that afternoon. I pulled the trigger on her, just like that, ending everything. As though there hadn't been another future for us swirling, shimmering with possibility like the sun setting on the Pacific, in my mind for days.

CHAPTER FORTY-THREE

Maia

I biked back towards Boulder in the stinging rain and hail. Up ahead on the mountains, lightning sliced the dark sky in jagged white while the pumping of my legs split the seam of the dress to the top of my thigh. I had to ditch the Chinese dragon platforms somewhere off Canyon; my feet kept slipping off the pedals.

Cool water and wind soothed my hives. All around me, the hot earth hissed, steaming, in the pelting rain. And I thought, if I got hit by lightning now, it would not be the worst thing that could happen.

I made it home in less than thirty minutes, drenched. All I knew was I needed my dog and a change of clothes, a moment to get out of the weather and formulate a plan.

Inside, it was loud and smoky, weed wafting in from the living room, and I saw lines of cocaine by the turntables, Luke's bare, muscled back bent over them. I could hear people shrieking outside in the hot tub, popping with rain, hysterical beer pong laughter coming up from the basement.

"Maia!" It was Will, coming toward me with a plate of food, Vader at his side, tail wagging.

"You're soaked. Here." Will put his sandwich down on the coffee table. "And you're barefoot again? You're like Peter Rabbit; can't keep a pair of shoes."

He held out his arms to wrap the blanket from the couch around me.

I wanted to fall into him, but I couldn't. Not now.

"Come here, sit," he made room beside him on the couch, Vader nudging me from the other side, like comfortable bookends, but my thighs vibrated, adrenaline singing in my veins—an itch to run, only…

I had nowhere to go.

"Hungry?" Will picked up his plate, tilted it toward me. "It's peanut butter and honey on wheat."

"What's that?" The living room was dark, lit only by the purplish glow of Beau's fish tank. I squinted; on the coffee table next to Will's plate were black squares of plastic garbage bags, untied dental floss, and like a cliché, a spent hypodermic needle. Two more eight balls sat beside them, bound.

"Jesus, Will, who's doing heroin?"

"Hammer brought it. A couple of Monique's friends were trying it. Luke."

"One needle. Classy."

"Eat something?" Will tried again.

But I had the sickening sense that the evening wasn't even close to over.

I curled my fingers over Vader's collar. I had my dog. What else?

Will tilted his head toward my ear over the music.

"I gave Luke my notice tonight, after how he acted. With you. I've had it. End of the month, I told him, just like Stan. I guess I can't run with the big dogs." He ruffled Vader's ears, our fingertips brushing.

"Maia, can I say something I thought I'd never say?"

I nodded and he said, "You look terrible. Like, really awful."

He looked relieved when I laughed, hiccupping back a sob, swiping my plastered hair off my forehead.

For a second, I relaxed. Will was still talking; a place, a house he'd seen out near his parents, a fixer-upper, a huge, fenced yard and garden, and a coop for chickens. He was going on about putting in cold frames for fall vegetables. Our hands touched on Vader's warm back, and it sounded beautiful and also heartbreaking, because I knew I wouldn't be a part of it. Not when my past surrounded me like a cloud of flies.

Just like a movie, there was a bam-bam-we-mean-business knock at the front door. It wasn't locked; three drunk girls had just stumbled out to smoke five minutes earlier.

They opened it, two of them: "Boulder County Police."

Will looked at me, then the coffee table, but it was too late.

"It's you again." The one with the shaved head said to Will. "And it appears she's home now. Maia Jane Kramer?" he said.

I nodded, twisting my wet hair up off my neck, readying myself.

It was time.

His eyes followed the path Will's had taken, from me to the drugs on the chessboard in front of us. "Well. Before, I just had some questions from our friends back in Philadelphia. But now," he nodded to the drugs, sighing, pulling on rubber gloves, "now we've got another little problem. Am I talking to just you, or is your boyfriend here involved too?"

In Boulder, there were a lot of things I did I wasn't proud of.

When I took the fall for Carolyn and the credit card, and then for the Juniper Court drugs that night in July, when I told the police they weren't anyone's but mine and shook my head at Will to silence him, these felt like the first good choices I'd made in months. The irony that they were lies didn't escape me.

EPILOGUE

December

It is dark, the party disintegrated, that night in July when a wildfire burns outside Boulder and a woman carefully buckles her little girl in the backseat, plying her with stories of a magic pink waterfall and warm peanuts from farm stands, a promise to run with her, holding hands, into the first ocean they can find. They leave a note. The girl's father is asleep in his bed, breathing like a broken air conditioner.

One thousand eight hundred ninety-eight miles. They stop when needed, sing a thousand songs. They tell each other a rambling, hours-long story about an elephant who dreams of dancing *The Nutcracker*. They see Ruby Falls and find a roadside petting zoo with llamas. They eat peaches and blueberries from farm stands in Illinois, and French fries in every state in between. When they reach Florida, they keep driving, all the way to the ocean at St. Augustine.

They do not run into the ocean naked, but stop at a gas station and shimmy into bathing suits first—it is midday in July and the beach is crowded. They dash, mother and daughter, across the scorching sand and straight into the welcoming Atlantic holding hands.

⌣⟩

The baby is born in Florida—three days after his due date—an easygoing, wise-eyed boy. The grandparents are fiercely protective. They remember their shock when they arrived, a bedraggled mother dog and her sea-wet pup, spewing stories of betrayal.

Her father paces the balcony of their condo, palming his grandson's narrow back, singing him show tunes and sighing his regrets. "I should have said something, years ago. I was the only one who never trusted Joel."

The grandmother rolls her eyes a little during the weekly phone calls between long-distance father and daughter. She is learning to keep her comments to herself.

In the fall, Carolyn and Sasha both begin school. Sasha makes friends easily, and her teacher notes on her first report card: *strong imagination; v. strong personality*!

"That's my girl," her Pop-Pop says, swinging her up into his arms by the pool while the old people look on with love and annoyance that Carolyn's mother, president of the HOA, insisted on temporarily ammending the 55+ only rules for her daughter and grandbabies.

"Brilliant and resilient, wonder where she gets it."

While Judith power-walks the neighborhood, pushing the double-stroller around the canal streets and teaching Sasha the complete score from *Evita*, Carolyn takes a twelve-week course in home staging.

"You should see the warehouse at the institute, rows and rows of furniture and accessories and art, bins of knickknacks. Creating the scenes for the sellers, it's like shopping without spending money, playing grown-up dollhouse," she tells her parents over delivery sushi, the baby lolling across her knees. "Sometimes I can't believe this is my life, that work can be so fulfilling, so much fun."

She will finish in January, with offers from two different firms, though money is no longer the most pressing issue. The house outside of Boulder has sold in a favorable real estate market, more than twice what they originally paid. When the realtor transfers the money, Carolyn will move them out of the guest bedroom in her parents' condo. There is a bungalow on Summer Island with ocean views, the smell of sea air, and a gated, private pool. There is talk of Christmas, the three of them together, in the new house, a fresh start.

Of course, it is not all that easy.

Carolyn and her classmates at the institute commiserate over cafeteria chicken salads about the challenge of juggling work and parenting. One of them, Grace, is becoming a friend. She has twins Sasha's age. On the weekends, they sometimes take their children to the beach where, with water wings, Carolyn is able to let Sasha play in the subdued surf.

Carolyn's weekly therapist helps her form an identity built on honesty and trust. Carolyn tells him everything about her, "the worst thing she's ever done," like Joel had once suggested the fateful night before the BBQ. In a steady voice, she tells him about Matthew Stein, and the accident, and—like Maia, she remembers with sharp pain—he insists she let it go, that it wasn't her fault.

She continues, telling him about the punishing binges and the secrecy and the shame, the compulsive shopping, about her guilt over losing the first baby, how the self-loathing had lived, like a whole other person, inside a marriage.

"I didn't want anyone to love me. I didn't think I was worthy of anyone's respect."

"And what changed that?" her therapist prods, the wind shushing through the palm fronds out his open winter window.

"Maia."

There is a place northeast of Philadelphia, in Bensalem, where all points of the compass rose converge in interstates, the east-west Turnpike, and the north-south coastal I-95.

It is not far from here that she steps out of the Riverside Women's Correctional Facility for the first time in five months, under-dressed in jeans, a sunflower T-shirt, and yellow flip flops, the outfit she changed into the last night in the Juniper Court basement bedroom, while Will and Dean waited upstairs, before she was extradited. The December day is brittle and sunny, the wind whipping up off the Schuylkill and she squints after the darkness inside.

The dog spots her first, barking, straining against his leash, dragging the poor man across the parking lot.

She half-runs toward them, arms flung wide, her first time outside in five months, except for the day pass allowing her to stand beside her sister, to bury their mother.

In a flannel shirt and wool socks under his Birkenstocks, he looks out of place against the backdrop of her silver hometown skyline. He is scruffy from days on the road; he looks perfect.

Behind them: the gleaming black vintage Porsche.

"I hope your dad took your mom for her ride?" She is breathless when they are finally face to face.

"Of course." He smiles, so honest and wide.

There is a moment of shyness, before he cups her jaw, tilting his face down to hers, kissing her.

"It's really you," he whispers into her hair. "All these months, nothing but letters, and it's finally you. In person."

Vader nudges his nose between them; their hands meet on his black head. Will has a bouquet—her cosmos and Black-eyed Susans, kept alive in the cold frame, driven across the country in a mason jar.

"What, are, you, doing, here?" she whispers, between kisses. She was expecting her sister, who visited every weekend, fingers spread wide against the scratched glass as they talked.

"Waiting for you."

They drive toward the turnpike, Will explaining the surprise, worked out with her sister beforehand. "And she says to tell you you'd better send her shirt back one of these days."

Vader perches on a plaid blanket on the tiny backseat, his head between them, resting his grizzled chin on her shoulder, Maia's fingers laced over Will's on the gearshift.

They stop in Bensalem, at the crossroads, for gas. Will goes in to pay, and when she gets the dog out of the backseat to walk the strip of winter-beige grass, she sees it: a large cardboard box in the backseat: Kemo Sabe.

When Will comes back, she already has the boots on, wrapped in the plaid blanket against the wind whipping up off the river. She opens her blanket wings to envelop him and because they finally can, they lean against the car, drinking each other's nearness in, until the dog's barking breaks them up.

"Ready?"

Inside the Porsche she stretches her long legs, and he pats the dashboard.

"Really?" she asks.

"Please. It was made for them. Picturing your beautiful feet up there is what got me through the last five hundred miles."

So she rests her boots lightly on his dashboard, hands tucked between her knees.

"Perfect," he murmurs.

"Will? Where did these come from?"

"It was the strangest thing: This woman came to the house, the worst night of my life, after they took you. She was pretty," he shows with his hand the arc of a belly. "I told her you weren't home. She looked surprised, or sorry, or I don't know, sad? There was a little girl, asleep in the back of the car."

Maia regards her feet, silhouetted by the western sun. The plan, Will has said, is to take the turnpike, West. A Colorado pine for a Christmas tree. He starts the engine.

"She said when I saw you, to give the boots to you, that you'd know what they meant."

Maia puts her hand lightly over his on the gear shift, heart pounding, *wait.*

"Will, can I ask you a question?"

His open smile says, *ask me anything.*

"You look like the kind of guy who might be up for an adventure."

"That's not exactly a question," he says, beaming. "Technically, it's more of a statement."

"Are you?"

His kiss over the gear shift is his answer.

"I'll tell you the whole story on the way."

"Like I keep saying," Will smiles, "I've got nothing but time."

Then, with her giving directions, they change course, and take 95, south.

AUTHOR'S NOTE

The idea for this story formed twenty-three years ago. I had a friend who was incredibly gorgeous, so stunning that people thought they'd had a celebrity sighting when we went out together. The trouble was, she had a seriously undeveloped moral compass, and so I watched in horror and fascination as she blitzkrieged through lives, stealing/lying/cheating, leaving chaos and broken relationships in her wake.

But because she was beautiful, there was always a new group willing to welcome her in. It started me thinking about how beauty without substance could make life both easy and lonely. I wondered what someone who used their looks as currency might bump up against that would stop these destructive patterns, what would be bigger, more sacred than the surface? Of course, the answer was a family.

If you want to continue the conversation, please check out the Book Club Discussion Questions section on my website. I am also happy to stop in with a glass of wine for a virtual visit!

https://www.chandrahoffman.com/for-book-clubs

If you loved the story and want to shout it from the virtual rooftops, please share a review on GOODREADS(https://www.goodreads.com/chandrahoffman), BookBub https://www.bookbub.com/profile/chandra-hoffmano or the retailer where you purchased this novel.

In the meantime, I am hard at work on *The Summer After,* a love story with a twist set in the Cayman Islands. To stay up to date on my newest releases, please sign up for my newsletter (https://www.chandrahoffman.com/subscribe)

www.chandrahoffman.com

ACKNOWLEDGMENTS

My thanks...

First, to all the friends and writers who believed in this story for the past twenty-three years. This might be the longest literary gestation ever, but you are all excellent midwives: Linda Davis, Linden Nowak, Lisa Kistner, Kira Mergen, Michelle Lordi, Abbey Nash, Janna King, Caeli Wolfson Widger and Jessica Hohmann.

To my astute editor Romy Somner, who is equal parts mentor and wordsmith.

To Asya Blue, whose vision and design talent is a wonder.

To my gracious and enthusiastic street team of early readers, who inspire me to write faster.

To Matt Messinger, for being my guru on all things law enforcement.

To Kakie Mashburn, my fellow spectator all those years ago.

To Finn, who made sure I never got too comfortable and listened as I narrated in the north campus fields.

To Hayden, Macrae and Piper, who are patient and independent when I slip down the writerly rabbit hole.

Finally, to Jonathan, the other half of my whole.

9 781736 725818